PROHIBITION A

by

Mike Hockney

Hyp

With special thanks to Suzanne Newell, Ian Breckon, Ros Cook, Emma Hooper, Nikita Lalwani, Joachim Noreiko and Jules Williams.

'Can we get control of an individual to the point where he will do our bidding against his will and even against fundamental laws of nature such as self preservation?'

CIA memorandum, January 1952

If there were no sinners, whom would God forgive?

Prologue

The Red Queen of Central Park

John had sounded weird when he called. 'Meet me at one-thirty at the Strawberry Fields entrance to Central Park. You have to do something for me. Wear something people won't forget.' Then he hung up.

It was 1.55 now. *Where the hell are you, John?* In rainbow-striped hot pants that dug into her backside and a scarlet crop-top that stretched too tightly across her chest, Sarah Harris was certain people were sniggering at her. Her feet had swollen up because of the heat and ached inside her new red Adidas sneakers.

'Wow, it's a hot one,' the weathergirl had said on the morning news. 'A hundred degrees in the shade.'

The glare from the sun was giving Sarah a headache. She glanced down at the metal stud sticking out of her bellybutton, wondering why she was doing this. She hadn't dressed this way since university. A respectable thirty-year-old FBI Special Agent should know better. No wonder the suits were eyeballing her. They were standing yards away, talking loudly, as if they wanted her to overhear.

'A hundred bucks says she does it.' The taller guy was adjusting a metallic earpiece. A matching microphone positioned near his mouth glinted in the sunshine. He and his colleague were checking out everyone who came into the park. They could easily be in Sarah's own line of business, but ops in major public spaces had been banned for years.

What were they talking about? Sarah was sure the shorter guy was staring at her handbag. A snatch? He seemed far too well dressed. Maybe they thought she was a hooker.

In the sweltering conditions, most visitors to the park were wearing T-shirts and shorts, but these two men were dressed in identical grey suits. Bulges spoiled the line of their jackets. Shoulder holsters? Sarah prayed they were nothing more than detectives on their lunch-break, making dumb bets to burn time. John called guys like that *The Undead* because they needed to get a life. Where *was* he?

'This is nuts,' the shorter man said. 'If you think she's going to do that right here in broad daylight, then...'

The tall man tapped his microphone with his index finger. 'Watch and learn.'

1

Prohibition A

Sarah was certain they were talking about her, but it made no sense. She ought to get out of here, but there was still no sign of John. He hadn't called to let her know why he was running late.

With the bright sunlight making her eyes water, she reached into her handbag and grabbed a pair of shades with mirrored blue lenses. She'd bought them on vacation in Vegas because they went well with her blonde hair, but the lenses were poor quality and gave everything a grainy appearance.

A traffic light had malfunctioned in West Central Park and the *Walk* and *Don't Walk* signs were showing at the same time. Drivers pounded on their horns as pedestrians weaved between the stationary vehicles. *Everything's screwing up*, Sarah thought, wiping a line of sweat from her forehead. How could the suits bear this furnace?

'Those two magic words, that's all it takes.'

Sarah stared at the tall man, trying to make sense of what he was saying. Then – shit – he winked at her. The training manual said she ought to get out of this situation, observe it from a distance and figure out what was going on, but it had been a long time since she last stuck to the rules.

'Quiet,' the second man said. 'Package identified.'

Sarah strained to see what they were looking at. A white Chevrolet van with scratch marks on the doors had parked illegally on a patch of grass near the entrance gates, with the volume of its radio turned right up. *What a Wonderful World* was blaring, the song that had been playing on the jukebox in the student bar when she first met John. The van looked like it belonged to a builder, but the man in the driver's seat was another grey suit. Holding an ice cream, he was making no attempt to eat it.

This is all fucked up. Then Sarah caught sight of John striding towards the park entrance, wearing a garish yellow suit and a wide-brimmed yellow hat. Everyone stopped to stare at him. Dark-haired and blue-eyed, John was six feet two, one hundred and eighty pounds and his muscular build showed he worked out regularly. He normally got admiring looks from women, but now, in this get-up, he looked like a crazy man.

After the accident, doctors had told her to be on the lookout for anomalous behaviour. She thought he'd been getting better, but now this.

A kid with a red balloon ran in front of him, forcing him to break his step. The little boy was rushing to join his friends playing near a set of rusting swings. Dressed in a Spiderman costume, he giggled every time he fired fake cobwebs from a toy gun. His parents, sitting on the grass nearby, were busy preparing a picnic. They looked up to peer curiously at John. As he approached, Sarah felt his eyes roaming over her body.

'The hot-pants are perfect,' he said.

'John, what's this all about?'

His eyes sucked in the two men in grey suits and the third one in the van. 'I didn't want to risk meeting you indoors. They tried to bug the apartment.'

'Please tell me what's going on.'

'They won't do anything; not here. Too many witnesses.'

'Who?'

'There's no time. I'm getting out.' John glanced at the park gates. '*Today*.' A coach and horses went by, carrying a newly married young couple. 'I want you to come with me.' John had been gripping something and now he extended his hand.

Sarah gazed at a black velvet box with a pink ribbon round it.

'I…' John hesitated. 'Why have we put it off for so long?'

'John?'

'You know how I feel. The only thing in my life that never changes is how much I love you.'

Sarah trembled as John lifted the locket hanging from his silver neck-chain and gently kissed it. He said it was his most prized possession. Within hours of first being introduced to her, he asked to take her picture. The next day he miniaturised the photo, put it in the locket and hung it from his neck-chain. 'So I'll always remember you,' he'd said.

Soon, she made a matching locket. They'd been inseparable after that, until John's assignments took him abroad. His long absences didn't sour things. Only the accident managed to put a dent in their relationship, and only because John was obsessed that 'they' did something to him. He claimed they were out to get him before he could prove anything. Sarah prayed things would go back to normal.

'Aren't you going to say anything?' John asked.

Now Sarah lifted her locket and kissed it too. She slipped her arms round his back. 'I love you to death.'

There was a shriek and Sarah glanced to her right. A small girl had crashed her bike and was sprawled on the grass a few metres away. John went over to help her to her feet. She was snivelling but smiled when she saw him. Before she rode off, she gave him a red rose she'd had in a basket on the front of her bike.

Sarah noticed a man in a grey suit walking in her direction – the guy from the van, still with a full ice cream. It hadn't melted.

Prohibition A

It hadn't melted.

It's plastic, she realised with a jolt. He was whispering into it. Some sort of microphone.

The man stopped right in front of her. Between his thumb and index finger, he held a small metallic gadget, the size and shape of a silver dollar.

'Red Queen,' he said, pressing the gizmo.

A high-pitched sound tore through Sarah. Immediately, she removed her shades. The world had become red. The grass, the trees, the buildings, the cars, the people, the sky itself – all red.

'Red Queen,' the man said again.

'I understand.' Normal colours reappeared. Sarah knew if she hadn't said the right thing, the world would have stayed red forever.

'I'm the Delivery Manager. The customer is John Dexter.' He gazed straight through her. 'Delivery must be made immediately.'

Sarah noticed a black cat slinking past the man and gazing up at her with intense green eyes. She reached out with her hand and realised she was invisibly trying to stroke her own cat, Clever Kitty. It had been missing for the last two days and she was concerned. She snatched her hand back to her side, confused.

'What you need is in your handbag,' the man said. 'Now take this.' He gave her a card then strode away into the crowd. She dropped it into her handbag.

John was walking back now, followed by Spiderman and several of his pals dressed as rival miniature superheroes, each holding a balloon in one hand and a messy, dripping ice cream in the other.

'A red rose for the beautiful lady,' John said. He was about to present her with the flower, but changed his mind. 'That comes after.' He placed the rose in the buttonhole of his lapel then raised the presentation box and opened it. Inside was a brushed-silver engagement ring engraved with ocean waves. Leaning forward, he kissed Sarah lightly on the forehead. 'How quickly can you pack? We need to travel light. Just grab your passport and a few things.'

Sarah reached into her handbag. Her fingers touched the grip of a pistol – a Heckler & Koch P9S, the sort she'd used in training at Quantico. A round was already chambered. She clicked off the safety. Raising the pistol in front of her, she pointed it at John's head then moved it down until it was opposite his chest.

'Sarah, what…' John stopped in mid-sentence. Some of the kids laughed.

She fired one shot. A splatting noise reminded her of a game boys played when they used watermelons as target practice for their air pistols.

Prologue

John collapsed. The side of his head cracked against the ground and his hand flailed upwards. Spiderman took his outstretched hand and burst into tears, losing his grip on his balloon. A second later, his mother snatched him away.

Sarah gazed upwards to track the balloon as it soared into the sky. Soon, it was moving so slowly she wondered if it had stopped. Shifting her attention to the ground, she saw a line of blood creeping towards her sneakers. A shiver ran up her spine: she couldn't remember her name.

She grabbed an ID card lying in her handbag. It said she was Jane Ford and worked for the Secret Service. She breathed out hard. An object glinting in the sun caught her attention. It was a ring nudging against a discarded Coke can lying a few feet away. She stared at it. Her stomach cramped and she thought she might collapse. She was aware of a foul taste in her mouth.

She closed her eyes, hoping everything would return to normal, but when she opened them again, everything had gone crazy. People were walking in slow motion, their voices sounding as if they'd been fed through a machine playing at half-speed. She heard everything everyone around her was saying, all at the same time.

Two police cars arrived and pulled up next to the kids' playground. Sarah was amazed that she could count each pulse of the flashing lights. Paramedics got out of an ambulance and came towards her, avoiding a puddle of vomit lying near a hot-dog cart. Voices marched through her mind. For a second, she was sure everyone was speaking in different languages. Then she became aware of one voice, very close. Someone was talking to her.

...under arrest. You have the right to remain silent. Anything you say...

Something cold and hard was put onto her wrists. She searched for the word. Handcuffs? Her eyes locked on to the man who had spoken: Italian looking with jet-black hair. His shoes were pointed at the toes, his suit too fashionable. Did he say he was a detective?

A black four-door Cadillac with blacked-out windows pulled up and two men in grey suits got out. She flinched. *Them.* The taller one flashed an ID shield that she didn't recognise.

She overheard a female paramedic saying, 'Get him in the ambulance right away.'

'Is he dead?' one of the suits asked.

'Who wants to know?' the detective interrupted.

The paramedic ignored both of them. 'Get a body bag ready.'

'We're handling this now,' the suit said, turning to the detective.

5

'What are you talking about?' the detective said. 'You can't do that.'

'You've seen our ID. You're way out of your depth, pal.'

'Who says?'

The suits looked at each.

Sarah studied the detective's mouth. It was quivering with frustration, the lips moving silently, cursing.

'What am I supposed to tell my boss?'

'That's your problem.'

The detective shook his head. 'I'm not taking this.'

'It's your funeral.' The taller of the suits removed Sarah's handcuffs, pushed her into the back of the Cadillac then slapped his colleague on the back.

'That's a hundred bucks you owe me.'

****

As the car moved off, Sarah listened to the tall man making a call on his cell phone.

'Termination completed at 14.15 hours. Red Queen has been deactivated. Possible signs of psychosis. Cleaning operation in progress.'

Why was the man saying these strange things? It was such a lovely day. What were all these policemen doing here? She felt anxious. Where on earth had John got to? He'd been behaving so oddly lately, but she wanted him to know that, no matter what, she'd always stand by him.

'OK,' the man said, 'I'll let the Director know. Bringing in asset now for reprogramming.'

Sarah stared out of the tinted window at an ambulance. There must have been an accident. Someone was taking pictures. She wondered who this Red Queen was. She sounded so glamorous.

1

Epidemic

<u>Two Years Later</u>

S arah Harris, in a black overcoat, pushed through the security turnstiles and hurried across the lobby to the elevators, avoiding slippery patches where snow, carried in on people's shoes, had melted. When her boss called her the night before to tell her something had come up, he sounded uncertain and James Dargo was famous for *never* sounding uncertain. The only clue he'd given her was a cryptic remark about red circles. What was *that* supposed to mean?

She glanced at the large sign over the elevators – *FBI: Critical Incident Response Group (New York)*. CIRG's job was to coordinate a rapid Federal response to any major criminal incident and it could draw on specialist units such as the Hostage Rescue Team and the Crisis Negotiation Unit, as well as the Behavioural Analysis Unit with its expert psychological profilers. Sarah wondered how red circles could in any way be connected with a critical incident.

This was her first working Sunday in six months and her body clock was struggling to adjust to an early start on a day when she normally caught up on her sleep. She looked at her watch. *Shit*, twenty minutes late. She was in line for Dargo's '80/20' speech. She knew it by heart. 'Twenty percent of any organisation are potential high flyers. You can make dog meat out of the rest.'

She showed her ID to the guard and he waved her on. He was a miserable old man called Bob. Every time she saw him, with his sleepy grey moustache, she thought of dust gathering on old, unread Bibles.

The CIRG office in Pearl Street in Manhattan's financial district housed around three hundred agents and ancillary staff. Today, apart from security personnel, few people were around. An unsettling quiet hung over the place.

As Sarah approached the elevators, she veered left. Five of the six elevators were painted battleship grey while the odd one, on the extreme left, was burgundy. It stopped at a single floor – the tenth, home to the senior staff.

The rapid ascent usually left her slightly light-headed, but this time Sarah didn't notice. When she got out, she almost collided with Eva Kranic.

7

Prohibition A

Kranic, from the FBI's Jacob K. Javits Manhattan office, was an elite undercover agent who sometimes worked on CIRG cases. Undercover Operations – UCOs – interested Sarah and she liked to chat with Kranic, but there was no time this morning. They nodded at each other, then Sarah made her way to the Phoenix Suite of interview rooms.

After knocking on the door of No. 3 interview room – nicknamed 'Sing Sing' because it was where FBI personnel under investigation by the Office of Professional Responsibility were supposed to 'sing' their secrets – she slipped inside. A small office painted peppermint green, Sing Sing smelled of lemon air freshener. Dargo, dressed in a navy blue suit and seated at a maple table, was studying a document. With his steel-grey cropped hair and sharp grey eyes, he looked like a made-man from a Mafia movie. He gave the impression that he knew the whereabouts of quite a few unmarked desert graves, and if you got on his wrong side he'd dig one for you too.

'*Harris,*' he said with an ostentatious look at his watch.

'I'm sorry,' Sarah apologised. 'There was a...'

'Sit down. We've wasted enough time.'

Sarah had once heard a story about Dargo forcing an agent to take a lie detector test because the guy's excuse for being late was so feeble. He failed and was fired. She nervously poured herself a black coffee and took the seat next to him. In front of her was a document with the title: 'Epidemic of Dissociative Identity Disorder in Manhattan?'

Dargo turned the first page for her, and gave a sly smile. 'A little surprise for you?'

Sarah saw the name of the author – Mike Lacey. *That's all I need*, she thought.

Dargo picked up the phone and called an extension. 'She's here, Mike. We're in Sing Sing. See you in five.' He put the phone down again and picked up his copy of the document. 'While we're waiting for Lacey, I'll give you a rundown of what this is all about.' He explained that Lacey had been collating reports from social services, police, hospitals, drug rehab centres and mental institutions about a growing number of young men and women who'd come to their attention over the last few months, all with an unlikely connection.

'Here's the thing,' Dargo said. 'First, they all suffer from bouts of amnesia. Second, they have at least three red circles tattooed on the insides of their left wrists. And every one of these people earned more than a quarter of a million dollars last year.'

8

Sarah, suddenly uneasy, stiffened and folded her arms.

'There's one last thing,' Dargo added. 'All of them have been voluntarily sterilised within the last six months.'

Sarah took a sip of coffee and stared blankly ahead, baffled.

'Over a hundred people have been affected so far,' Dargo said, 'and new cases are being reported every day. No newspapers have got hold of this story yet, but you can imagine the headlines if they do.'

'But there's no evidence of any crime, let alone any critical incident,' Sarah said. She was interrupted by a knock on the door and cleared her throat as Mike Lacey entered. 'Hi, Mike,' she said quietly.

Lacey gave a little nod and sat down opposite her. From Brooklyn, he was slim, black, twenty-seven years old and over six feet tall. A purple silk tie with a large knot offset his conventional dark suit and white shirt, apparently his way of demonstrating that he hadn't become just another agent. He'd become a rising star of the Behavioural Analysis Unit after providing a profile that proved decisive in allowing the FBI to apprehend a notorious serial killer.

'Sarah has some doubts about all of this, Mike. Why don't you reassure her?'

Lacey nodded. 'I'll begin by showing you a police video.' He rotated his swivel seat so that he faced the plasma TV on the wall behind him. 'The young woman you're about to see is Theresa Martinez. She's twenty-eight, a creative director in an advertising agency and she earns three hundred thousand dollars a year.' He pressed a button on a remote control and low-quality video footage appeared on the TV.

A striking Hispanic woman with shining skin, large gold earrings and a gold tongue stud was being interviewed by a detective, with the interview timed at four o'clock on a Saturday morning. The woman's eyes initially refused to focus then focused too much, making her stare like a lunatic. She held up her left hand and three small red circles in a neat row were visible on the inside of her wrist. Her speech was slurred and she didn't answer any questions. 'The voice in the darkness,' she mumbled a few times. Another comment stood out: 'The river can save us all. Back to the beginning.' Everything else was babble.

A second interview timed at nine o'clock on the same morning showed the same woman, now looking smart and composed. She politely answered questions, but was unable to say anything about where she'd been earlier, or what had happened to her. 'Mi vida loca,' she said with a shrug. It became obvious that she had, or was pretending to have, amnesia concerning the previous few hours.

'Rohypnol?' Sarah commented. She prayed it was something as simple as that, but Lacey shook his head.

'This Martinez woman has been to her doctor several times since that interview,' he said. 'Each time she visits, a new circle is on her wrist, but she has no idea how it got there. There are seven circles now, in a line going most of the way round her wrist. There's room for three more. Also, she complains about hours of the day going missing. She says friends have told her she occasionally starts gibbering and doesn't recognise anyone. She's on sick leave now. It's a similar story with the others.'

Sarah turned several pages of the report at once. 'I don't understand why we're looking at this. Some new designer drug has hit the streets, that's all. Leave it to the narcotics guys.'

'We're getting involved because more than a hundred rich young people have reported the same thing,' Lacey said. 'All of them have multiple red circles on their wrists and they're acting weird. We don't know what's causing it and we don't know how big it might get.' He leaned forward. 'What happens if Martinez completes the set? – all ten circles.'

'Tell us your theory,' Dargo said.

'The report you have in front of you states the facts, that's all. I haven't offered any speculations other than to point out that all of the people in this report appear to be suffering from varying degrees of dissociation.'

'Dissociation?' Sarah blurted. This case unnerved her and she had no idea why.

'Dissociation is a process of mental disconnection in a person's thoughts, feelings and memories,' Lacey said, 'maybe in their whole identity. While a person is dissociating, normal mental activity is partially or completely disrupted. The classic example is of a child being severely sexually abused. The abuse may be so bad that the kid dissociates it from his normal memory and hides it in his subconscious so that he won't have to confront it every day. It's an effective escape mechanism for someone facing unbearable trauma, but it leads to memory gaps. In extreme cases, it can lead to what used to be called multiple personality disorder where a person has one personality for dealing with the normal world and another for dealing with abusive situations. Sometimes there can be more than one personality.'

Epidemic

'Are you saying the red circle people have been sexually abused?' Dargo asked.

'I'm saying it's possible they've been exposed to severe trauma, somehow connected with those circles.'

'How do you propose we move this forward, Mike?' Sarah asked. The circles seemed such a small thing, she thought, but somehow they signified something much bigger.

'We should set up surveillance on all of these people, see what they get up to, where they go; find out if we can identify a common link.'

'What do you think, Sarah?' Dargo asked.

'We don't have the resources for this, sir. I agree it's intriguing, but if some new designer drug is in town, it's not our job to sort it out. I can't see how we can justify an investigation at this stage. Our budgets have been capped again this year. We simply can't afford it.' She tried to smile supportively at Lacey, but feared it came out as patronising. 'I'd say that Mike should continue to monitor the situation and let us know if there are any significant developments.'

'I have to go along with Sarah on this one,' Dargo said. 'This is good work, Mike, and thanks for bringing it to our attention, but there's nothing we can do right now. Even so, I have a gut feeling this could be trouble.'

Lacey, who had been spinning a pen between his fingers for the past few seconds, now carefully placed the pen on the table. 'Sir, a lot of wealthy people are affected by this, maybe people of influence, or related to people of influence, if you know what I mean. I think we have to gamble and take the initiative right now. If we get it right, it will be a coup for the department. We may get a bigger budget for next year.'

Dargo smiled. 'Mike, you're saying the right things, but if you're wrong, CIRG will get burned. We're keeping out of this for now.'

Sarah fought to keep her face expressionless, but she couldn't disguise her relief.

Just then, Dargo's cell phone beeped. He glanced at it then stood up. 'Excuse me. I'll be back shortly.'

'We don't meet much these days, Sarah,' Lacey said when Dargo left.

As always, Sarah's mind flashed back to their infamous kiss at a Christmas party. It had come out of the blue. It was so hot that her boss at the time spoke to her afterwards to say that kind of thing wasn't appreciated. 'It could compromise your reputation,' he warned. Ever since, she'd been abrupt with Lacey. Now, she was on edge, hoping Dargo would return fast.

11

Prohibition A

'According to the polls, your boyfriend's looking good for the *big job*,' Lacey said. 'I don't know, would that make you First Lady?'

'We're not married.'

'He has a rally planned for tonight, doesn't he? Craigavon Hall, right? I was thinking of going.'

'Are you interested in politics?'

'Not really. I heard Montcrieff is planning to make a major announcement. I'm curious. Do you know what it is?'

Sarah shook her head, but she did know something unusual was on Robert's agenda. He'd made her promise to go to tonight's rally. He wanted her to wear her most glamorous dress and get her hair done. 'You mustn't be late,' he insisted.

She felt as if a storm were about to break. Maybe that would be a relief from the strange wintry freeze that had settled over Manhattan lately. The city had been locked in snow and ice since the start of October with record low temperatures being logged daily.

The door opened and Dargo came back in. 'OK, where were we? Just wrapping things up, right? I have to emphasise that the media mustn't get a scent of this. They'll turn it into a circus like they always do. So, not a word to anyone. Clear?'

Sarah and Lacey nodded.

'Oh, one more thing while you're here,' Dargo said, turning to Sarah. 'With Robert Montcrieff in town, there's bound to be a lot of media attention coming your way. I've asked the PR department to contact all media outlets to say we don't want anyone hassling you while you're doing your job. I've reminded them it could be deemed a Federal offence.'

'*Thanks*.' At times like this, Sarah wished Robert were a regular guy. Whether she liked it or not, the spotlight was about to single her out big time. She stood up to leave.

'Robert's a wealthy guy, isn't he? – not so different from the folks in my report,' Lacey commented with a smirk as she headed for the door. 'Better check his left wrist tonight.' He winked. 'You never know what you might find.'

2

Ghost

This can't be. General Clark, his heart thudding, looked across the table at David Warren.

Warren pushed the photograph away, as though it were scorching his fingers. He closed his eyes and nodded his head.

Clark stood up and walked to the window. The Hudson Tower was a black glass skyscraper overlooking Manhattan's Lincoln Tunnel. The penthouse boardroom where the six members of the Committee held their secret meetings offered some of the best views of Manhattan on clear days, but the sun didn't show up much these days. Darkness clung to the city; a darkness that Clark imagined was reaching deeper and deeper inside him as the critical day approached. Now, without warning, an impossible new darkness had appeared.

Could it really be *him*? Clark stared at a picture on the far wall, depicting the Neulander Institute with its high white walls like those of a maximum-security penitentiary. Many men would have chosen to hang a picture of their family on the wall, but, for Clark, nothing could have been worse than to see the face of his ex-wife Jane and his daughter staring back at him. So, the Neulander Institute was there instead.

It wasn't a sight he found reassuring. Even though bright white light fell on every surface of that building, every member of staff wore white, and every piece of furniture was white, it was the darkest place in the world. If everyone had a place that haunted them, the Neulander Institute was it for him. It was where *he*, the man whose photograph was now being passed around, was created.

Clark turned away from the window and switched his attention to FBI Director Gary Lassiter – a tall, grim man with a skeletal head and black sunken eyes. Despite problems in the past, Clark now found Lassiter rock solid.

'God help us,' Lassiter said as he took the photograph and squinted at it.

Clark's gaze shifted to the cold, aluminium-clad walls of the boardroom. 'You're absolutely sure?' It was crazy that he was asking these questions since he already knew the answer, but somehow he had to hear others confirming it.

'I knew him well,' Lassiter replied. 'He did three missions with my guys.'

'There's no chance you're mistaken?'

Lassiter shook his head.

Could this really be happening? Cooke had called this emergency meeting because a photograph taken by an agent had been classified *Intcon 1* as soon as it was seen by a senior station officer that morning. Clark never believed a picture could make him physically sick, but this one did.

'There's no question.' Lassiter bowed his head.

Despite the cold outside, Clark sweated and shivered at the same time. Of all the things he expected to see today, this picture wasn't just the last, it was impossible. Ghosts didn't exist: Sarah Harris *killed* John Dexter in Central Park two years ago.

He tried to remain calm as he measured his reply. 'Dexter was declared DOA at the hospital.' Even as he said it, memories of Dexter flooded back.

John Dexter was the proof of the effectiveness of Alice Through the Looking Glass. When the finance committee came to town, Clark needed only to point to Dexter's record and the funding for this most secret of all projects was renewed instantly. No one was more highly trained than Dexter, but, ultimately, training has its limits. Then innate skills are required: intuition, the ability to improvise, sheer nerve. Dexter had it all, plus, of course, the unique advantages conferred by the Looking Glass project.

'He fooled us,' Lassiter said, shaking his head. 'Jesus, maybe he knows about Alice.'

'*No.*' The thought that Alice's security had been breached terrified Clark. *Everything* depended on it. The idea of the project failing after all the time and effort that had been invested in it was unthinkable.

'We thought we'd killed Dexter,' Warren remarked. 'We were wrong about that. Maybe we're wrong about Alice too.'

'Perhaps Dexter's death was staged,' Ted Boca, Director of the National Security Agency, said. 'Maybe Dexter and Sarah were in it together all along.'

Clark liked Boca. He was a quiet man, but strong and tough. With a pockmarked face and a severe crew cut, he gave off a vaguely threatening vibe. When he spoke, everyone listened, but this time he'd gone too far.

'The whole team did its duty,' Clark snapped. 'I can't explain what happened, but I'm certain nothing went wrong with Alice. We weren't betrayed.'

'Dexter must have guessed,' Lassiter intervened. 'He took counter-measures.'

Clark wanted to hear the opinion of Jim Carson, Director of the National Reconnaissance Organisation. He had a PhD in quantum physics from MIT and his opinion always carried weight.

'Dexter was a big fan of customised bulletproof vests,' Carson said in his soft Texan accent. 'Sarah should have gone for a head shot.'

Clark nodded. 'It's the only rational explanation.' He took a moment to compose himself. He mustn't show any signs of weakness. 'OK, let's run through what we know. Three weeks ago, an American national arrived from Russia. Initially, he didn't raise any suspicions. However, his passport was copied for a random background check. The following day it was exposed as an expert fake, like ones used by our own agents. It was passed to intelligence analysts who made an assessment that the man was probably a former agent of ours. In the absence of any other information, the analysts presumed a worst-case scenario as per standard operating procedure, assuming he was a terrorist or assassin. They concluded their report with the following: identity of assassin – *unknown*; true appearance of assassin – *unknown*; target of assassin – *unknown*. They classified him as 'unsub' – *unknown subject*.

'Later, we discovered that a man newly arrived from Russia had joined a network of suspected terrorists we'd been monitoring for months. It was likely this was our missing unsub. Two of our agents had already successfully infiltrated the organisation. One of them – Eva Kranic, code-name March Hare – recently identified the newcomer as the leader of the network and managed to get the picture you have in front of you. In this room, we've now all positively identified him as John Dexter.' Clark stopped, still struggling to accept the reality of it.

'If this *is* Dexter,' Warren said, 'what's his objective?'

'It's obvious,' Carson commented. '*Revenge*. He's here for Sarah.' His next words came more slowly. '*And us.*'

'What are we going to do?' Warren asked.

Clark breathed in hard. 'Nothing drastic for now. We'll put our two undercover agents – March Hare and White Rabbit – on full alert.'

'Isn't it too risky to let Dexter stay on the loose?' Lassiter interrupted. 'Election Day is just a week away. All of our preparations are at a critical stage.'

Prohibition A

'March Hare told us Dexter was moving constantly, using every counter-surveillance technique in the book,' Clark responded. 'Remember, Dexter *wrote* the book. If we want to kill him we need more intel. about his plans.'

He waited for someone to disagree. He realised Frank Doyle, Director of the Defence Intelligence Agency, hadn't spoken yet. The DIA, the military equivalent of the CIA, was a huge organisation with over eight thousand employees, responsible for providing high quality military intelligence to the Department of Defence. As for Doyle, he was a three-star general and the principal intelligence adviser to the Secretary of Defence and the Chairman of the Joint Chiefs of Staff.

'You're very quiet, Frank,' Clark said.

Doyle looked up. 'Dexter won't be waiting to gather information.' His face had turned pale. 'He already knows what he's going to do. And we all know he's one of the most dangerous men on earth.'

3

The Speech

'Sarah, what kept you?' Jacob Spiegel's voice echoed in the great expanse of Craigavon Hall's marble lobby. 'I promised Robert I'd have you side-stage by the end of his speech.'

Dickhead, Sarah mouthed. She loathed Robert's campaign manager with his face like a store-detective's and his shiny suits that he probably thought put him up there with the slickest dressers. It wasn't her fault that she was late. The two secret service men assigned to her had spent so much time fussing around they'd fallen half an hour behind schedule.

'Robert's about to make his announcement,' Spiegel said. 'I don't know what he plans to say, but he definitely wants you there.'

'When does his speech finish?'

'Ten minutes. Go through the door behind me and stand behind the curtain at the side of the stage. Robert will signal when he's ready.'

Sarah made her way to her position. She'd done what Robert suggested and visited Amanda, her favourite hairdresser. Her hair was now cut in a sharp, jaw-length bob that clung to her head like a helmet. A killer hairstyle Amanda had assured her after spending two hours getting it just right. They'd joked about their common journey over the years from blonde to raven hair, long to short. To complete her look, Sarah was wearing three-inch stilettos and a designer black chiffon dress. '*To die for*,' Amanda had enthused.

Through a space in the curtains, Sarah glimpsed Robert standing at a lectern in front of thousands of supporters. Everywhere, his face gazed back from his supporters' placards. 'Vote for the Dream Ticket,' each proclaimed. 'Robert Montcrieff for President. Grace Rebello for Vice President.'

Robert's supporters had a special gleam in their eyes, as though they'd been shown the secret shortcut to heaven. The front ranks were filled with attractive women, all greedily pressing forward, stretching out their hands towards their idol.

Robert really *can* be President, Sarah thought. He would be the first true independent to sit in the White House. She remembered what one women's magazine said about him in its latest edition. *Wanted – Robert Montcrieff for total gorgeousness*. It still astonished her that she'd managed to hook such a special guy.

'He sure knows how to work a crowd,' a voice behind her said.

er best friend, Nicki Murphy. The New York
gton Post, Nicki was following Robert on the
'tion special on him. Originally from Dublin,
long Pre-Raphaelite hair.
....airdo,' Nicki said. 'Going for the Louise Brooks

....uled.

it's some story, isn't it?' Nicki gestured at Robert. 'The man from
nowhere running on an independent ticket. The Republicans and Democrats
turn their big guns on him and the shells just bounce off. Then he picks
Grace Rebello as his running mate. I mean, he has every base covered,
doesn't he?'

Grace Rebello was a beautiful black woman, chic and smart, with a
degree in economics from Yale and a PhD from Harvard, and she was
reputedly in the running for the Nobel Prize.

'Robert and Grace – let's hope they're not the dream team in more ways
than one, huh?' Nicki teased. 'Of course, you know Spiegel's trying to
arrange a permanent union between them. He's obsessed with _The Project_.'

Screw Spiegel and his project, Sarah thought. She didn't like any of
Robert's close friends; in particular the two ex-Marines, Ian Longbottom and
Tommy Henshaw, who headed up Robert's security team. Their constant
presence irritated her. It was hard enough to spend time with him without
those clowns hanging around.

She turned her attention back to the rally. The Stars and Stripes were
everywhere. Even the stage curtains formed a gigantic Stars and Stripes. Red,
white and blue spotlights criss-crossed over the heads of the crowd and
highlighted Robert as he stood in front of a semicircle of pristine flags.

'He sure knows how to play the patriotic card,' Nicki said.

Every few seconds, the crowd cheered and stabbed their placards into the
air to greet the main points of Robert's speech. Campaign workers held up
large signs saying, alternately, _Clap_! _Cheer_! At the side of the hall, long-
legged cheerleaders in Stars and Stripes uniforms added more excitement.
The whole thing seemed closer to a Broadway show than a political speech.

As Robert spoke, cameras flashed repeatedly. Several TV crews were in
position to film the speech for the major networks. It was a key moment of
the last week of the campaign, one of the set pieces to be endlessly recycled
on news reports.

'There's one week left to save the country,' Robert said, adjusting the
angle of his microphone then jabbing his finger at a poster showing President

The Speech

Adam Rieper as the Grim Reaper – Spiegel's idea for milking the President's distinctive name. 'Under that guy's watch, we've become clapped out, junked out, burned out. We're lying flat on our faces in the gutter. Forget the American dream: we're not curing the world, we're infecting it.' To a background of cheers, he beckoned Grace Rebello onto the stage to join him. 'You all know what you can do about it. Take a step into the future. Choose the dream ticket. Vote Montcrieff and Rebello next Tuesday.'

Sarah took an impulsive step forward, cheering with the rest of the crowd, as Robert shouted over the hubbub: 'And remember – Don't fear the Reaper.' On cue, the *Blue Oyster Cult's* famous rock anthem blasted through Craigavon Hall. Robert and Grace moved to the front of the stage and waved to their supporters.

Sarah gave Robert a thumbs-up. He gestured to the crowd to let him speak again. The music stopped.

'Is it possible to make this great night even more special?' he said. 'There's a person here tonight who I just can't get out of my head.'

Sarah was uncomfortable now, feeling as if she had an icy hand squeezing her stomach.

'I know I'm standing here in front of thousands of you but my next remark is up close and personal.' Robert gestured for the lights to be lowered. 'Sarah, please come out here.'

Sarah noticed Spiegel scowling at her.

'You're *on*,' Nicki said, giving her a slap on the back.

Blinded by a spotlight, Sarah made her way across the stage. In her stilettos, she had to walk painfully slowly. She sensed Grace Rebello studying her. It was hard not to think of Rebello as a rival, but the truth was she'd never noticed any sexual chemistry between Robert and Rebello.

Robert approached, looking serious. As he got closer, he winked. 'Love the hair.' He put his hand round Sarah's waist and kissed her neck.

What happens now? Sarah's answer came right away. Robert dropped onto one knee and took a blue Tiffany box out of his pocket. Sarah wasn't sure if time had speeded up, slowed down or gone into some indeterminate state.

'Sarah, *will you be my wife?*'

Jesus.

Sarah was hurled back to her childhood. Twelve years old, she stood cowering in front of her head teacher at convent school. Everyone had been asked to bring in a picture of their parents on their wedding day so that a collage called *Marriage* could be put on the classroom wall. She had no

19

pictures to show and everyone knew exactly why. Her classmates called her 'Gappy' because of the space between her front teeth: *Gappy, the orphan.*

When the others went home, she stayed behind. Soon the wall was bare, and the garbage can contained three piles: one for all the brides that she'd carefully separated from the grooms, one for the grooms, and one for the grooms' heads, snipped from their necks.

She still had no idea why she did it. Miss O'Mallen, the headteacher, nearly expelled her. 'Sarah Harris, you're a wicked child. You've sinned against the sacrament of marriage. I promise you, you'll never wed. *Never.*'

The present snapped back. What was Robert playing at? This was lunacy. They'd never discussed marriage. Now this. No time to think. What if she said *no*?

A few photographers, then more, emerged onto the stage. A camera crew appeared too. Robert's friends – Spiegel, Henshaw and Longbottom – materialised, albeit with stony faces and phony smiles.

Sarah looked down at Robert, still on one knee, as dozens of cameras clicked. He opened the Tiffany box, revealing an exquisite platinum ring, mounted with a sapphire stone. Sarah felt faint. For some reason, she imagined the ring lying beside a discarded Coke can.

The silence in the hall verged on the deathly. Robert looked up, sudden fear in his eyes.

The more Sarah stared at the ring, the more it frightened her. Something was *wrong*. Then she remembered O'Mallen curse that she'd never marry. *You always thought you were so right, O'Mallen, didn't you?*

'Yes,' she said without conviction. She was practically knocked over by the whooping that exploded from the crowd.

Robert stood up. With a slick movement, he pushed the ring onto her finger and gave her a spectacular Gone-With-The-Wind kiss. She didn't enjoy it here like this in front of gawping strangers and eased herself away.

The media surrounded them, barking out questions.

'Thanks for coming,' Robert said. 'God, it would have been embarrassing if Sarah had said no.' Everyone chuckled. They couldn't help themselves. Robert could charm anyone. 'Isn't she gorgeous? I'm such a lucky man.'

Sarah knew she had to say something and tried to compose a few inadequate sentences. 'Hi, everyone. As you probably know, I work for the FBI.' She felt her voice quaking, making her wish she had some of Robert's easy charm.

The Speech

'If I screw up, she'll be reading me my rights,' Robert interrupted. They all laughed again.

Someone pushed a microphone towards Sarah. Photographers jostled for position. 'Speak up, Sarah,' a reporter shouted. 'Tell us what you think of Robert.'

'I, er...' she began feebly. *Get a grip.* 'Robert's the most extraordinary man I've ever met,' she said more confidently. 'He's smart and charming, an amazingly dynamic man. Throw in the obvious stuff that he's tall, dashing and handsome and you have to ask how could I resist? Well, I couldn't, of course. Robert will make a truly exceptional president.'

Robert was delighted. She could see it in his face.

'This is one *hell* of a woman,' Robert declared. 'Sarah will revolutionise the role of First Lady. She'll be an inspiration to young working women everywhere.'

Sarah glanced at the faces of the hacks. Even the old cynics with their hard eyes looked like they were about to shed a tear.

'Well, that's it, everyone,' Robert said. 'Now I want to whisk away my beautiful fiancée for some quality time.'

As the cheers boomed around Craigavon Hall, Sarah hoped she could disappear as people thronged around, patting her on the back.

'Good job.' Nicki gave her a high five.

'I must speak to you later, Nicki. I have a favour to ask.'

As usual, Spiegel was lurking around. 'This way.' He led them to an empty room, laid out for a kids' party. 'Sorry about this but I've been told the caretaker's son is having a party in half an hour,' he explained. 'Robert, you took me by surprise out there. Stay here and I'll be back in a few minutes once I've got rid of the media.' He disappeared again, leaving them alone.

'Spiegel was right about one thing.' Sarah threw her arms round Robert to hug him. 'That was a hell of a surprise.'

Robert kissed her with the same passion he'd just put into his speech. Sarah felt ecstatic. Then she broke off and took a step back. When she looked at her engagement ring, her stomach lurched. Almost mechanically, her eyes tracked down to Robert's left wrist.

Nothing there. Thank God. She wondered why she'd even considered it. Something was spooking her and it wasn't just the red circles. When she first met Robert, there was something unreal about it. Even the location was odd – the FBI's Art Gallery, where she spent a short stint before beginning her current job. It was nicknamed the *Ghouls' Gallery* – a place she was never likely to forget.

4

The Ghouls' Gallery

One Year Earlier

People always asked the same question: why do you them call them *Ghost* deliveries? Sarah used to enjoy teasing them. Now she just snapped out the response: 'Because they're from beyond the grave.'

Every year, the paintings of prisoners who had graduated from Death Row to the execution chamber were brought to an annexe of the main office of the FBI's Behavioural Analysis Unit in Manhattan, quickly furnishing the annexe with its Ghouls' Gallery label.

Most of the art was embarrassingly amateurish and was put into storage in the basement for behavioural psychologists to study, but the occasional painting showed genuine talent, and these were the ones Sarah selected for public display.

Today, she was less interested in the delivery of a new batch of paintings and more concerned with avoiding her assistant. Jenny Lavelle was obsessed with marriage. Engaged for two years, her wedding day was still eight months away, but that didn't stop her bringing in a new wedding magazine every week. 'Just looking for ideas,' she remarked gleefully each time.

Sarah was convinced Jenny's wedding would be the most intricately planned in history. Every detail had been considered from a hundred separate angles. She disliked Jenny's obsession for the simple reason that it invariably led to Jenny quizzing her about her own love life and asking about the type of wedding she would have.

Sarah had tried many times to declare her love life, or rather lack of it, off limits, but Jenny never took the hint. 'Don't worry, Sarah,' she kept saying, 'one of these days you'll meet your dream man. I've a feeling you'll have the mother of all weddings.'

Whenever she heard that sort of talk, Sarah made her excuses and fled for sanctuary. That usually meant a visit to the penthouse gallery where paintings by some of America's most notorious serial killers were displayed. Jenny thought it was creepy and rarely ventured here, turning it into a refuge for Sarah.

She didn't like to admit it, but sometimes she felt that if she were to paint a picture, it would resemble one of these. They were all about dislocation,

22

emptiness, and, especially, loneliness. They tended to be set in remote locations, way out in the countryside or in parts of the city where no one ever ventured. They rarely featured more than one person and that person always seemed to have his back to the viewer. There were never any faces.

Sarah could stare for hours at the strange, isolated figures in their desolate landscapes. She got the impression that the figures were consumed with loss – of love, innocence, freedom, dignity...whatever there was to lose. Although she couldn't see any faces, she knew they were all staring into the distance, seeking to retrieve whatever it was that they had lost.

That was exactly how she felt. Why did her parents have to die in that car crash? In a blink, she'd lost everything.

Rain lashed against the gallery's windows, battering the glass as if it were trying to break in. After days of sultry weather, a huge thunderstorm had arrived. Flashes of lightning ripped across the Manhattan skyline. Then came booming thunder.

Sarah gazed down into the street. People were scattering into whatever hiding places they could find. A group of men in dark suits hurried inside the gallery. They'd probably stay in the lobby for a few minutes and then leave when the rain eased off, Sarah thought.

It was only a few minutes later when a man in a grey suit and candy-striped tie entered the penthouse gallery. For a moment, Sarah felt a wave of extreme...annoyance was the first thing she thought of, but she realised it was stronger than that – much stronger – *revulsion*. Then it was replaced by the opposite. Tanned, blue-eyed and blond, the man was like a hero from some romantic legend.

He gazed at her in an odd way. 'Hello, I'm Robert Montcrieff. Have we met?'

'I'm sure I would have remembered.' Despite her answer, Sarah was also aware of some vague familiarity. 'I'm Sarah Harris and I run the gallery.' She extended her hand.

Montcrieff took it and seemed to hold on for an extra second.

'Your name,' Sarah said. 'I'm sure I've heard it somewhere.'

Montcrieff smiled. 'Well, I knew yours: your colleague Jenny was keen we should meet.'

Sarah grimaced. So, matchmaker Jenny was meddling again. She must have noticed that Mr Montcrieff didn't have a wedding ring and immediately concluded that two single people were in need of being thrown together.

'Jenny has some strange ideas.' Sarah began flicking her hair. She studied Montcrieff as he positioned himself in front of a large exhibit. He moved like someone who knew how to control a room, to direct everyone's attention towards him. *An actor*? She wished she spent more time reading newspapers and watching TV. Her lack of knowledge of celebrities often caught her out. Mostly, she stayed at home with her cat, drinking red wine and trying to remember why she wanted to forget.

Montcrieff was looking at the only item in the gallery that didn't legitimately belong in the Death Row collection. It was a framed photograph of a Peregrine falcon in Central Park.

'This is fantastic,' Montcrieff said. 'Did one of the prisoners take this?'

Sarah blushed.

'Ah, I see.' Montcrieff winked.

'What?'

'Don't worry, I won't tell anyone.'

Sarah stepped closer to him. She liked the way his mind worked so quickly. He'd probably realised straight away that a Death Row prisoner would never have been allowed to take photographs in Central Park. Her embarrassed reaction must have immediately revealed it was her own picture.

'You came in here to get out of the rain, didn't you?' she said. 'I wouldn't put you down as someone interested in Death Row art.'

Montcrieff gave a faint smile and turned to one of the most striking paintings. It showed a man in a black trenchcoat standing in a wilderness, gazing out over a lake. From a bright yellow sun in the top right corner of the painting, large blue drops fell.

'*Solar Cyanide*,' Montcrieff said, reading the title of the painting.

'The man who painted that killed five children in Tennessee,' Sarah said. 'His trademark was to kill his victims on the hottest days of the year. He took them out to dusty fields near isolated lakes and strangled them. Afterwards, he used an eye-dropper to drip prussic acid onto their faces.'

'Prussic acid is cyanide, right?'

Sarah nodded. 'The serial killer claimed he loved each of his victims, but that all love is poisonous. He said that when he thought of love he imagined poison dripping from the sun.'

'I see: solar cyanide. Isn't it depressing being surrounded by stuff like this?'

'I think everyone should come to see these paintings.'

Montcrieff scanned around. 'They're all so lonely. Sadness radiates from them. It's almost overwhelming.'

'When did an art gallery last make you feel that way?'

The Ghouls' Gallery

A man stomped into the room, with Jenny a few steps behind, looking excited.

'Mr Montcrieff, they want you over there in thirty for the set-up. We have to go.'

Montcrieff shrugged and turned to Sarah. 'It was nice meeting you, Miss Harris. I'm glad it rained.'

'Likewise, Mr Montcrieff.'

Moments later Montcrieff and his colleague had disappeared.

Jenny looked like she was about to faint. 'Have you any idea who *that* was?'

'The name rings a bell, but I can't place him.'

'Most of those men he came in with were bodyguards,' Jenny said. 'There was a media adviser too.'

'I'm not following. Is he a movie star or something?'

Jenny clapped her hands. 'Sarah, you've just met the next president.' She explained that Robert Montcrieff was en route to Craigavon Hall on Fifth Avenue to announce formally that he was standing for the presidency. Thousands of supporters were waiting for him. Five TV networks had sent teams to film the rally and reporters were present from all over the world.

At first it seemed incredible, but the more Sarah thought about it, the less surprised she was. Montcrieff was a rich, handsome man with charisma, a commanding presence, and a quick mind.

'And best of all,' Jenny said, 'he's *single*.'

'Come off it, Jenny. I'll never meet him again in my life. Not that I think he was interested in me anyway.'

'I saw the way he looked at you.'

Sarah shook her head and turned away.

****

The following day, Sarah was at the gallery as usual, but she wasn't paying attention to the Death Row pictures. The plasma screen in reception showed Robert Montcrieff's formal declaration that he was running for president. Far from writing him off as a hopeless outsider, analysts were saying he had a chance, maybe a good one. Opinion polls had already given him a rating only marginally behind the President and his main Democrat rival.

To Sarah, it seemed so random that she'd met a potential president. Without that thunderstorm, Robert Montcrieff would never have come into her gallery. He would have walked by and she'd never have known.

Prohibition A

Sometimes it frightened her to think of how much of life was shaped by chance events like that. Serial killers said that when they went out looking for victims they usually encountered several likely targets. It was frequently pure accident that they picked one rather than another. Maybe the victim looked at them at the wrong moment in the wrong way; maybe the victim turned right rather than left; maybe they stopped at a traffic light, or crossed the road seconds too early or too late. Maybe they had headphones on, were looking in a shop window, or had bent down to tie a shoelace. It might be anything. Insignificant details could mean life or death. People were walking around now who would be dead if they'd done something infinitesimally different. They'd never know how close they came to being a serial killer's next victim. Could life really be as haphazard as that?

It was midday when the flowers arrived; a grand bouquet of yellow carnations. The delivery guy had only just stepped into reception when Jenny leapt on him. She grabbed the bouquet with one hand, signed for it with the other then broke into a grin as she thrust the flowers at Sarah.

'I knew it,' she said. She waved the greetings card.

Sarah snatched it and read the message.

'Hi, Sarah,' it said. 'Enjoyed the lightning show. Maybe I got hit and didn't realise it. Dinner?' It was signed by Robert Montcrieff and there was an e-mail address underneath.

Sarah gazed at it and all she could think of was dice rolling in every direction. Her life had become a casino game.

'Start e-mailing, honey,' Jenny said. 'Even you couldn't be dumb enough to turn down Robert Montcrieff.'

Sarah took the elevator to her penthouse sanctuary. The last thing she wanted was Jenny delving into her feelings for Montcrieff. She'd only just met the man. OK, he was gorgeous and about as eligible as you could get, but something was wrong. Gazing at her picture of the Peregrine falcon in Central Park, she felt a sensation of – the word that jumped into her mind was betrayal. She shook her head and poured herself some water from the dispenser at the back of the room. *Nerves*, she thought.

****

Sarah had never eaten in the *Ludovico*. With every table reserved for months in advance, the idea of getting a last-minute table here was ludicrous – except, of course, she was now the guest of a presidential candidate. She nervously tapped her foot against the polished floorboards. It didn't seem right that she should be here. From art gallery curator to one of the glitterati in one bound, all thanks to a thunderstorm. She glanced around. It was weird having security men at the adjacent tables. Whenever she went to the restroom, one of them followed. Everyone kept staring at her, whispering. She'd never felt more self-conscious in her life. Every now and again she heard an odd snapping noise and wondered what it was and why it was making her so agitated.

Thank God for Robert. He seemed unconcerned about the waiters fussing around, the other diners gawping, the security men twitching. There were no intrusive questions, no awkward silences. She couldn't imagine a more charming man.

'You took a chance sending me those flowers,' she said. 'I might have had a boyfriend.'

'For the things I want in life, I'd risk everything. Besides, your friend Jenny said I ought to see her *single* friend.'

Good old Jenny. Never one for subtlety.

At the end of a lobster meal, followed by a delicious sorbet sweet, the waiter served them coffee in beautiful china cups. Their conversation during the evening had studiously avoided work, politics, religion, and old love affairs. They discussed art, favourite books, travel. Now they moved onto dreams and Sarah was incredulous when she discovered they had one in common. Both of them had dreamt on several occasions that several of their limbs went missing during the course of their working day. Complete in the morning, they were disembodied by nightfall, a trail of their body parts left scattered around their office.

'I've never asked anyone what it means,' Robert admitted.

'I have.' With easy access to the FBI's behavioural psychologists, Sarah had a ready supply of well-qualified dream interpreters. 'I'm told it means my life is incomplete. Apparently I'm not giving sufficient attention to important aspects of my life. Those are the limbs dropping from my body. They're crying out to me to take care of them. If I want to be whole again, I must stop neglecting them.'

'I don't like the sound of that.' Robert frowned. 'I guess the aspect of my life I've neglected lately is romance.' He leaned across and tidied a stray hair hanging over Sarah's eyes. 'What about you? What are you neglecting?' He put his hands beneath the table.

Sarah tried to waft some air over her face. Again, she heard a strange snapping sound. What *was* it?

Prohibition A

Robert leaned closer. 'Do you believe in instant connections? From the first second we met I felt there was a bond between us. We have stuff in common, I'm certain of it. That bolt of lightning – it was no accident'

'I feel the same way,' Sarah said quietly.

Robert took both of her hands in his. 'I'd like to see you again.'

Sarah looked at him but didn't reply. She felt as if thousands of butterflies were inside her, fluttering their wings all at once.

'I hope you say *yes*.' Robert shrugged awkwardly. 'But I'd need to have your background checked out to make sure there's nothing embarrassing there. Not that I'm expecting anything. You're in the FBI, after all.'

The thought of Robert probing her past appalled Sarah. Regardless of what the psychologists said, she'd always understood what her lost limbs dream was really about. The limbs were forgotten episodes from her past, and she didn't want to remember what they were.

'So, *do* you have any secrets?' Robert asked.

The question startled Sarah, but it was something else that grabbed her attention. She now realised what the snapping sound was – Robert was interlocking one hand with another and making a clicking sound with his knuckles. For some reason, the sound and the gesture made her feel sick.

5

Wedding Arrangements

'What is it?' Robert leaned forward and squeezed Sarah's cheek.

'I'm just trying to take it all in.' Sarah gazed around the small reception room in Carnegie Hall, and wished she could be at home, away from all of this. She hated the attention, the photographers, the reporters, Robert's cronies.

'Well, you were fantastic out there.' Robert hesitated. 'Hell, I forgot to announce the wedding date.'

'We haven't discussed it yet.' Sarah gave him a puzzled smile.

'The date's already arranged. It's next week – Monday.'

'I hadn't even said *yes* until five minutes ago.'

'Well...'

'Anyway, Monday's the day before the election.'

'Think of the feel-good factor. On Election Day, every newspaper in the country will have our wedding pictures on the front page.'

'Robert, you can't reduce our wedding to a campaign manoeuvre.'

Robert sighed. 'Sarah, remember we lay under that cherry blossom tree last year and said we hoped we were the kind of people who'd make any sacrifice for the one we loved? Well, I love you and I'm asking you to make this sacrifice for me.'

Sarah's face reddened. 'One week is do-able, I guess,' she replied quietly.

Robert took her hand, lifted it and kissed it.

Sarah's mind went back to that special day under the cherry blossom tree. It was *so* perfect it seemed almost unreal, as if some god had specially manufactured it for her. Didn't a Chinese philosopher say that you were blessed if, in a lifetime, you could have one hundred days that came close to your best day? She was hoping for thousands of days like that one.

'OK, we only have a week.' She managed a faint smile. 'I guess everything is already planned. Tell me what you have in mind.'

'The mother of all weddings.'

Sarah remembered that Jenny predicted that very thing. In a way, she was relieved that Robert was taking control. Maybe she would have enjoyed getting involved with the arrangements for a small-scale wedding, but Robert's plans were sure to be on the grand scale. Besides, as an orphan with no parents and no family, she couldn't get into weddings in the way most women did. And she cut up those wedding pictures in her childhood, didn't she? Weddings had always made her uncomfortable.

A bunch of kids burst in, escorted by a flustered mum struggling to keep them under control.

'I need to *go*!' a boy wailed.

'Right now?' His mum rolled her eyes.

'*Now*!'

'If you want, we'll keep an eye on the rest of them for you until you get back,' Sarah said helpfully.

'Well, I shouldn't really leave them. I mean, I don't...'

'*Now*!' the boy repeated, even more loudly.

'Oh, come on then,' the woman said and led him away, nodding awkwardly at Sarah and Robert.

Robert winked at Sarah. 'Did you see that? – not a flicker of recognition from her. She must be voting for the other guy.'

Sarah noticed that the remaining kids had stopped talking and were staring at Robert and her.

'I suppose you've already arranged the venue,' she said.

'We can talk about it.'

'Where do you suggest?'

'How does this grab you? *St Patrick's Cathedral*. TV cameras will be there. We'll bring Fifth Avenue to a standstill. It will be *huge*.'

Sarah was raised as a Catholic, but she had no idea about Robert's religious persuasion. 'Why not Vegas? Just the two of us and a couple of Elvis impersonators. You know the kind of thing.'

Robert eyed her curiously, obviously unsure whether she was being serious or not. 'I'll tell you what, let's put it to the vote.' He gestured towards the children. 'Let's ask the future electorate what they think. Deal?'

'*Deal*.' This would be a revelation. Sarah was certain the kids would choose Vegas.

Robert crouched down in the middle of the kids. 'You see the pretty lady? I'm going to marry her.' The kids booed, but Robert persisted. 'Where do you think the wedding should be? Right here in the fantastic Big Apple or in trashy Vegas way out there in the desert? I have a dollar for everyone who gives me the right answer.'

The kids held a quick conference. 'Vegas! Vegas!' they squealed. The smallest clapped his hands. 'My dad won a thousand bucks in the big black pyramid.'

Wedding Arrangements

Robert put his roll of dollars back in his pocket and returned to Sarah, while the kids surrounded him, demanding money. 'A buck each if you say St Patrick's,' he whispered out of the corner of his mouth.

'St Patrick's!' they all shouted.

'The people have spoken,' Robert announced.

The perfect politician, Sarah thought. He could even get kids on the bankroll.

'So, St Pat's it is.' Robert paid off his little accomplices. 'I'm glad that's settled. I had to call in a lot of favours to get it at such short notice.'

Sarah didn't answer. She felt dizzy and, for a moment, thought she'd faint. She heard herself saying, 'Have I been here before?'

'What?' Robert peered at her.

'You…don't you rush off now and bring back a red rose? A horse and carriage is going past, with a newly wed couple.'

'What are you talking about?'

Sarah saw herself in a dream in which everything was red. Wearing a red crop top and crazy hot pants, she was waiting for someone. Not Robert.

'Is something wrong?' Robert asked.

'I feel strange.'

'Strange feelings aren't allowed today. Listen, are you sure you're OK about St Patrick's?'

'It's great.' Sarah tried to give Robert an enthusiastic kiss. The kids made gagging gestures. 'Honeymoon?' she prompted. She was still uncomfortably conscious of something being way off beam.

'We're going to Monte Carlo,' Robert said. 'You said you always dreamt of going there. We'll fly out the day after the election. It will be a double celebration. I've booked the Wedding Suite in the Grand Hotel next to the Casino.'

Sarah couldn't argue with that. It sounded perfect. An image flashed into her mind. She was lying in a four-poster bed, rolling about in her wedding dress amongst hundreds of colourful playing cards. Robert was laughing. When she looked at the cards, she saw that they were all the same. She felt giddy again.

Why only red queens?

6

Alice Through the Looking Glass

General Clark sat alone in his office, thinking of Doyle's parting words about Dexter. *We all know he's one of the most dangerous men on earth.*

Christ, Dexter. It really *was* him. Dexter had pulled off many incredible things in his life. Faking his own death was well within his capabilities. As Warren had suggested, did that throw doubt on Sarah?

Clark shivered. He daren't think of any flaws in Alice Through the Looking Glass. It was the entire purpose of the Neulander Institute. Masquerading as a medical facility for the treatment of severe psychiatric disorders, the institute was the home of Special Military Intelligence's research team. All the stuff that Hollywood fantasised about in thrillers and sci-fi movies, all the stuff that conspiracy theorists salivated over, all the material that 'alien visitation experts' gave lecture tours on – all of it was in the Neulander.

It was named after the obscure 17th century German philosopher Friedrich Neulander who declared: 'The purpose of mankind is secret. Uncovering that secret is *everything*.' That was the inscription above the front doors of the institute. Everyone who passed through those doors believed it implicitly. They saw themselves as a super elite.

To an outsider, the institute's staff would have seemed like ghosts, floating through the strangest of universes. The institute offered direct access to the deepest, most elemental parts of the human psyche.

Cryptographers, cosmologists, sociologists, psychologists, psychiatrists, mathematicians, anthropologists, historians, philosophers, and scientists of every description were here. Their subject was the human mind. Why was it the way it was; what were its capabilities, its properties, its processes? Most importantly – how could it be changed? Why engage in costly and damaging wars if you could manipulate the minds of your enemies to make them obey you? That was the knowledge, the power, SMI sought to acquire. Complete mind control of everyone, everywhere, *permanently*.

He remembered the day two years earlier when he revealed the true nature of the Looking Glass project to the other members of the Committee. It was just three months after Sarah shot Dexter in Central Park. Things had started so well, yet in the space of a few minutes, he thought his world was about to disintegrate…

Two Years Earlier

'We've had problems,' David Warren said. 'Your daughter was in love.'

General Clark stopped, grabbed Warren by the arms and pinned him against the wall. 'Don't ever call that woman my *daughter*. Sarah Harris is an orphan. Understood?' People were staring at him, but he knew no one would dare to argue with a four-star general. Releasing his hold, his thoughts returned to the nightmare that had preoccupied him for days. Soon, he'd see Sarah in the flesh and that same anger that overwhelmed him every time he was near her would grip him. He couldn't let it get to him. There was too much at stake.

'OK, Sarah loved Dexter. So what? She killed him, didn't she?' Clark watched as Warren took out a handkerchief and mopped his brow.

David Warren, chief scientist of the Neulander Institute, was fat and pig-like with a swollen face. The former Columbia University professor of Psychology was fifty-eight but liked to pretend he was twenty years younger. A vain and pedantic prick, Clark thought. Nevertheless, he was a man on the up, earmarked as a future CIA Director. No one doubted he was a genius at getting inside broken minds. If he'd struggled to put Sarah back together again, she must have been in a bad way.

'Her mind was tuned into Dexter,' Warren said. 'Her memories, her emotions, even her dreams. To unravel that…I'm not sure we've succeeded.' He shrugged. 'She seems OK, but who knows what she'll be like years from now. It could all come back. A powerful enough emotional trigger would tip her over. I mean, if she ever found out she killed the love of her life…'

'Save the propaganda. I just want to know if she can do one more big op.'

Warren frowned. 'Probably. I can't say for sure. The love element is particularly unpredictable.'

'Love? Don't make me laugh.' Clark's body bristled. 'Listen, there's only one difference between love and mental illness. Both are distorted versions of reality, except with mental illness you don't have to fuck the thing making you ill.' He almost spat as he said it. Love was something he'd come to regard as a branch of pathology.

Warren took an object out of his pocket and held it up.

Clark examined it: a locket on a silver neck-chain. 'Why are you showing me this?'

'It contains a picture of Dexter. Sarah always wore it.'

'You think I give a damn? Get rid of it.'

Warren returned the locket to his pocket. They walked on in silence then Warren opened a door with his security smartcard and led Clark into the complex that housed the Neulander's experimental labs. They marched through the maze of whitewashed corridors, past men and women in white coats hurrying in and out of labs, clutching clipboards and palm-sized computers.

It was eight years, Clark realised, eight *long* years since he last set foot inside the Neulander Institute. Located in the outskirts of Albany, the remote capital of New York State, it was the perfect location for a top-secret facility.

He hated the smell of this place, like a hospital where the floors had been mopped with a foul-smelling cleaning fluid. As they went past each lab, he glanced up at the TV monitors positioned above the locked doors, showing the experiments going on inside.

Some of the rooms resembled torture chambers, full of mazes, assault courses and electric shock equipment. Others contained hi-tech machines, state-of-the-art devices costing tens of millions of dollars that could monitor every process happening inside a human body, especially inside the brain. In other rooms, shaven-headed men and women in white boiler suits were sitting like showroom dummies while someone in a lab coat stood beside them, taking notes. The room that particularly caught Clark's attention was empty apart from a plastic seat and a red light that flashed every half second. That was the room where Sarah was taken most often.

'The other members of the Committee are in Lecture Room One,' Warren said. 'Sarah's waiting in an annexe.'

Clark grabbed his arm. 'She won't recognise me?'

'She still believes she's an orphan, as per your original instructions.'

Clark wished he didn't have to go through with this, but he had to be sure.

As they approached the room, Warren halted. 'When you see your dau... em, when you see Sarah, remember that a week ago she was a basket case. She kept asking where Dexter was. It was driving me nuts.'

'I read your report. I'm fully aware of the problems you've had. If Sarah is usable again, you'll get your reward.'

'I want that promotion. I deserve it.'

'I told you, if everything's OK, you'll get what's coming to you.'

Alice Through the Looking Glass

'What about Grissom and Lassiter?'

Clark tensed up. Steve Grissom, Director of the CIA, and Gary Lassiter, Director of the FBI, might ruin everything. 'Have you got a plan?' he asked. 'They might have to be…' He thought of the right words. 'Dealt with.'

'I have it all worked out,' Warren said. 'What happens to Sarah after this, now that she's been normalised?'

'I'm making use of her art background.'

Warren laughed. 'You mean you're sticking her in the Ghouls' Gallery?'

Clark disliked that nickname, but it was accurate enough. The Ghouls' Gallery was one of the FBI's most controversial projects. Although it was regarded in many quarters as sick and tasteless, it had proved quite a commercial success and supporters claimed it allowed ordinary people to get an insight into the mind of murderers.

'It's ideal,' Clark said. 'It gets Sarah away from frontline duty for a while.'

'I guess so. The last thing we need is for Sarah to suffer any traumas in the field.' Warren paused. 'But the paintings are disturbing. Don't you think that's a risk?'

'Sarah studied Art History at Columbia. I'm sure she's used to seeing all kinds of stuff.'

As they walked on, Clark said, 'Tell me, why do you think she and Dexter wore those crazy clothes in Central Park?'

'Maximum visibility. Dexter thought we'd never try anything if there were too many witnesses. I mean, no one was going to forget a couple dressed like they were.'

'But we've never been worried about that kind of thing. Dexter knew that better than anyone.'

'His mind was coming apart.'

'Do you think he remembered everything that we did to him?'

'I wouldn't say that. At the end, his mind must have been like shifting sands: chaos, frankly. He wouldn't be sure what was real and what fabricated. It was amazing he kept his shit together at all. Most people would have gone completely psycho.

'What was for sure was that Dexter's stunt in Central Park made it easy for us to cover up the incident. The cleaning unit told witnesses they were filming a scene from a fantasy movie, hence why Sarah made no attempt to escape. One detective kicked up a fuss, but he shut his face when he was told his crack-cocaine habit might not look too good if anyone asked questions. In any case, he never got the chance to find out Sarah's real name. As for her appearance, it has changed dramatically since then. There's no way the detective or any of the other witnesses would recognise her.'

Warren opened the door to the lecture theatre and the two men went in. The other members of the Committee were seated in the front row of the tiered auditorium: Frank Doyle, Director of the Defence Intelligence Agency, Jim Carson, Director of the National Reconnaissance Organisation, Ted Boca, Director of the National Security Agency, Gary Lassiter, Director of the FBI and Steve Grissom, Director of the CIA. Clark knew that three of them were 'safe'. As for Grissom and Lassiter, Warren had assured him everything was 'under control'.

A white table and chair had been placed at the front of the room. There was a lectern for Warren and a plasma screen on the main wall.

Once he was seated, Clark signalled to Warren to begin.

Warren cleared his throat and glanced at his notes. 'Well, gentlemen, you've seen the video of what happened in Central Park three months ago. As you now know, Special Military Intelligence has been working on a classified project. It's fully described in the documents I've issued to you, so I'll run through the highlights only.

'In 1943, the OSS gave President Roosevelt a top-secret briefing after they intercepted Soviet intelligence communications saying that there was credible evidence that Jews released from Auschwitz had fought for the Nazis on the Russian Front as suicidal shock units. Somehow, the minds of the Jewish prisoners had been hijacked and they'd become human robots, dying in the service of their worst enemies. A weapon like that couldn't be ignored.

'Under Operation Paperclip of 1947, Nazi scientists, psychologists and psychiatrists who worked on mind control programmes and other high-profile scientific projects were secretly brought to the States. Nazi mind-manipulation techniques were then used on African-American prisoners in jails in Mississippi and Alabama, and on retarded inmates in mental institutions all over the country. Hypnosis, narco-hypnosis, drugs, radiation, psycho-electronics, electroshock, even brain surgery were all used in the search for effective mind control.

'Eventually, in 1950, all the unofficial projects were brought together under the code-name Bluebird. Its scope was later broadened and it was re-christened several times, most famously as MK-Ultra. In 1990, General Clark gave it its current name: *Alice Through the Looking Glass*.

'In the documents I've given you, you will see exactly how we...'

'Pavlov's dogs, huh?' The man who interrupted was Jim Carson, Director of the National Reconnaissance Organisation.

'Is this why we've been dragged out to this godforsaken place?' Gary Lassiter grunted. 'This is a retread of the stuff the CIA tried decades ago. They dropped that shit because it was going nowhere. Are you telling us SMI have been jacking off to it ever since?'

Clark frowned. Lassiter was living up to his billing. It was true Alice Through the Looking Glass in its earliest incarnations was a CIA operation, but they'd never appreciated its true worth. Clark expected Steve Grissom to support Lassiter, but the CIA man said nothing.

Warren took the interruption in his stride. 'Naturally, we began with classical techniques. As everyone knows, Pavlov fed a dog every time a bell was rung and eventually the dog salivated just on hearing the sound of the bell. He had trained the dog to do something unnatural – to dribble when a bell is rung. People are no different. You reward them when they do what you want and punish them when they don't. Before you know it, they're as compliant as any dog and dribble at the right times. It's the basis of religion, society, of all forms of social control.

'After, we moved on to sophisticated operant conditioning involving positive reinforcement and negative punishment, positive punishment and negative reinforcement.'

Lassiter laughed. 'All the usual hokum, huh? Sensory deprivation tanks, solitary confinement, sleep disruption, subliminal manipulation. For Christ's sake, you probably recruited animal trainers. I know the CIA did.'

Clark swapped a glance with Frank Doyle, Director of the Defence Intelligence Agency. Today, Doyle had his arm in a sling after a riding accident. He might be a little worse for wear but he was one of the most reliable men Clark knew. Doyle wouldn't let him down today. Would Warren?

'All of the above,' Warren said. 'And some extras. We drugged our subjects, bombarded them with microwave transmissions targeting the temporal region of the brain. We stuck electrodes in their brains, made them ill with LSD, subjected them to days of narco-hypnosis. Bottom line is that we succeeded in washing their minds perfectly clean.'

'Yeah, *right*,' Lassiter retorted sarcastically, looking at his colleagues for support.

Clark was relieved to see that the others, even Grissom, were ignoring the FBI Director. Then he noticed Grissom dipping his hand in and out of his pocket. What was he doing? Reaching for his cell phone; a pager? Something seemed wrong.

'We controlled everything,' Warren continued, 'even when our subjects went to the restroom to take a leak. We chose when to let sights, sounds, smell, touch, tastes enter their lives. We played Beethoven's *Moonlight Sonata* or Louis Armstrong's *What a Wonderful World* to them. We recited the poetry of Blake, Dante, Milton, Pindar and others. We filled their heads with dozens of psychological triggers that could be used to control them. Subliminal messages were implanted at every level of consciousness. We made personal movies for them showing life-changing events that never happened; yet, they believed them implicitly. In short, we became their God.'

'I get the picture,' Lassiter said. 'But the CIA could have said most of that fifty years ago. What do you have that really makes a difference? What's new?'

'Multiple Personality Syndrome is the key,' Warren answered. 'We've discovered how to reliably create a second, hidden personality within any person. This hidden personality is entirely under our control. It's always switched on and it's fully aware of the individual's normal personality. The relationship is asymmetric – the normal personality has no awareness of the hidden personality. We can transfer control to the hidden personality by use of a trigger. This is usually a codeword or password, accompanied by a specific acoustic tone to safeguard against accidental use. As you know, Sarah Harris's password is *Red Queen*.

'It's the task of the hidden personality to execute our mission orders. The hidden personality is able to manipulate the normal personality. It remains in control until delivery is complete then it withdraws into the subconscious again. While the mission is underway, the normal personality stays practically intact, so no one should notice any abnormal behaviour by the subject. The only exception is if the mission traumatises the normal personality. Then signs of psychosis may appear. The subject must be recovered for re-programming whereby we erase all negative memories before redeployment.'

'That's what happened with Sarah, isn't it?' It was Jim Carson who spoke.

Clark looked at Carson. With an over-sized head and buckteeth, Carson's appearance was unprepossessing but he was a straight-down-the-line guy, completely loyal, unlike Lassiter and Grissom. Once again, Clark's gaze was drawn to Grissom's pocket. What did he have in there?

Alice Through the Looking Glass

'OK, you have a degree of control over certain people's minds,' Lassiter butted in. 'So what? We were told we were here to be briefed on a revolutionary plan, something that could change everything. Mind control didn't change anything in the '50s and '60s. What's so different now? I bet you haven't overcome the problem of residuals.'

'Warren, bring Sarah out.' Clark stared at Lassiter. 'You're welcome to ask her any question about the Dexter mission.'

Warren opened a side door and called to Sarah.

Keeping his head down, Clark didn't look at the young woman who then walked into the room, whose soft breathing he could now hear. He remembered the false ID she'd been given in Central Park. *Jane Ford*: the maiden name of his ex-wife, Sarah's mother.

Jane? It should have been Jezebel. Where was the bitch now? He'd resisted the temptation to track her down, to find out what sordid life she must have fallen into when she left him to take up with some fast-talking bum. Even now, all these years later, his rage was raw. It was the one defeat he'd suffered in his life. He'd been besotted with baby Sarah until his wife told him he wasn't the father. The cuckoo in the nest. All the love he'd lavished on her was for nothing. Now the sight of her made him want to retch.

He pretended to his colleagues that it meant nothing, but inside it was rotting him, dissolving everything within him capable of redemption. Sometimes he felt he was being eaten alive by his memories of his unfaithful, lying wife. The irony was that when he took baby Sarah to hospital for paternity tests as part of divorce proceedings, the results confirmed that she was his after all.

But there was no way back.

'Sarah,' Warren said, 'your debriefing will be over soon and you can go home.' He gestured at his small audience. 'As you can see, we have several VIPs here today. I don't believe you've ever seen the Committee all together before. You won't recognise one of them. I can't tell you who he is for security reasons.'

'I understand,' Sarah said.

The voice sliced through Clark. So like his ex-wife's. For the first time, he raised his eyes. Sarah was dressed in a simple white blouse and black pencil skirt, and was smiling politely. Her long blonde hair had been shaved off after the Central Park mission and had now grown back in its natural chestnut colour. With her short hair giving her a Joan of Arc air, she looked particularly striking. Clark's heart thudded against his rib cage. Nature is cruel, he thought. It shouldn't remind you of your failures…your humiliations. Yet, whenever he looked at his daughter that was how he felt. That face, those copper eyes, every expression, so like her mother. *I can't do this*, he thought. But he had no choice. He poured himself a glass of water, barely stopping his hand from shaking. Lassiter smirked at him.

'Sarah, for the benefit of our audience, we want to run over some of the details of your mission,' Warren said.

This is it, Clark thought. Now we'll find out. He breathed in hard, trying to control himself.

'I gave you everything in my written statement,' Sarah replied.

'I know, Sarah, but we have to check some details, make sure nothing was missed.'

Sarah shrugged. 'OK, one more time. The Delivery Manager contacted me and gave me details of the target. I was told John Dexter would be in an underground parking garage in Baltimore, expecting to meet a member of his organisation. I was given the location of the parking garage and details of where I should position myself to take the shot. I was told I'd have only one chance.

'Dexter showed up on time. No one else was in the parking garage. I fired at Dexter's chest from ten yards, using a Heckler & Koch P9S pistol. The shot attracted some people from another level of the parking garage. I got out, using an agreed escape route. I learned later that Dexter was declared DOA at the hospital. End of story. It's all in the report.'

Warren had done his job well, Clark thought. Sarah had been implanted with a false memory of what happened with Dexter. But it was so much more than that. Her whole life with Dexter had been airbrushed away. Dexter had become like one of those old Soviet politicians: standing next to Stalin one day, erased from history the next. Triumphantly, Clark looked over at Lassiter and Grissom. His pleasure didn't last. Lassiter appeared thoughtful but Grissom had stopped reaching into his pocket and was now glancing at his watch every few seconds. Why was he so interested in the time?

'Sarah, how much did you know about Dexter before the mission?' Grissom asked, speaking for the first time.

She looked at him in obvious surprise. 'I knew what everyone knew. He was our top agent but he'd gone rogue. He set up his own organisation and tried to recruit our agents.'

'Did you have any feelings for him?'

40

'Pardon me? First time I saw him in the flesh was that day in Baltimore. I was curious about why a guy like that turned against us, but I figure you're not going to tell me.'

'One last thing, Sarah,' Grissom said. 'Tell us what you remember about your father.'

Bastard. Clark had to stop himself grabbing Grissom. Everyone knew that subject was permanently off limits. Grissom held up his wrist and ostentatiously looked at his watch. What was the jerk trying to say? That time was running out?

'OK, I think that's enough,' Warren intervened. 'Thanks, Sarah, you've been very helpful.'

'Can I go now?' Sarah shot a puzzled glance at Grissom and then back at Warren.

'In a minute, Sarah.' Warren pressed a button on the lectern and, a moment later, the door opened and a man in a grey suit came in carrying a black cat with amber eyes. He dropped the cat and it scampered over to Sarah.

Clark gave the newcomer a double take: *The Delivery Manager.*

Sarah laughed, scooped up the cat and pressed it against her cheek, before giving it a kiss. 'God, where did you find him? I was so worried.'

'A little surprise,' Warren said. 'What's his name, Sarah?'

'Clever Kitty,' she beamed. Smiling, she tickled the cat under its chin, making it purr.

Warren nodded to the Delivery Manager. He took Sarah by the arm and led her away. A second later, the door closed and she was gone.

Clark shook his head. Thank God, it was over...just Lassiter and Grissom left to worry about.

'So, Mr Lassiter, what do you think of the job I did on Sarah?' Warren asked.

'She seems normal,' Lassiter answered flatly.

Clark almost smiled. Warren had done excellent work. It was incredible – *miraculous* – the way Dexter had been flushed out of Sarah's system. But, always, there was that same worry – would it stay that way? A single emotional shock, if it were big enough, could change everything. He'd never tell Lassiter and Grissom that, of course. They mustn't know of any drawbacks. The Committee had to back the plan unanimously. One way or another, those two must be persuaded.

'Did the CIA ever manage anything like this?' Warren asked Grissom.

Prohibition A

Grissom shook his head. 'Residuals usually kicked in quickly. Most of our subjects went loco straight after an op.'

'What exactly are residuals?' asked Ted Boca, Director of the National Security Agency.

'You can't fully reprogramme a mind,' Warren replied. 'There are residual memories, residual behavioural patterns. Traces of the past manage to cling on in places. It can lead to mental health problems, and ultimately to psychosis.'

'So, you admit Sarah will go nuts one day?' Lassiter said. 'She's a ticking bomb, huh?'

'I acknowledge that residuals may still be a problem,' Warren commented, 'but we think we have much better control nowadays. The bomb, as you put it, may never go off.'

'Yeah, but now we know the truth about Dexter. You haven't said so, but it's obvious he was part of your mind control programme too. He left the reservation, didn't he? That's why Sarah killed him.'

For the first time, Warren seemed embarrassed. Clark felt the same way. Until today, none of the other members of the Committee were aware of Alice Through the Looking Glass. Of course, they were fascinated when they heard that Sarah shot SMI's star agent, especially since it was common knowledge that they were lovers. Obviously, it was no ordinary op. They started asking questions and now he and Warren had been forced to supply answers before they were ready.

'Yes,' Warren said, 'Dexter was a programmed assassin.' He coughed nervously. 'And, yes, he suffered from residuals. But you must remember that he completed forty-nine successful missions. As you know, he was given the Distinguished Intelligence Cross three times – awarded by the President himself. That makes him the best agent this country ever had. What better proof could there be of the effectiveness of Alice Through the Looking Glass? And when things began to go wrong, we were able to carry out an effective cleaning operation, using a second brainwashed agent. Even though Sarah loved Dexter, our programming was strong enough to make her obey our orders.'

'What happened to Sarah's memories of Dexter?' Lassiter asked.

'They're still there, but we've pushed them deep into her subconscious.' Warren gave an odd smile. 'I've given her other things to think about. A dead falcon, Mississippi and wedding photographs, amongst other things. Cognitive dissonance is the key. Would you like me to explain?'

'Spare us the psychobabble,' Lassiter snapped.

42

'Aren't you impressed?' Clark interrupted. 'Surely, you can see the potential?'

'OK, I concede that this is clever stuff, but how is it going to change the world? The CIA did tricks with this baloney decades ago. In the end, it didn't amount to a hill of beans. That's why they dumped it.'

Clark ignored Lassiter and turned to Grissom who'd remained oddly restrained throughout, apart from that one intervention when Sarah was present. Again, Grissom looked at his watch.

Now Clark did the same. It was 12 o'clock, time for the news round up. He noticed two things: Warren was peering at him and Grissom was again reaching into his pocket.

No time to worry about it. Clark switched on the plasma screen. It showed a live feed from CNN. A message ran across the bottom of the screen saying, 'Breaking News...'

A newsreader said, 'Multi-millionaire property magnate Robert Montcrieff, owner of a chain of a highly profitable upmarket health clubs, nightclubs, restaurants and leisure centres, has refused to deny growing speculation that he may launch a bid for the presidency on a radical independent ticket. Analysts believe that the charismatic 37-year-old bachelor will throw his hat into the ring if a series of private polls currently being conducted by his advisers suggest he will be a serious contender. It's thought that his running mate is likely to be Grace Rebello, the glamorous African-American professor of economics at Harvard, widely tipped as a future Nobel Prize winner. Commentators have said this would be a formidable team that could capture the imagination of many voters disillusioned with mainstream politics.'

A video-clip showed Montcrieff addressing a prestigious audience at a business conference in Chicago. He stood in front of a line of American flags, making him look the perfect patriot. 'For the Washington elite,' Montcrieff declared, 'politics isn't public service, it's *self-service*.' To rapturous cheers he concluded by saying, 'If the political establishment refuses to give America a government she can be proud of then the time has come when others must provide the leadership that this great nation demands and deserves.'

Warren, a friend of Montcrieff, had long predicted that this energetic, handsome man was destined for great things. If he ran for the presidency and won then the Committee would have easy access to the new president. That was the easy option. Clark had something very different in mind.

Prohibition A

'What has any of this got to do with…' Lassiter stopped in mid-sentence then nodded. 'I get it. Sarah Harris is going to have a close encounter of the fatal kind with the President, is that it? Or maybe you think this Montcrieff guy will make it to the White House and you want to…'

Clark turned off the TV. 'It's time for me to tell you all exactly why I asked you to come here today. You've been given the flavour of Alice Through the Looking Glass, but I've said nothing about…' He looked at each of them in turn. 'The precise objectives.'

'I've heard enough.' Steve Grissom stood up. 'What you're talking about is treason.'

Clark stared at his rival. 'Every patriot has a duty to preserve his country. We're in a position of unique power. If the time comes when the prevailing administration cannot protect the interests of the country, the burden falls on us to give the country the government it needs. We must be ready to move at any moment. All the necessary machinery is in place.'

'It's the people who change governments, not us. There's a thing called an election, or had you forgotten?'

Clark bristled. 'You support *this* administration? After everything that's happened?'

'Maybe the government isn't America, but the people are,' Grissom replied. 'And they voted the government into power. Live with it.'

'I told you, we must be ready for all eventualities. In these uncertain times, civil administration may not always be appropriate.' Clark glanced at his colleagues and saw several of them nodding. 'If terrorists wiped out the administration, we all know that regardless of the legal niceties we'd take charge. There would be no alternative. Equally, if the administration lacks the will to do the things required to protect this country, are we not duty-bound to intervene?' Astonishingly, Lassiter was nodding. Everyone was on board except Grissom. 'Drastic times demand drastic actions,' Clark said. 'I believe this decade will be the most critical in America's history. The question is whether we're strong enough for the challenges that lie ahead.'

'But it's much more than that, isn't it?' Grissom said. 'You guys want to be the judges of whether the government is up to the job. Hell, it sounds as though you've already reached the conclusion that it isn't. Are you planning a coup?'

'We want you to join us.'

'I believe in the Constitution.'

'Get real,' Clark said. 'If you love your country, you'll know that sometimes to protect your country you must be strong enough to protect it

44

from itself. Survival isn't compulsory. We must have the will to do the unthinkable.'

'What are you saying?'

'When Adolf Hitler wanted to seize power in Germany, he knew he needed a crisis. When one didn't come along, he created it himself. He burned down the German parliament and claimed a Dutch Jew was responsible. He demanded emergency powers and got them.'

'So, you're going to engineer a crisis; manipulate the election somehow and get yourselves into power, or one of your puppets. This Montcrieff guy, is he...'

'Mr Grissom...who says the next election will take place?'

'You're joking, right? Let me see if I'm getting this. Alice Through the Looking Glass has provided you with a whole gang of brainwashed, pre-programmed sleeper assassins to get rid of anyone who opposes you. One for the President, one for the Vice President, one for every person in the presidential succession. Then you guys will step in to fill the vacuum. Am I warm?'

'You can choose to ignore the lessons of the modern world, but we won't. Military operations against our enemies aren't the answer – just look at the mess we got into in Afghanistan and Iraq. Now we're zeroing in on something completely different. I'm talking about mind control, private and public, local and global. All of our enemies will be subdued without a bullet being fired, without a single body bag being flown home. Total security for America. *Forever.*'

'You really mean this, don't you? You've actually planned it.'

'Are you with us or not?'

'Pax Americana and all that bullshit?' Grissom said. 'America über alles. You want to make the rest of the world our slaves.'

'I take it that's a *no*.'

Before Grissom replied, the doors on either side of the auditorium burst open. Ten agents in dark suits flooded in, accompanied by a man whom Clark immediately recognised – the Attorney General.

'Right on time.' Grissom pulled a document from his pocket then looked at Lassiter. 'Gary, whose side are you on?'

Clark expected Lassiter to join Grissom. Instead, Lassiter said, 'I'm sorry, Steve. 'It's like Clark says – to defend America, we must have the will to do things we can barely imagine.'

'In that case, I have a warrant for the arrest of every one of you, signed by the Attorney General. As you can see, he has now joined us with several of my agents. The charge is treason. I've recorded everything said in this room in the last half hour. It confirms what we already suspected.'

Clark looked at his colleagues. This was impossible. Warren had assured him that every aspect of security had been handled. There had been no leaks. He watched in silence as Grissom made his way to the front of the room and stood beside the Attorney General.

It was over. He was finished. They all were. Lassiter too. Why hadn't the FBI man taken the chance to join Grissom and save himself? Then he noticed Warren moving towards Grissom. Grissom's agents glanced at Warren, but did nothing. Warren pulled out something from his inside pocket. A hypodermic needle? He plunged it into Grissom's neck. It was over in a second. Grissom slumped to the ground making a gurgling sound. Froth trickled from his mouth.

Clark gazed at Warren, remembering what Warren had said earlier about having it all worked out. He must have discovered Grissom's plans. Did Lassiter know too? He realised two things. Warren had secured his promotion...and the final obstacle to Alice Through the Looking Glass had just vanished.

He thought of what would happen now. The preparations for seizing control of the government would be rolled out soon. They would revolve around Robert Montcrieff; a candidate whom Special Military Intelligence analysts predicted had an excellent chance of being elected the next president. A single man, though not for want of offers, Montcrieff was in need of a wife for political reasons. The signal to begin the final phase of the coup d'état would be an incident that would shock the world, involving Montcrieff and a uniquely eligible young woman.

Sarah Harris.

7

Memories

Those damned circles. Several times that night, whenever she saw any glamorous young men and women, Sarah found herself staring at their wrists. That wasn't the only thing preoccupying her. Every time she caught sight of her own engagement ring, she shuddered. No matter how beautiful and expensive it was, it seemed wrong in every way.

She forced herself to smile, convinced that if she stopped she'd look like the saddest woman on earth. Why had she got herself into the dumb situation of having to answer an embarrassing personal question for Nicki's benefit? Her friend was peering at her, awaiting her answer. Robert was sitting back on the expensive green leather sofa, grinning. Spiegel was there too, taking a sudden and unexpected interest. She thought back to how she'd got into this ridiculous position.

At Craigavon Hall, Spiegel and Nicki had returned to rescue Robert and her from the kids' party. Minutes later they were back in Robert's campaign headquarters in Fifth Avenue, being sprayed with champagne, Formula-1 style, by Robert's campaign team. Everyone said the pictures from Craigavon Hall had played fantastically on TV. The on-air proposal was a sensation and news commentators were already talking of a new Camelot.

Sarah had stepped back as Robert made a neat little speech to his team. 'This is the best day of my life,' he announced amidst the cheers. 'But you know my philosophy – the best is yet to come.'

His staff were ecstatic, no doubt picturing themselves in Washington DC, going in and out of the White House every day, giving interviews to CNN, dining in the finest French restaurants. They could smell how close to power they were. She wished they could transmit that same exuberance to her. She'd never felt so flat.

'Ten jeroboams of champagne are on their way,' Robert declared, 'and the finest beluga caviar. No one deserves it more than you guys.' Then the final payoff. 'A week tomorrow, I'll be married. The following day I'll be President Elect. The day after, Sarah and I will be in Monte Carlo on honeymoon, but you guys will be partying in the Bellagio Hotel in Vegas for five days, all expenses paid. I've reserved a High Rollers table for you.' Wild yelling at that.

That was the moment when Nicki seized her chance. 'Sarah, that favour you were asking for back in Craigavon Hall?'

Ah yes, the favour. Their conversation was brief. 'Nicki, I want you to be my Maid of Honour.'

'Well, I have to warn you,' Nicki replied with a wink, 'I'm no maid and I have no honour.' The infallible law of TINSTAAFL – *there's no such thing as a free lunch* – then applied. An exclusive interview with the happy couple was Nicki's price. *Happy couple*? Sarah hoped she'd cheer up soon. She didn't want to spoil things for Robert.

She expected Robert or Spiegel to have objected to Nicki's suggestion, but they all thought it was a great idea. So all four of them had retreated to the Media Room and were now sitting on luxury leather sofas, sipping champagne, surrounded by paintings by up-and-coming artists. As for Nicki, she was going for the personal angle, 'the stuff the readers really want to know.'

It was Robert who playfully prompted Nicki to ask the dreaded question. 'Go on, Nicki,' he said. 'Ask Sarah why she has a model of an old Mississippi steamer in her apartment.'

Sarah had never managed to work out a smart response to that question. 'You can thank my teeth,' she responded at last.

'Teeth?'

'The gap between my two front teeth.' Instinctively, Sarah brought her hand up to cover her mouth. 'I've been self-conscious about it ever since I was a kid.'

'I'm not getting it. What's the connection?'

'I got a complex when a teacher at school made me spell Mississippi,' she said quietly. 'I tried so hard, but when I got to "s", I made this high-pitched whistling sound through the gap. The other kids thought it was hilarious. "Stand on the table, Sarah Harris," the teacher ordered. "Spell the word all the way to the end." The taunts from the other kids got so bad I ended up going to speech therapy for months afterwards. I had to learn how to breathe differently, change the way I moved my lips, even use my tongue differently. It was horrible.' She ran her finger over her lips. 'Now, when I smile, I make sure I keep my lips together.'

'Why don't you get veneers or something?' Spiegel interrupted. It was what everyone asked, as if to have less than perfect movie-star teeth was an affront to nature.

'I've never got round to it,' Sarah replied. 'I can't imagine myself without my gappy teeth now.'

Memories

'I don't know why you want to be reminded of that kind of childhood trauma,' Nicki said. 'Shouldn't you ditch the steamer?'

'Who can forget?' Sarah stared glumly at the floor. 'I suppose it reminds me of where I've come from. Who I am.'

'Robert, what do you think?' Nicki asked.

'I wouldn't change a single thing. I love Sarah just the way she is.'

'And have *you* got any Mississippis in your cupboard?' Nicki said to Robert.

'How about this? I'm fascinated by an obscure poem called *Samson Agonistes* by Milton. Every day I find myself saying a few lines from it, sometimes whole verses, but I don't remember ever having learned.'

'Weird,' Nicki said. 'What's the poem about?'

He's never told me about this, Sarah thought.

'The trials of Samson after he was captured by the Philistines.'

'Samson, as in Samson and Delilah?'

'Yeah, that one – so don't let Sarah come anywhere near me with a pair of scissors or I might never make it to the White House.'

Nicki laughed and scribbled a few notes in her notebook, but a moment later, she couldn't stifle a yawn. 'I didn't get home until six this morning,' she explained. 'I was covering another story.'

'What story?' Sarah asked.

'I'm researching an article on the world's most controversial nightclub.'

'You went *there*?'

Nicki nodded. 'My fifth visit.'

'Does it live up to its rep?'

'Believe me, there's no place like *Prohibition A*.' Nicki turned to Robert. 'Have you been?'

Robert shook his head. 'I've heard so many things about that place.'

'It's all true,' Nicki said gleefully. 'You know what, it's the perfect place to take Sarah for her hen night. Trust me, it's an *experience*, a once-in-a-lifetimer.'

'You must be kidding.' Sarah couldn't imagine ever going to *Prohibition A*. It was one of the most secretive places in Manhattan – Jesus, in the world – and was a magnet for every rich young socialite in Manhattan. It probably had the wealthiest clientele of any place on earth. The most bizarre rumours circulated regarding what the super-rich partygoers got up to. It occurred to Sarah that it was exactly the sort of place that would attract the red circle people.

Prohibition A

'Come on, just the two of us,' Nicki enthused. 'Wednesday or Thursday night is good for me.'

'A future First Lady to go to a place like that,' Robert said. 'You just want to get yourself a scoop, don't you, Nicki?'

'Suit yourselves. Sarah, if you change your mind, let me know.'

Spiegel's cell phone rang. 'Let me take this.' He had a brief conversation then stood up. 'Sorry, Robert, I'm afraid I have to take you away. A consortium from Wall Street is in the Red Room. They want to make a big donation. I need you to meet and greet them, maybe give a quick speech.'

'Money talks,' Robert said with a shrug. 'Got to go.'

'That means I'll need another anecdote from you, Sarah.' Nicki frowned. 'I can't believe I've never asked you about that steamer. I've seen it loads of times and never thought anything about it.' Waving her pen, she said, 'I think I have something – another thing I missed.'

'*What*?'

'Above your fireplace, there's a large, framed photograph of a bird perched on a falconer's glove. I think you told me it used to hang in the FBI's art gallery. I thought you just liked the picture, but maybe there's a story there.'

Sarah sat back. 'I took that myself when I was a kid.' A knot of emotion grew in her throat. 'It was a beautiful day. A falconer was giving a demonstration in Central Park. I saw this little dot circling high up then plunging down at incredible speed. As it swooped, my stomach lurched.'

Whenever she talked about it, she felt tears building. 'When the dot came closer, it transformed into this most fantastic bird. I've never seen anything so exciting. It snatched a piece of meat left for it, before soaring into the sky again. Later, it came back to rest on the falconer's glove and let me stroke it. It was a Peregrine falcon, with a black head and dark brown eyes with yellow rings. I remember it had a fabulous white-tipped tail and an amazingly proud look in its eye.'

'It made a big impression, huh?'

Sarah bowed her head. 'It was dead ten minutes after that picture was taken.' The horror flooded back. 'It took off on another flight but when it came back, it wasn't flying right. One of its eyes had been put out. Someone had shot it with an air rifle.

'With its good eye, the falcon stared at its master. It's weird but I remember thinking I could hear it thinking: "I can't bear to live like this."

'The falconer started crying. He said – and I'll never forget this – "The strong *can't* be weak." With one twist of his hands, he snapped its neck.' She felt herself choking. 'I dreamt about that bird for days afterwards, remembering how high it flew, that bewildering speed, how beautiful and free it was.'

'Sad story,' Nicki remarked.

Sarah nodded. 'Things like that stay with you.'

'Did the falconer do the right thing? Shouldn't he have tried to patch it up?'

Sarah shook her head. 'I would have done exactly the same thing.'

'I don't know. It seems such a waste.'

Sarah didn't want to talk about it anymore. She steered the conversation onto trivia. Mercifully, the time passed quickly, without any more painful questions.

The door opened and Robert's head appeared. 'Sarah, can I have a private word?'

Sarah apologised to Nicki and stepped outside, wondering what was up.

'David Warren called a few minutes ago,' Robert said. 'He was offering his congratulations on our engagement. He's invited us over to that crazy castle of his tomorrow night to celebrate our engagement. He's having a special party.'

'I can't stand him, Robert. Can't we go some other time?...like next century.'

'I don't want to offend him. He's always been friendly towards me. Don't you want to see his castle again? He claims he's hired a top French chef. Some movie stars are turning up too, he says.'

'What about Nicki? Can she come?'

'You know Warren loathes her.'

Sarah shrugged. She wasn't keen but she had to admit there was nowhere quite like Dromlech Castle. But first, she had other things on her mind. She grabbed Robert and kissed him. 'Let's go back to my apartment.' Tonight of all nights, she wanted to feel genuine elation. Was sex the answer? She prayed it was. 'The champagne has gone straight to my head.' Even as she spoke, she found red circles dancing in front of her eyes. Thousands of them, dripping with blood.

8

The Neulander Institute

General Clark sat in his office in front of his computer, staring at the final paragraph of the amended plan. Soon, he'd present it to the other members of the Committee and then he'd discover how committed they really were.

When he heard Sarah and Montcrieff's decision to have their wedding in St Patrick's Cathedral on the eve of the election, it gave him an opportunity he could never have anticipated, yet perfect in every way.

It took him only a moment to devise the new plan. To ordinary people, it might seem grotesque, but the Terror Age, like every other age, required its martyrs, its sacrifices, its acts of breathtaking boldness. He'd do anything for America, to see it rise above all other nations with a power and glory the world had never witnessed before. He'd even feed his own daughter into the flames of destruction. That was what was required of patriots.

Everyone is scarred by the past, but all of his scar tissue had a single cause. It was created, layer by sickening layer, by his broken marriage. This was a particularly bad time for him, days before the thirtieth anniversary of his wife's leaving him. Sarah was now the same age as Jane was back then. It gave him such an odd feeling when he watched her shooting Dexter in Central Park. A traitor to love, just like her mother. Was it a congenital defect, passed from mother to daughter? Sarah was a monster, capable of the worst possible crime against the man she claimed to love. No, even he couldn't believe that. Unlike her mother, Sarah didn't know what she was doing.

He remembered a conversation where he pointed out to Warren that Sarah had killed the love of her life.

'We brainwashed her, remember?' Warren had retorted.

That was true, but was it an excuse, *really* an excuse?

Even now, Clark couldn't shake free of the memories of what the Looking Glass project had done to Sarah. By the end of the first three months, it was obvious she didn't know who she was. When they held up a mirror in front of her, she didn't recognise herself.

He remembered entering a top-security laboratory and finding himself confronted by a spectacle that stunned him. Sarah and Dexter were suspended in huge, transparent isolation tanks filled with yellow liquid and streams of bubbles. All kinds of tubes were sticking out of them. The extraordinary thing was that they were naked and hairless. Even their eyebrows had been removed. Until then, Clark had never realised how hair defines appearance. Take it away from people and all that's left is a collection of indistinguishable shop dummies.

Does *that* belong to me, he had thought. If only it were Jane and not Sarah. How had it come to this? How had *he* come to this? He wasn't religious. Even as a kid, he lacked the inclination, the ability, to have faith. His parents were Jehovah's Witnesses and did everything they could to 'save' him. Escape couldn't come quickly enough and it arrived in the shape of a *Turing* scholarship to study cryptography at Harvard. His youthful love of chess, crosswords, puzzles, mathematics and computer programming provided him with the ideal background.

He came top of his class at Harvard. No late-night boozing for him, no nightclubs, no frat parties, no girlfriends, other than the occasional fling to prove he wasn't a freak. He smiled wryly – even the Jehovah's Witnesses might have approved of his prudish lifestyle.

From Harvard he went to the Defence Intelligence Agency, via the Marine Corps training programme to get him physically fit and introduce him to the military way of life. He was still proud of his trim waistline. He was only ten pounds heavier than he was at twenty-one. His mentors allowed him to attend classes on military strategy at West Point, where he became an expert in the tactics of the great Carthaginian general Hannibal. He had no complaints about the training he'd received. They had identified him as a high-flyer and he didn't disappoint. Everyone was impressed with his efforts, his dedication. So, at just twenty-six, he was assigned to the Neulander Institute, a new facility at the forefront of research for the intelligence community. In this disinfected setting, like the most high-tech of hospitals, he was introduced to the bizarre world of Special Military Intelligence. Officially, no such agency existed. Unofficially, it was the most powerful in the world.

After the public relations disasters of the Nixon era, all of the CIA's most controversial projects were terminated, judged unacceptable to the American public. That was the usual bureaucratic camouflage. A new group was established that had learned the lessons of the past. Special Military Intelligence was the CIA with the gloves off, so secret that scarcely anyone who wasn't in SMI was in a position to know anything about it.

A web of 'shell' organisations shielded the SMI from prying eyes. All SMI personnel were registered as employees with the shells and had fictitious jobs. SMI's money was filtered through the shells, which also owned all of its property. As far as the outside world was concerned, only the shells existed. So, no awkward questions, no committees from Capitol Hill to be appeased, no journalists snooping around. Only the finance committee, comprised of retired members of the intelligence community and reporting directly to the National Security Adviser, was permitted any access to SMI, simply to prove that the budget wasn't being squandered.

SMI now handled all of the old, discredited CIA projects, but it had analysed in detail where each went wrong, and remedied the errors. Now the past's failures had been transformed into miracles of innovation and effectiveness.

It was SMI's job to bring the impossible into the world. Their work had reached its culmination in Alice Through the Looking Glass. But Clark wasn't so much concerned about how to make someone a brainwashed assassin as what to do with the assassins when you had them. He left the other details to Warren, a man born with an excessive curiosity about the minds of others. Perhaps, he shouldn't have given Warren so much autonomy, but SMI's leading scientist had never done anything to suggest that the trust placed in him was misplaced, even though he was fond of making the most provocative of remarks. Warren once said that his greatest wish was to be the perfect conman, capable of conning everyone all of the time. He wanted to be so adept in understanding behaviour that he would always know the right buttons to push.

Am I conducting an experiment on my own mind? How often had Clark entertained that thought? Maybe 'soul' was a better word even though he hated its religious overtones. Was it possible he was testing his own soul to destruction? Following the Looking Glass project to its logical conclusion led, he knew, to Sarah's death. He might not deliver the fatal blow, but it would be his work all the same. Simple cause and effect. Could he stand by and watch his own flesh and blood die? The time wasn't far off when he'd learn the answer.

He could almost bring himself to feel sorry for Sarah, but that would practically be an admission of guilt. None of it was his fault. Jane was the one who deserted Sarah when she was a toddler. What did he, a military man, know of raising children? As every year passed and Sarah's resemblance to her mother grew stronger, he treated her more harshly, taking all his rage out on her. He sent her to a Catholic convent school knowing how much it would infuriate his parents who loathed the Catholic Church. His hope was that he would be able to forget her, but instead he sent her a birthday card every year, reminding her of the treacherous, poisonous nature she'd inherited from her mother. Their common sin.

Now, though, he didn't want Sarah to have any knowledge of his existence. He'd given Warren very specific instructions, so Sarah had been brainwashed into believing that he and his wife were killed in a car crash when Sarah was five, leaving Sarah as an orphan. To help conceal her true identity, she was given the name 'Harris' – the maiden name of Clark's mother.

Ordinary people would never comprehend the way he treated his daughter, but his world was far beyond them. That's why he was in charge of SMI while they stacked shelves in supermarkets. They could no more understand his motivations than he could sit down and watch one of their daytime chat shows.

Not one of them could have conceived of his alarm call to America, the final act that would show the people that everything had changed once and for all. He had decided to attack the bedrock of civilisation, the true evil from which all the rest of the corruption flowed – *marriage*. To defile that, to associate it with the greatest of sins, to link it forever with tragedy and horror, that seemed to him like an act of the greatest benevolence towards mankind. Such acts demanded the ultimate sacrifice.

In a week's time, Robert Montcrieff, the likely next president, would stand with Sarah in front of the high altar of St Patrick's Cathedral. The whole world would be watching his televised wedding. But Montcrieff would never leave the cathedral alive.

9

Mirrors

'Give the guy a break. Sometimes I think you don't like any of my friends.' Robert shrugged as he pressed the elevator button. 'Anyway, I won't let you spoil my story. Tommy told me this amazing thing about how a new hotel solved a PR disaster. Complaints were flooding in about how slow the elevators were, and the hotel realised it had a crisis on its hands. The cost of redesigning them or building new ones would have put them out of business, so they brought in a psychologist and asked him to come up with a solution. Within five minutes, he had the answer. By the end of the day, his solution had been implemented. The following day all complaints stopped. Many customers enthused about how much faster the elevators were even though they hadn't been touched in any way.' Robert smiled. 'Want to guess what the psychologist's answer was?'

Sarah shook her head. She didn't have the energy for this game. She wanted the elevator to go faster, to get back to her apartment, close the door and shut out the world.

'*Mirrors*,' Robert said. 'Next to every elevator, they fitted a long mirror. Instead of waiting impatiently, the hotel's customers could now stare at themselves, and time suddenly passed in a blink.'

Sarah usually enjoyed anecdotes like that. Tonight it was different. For a moment, Robert seemed like a stranger. Or was *she* the stranger? Last time she felt this way...she shivered. She was back in that dark underground parking garage in Baltimore, waiting for John Dexter to show up. Dexter was the best in the business, America's top agent. Would she be able to surprise him? Everyone said he had a sixth sense for sniffing out trouble.

'Are you all right?' Robert asked.

'Too much excitement for one night.' Sarah gave a feeble smile as she ushered Robert along the small hallway and into the lounge. A compact, fashionable room, the lounge had gleaming maple floorboards and lilac-painted walls. There were two expensive white leather sofas, a glass dining table with matching coffee table, a plasma TV and a top-of-the-range Zarconium sound system. She was glad to be home.

'What's so funny now?' she asked. Robert was chuckling almost sinisterly as he stepped into the lounge. 'Another of Henshaw's anecdotes?'

'This should cheer you up. I'm reading a description of you from the evening newspaper.'

'What's the damage?'

'Listen to this. Tall and slim, Sarah Harris is five foot nine and one hundred and thirty pounds, with an athletic build, no doubt first honed by the tough training camp she attended at the FBI's academy in Quantico. Of course, her standout feature is that killer Louise Brooks bob of hair. To top it all, she's smart and capable – a prominent figure in the New York FBI. Mr Montcrieff has picked himself a winner. As you may have noticed, I'm a bit of a fan too. But, for some of us, casting envious glances is our allotted task in life. Welcome to the battalions of losers, dear reader. Miss Harris need have no such worries.'

'I don't believe you,' Sarah said.

'I'm serious. I think I'd hire extra security if I were you. Sounds like this journalist is going to be stalking you soon.'

Robert thrust the newspaper into her hand. He'd used a red pen to ring the article.

But the reality is *so* dull, Sarah thought. And no mention of her gappy teeth.

Robert hung up his overcoat. 'So, when do I get the hot action you promised me?'

'Whenever you like.' Truth was Sarah just wanted to go to sleep, but she was scared of what her dreams would bring. Red circles and red queens, no doubt. No other case had affected her like this. It wasn't even a formal investigation yet. Why was it getting under her skin so much? It had wrecked her enjoyment of her engagement. She felt so much pressure to say everything was just great when she felt as though the ground was giving way beneath her feet.

Robert put up his hands in mock surrender. 'Actually, I need some food first or I'll have no energy. I've had a glass in my hand all night – I haven't eaten.'

'Food?' Sarah teased, trying her best to maintain the illusion of being a seductress. 'I bet that reporter from the evening newspaper wouldn't be worrying about food.'

Robert flopped onto the sofa. 'I'm shattered. That took it out of me tonight. Maybe it was having all that champagne on an empty stomach.'

'Excuses, excuses.' Sarah poked him in the stomach. 'You're such a let-down.'

Robert shrugged. 'I'm pathetic, huh?' He seemed to have tuned into her downbeat mood. 'What are we like?'

'We're just winding down, that's all.' Sarah started pacing round the room. 'You'll need to let me see all of the arrangements you've made for the wedding.'

'Is that what's getting to you?'

'No, um, something at work. What about you?'

'I can't be myself. I have a fake smile permanently stuck to my face. Everywhere I go I have to be upbeat, shaking everyone's hand. I *hate* it.'

She sat down beside him and stroked his hair. 'I could never do it.' But she was doing it right now, faking it. In fact, her whole life seemed fake in some indefinable way.

'I've become this ridiculous, phony showman.' Robert rubbed his head. 'Maybe conman would be a better word.'

Where had all of this come from so suddenly? It made Sarah nervous. She thought of how weird Robert was the last time they had sex; that crazy moment when he almost bit a chunk out of her ass. *Flesh*, that's what he said, as though he were some kind of cannibal. What did he mean by it? She'd been too scared to ask.

'You know what,' Robert said in little more than a whisper, 'I'm a person impersonator. Everything about me is false.' He leaned over and kissed Sarah. 'I only feel real when I'm alone with you.' He put his finger on the tip of her nose.

Sarah kissed him, and felt sick. They sat silently for about ten minutes, holding hands. A *person impersonator*? What a strange phrase to use, but it summed up how she was feeling about herself. 'I'm going to rustle up that food you were talking about.' She hoped it would take her mind off things.

Robert put his hand on her thigh. 'Let me do it.'

'Since when did you know how to cook?'

'This will be a presidential special.'

He went into the kitchen, put on an apron and began slamming things around. Curling up on the sofa, Sarah sipped some red wine. She put on a compilation of chill-out music, hoping it would soothe her. Instead, she felt more agitated than ever. *I should be calling mom and dad to tell them about my engagement*, she thought. Tears welled in her eyes. *Why did my parents have to die?* She could hear Robert swearing in the kitchen. He was frying bacon. Would it make her throw up?

He emerged, holding the large silver tray she reserved for Thanksgiving dinner, with the food concealed under a silver dome.

Mirrors

'Dinner is served,' he declared, placing the silver dish in the middle of the table. He poured two glasses of champagne from a bottle of Krug that had been chilling in the refrigerator. 'You *lucky* woman,' he said with a grin.

'OK, what have you come up with?' she asked as they sat down at the dinner table.

Robert lifted the domed lid with a grand flourish.

She stared in disbelief at what was underneath: four white-bread sandwiches with butter melting from the sides. She cautiously lifted the top slice off one of the sandwiches. Underneath were several rashers of bacon smothered in tomato ketchup. Revolting.

'I'm fired, huh?' Robert said.

All Sarah could do was laugh. 'If you were as bad in bed as you are in the kitchen, I'd call the whole thing off.' She picked up one of the sandwiches. 'Is this safe?' After one bite, she put it down. 'I'm not hungry.'

'That's a no-no to the presidential special, huh?' Robert ate his own sandwiches in silence.

As she studied her future husband, Sarah thought back to the day at school when she cut the heads off the pictures of the grooms. Why had she done it? A fear of marriage? Did she have some sort of phobia? Maybe she should see a shrink. Nicki did a few years back and said it was really helpful.

'I'm sorry for springing all of this on you,' Robert said when he'd finished. 'It was unfair.' He picked up the bottle of champagne and led her back to the sofa. 'I'll make it up to you, I promise.'

She nestled into his lap. As she reached up to stroke his hair, she noticed he was gazing at the picture above the artificial fireplace – her framed photograph of the Peregrine falcon, the one he'd first seen in the Ghouls' Gallery.

'It's beautiful,' Robert said. 'You could have been a photographer.'

Whenever Sarah stared at it, she felt odd. Sometimes, it seemed to put her into a trance-like state and she was convinced she could stand in front of it for hours, gazing at it like a zombie. It was spectacularly well shot. Everyone always commented on how professional it was. The odd thing was that she had no memory of actually taking the picture, or what camera she'd used, and she'd never got close to taking any picture as good since.

Robert's attention turned to the glass display cabinet. 'So, there's your famous old steamer. I'm sorry for embarrassing you in front of Nicki.'

His cell phone rang and he got up to answer it. The ring tone was the *Mission Impossible* tune. Sarah figured you could tell a lot about someone from which tune they chose for their ring tone. Someone who thinks he's a joker always has a zany tune. A film buff chooses an obscure movie sound clip. Fashionable people had the latest trendy TV programme or hip cartoon. Drama queens chose an operatic tune. Sometimes it scared her just how easy it was to pigeonhole people. She wondered what people would think of her choice – the sound of the helicopter blades from *Apocalypse Now*.

Robert spoke briefly to Tommy Henshaw who was outside with the security team. When he was done, he glanced at this watch. 'I have to be out of here at seven am. That means we have all night for…' he glanced towards the bedroom. '…what you promised me.'

Sarah looked at him. Any woman would give anything to be here with him like this.

He put an arm round her waist, another under her legs and scooped her up. 'You know, I had a dream about you last night.'

'What was it about?'

'Let's just say it put a smile on my face. You were wearing a silver satin camisole that really *clung*. You had open-toed silver high heels and your toenails and fingernails were painted silver. But your best feature was a silver mask that fitted your face like a second skin. You were like a beautiful cyborg.'

'And I guess I did all kinds of disgusting cyborg things to you?' Sex, suddenly, was the only thing that Sarah thought might relax her. The harder and faster, the better. An explosion of energy. Then deep sleep. Oblivion. No more red circles or red queens.

'You'd better believe it.'

'And now you're going to describe those things to me, huh?'

'I'm going to do better than that,' Robert laid her down on the bed. 'I'm going to show you.'

Sarah closed her eyes. *Oh my God*. She had a terrifying picture in her mind of decapitated bridegrooms in their wedding-day morning suits, hundreds of them. Not cut-up photos, but real people. She recognised two of them.

One was Robert. The other was John Dexter.

10

Connections

'Hey, wait up Sarah.' Mike Lacey's Brooklyn accent was unmistakable. 'Man, I didn't expect to see you in the office today.'

Sarah had just emerged from the elevator and was hoping to reach her office without bumping into any of her colleagues. No such luck.

'Hi, Mike.' She wearily turned to acknowledge her colleague. Wearing a cream suit, pink shirt and bold red tie, Lacey resembled an extra from *The Great Gatsby*.

'In fact, I wasn't expecting you back here ever again,' Lacey said. 'Aren't you resigning, or at least taking a long, *long* time off?'

'I'm not sure *what* I'm doing right now, Mike. I'm going to see Dargo to talk it over.'

'Well, I guess I should do the traditional thing and offer my congratulations. I knew Montcrieff was making a big announcement, but I wasn't expecting *that*.'

'Tell me about it.' Sarah frowned. It still hadn't sunk in that she was going to be Mrs Montcrieff in a few days. God, maybe First Lady. As for her job, she'd only touched on it with Robert. Was she being impractical by wanting to keep doing it? Luckily, Robert seemed to approve, although he insisted she'd have to put up with two secret service men shadowing her. She'd left them in the reception area and said she'd hook up again when she was ready to leave. They weren't happy, but she was determined to stop them trailing after her the whole time. Besides, she was in an FBI office. You couldn't get much safer than that.

'Is it scary?' Lacey asked.

'Is *what* scary?'

'Your picture,' Lacey said, 'it's all over the newspapers. You're on every TV channel.'

'Let's not go there.'

'That bad, huh?'

'I've been under siege.' Sarah recalled with a shudder the army of media people camped outside her apartment block that morning, doing everything they could to hassle her. Robert, by leaving early, had managed to avoid most of them. She had certainly needed her secret service escorts to help her shove her way through the throng to get to her car. A TV camera almost hit her in the face when some jerk pushed forward to get a better picture.

'Well, those engagement pictures were certainly excellent publicity for Montcrieff's campaign.'

'Don't be so cynical, Mike. We're in love.'

'If you say so.' As soon as he said it, Lacey apparently regretted it. 'I'm sorry, that was mean of me. I guess I'm feeling a bit tender at the moment. I've gone from hero to zero in the romance stakes. I keep striking out.' He shuffled uneasily. 'I just can't seem to get my shit together when it comes to relationships. I think I've acquired a fondness for, um, out-of-reach women.' He stared at the floor.

Sarah quickly changed the subject. 'Mike, ever since you mentioned those red circles yesterday I've been having such weird experiences.'

'Hey, me too. You see, we have *so* much in common.'

Their conversation dried up. Sarah felt her old awkwardness returning. 'I have to go now.'

'Am I becoming like Dargo?' Lacey asked. 'Could you ever imagine him dating?'

'It's been tough for him.' Bizarrely, Sarah found herself defending her boss, something she scarcely thought possible. 'After his divorce, he just bottled everything up,' she said. 'He loved his wife, talked about her all the time. I hear he was quite a nice guy in those days. Then the ice age descended and every emotion froze solid. He's not the first to react that way to a bad break-up.'

'Old iron-ass, huh? Anyway, what's next for you? Is Robert taking you out tonight to show you off to his admiring public?'

'We're going to Dromlech Castle, actually.'

'Man, I've always wanted to visit that place.'

'Yeah, but that means I've got to endure a night with David Warren. I think I'd rather hang out with Count Dracula.'

Lacey nodded. 'Warren gives me the creeps too.'

'I didn't realise you'd met him.'

'No, I've only seen him on TV, but there's something about his eyes.'

Sarah knew exactly what he meant. Warren had a way of looking at people that made it seem as if he could see inside their heads. No one with secrets ever felt comfortable in his presence. Oddly enough, the rumour was that he had more secrets than anyone.

11

Towers and Dreams

Warren's nickname was 'Piggy' and that was exactly how Sarah regarded him. The only thing he had in his favour was his crazy castle. He liked to tell interviewers that it was an old-fashioned folly, pointless but beautiful, like most of the best things in life. If Sarah remembered right, it was a re-creation of some Scottish castle that Warren visited as a kid and couldn't get out of his head. The story went that he swore to build a *homage* to it back home in the States one day and Dromlech Castle was the result. It was located in Long Island's most scenic bay, in a spectacular Gothic setting overlooking the Atlantic. No one knew where the money came from: thirty or forty million dollars by all accounts. Word had it that Warren had his stubby fingers in several pies that weren't altogether legal, but no one could prove a thing.

'Who's going to give you away at the altar?' Warren asked. 'I mean, without your father...'

'I haven't decided.' Sarah couldn't believe she'd ended up stuck with Warren. He always peered at her in an odd way, as if studying a sample under a microscope. She had to be polite to him given who he was, but she wanted to get out of this situation fast. At least her conversation with Dargo earlier that day had gone well. He was relaxed about her engagement and said he'd give her ample time to decide what she wanted to do. In the meantime, he was happy for her to come and go as she pleased. He thought the publicity would be good for the FBI.

As she gazed at the castle's grand hall with its timber frame, stone floor, crystal chandeliers and abstract paintings, she couldn't hide her agitation. Every now and again, she caught sight of a tall, dark-haired man in a tuxedo, weaving through the party guests but not stopping to talk to anyone. Although she never managed to get a good view of him, he bore a startling resemblance to a former boyfriend. That was all she needed. Her break-up with Tom had been ugly. If that's who it was, there was bound to be a scene. She had a weird feeling he was watching her constantly, not in any obvious way – like a guy in a surveillance op. A *pro*.

She glanced over at Robert. Jacob Spiegel had steered him in the direction of Ed Reese and Lana Farezi, stars of the new blockbuster *Bluebeard's Revenge*. The movie was getting its world premiere here tonight,

63

ensuring that the media pack had turned out in full force, especially since the young movie stars' on-screen chemistry had raised feverish speculation about an off-screen romance.

'It will be excellent publicity for you to be seen with the stars,' Spiegel had assured Robert. 'You're sure to pick up the 18-25 vote.'

Now Robert was chatting with the glamorous couple and getting checked out by the beautiful Lana. Bright lights shone on them as photographers and camera crews jostled for good positions.

Sarah stood in semi-darkness, watching from a distance. Dressed in a glitzy silver cocktail dress she ought to be shining, but all her sparkle had gone. Being alone with Warren was a pain in the neck.

'A coup, huh?' Warren said in his smarmy voice.

'What do you mean?'

'It's not every day you get the premiere of a Hollywood blockbuster in your own home, is it? He gestured around. 'Did you realise the whole thing was filmed right here?'

'I thought I recognised a few things.' Sarah was wondering how long she'd have to spend with him. She wanted to find the right tone for him to take the hint and leave her alone.

'I got a decent pay-day from the producers,' Warren remarked. 'I needed it. You wouldn't believe how much it costs to run this place.'

'I guess a maid coming in twice a week for three hours doesn't do it.'

'No, not quite.' Warren swirled his glass of brandy. 'It keeps getting more expensive. I've just hired a new gardener to look after the maze. I got a designer in from England to build the thing. He finished it last week after a year's work. It's the most elaborate in the world, so he tells me, with a unique trick feature. It has a mechanically operated section of hedge that can be activated to make it close over the entrance moments after a suitable victim enters. Then the only way out is through a hidden trapdoor in the centre.'

'Ingenious,' Sarah commented.

What a jerk, she thought. Spending a fortune on every kind of nonsense.

'I showed it to Robert earlier. He loved it.' Warren took a slow sip of his brandy. 'Did you like the film?'

'That image of the bride,' Sarah said, 'The way the blood spread over her white wedding dress...' She trembled. The dress was uncannily like the Pino Monzelli design she'd chosen for her own wedding.

Warren peered at her. 'The castle was the real star. Best of all was the Forbidden Room.'

'Which room is that?'

'The library. It's a perfect octagon. They took out all the books before they shot the scene. Would you like to see it?'

'Maybe later.' She wanted to make her excuses and leave, but Warren wouldn't let her go.

'There's a book in the library called *The Legend of Bluebeard*. Do you know what Bluebeard's true secret was?'

'I really have no idea.'

'In a time of religious persecution, he was a heretic. The room was forbidden because it contained prohibited knowledge.'

'Such as?' Sarah was intrigued for once.

'That everything we believe in is a lie.' Warren gave a sly smile. 'Knowledge like that can kill people, don't you think? I mean, if you've spent your whole life believing in God and then you discover he doesn't exist, or that you've been worshipping the wrong one, it would devastate you, wouldn't it? Bluebeard didn't murder his wives, he showed them forbidden secrets, that's all.' He reached out and gripped her wrist. 'Do you think everyone has their own forbidden room? Where the bodies are buried.'

Sarah felt a shiver running through her. What was he driving at? After the mysterious death of Steve Grissom, the previous CIA Director, Warren got the job to the amazement of nearly everyone in the Intelligence community. To many people, it seemed as if Warren had come from nowhere. He had influential backers and no one quite knew why.

'Tell me about Robert,' Warren said. 'You must feel very lucky.'

'I never thought I could love anyone the way I love Robert.'

'*Really*?' Warren looked at her with the most distasteful smirk. 'Do you think your father loved you?'

'What are you talking about?'

'Have you ever considered that he's still alive?'

'I have no idea what you're pulling here, but this is in very poor taste.'

'I see I've touched a raw nerve. It's just a hypothetical question.'

Sarah was getting more and more wound up. 'No, I want to hear what you're getting at. Are you saying my dad didn't love me; he abandoned me?'

'Only a sick man would do something like that, huh?'

'Yeah, *sick*. But my dad's not sick – he's dead.' Sarah stomped away, angry with herself for having put up with Warren for so long.

Scanning around for any sign of her ex-boyfriend, she saw a young woman with an angelic face and spikey blonde hair heading straight for her. In a shrink-wrapped black dress with holes cut in revealing positions, the woman was stunning. One of her breasts was almost sticking out. Further down, another of the holes had been cut too close to her bikini line.

'David, you're always harassing beautiful women,' she said loudly.

Sarah turned and found Warren right behind her.

'This is my girlfriend, Carolyn Voronski,' he said, his voice smarmier than ever. 'Carolyn, meet Sarah Harris.'

'I know who she is.' Carolyn held out her hand. 'Pleased to meet you, Sarah.'

Sarah wondered how an old man like Warren could get a gorgeous girl like this. 'Pleased to meet you, too.' As she shook Carolyn's hand, she noticed that her fingernails were painted with glossy black nail varnish. She oozed sexuality.

'Delicious, isn't she?' Warren squeezed his girlfriend's waist. 'Carolyn should have been starring in the movie.' He patted her ass. 'You like performing, don't you, honey?'

'The whole of life's a show.' Carolyn made a point of looking over at Robert. 'In fact, it's the only show in town: a one-time performance with no encores.'

'Quite the philosopher, isn't she?' Warren commented.

'Come with me, Sarah,' Carolyn said. 'I want to show you something.' Turning to David, she blew him a kiss. 'See you later.' She gave him a little wave.

Sarah stared at Carolyn's wrist and kept staring. 'Where did you get that?' She could hardly believe what she was seeing. There it was, unmistakable, a red circle – exactly like one of those on the woman in Lacey's police video.

'My circle? Ah, that would be telling.'

'You *know*?' Sarah was incredulous, remembering that none of the people on Lacey's list claimed to have any idea of where they got their circles.

'What kind of dumb question is that? Of course I do.'

'Well, *where*?'

'Thinking of getting one, huh?'

****

'You must love this view, Carolyn.' Shielded by double-glazing, Sarah and Carolyn were sitting on leather bar stools in a small observation booth at the top of Dromlech Castle's west tower, looking out over the Atlantic Ocean.

Towers and Dreams

They were drinking Sicilian white wine and nibbling caviar canapés. It was a wild night and a strong wind swirled around the castle, making doors creak on their hinges.

Sarah gazed at the moon. It threw a pale light over the waves battering against the sandy seashore, just yards from the rear of the castle. She was preoccupied with just one thing – how did Carolyn know where she got her red circle done when none of the others did? Were they lying, or was she?

'It's spectacular, huh?' Carolyn said. 'I dream better when I stay here in the castle. Did you know that people are paralysed when they dream? It stops them harming themselves.'

'What do you mean?' Sarah was still trying to figure out why she'd been invited up here.

'Think about it. You could harm yourself if you moved about while you were dreaming – you know, physically acting out the things happening in your dream.'

'I suppose so.' Sarah felt spooked by the way Carolyn kept studying her, looking her up and down as if trying to work out how she'd ever managed to hook Robert. She had to pick the right moment to ask about the red circle.

'I read the other day,' Carolyn said, 'that if you eat chocolate just before you go to sleep, the chemicals in the chocolate somehow screw up the natural processes for paralysing you.'

'Another reason for not eating chocolate, huh?'

'Yeah, but who could give it up?' Carolyn smiled, running her hands through her short blonde hair. 'Do you like movies, Sarah?'

'Some.'

'What sort? Thrillers, rom-coms, disaster movies? I've got you down as a bit of an art house type.'

'I like films about long journeys, from light into dark.' Sarah realised she was deferring to Carolyn. It was ridiculous but she felt intimidated by the younger woman. Got to snap out of it.

'*Cool* – I like those, too. You must have enjoyed tonight's movie then? We all want to know what's on the other side of that secret door, right?'

'Not if they end up like Bluebeard's bride.'

'I guess not.' Carolyn grinned, showing off her perfect teeth. 'Do you kick ass when you're on your assignments, Sarah? There's something deceptive about you. You look sweet, but there's a toughness under it all.'

'I try to do my job as professionally as I can.' Sarah tried not to open her mouth too wide for fear of exposing her gappy teeth. 'What about you, Carolyn? What kind of job do you have?'

'I don't. David pays the bills. I refuse to have some fucking boss telling me how to spend my time.'

'Yeah, but doesn't David...'

'Doesn't David *what*? You think he's my boss? My sugar daddy? Listen, honey, I can come and go whenever I please. David knows he'd lose me if he wanted it any different. He's a fascinating guy, but no way is he my boss.'

'He's a bit older than you.'

'Old enough to be my daddy, is that it? So what? I like older men. They know more and they try harder. And they're better with their tongues...'

'I'm not having a go at you.'

'It sounds like it. Anyway, I hate my father, so if you think I have a daddy complex, you couldn't be more wrong.' Carolyn poured more wine, but didn't offer any to Sarah. 'My father's working over in London for some big investment bank. I never see him and I don't care. He treated my mum and me like shit. She divorced him, but it was too late. She's an alcoholic now. I just keep away. The whole thing does my head in. Fucking happy families, huh?' She fixed Sarah with a stare. 'What about your family, Sarah? Is it go to Pleasantville east of Smallville, take the first turning at Normalopolis and Harrisburg is first on the right with your mom and dad waiting in the porch with grandma's apple pie and home-made lemonade?'

'I'm an orphan.' Sarah lowered her head. 'My parents died in a car smash when I was five. I was in state care until I was eighteen, then I won a place at Columbia.'

'Tough and smart, huh?' Carolyn took another sip of wine. 'Sorry to hear about your parents. Do you have any memories of them?'

'Nothing, really.'

'Well, at least you don't have bad memories.'

'But you always ask yourself what it would be like if they hadn't died. Would everything be different? Would I be, you know, *happy*, deep inside?'

'I don't know anyone who's happy like that. Everyone wants to party all the time: they're all just running away though, aren't they?'

'Are you running, Carolyn?'

'Faster than anyone.' Carolyn finished off her wine. 'Speaking of parties, the reason I asked you up here is that we're having one tomorrow night. I want to invite you and Robert. David has something special in mind. Adult stuff, if you know what I mean. Strictly confidential.'

'You have to be kidding. That type of party is off limits.'

'Off limits, huh?'

68

Towers and Dreams

Sarah realised she was losing Carolyn. It was now or never. 'Listen, Carolyn, I've seen some other people with circles on their wrists. Is it a new fashion? Can you tell me where you got it done?'

Carolyn smirked. 'I guess that's off limits too.'

Warren appeared. 'Good news,' he said to Carolyn. 'Ed Reese and Lana Farezi are interested in coming along to Prohibition A with us tomorrow. They might join our party afterwards. It should be the best yet.'

Sarah sprang to her feet. *Prohibition A.* She was certain it had something to do with the red circles. Should she mention it to Dargo and Lacey? 'I'm going to find Robert,' she said, then hurried down the spiral staircase.

When she reached the bottom, she almost collided with a tall man – the very one she thought had been following her. Their eyes locked for a moment. She stared at him, incredulous. He returned her gaze with equal shock, then moved away fast and disappeared into the throng.

The door of Bluebeard's room had swung wide open. It wasn't her ex-boyfriend after all. It was infinitely worse. Sarah's whole body began to shake.

It was John Dexter.

12

Private Movie

John Dexter is back. General Clark, sitting in his office in Hudson Tower, poured another glass of Scotch, another chance to deaden the panic. Dexter could ruin everything. Once, he killed a Chinese general at a parade in front of a hundred thousand soldiers. He was gone before anyone noticed what had happened.

Dexter was meticulous, able to detect the weak points in any defence, to use his imagination to find the simplicity buried within complexity. Forget the hundred thousands soldiers. Concentrate only on the handful near the general. Perhaps only the man standing beside the target. Can he be manipulated, bribed perhaps? Take care of him and everything else follows.

Dexter had proved that a programmed assassin is always better than a normal agent. The programming removed the human weaknesses that so often betrayed agents at critical moments. Dexter himself was once soppy, sentimental, weak, but Alice Through the Looking Glass removed those defects. It was a catastrophe when he stopped responding to his mind control commands. Every attempt at reprogramming failed, and, worse, Dexter started asking questions about Alice. He had to be eliminated, but taking him out wouldn't be simple.

Clark turned to the man sitting opposite him. He found it odd that he hated David Warren yet continually confided in him. It took him years to work out why, but it was obvious really: Warren had to be twice as good as everyone else to overcome the hostility. He'd proved himself many times over, particularly in the way he handled the Grissom crisis.

'I want to know what will happen if Sarah sees Dexter.' The question had been preying on Clark's mind. Warren once said an emotional trauma could trigger Sarah's buried memories. Clark gripped his glass. Everything was so finely balanced.

'Pray she doesn't,' Warren said. 'One of two things might happen. She could remember everything all at once and become psychotic. Or it will be like a dam slowly bursting. There will be a gradual awakening, with bits and pieces of her past breaking through, odd memory fragments, getting more frequent as time goes on. Eventually, the dam will burst.'

That was the last thing Clark wanted to hear. He had already assumed Dexter was tailing Sarah. An encounter was possible, even probable. He needed to find out more so that he could calculate what might happen. In the past, he'd never concerned himself too much with Warren's work. The results were what interested him, not the processes that underlay them. Now, the situation demanded that he delve into Warren's bizarre world of fabricated memories. 'How did you do it?' he asked.

The CIA Director smiled, and Clark knew his question had been fully understood.

'A movie,' Warren said. 'We gave Sarah the starring role.'

Warren described a movie with five main scenes. The first was a reconstruction of Sarah's shooting of Dexter, but this time it wasn't in Central Park but in an underground parking garage in Baltimore. The camera was placed in the position Sarah's head would have occupied, to act as her eyes. A Dexter look-alike was used.

'Then we subjected her to weeks of sensory deprivation,' Warren said, 'making sure she did nothing but sit in an empty white room. There was nothing to distract her. No TV, no radio, no music, no books, no people. When that happens to people, their minds become sponges, desperate to soak up the tiniest item of information. We played the Baltimore scene repeatedly on a loop, a thousand times in total. By the end, Sarah was much more familiar with our fabricated assassination than the real thing.'

Warren explained about the other scenes in Sarah's personal movie. They filmed a scene in which a young girl was persecuted by her schoolteacher and classmates because she whistled when she pronounced the letter "s" in Mississippi because of the gap between her front teeth. The purpose was to make Sarah neurotic, paranoid, wary of others. The best assassins were always antisocial loners. Sarah had only one close friend – Nicki Murphy.

They filmed the death of a falcon to show the necessity of things you love having to die if they're damaged. Deep down, Sarah was aware she'd shot the man she loved. How could she live with herself? But if it were her duty to put her lover out of his misery, she could justify it to herself at some deep level. Dexter was damaged goods long before Sarah shot him. They both knew it.

The fourth scene showed Sarah as an orphan cutting up wedding photographs. It was designed to give Sarah an ambivalent attitude towards marriage. She hated it because she associated it with the sort of happy families from which she seemed permanently excluded. But she also craved it because then she'd be 'normal.'

'The fifth?' Clark asked.

Prohibition A

'I discussed it with you a while back.'

Clark sipped his whisky. If he remembered right, it was something to do with a cherry blossom tree.

'Sarah turned out exactly right,' Warren said. 'Dargo says she's excellent at her job. She has few friends. She's independent and capable, but also sad and vulnerable. You don't want them too happy, or too depressed. Complex is what you're looking for. Sarah is definitely *complex*. And her relationship with Montcrieff is everything we planned.'

Clark smiled. He preferred discussing his daughter as an object of study, or to think of her as an actress playing a part. 'But those scenes you've talked about don't have any emotional context. It's one thing to see something, but you have to feel it too, don't you?'

'Haven't you ever felt anything when you watched a movie?' Warren retorted. 'It's all down to empathy. When you watch a good movie, you're not on the outside looking in. You're imagining yourself in the hero's position and then the movie's about your feelings, not his.

'Believe me, everything can be faked. Remember all that stuff they used to say about people not being able to act against their fundamental instincts? It's garbage. When you get inside someone's mind, fundamental instincts are as meaningful as popcorn.' Warren smirked. 'There's a famous story of a rail-worker who suffered a terrible accident – a metal spike went clean through his head. He didn't die, but he changed from being a kind, calm man to a violent bully. So where had his fundamental nice-guy instincts gone? Fact is they were a function of his brain. When that was damaged, so was his personality.'

Clark was pensive. 'There's one thing I still don't get. I know you've touched on it before, but how is it possible for Sarah to forget Dexter? I mean, how can anyone replace all those memories, all that love?'

'You can thank cognitive dissonance. It's the closest you'll come to magic. People are only now discovering how powerful it is.'

'I don't know anything about cognitive dissonance.' Clark knew his admission would open the dam, but he had to understand, even if it gave Warren a smug sense of satisfaction.

'The theory was formulated by Leon Festinger in the late 1950s. It's about the psychological state a person has when two of his ideas about the world contradict each other. If the contradiction is severe enough it can make the person distressed, even ill. In extreme cases, it can drive them insane. Festinger says that when we're faced with that situation, we'll take the simplest way out to resolve the contradiction, to stop us feeling torn in different directions by the inconsistencies. So, with Sarah, she has years of memories of John Dexter in her head, but she has a programmed false memory of shooting Dexter in Baltimore. She also has a true memory of shooting him in Central Park. The contradiction of loving Dexter and shooting him is too great, so she has to resolve it to protect her sanity.'

'She has to choose between the memories of loving Dexter and shooting him, is that it?' Clark asked. 'She can't get rid of the memory of shooting him because we've hardwired it into her, so it's the other one that has to go.'

'Not quite. She can't forget loving a man for all that time. It might sound crazy, but what she can forget is who the man was. One last thing we did for Sarah was to show her the picture of another man – another SMI agent – who looked quite like Dexter. Through the magic of cognitive dissonance, all of Sarah's memories of Dexter have been converted into memories of this other guy. Everything is consistent in Sarah's head. No contradictions. Just a slightly hazy picture in her mind of what her former lover looked like.' Warren gave an odd smile. 'I confess, I have the same haziness when I think of some of my exes.' He clasped his hands together. 'We dramatised a break-up between Sarah and this other agent to account for why they're no longer together. Then we transferred this man abroad – permanently.'

'I presume you gave a fictitious name to this other agent?'

'Tom Dexler,' Warren said with a smile. 'It sounds like John Dexter, obviously. As far as possible, you want the fake memories to mimic the real ones. Less dissonance, you see.'

Clark couldn't hide how impressed he was. 'You've done a good job, Warren. But I have another task for you.' He stood up and looked out of the window. 'You know exactly what's at stake. We can't take any chances. I want you to prove that Sarah is still with the programme. You must arrange for her to kill someone.' He turned to face his colleague. 'By close of business today.'

13

Red Square

It was her lunchtime and Sarah had agreed to meet Robert for another of his PR stunts. He was doing a photo-op, this time in *Red Square* on the outskirts of Little Italy, the home of New York's flourishing Russian community. His plan was for both of them to be photographed with Russian bears, kids in traditional costumes, that kind of thing. Afterwards, he was flying to Boston to make another campaign speech.

Sarah's current priority was to stay clear of Tommy Henshaw's security team, standing feet away in their long black coats, like undertakers. Her own two secret servicemen were vastly preferable to that bunch. Equally important was avoiding the scores of journalists and reporters with cell phones glued to their ears, itching to get any angle on Robert.

Leaning against a whitewashed wall, watching as her breath condensed in the freezing air, Sarah's mind insisted on returning to last night. What had happened? Must have drunk too much. Should she visit a doctor? Jesus, maybe a psychiatrist. How would she begin? Dear Professor…I just saw a dead man.

As she waited for Robert to emerge from a private meeting with the community leaders, Sarah refused to let go of that image – that mirage? – of Dexter. When she saw him, it was as if someone with freezing hands had gripped her stomach. She was in a daze for hours afterwards. Then came a nightmare so vivid she could still see it in her mind even now. Someone was dead in Central Park, and police were interviewing witnesses.

I tell you, the dead guy had just proposed to her. He was giving her an engagement ring. Next thing she pulls a gun and blows him away. Finito. What more can I say? Yeah, that broad over there in the jazzy hot pants.

I'm telling you, they were kissing. Then she pulled the pistol from her handbag. It was over in a second.

Man, never saw anything like it. Whacked the guy. Didn't say a word. Didn't try to run nor nothing. Wouldn't have believed it if I hadn't seen it myself.

Was she cracking up? Then there was the shock of seeing that red circle on Carolyn's wrist. She tried to get in touch with Lacey to discuss it, but he wasn't in the office, so she left him an e-mail and a voice message. He still hadn't got back to her.

She had to think of other things or she'd go crazy. Slapping her gloved hands together, she did her best to warm herself up. Even though she was wearing a bottle-green Puffa jacket, black ski-pants and fur-lined boots, the chill was still getting through. It was years since she last felt her teeth chattering like this. Almost without thinking, she ran her tongue over the gap between her front teeth. She could imagine a layer of ice forming over it, triggering the old thoughts about whether she should get her teeth fixed. She was falling apart. The crows' feet around her eyes were getting more noticeable, and the mirrors in her bathroom insisted on exposing signs of creeping cellulite.

A vagrant edged towards her. The guy, with a Fidel Castro beard, was dressed in a tattered gold cowboy hat and mud-encrusted US Marine jungle gear.

'Dress your best,' he chanted in a thick, mid-West accent, 'the Grim Reaper is coming.' For some reason he was carrying a square wooden frame. Sarah noticed her secret service men starting to twitch. 'Self portrait,' the vagrant said, sticking his head into the centre of the frame.

Sarah smiled and reached into her pocket for a buck.

With a forceful flick of his wrist, the vagrant refused the money. 'Killed any boyfriends lately?' he snapped.

'*What did you say?*'

Sarah's secret service men stepped closer and a few journalists looked over. The vagrant retreated into the crowd. *Forget it*, Sarah thought. The guy's drunk; doesn't know what he's saying.

A door slammed and everyone turned round. Robert emerged from the community centre and put on his sunglasses, even though the sun hadn't put in an appearance for weeks. The shades were real *look-at-me* specials in metallic black that she'd bought him as a birthday present a few weeks earlier. Henshaw's security men formed a protective cordon while the media pack swarmed around Robert, screaming questions at him.

Beneath his overcoat, Robert was dressed in a dark suit and light-coloured tie. 'I read my horoscope this morning,' he said to the assembled media. 'It predicted I'd soon be moving to a prestigious new address.' He winked at the TV cameras. 'My new house will have a strong white theme.' Everyone laughed.

A peroxide blonde reporter with a Botox-assisted face pushed forward. 'Would any serious politician read a horoscope?' she asked. 'If you become

Prohibition A

President will you have astrologers in the Cabinet, maybe a clairvoyant as the Secretary of State?'

'No one needed a crystal ball to see a recession coming last year,' Robert replied coolly. 'Except the President, of course. He was predicting annual growth of six percent. You wouldn't catch any fortune tellers talking crazy like that.'

It was an effective response and there was no comeback.

'Thanks for coming along today,' Robert said. 'Now, if you don't mind, I'd like to see my fiancée before she goes back to work. I'll catch up with you all later.' He pushed through the throng, heading in Sarah's direction, with his security team close behind.

Sarah couldn't help thinking how handsome he looked. Sometimes, over-familiarity made her forget. Then, suddenly, something would be different and it would be like seeing him for the first time. Maybe the light framed his face differently, maybe his haircut was different, maybe he was wearing something new. Whatever, every now and again she felt herself almost overwhelmed by his beauty. She didn't like using that word about a man, but it was right for Robert. It wasn't surprising that many women reported feeling faint when he was around. She shuddered – John Dexter was handsome too. How could she even begin to think something like that?

The vagrant stepped out in front of Robert, causing the security team to brace for action. Sarah readied herself too.

'Any spare change for a veteran?' the man asked.

'Veteran, my ass,' Robert growled. 'Get lost.'

Sarah was nervous. The vagrant insisted on standing his ground.

'I told you to take a hike,' Robert said. A photographer snapped wildly, hoping for a money shot.

Sarah grimaced. She knew Robert was on edge. He'd been hyped up ever since returning to New York. With a forced smile, he took out a ten-dollar note and stuffed it into the vagrant's chest pocket. 'Have a meal on me, friend.' The vagrant didn't look happy but moved away without further fuss.

Robert took Sarah by the arm and steered her through the crowd towards a podium where he and the community leaders would watch a parade. Most of the dignitaries were seated, but Sarah was glad that Robert wanted to stand.

'You look sensational,' Robert said. 'Those ski-pants fit you in all the right places. I wish I wasn't going to Boston.'

76

Red Square

Before Sarah could reply, a drum roll of bangs signalled the start of a daytime fireworks display. Multi-coloured sparks showered over Red Square as hundreds of fireworks went off in quick succession.

A procession of locals dressed in Russian folk costumes snaked into view. At the front, a bald man led a black bear with a red harness round its neck. Despite the freezing conditions, the man's torso was naked, but he benefited from a disgustingly hairy chest, the hair extending right over his shoulders and down his back. Sarah hated that. She was glad Robert was always immaculately smooth, not that he admitted to removing any body hair. Her gaze returned to the bear. Children were dancing round it, clapping whenever a nearby fire-eater discharged a jet of flame from his mouth.

Looking into the crowd, Sarah was unnerved to see the vagrant standing near the front, scowling at her. His eyes were fixed on her so intently, it was easy to imagine he was trying to burn a hole through her head. She had a sensation of someone sticking syringes into her flesh. At the same time, her mind filled with vivid pictures. She was in Central Park again on a beautiful sunny day, standing perfectly still, in crazy gear that a teenager might wear. Then someone behind her pushed her forward, thrust her head downwards and forced her into the back seat of a police car. A policewoman opened the door on the other side and got in beside her. The policewoman didn't speak. More and more cops clustered around the car, taking a look…

'What have we got so far?' a smartly dressed detective said to a cop scribbling something in a notebook.

'Major shit, that's what,' the cop answered through a mouthful of gum. 'Lots of witnesses, all saying the same thing. A couple is doing the romance thing then the broad pulls out a gun and zaps the guy. Word we've been getting is that the dead guy had just proposed.'

'Man,' the detective snorted, 'wouldn't a simple no have done?' He looked into the car, but didn't say anything.

'So, let's see,' the detective said. 'A presentation box lying beside the dead guy. Big pink ribbon on it and a gold ring inside. A no-brainer, right? Except for the motive. Women these days. What the fuck are they thinking?'

'Poor jerk couldn't have done the marriage proposal right,' the cop sniggered. 'Or maybe she didn't like his suit. Who wears yellow nowadays?'

The pictures vanished and Sarah found herself staring into the crowd again. She was so nauseous she thought she might collapse. That vagrant – there was something disturbingly familiar about him.

14

Clever Kitty

In a few minutes, General Clark would see Sarah. Not on a TV screen, in a newspaper or in a crowd, but up close and personal – the worst kind of ordeal for him.

When he reached Lab 16 of the Neulander Institute, he stood outside for a moment, trying to compose himself. When the door opened, he knew it would be like seeing his ex-wife again. It made him feel sick.

Sarah had been brought here on the pretext that Warren wanted to interview her about an old mission that affected the CIA.

Clark knocked on the door and a moment later Warren appeared.

'Is everything ready?' Clark whispered.

Warren nodded and showed him inside.

Walking across the room, Clark felt Sarah's eyes on him. He sat down opposite her with his head bowed. Several seconds passed without anyone speaking.

'What's going on?' Sarah asked.

Warren pressed a buzzer, the door opened and the Delivery Manager came in, clutching a cat.

'That's Clever Kitty.' Sarah stood up. 'What the hell are you doing with her?'

The Delivery Manager let the cat drop to the ground then took a silver tone generator from his pocket.

Sarah stared at her cat, then at the Delivery Manager.

'Red Queen.' The Delivery Manager pressed the tone generator.

Sarah's expression instantly changed, a deep frown settling over her face.

'I'm the Delivery Manager. The customer is Clever Kitty. Delivery must be made immediately. What you need is in the drawer in front of you.'

Sarah's right hand rose and fell again. She stood perfectly still.

Clark exchanged glances with Warren. After several seconds, Sarah opened the drawer and took out the Heckler & Koch pistol lying inside. She turned towards her cat and pointed it at its head. Slipping off the safety, she steadied herself then fired. The cat's head exploded, its blood splashing onto the back wall.

Cause and effect, Clark thought grimly.

Clever Kitty

Then...God Almighty. Sarah raised the pistol again and pointed it straight at him.

Christ, she's going to kill me.

Sarah swivelled and shot the Delivery Manager in the chest. For a second, the man stared at her in disbelief, then slumped to the ground. Sarah dropped the pistol and it clanged against the floor. Her expression was utterly blank.

'What the hell happened?' Clark leapt to his feet and snatched up the pistol. 'What a fucking mess.'

'What happens now?' Warren's face had lost its ruddy appearance. He looked as though he was going to pass out.

'You tell me.' Clark rubbed his forehead with the heel of his hand. 'Will she have any memory of what she's just done?'

'It will be a dream image,' Warren said slowly, 'like when she shot Dexter. She'll be in post-event shock for half an hour or so. We'll give her a sedative. If you want, we can do a full reprogramming job on her, give her a new set of memories about what happened today. We'll say her cat was run over.'

'Whatever.' Clark slumped into his seat. 'Now get her out of here.' He stared at the cat's blood on the wall. 'And send someone to clean that up.'

He sat there, numb. Had the demonstration proved that Sarah was fit for another op, or that she should never be used again? She had just killed the cat she loved, exactly as she once shot the man she loved. But those were by order: now she'd executed the Delivery Manager without any instructions. Jesus, almost killed *him* too. Was the programming breaking down, just as it had with Dexter?

He held his head. Cracks were appearing in the Looking Glass. The tight control the project demanded was slipping away. His mind returned to the question that haunted him. If Sarah saw Dexter, would she break down completely? Then a more shocking thought seized him.

Had she already seen him?

15

The Restroom

Sarah hated this place. Whenever she visited the women's restroom in the far corner of Grand Central Station, it was always dirty and crowded. Today, for some reason, things were different. Miraculously clean, it was also deserted. She was just back from the Neulander Institute in Albany and she had a bad headache. Ever since her meeting with Warren, she'd been unsettled. The whole thing was a strange blur. She remembered practically nothing of what they discussed. More than that: she didn't want to remember. The Neulander Institute was a place that terrified her. Anything that went on in there was best forgotten, as fast as possible.

She rinsed her hands, dried them and gave thanks that no one had come in to interrupt her. Glancing at herself in the mirror, she thought she should touch up her makeup. Just as she was taking out her lipstick from her handbag, she gave a silent groan as the door opened and a woman entered. Watching the woman in the mirror, she noticed straight away the odd expression that crossed the woman's face – surprise turning rapidly to astonishment.

'I don't believe it: *Sarah Harris*!'

Sarah stared at the woman's face and was mystified. She'd never seen this woman before in her life. Judging by her body language, there was no question she believed they knew each other intimately.

'Jesus, you don't recognise me. Sarah, it's *me* – Helen Reeves. Come on, your appearance has changed much more than mine. You used to have long blonde hair and brown eyes. Look at you now. Are you wearing blue contacts?'

Sarah was flummoxed, but the fact that the woman knew her name was no big deal. She appeared in the media all the time thanks to her relationship with Robert.

'I'm sorry,' she said politely, 'I've met so many people lately. I can't place you, I'm afraid.'

'Sarah, what are you playing at? Christ, I was your best friend at Columbia. Ben and me, and you and John. We were together all the time.'

John and me? Now Sarah began to panic. Sure, she'd been at Columbia, but she didn't know a couple called Ben and Helen. And not once in her life had she ever gone out with anyone called John.

The Restroom

'Stop fooling around, Sarah. I bet you and John are married now with kids.'

'This in very poor taste,' Sarah said. 'I'm engaged to Robert Montcrieff.'

The woman was incredulous. '*Robert Montcrieff*?' she blurted. 'Jesus fucking Christ, you have to be kidding me. You despised Robert Montcrieff. We all did.'

'I have no idea what you're talking about. I've never seen you before.'

The woman shook her head. 'What's happened to you, Sarah? After that dumb experiment in the water tanks, you and John ran away without telling anyone where you were going. Ben and I were worried sick. We even went over to Europe to look for you. We ended up getting jobs and staying over there. Ben came back last week, and I just flew in from Paris today.'

'You must be confusing me with someone else,' Sarah said.

The woman fell silent, her arms flopping to her sides.

Sarah pushed past her and headed for the door.

'You must have had an accident,' the woman shouted after her. 'You have amnesia. You need help, Sarah.'

Sarah hurried out and was joined by her two bodyguards.

'Are you all right, ma'am?' one of them asked. 'You look pale.'

'I'm OK. Let's get out of here.'

16

Immersion

Helen Reeves emerged from the restroom and stared at Sarah as she disappeared in the company of two burly men. Christ, she was acting like a crazy person. How could she be going out with Robert Montcrieff? It was ridiculous beyond words. As for John, Sarah genuinely seemed oblivious to his name. How could that be? Those two were inseparable. What on earth happened to them that day eight years ago?

Eight Years Earlier

Helen took her boyfriend's arm. 'I'm nervous,' she said.

'I'm not looking forward to it any more than you are, Helen,' Ben Canvey said, 'but what choice do we have? Sure, it's a sensory deprivation experiment, and that sounds scary, but all we're really doing is relaxing in a glorified bath for two weeks. We can spend the time dreaming about what we're going to do when we get to Italy.'

Even though Helen was a Columbia University philosophy senior, she'd heard on the grapevine of the lucrative summer experiment being run by the psychology department. She and Ben had been searching for ages for a money-raising job to finance a trip to Venice. This seemed like the perfect opportunity.

Ben went through the technical details again. The experiment involved lying in a flotation tank filled with ten inches of water containing eight hundred pounds of dissolved epsom salts. The solution was so dense it would push you to the surface like a cork. It was simply impossible not to float. Your face would stick out of the water, while your ears, protected by earplugs, would be below the surface. The tank environment was humid, but not uncomfortable. An air circulation system brought in fresh air from the outside.

'I mean, it's a thousand bucks a week,' Ben said. 'At the end, we'll have four grand between us and we can get out of here. I can't wait to have a moonlight gondola trip along the Grand Canal.'

They were approaching the end of the long queue of students who'd also heard about the summer's quickest get-rich-at-minimum-effort scheme; the slacker's dream.

Immersion

'There's no other way?' Helen asked. Sure, it sounded like easy money, but lying suspended in a watery coffin was like something from a horror movie.

'Not if we want to get to Venice this summer.'

Helen nudged Ben and pointed at the back of the queue. Their best friends John Dexter and Sarah Harris were there, waving.

'Joined at the hip, as usual,' Ben mouthed.

'Don't be nasty,' Helen said. 'It's sweet that they're so into each other.'

'What the hell's Sarah wearing?' Ben blurted. 'She looks like a hooker.'

Helen gazed at Sarah and couldn't help shaking her head. Ben was spot on. Drastically underdressed in a skin-tight scarlet crop top and rainbow coloured hot-pants, Sarah also had red sneakers on, without socks, and a gleaming silver stud in her belly button.

Helen took Ben's hand and they joined their friends in the line. 'Hey, you two,' she said.

'No one's going to forget you in a hurry,' Ben said to Sarah. 'Is it a bet?'

'I just wanted to wear something different.' Sarah sounded typically defensive.

John quickly jumped in and said fifty places were available on the programme. He'd estimated there were over two hundred students in the queue.

'One in four chance, huh?' Ben said. 'But they're not going to turn us down, are they?' Again, he peered at what Sarah was wearing. 'I mean, who'd say no to a party girl and her best pals?'

Helen listened distractedly as John announced how much he was looking forward to chilling out for a while. He'd worked hard during the term, he said, and now just wanted to take it easy. 'What better way than soaking in a big tub for two weeks? And getting paid for it too.'

'Yeah, leaving all the shit behind for a while,' Ben said.

Helen watched as John winked at Sarah. Sarah leaned towards him, putting her hand round his neck. Helen heard her whispering, 'I love you to death.' She thought Sarah looked so sad and beautiful at the same time. Sarah and John both seemed lost sometimes. She put it down to the fact that both were orphans. They didn't speak about it much but you could tell it had hugely impacted on their lives.

'Cut it out, you two,' she said and playfully punched John's shoulder to separate him from Sarah. It didn't work.

Prohibition A

As John gazed at Sarah with ludicrous intensity, Helen giggled in embarrassment and nudged Ben in the ribs. 'Why do you never look at *me* like that?'

Ben threw up his hands in mock horror. 'Hey, those two are on the marry-go-round – we're just having fun, babe.'

'Gee, thanks.' Helen scrunched up her face. 'When's the wedding?' she asked Sarah. 'It can't be long now.'

Sarah and John both blushed. Then Helen noticed a group of three men looming up behind them. *Shit.*

Robert Montcrieff, Tommy Henshaw and Ian Longbottom were MBA students who loved flaunting their expensive designer suits. They weren't exactly popular figures on campus. They'd come to Columbia from the Marine Corps and were practically a decade older than most of the other students. They became notorious when they were accused of beating up a vagrant who'd taken to hanging around the campus's ATM machines. The man was hospitalised and couldn't remember anything about the attack. There were no witnesses, but no one doubted who was responsible.

'Hey, Gappy, are you trying to raise some money to fix those witch's teeth?' Ian Longbottom's booming voice made people in the queue look round to see what was happening. As Helen had witnessed on several occasions in the student bar, Longbottom had an unhealthy interest in Sarah.

She winced, knowing how sensitive Sarah was about the space between her front teeth. It was a feature that John claimed didn't bother him; in fact he said it added to her beauty, in the way that imperfections are always more interesting than flawless looks. But Sarah hated it and was always speculating about getting her teeth fixed.

'I bet that when you give your boyfriend a blow-job, all the jism dribbles out of the gap,' Longbottom said, eyeballing Sarah. 'Fucking disgusting.'

John clenched his fists, but Sarah put her hand on his arm and shook her head. Helen wiggled her little finger at Longbottom. There was a rumour that when Longbottom went to Paris on vacation, the woman at passport control stopped him then announced to her colleagues that a Monsieur *Grand Derriere* had just arrived from the States.

'Hey,' Helen hissed, 'can't you haul that huge butt of yours somewhere else.'

'Fucking whore,' Longbottom shouted.

Montcrieff restrained Longbottom, then looked at Sarah and whispered something that made Longbottom snigger.

Immersion

When Sarah swung her hand at Montcrieff, he grabbed her by the wrist and pulled her towards him. 'You know, if you sorted those teeth, I might be interested.' He looked her up and down. 'How much do you charge? Fifty?'

'Fuck off,' John yelled.

Longbottom and Henshaw stepped forward, but Montcrieff simply smiled. He interlaced his knuckles and made an irritating cracking sound. He did it repeatedly, at least six times. The sound went right through Helen. Sarah seemed to hate it even more, pressing her hands against her ears.

'Let's go,' Montcrieff said.

Helen watched as the three men strode past the head of the queue and marched up the steps. An overweight, middle-aged man in a white lab coat came out to greet them, shook Montcrieff's hand then ushered them inside. *Why the red carpet treatment for those three?* she wondered.

When she glanced at Sarah, her friend was clutching her arms against her chest, with her head bowed. She looked like she was about to cry. Ben told a joke to defuse the atmosphere and Sarah tried to play along, but she kept covering her mouth with her hand.

John was agitated. He always got strung out when Sarah was distressed.

It was forty-five minutes before they reached the front of the queue and entered the building. The piggy man Helen had seen earlier with Montcrieff and his cronies was there. He introduced himself as David Warren, Professor of Psychology. His three assistants directed some people towards a room on the left, and a smaller number to a room on the right. Everyone was handed a questionnaire to fill in.

John was first to give his name to the professor.

Warren glanced at his clipboard and smiled. 'Ah, come with me...and your girlfriend.'

Helen wondered why John and Sarah were the only ones not to get questionnaires.

John was obviously thinking the same thing. She could overhear him talking to Warren as they went round the corner.

'Oh, that's to sort the wheat from the chaff,' Warren was saying. 'You and Sarah are just the sort we're looking for.'

'What do you mean?' John asked. 'You've never met us before.'

'Each of you will have to be evaluated psychologically, to make sure you can cope with two weeks in a tank,' Warren replied. 'We don't want anyone going psycho on us, do we? You're coming with me, Mr Dexter. One of my assistants will look after Sarah.'

Prohibition A

Helen felt alarmed by what she'd heard. It was a relief when they all met up again a couple of hours later. After an induction class with the other successful candidates, they changed into special underwater suits and stored their possessions in a locker room.

Helen was certain she saw John putting away a presentation box. Jesus, maybe he was planning to propose to Sarah. They had spoken about going to Paris after the experiment. What better place than Paris to pop the question?

A siren sounded and the professor clapped his hands. 'OK, folks, you all know what you're here for. We'll have someone supervising the tanks 24/7. Remember, if any of you suffers a panic attack or any kind of illness or distress over the next two weeks then just hit the red button and we'll come and get you out of there. Good luck to all of you.'

Helen grimaced. This experiment was getting less appealing by the second. Within the sensory deprivation tanks, they'd have access to two tubes; one for drinking water and the other for a bland soup. As for waste disposal, they had special attachments on their suits that were hooked up to two tubes that could be flushed with high-pressure jets of water. Apparently, everything that left their bodies would be carefully examined to see if any changes occurred over the course of the two-week experiment. She was glad they were all in adjacent tanks, even if they couldn't see each other.

When she noticed Sarah nudging John and giving him a final kiss, she immediately did the same with Ben. She fitted her earplugs then swung through the porthole of the white tank and pushed herself into the water.

Just as she'd settled into the tank and was waiting for one of Warren's assistants to close the hatch, she noticed a tall, silver-haired man in a black uniform appearing from nowhere and approaching the professor.

Why the hell are the military here? she wondered as the hatch slammed shut and everything went dark.

****

Helen shook her head as all the details flooded back. It was supposed to be easy money, but it ended up being the hardest two weeks of her life. Jesus, did something happen to Sarah inside those tanks? Maybe she suffered some kind of breakdown.

As she fished in her handbag for her cell phone, she saw two men in grey suits coming towards her.

'Helen Reeves?' one of them asked.

'Yes. Can I help you?'

86

Immersion

'We're from the Department of Homeland Security. You've just returned from France, ma'am, haven't you? According to our records, you spent eight years there. We have a few questions for you about various people you associated with while you were over there. If you'd like to come with us, we have a car waiting outside. Ben Canvey is coming with us too.'

'I was just going to phone Ben.'

'Well, now you can speak to him in person.'

'Where are we going?'

'Our office is downtown. In a couple of hours, you'll be free to go.'

17

The Trick-or-Treat Killers

Trick-or-treat masks hid their faces, but these guys were all trick and no treat. David Warren wasn't sure whether there were four or five of them. His head was jerking around so much it was disorientating him. The adrenalin that had flooded his body minutes earlier had doubled his heartbeat. Christ, he couldn't deny it any longer – he was running for his life.

He looked back towards Dromlech Castle, lying in the darkness beneath a fresh snowfall. The night was so thick it felt like a prison. Who were they? In a few more minutes, the ceremony, the climax of the night's adult fun, would have been over. Instead, the world had gone crazy. Now his body was itching uncontrollably, as if an army of hot spiders had spilled into his bloodstream.

Lightning cracked the sky. A storm was closing in. A storm? That had already been, hadn't it? His mind returned to those masks. Whose faces were behind them? He remembered the day he killed Steve Grissom, plunging a needle full of untraceable poison into his neck. Within the hour, he was appointed Grissom's successor. Had Grissom somehow reached out from the grave? He shook his head. There was no doubt who was responsible – John Dexter was back.

God, can't breathe. Warren gripped his chest. A spasm of shivers shot through him so violently that his legs almost buckled. All he had on was the red silk robe he'd worn for the ceremony. But there was something else, wasn't there? What would they think of him when they discovered what was strapped to his butt? Carolyn had suggested it. This was her all-time favourite trick, she said. She was the sort who knew more than a few. She called it the *osculum obscenum* – the obscene kiss. The idea was that at the climax of the ceremony he would bend over, raise his robe and stick his ass into her face. Carolyn would see the face of the devil looking back at her, with the mouth strategically placed. She would then French kiss the devil. He was looking forward to it so much, but the ceremony hadn't got that far. Now the cleverest spin-doctor in the world couldn't bail him out. Even if he survived, he was finished. The mask could only be removed with a special key. He'd lost it when he fled from the castle.

Over there – the parrot cages, the main attraction of his ocean-side property. All the birds would be asleep now. If he could wake them, they'd start squawking and raise the alarm. But there was no one out there to hear, was there? He started wheezing. This cold air was terrible for his lungs. It was only a matter of time before he had an asthma attack.

There they were again. Four of them, standing in line in the moonlight. They were wearing suits, like businessmen. Was this a warning or a wake? Did they really think they'd get away with this? Why the crazy masks? If he wasn't mistaken, they all looked like the Big Bad Wolf.

Crack. Single gunshot. A spray of blood. *His* blood. Falling. Everything spinning. The parrots, screeching like crazy. No moon now. Must have some light to see by. Got to get up out of the snow. Keep moving. It was a shot from a Ruger P85 semi-automatic, wasn't it? He knew the sound well enough from target practice on his private shooting range. He pushed himself onwards. The chest pains were getting worse. Too old, too fat. His team called him Piggy behind his back. The doctor had warned him: cut this out, cut that out. Might as well be dead if you couldn't cut yourself some fun. Fun was what he'd designed Dromlech Castle for. Here, far from his pressure-tank life in Langley, was where he could relax. He was due to go back there to the boiler room after the election. Now, he knew, he'd never make it.

Everything was screwing up. Dexter was back from the dead and Sarah's mind had started to go AWOL According to Clark, Sarah might already have encountered Dexter. Jesus, the whole thing was a nightmare. He was glad to have escaped from it all for a while. Then this.

Another minute passed. He realised they weren't catching up. So, not going for the kill just yet. The single bullet had struck him in the shoulder. A precise shot, designed to give him a long, lingering death. Marksmen. The bastards were toying with him.

Just ahead – *the maze*. Thank God, a chance to save himself. They wouldn't know its secret. They'd get trapped and the cops would come and arrest them. But there was no one left to call him, was there? He'd given his own security team the night off. Didn't want them prying. Bad mistake. Should have invited them to join in. They were young guys out of Yale. They'd have loved it. Might even have been able to save him. But none of the other young men at the ritual survived, did they? Good-looking kids they were too. They were in top shape, making daily visits to the gym, pumping every kind of iron. It didn't save them. Cyanide gas: that's what they used, wasn't it? It was a miracle he got out, before the steel security shutters closed to seal off the main room and transform it into a death trap.

Into the hedges. Blood loss getting critical. Cock-sucking weather, beginning to rain. Snow turning to slush. So cold, like someone had stuck him inside a freezer.

Inside the maze now, with its eight-feet-high hedges. If he could reach the hidden trapdoor at the centre, he'd be safe. It led to an underground chamber lined with pagan statues. There he could activate the system to trap the killers. He had seduced so many women in that cavern. Such good times. Remember when...but not now, no time for the past. He staggered on, his vision growing fuzzy. Spasms of pains exploded all over his body like firecrackers.

He pulled up the hidden trapdoor and gingerly climbed down the rope ladder into the chamber, carefully replacing the trapdoor behind him. An automatic light came on as he descended. He let out a gasp of relief. For the first time since the nightmare began, he felt some kind of safety. Then he coughed. *Oh, Mother of God.* He gazed at the thick blobs of blood that had spurted from his mouth.

Got to press the button and trap the bastards. With a groan, he dragged his failing body over to the control panel built into the wall of the chamber. Flashing red lights indicated that the four intruders were already inside the maze. He pressed the button, almost fainting with elation. 'Got you, you fuckwits. No one screws with David Warren and gets away with it.'

He pulled his aching body along the thirty yards of rising stone corridor that led to the chamber's exit in a little, secluded garden, concealed by a square of tall Leyland cypress trees. This was his private space, his retreat from the pressures of his job, the only place where he could wind down. A pale blue light kept it illuminated in the dark. A canopy protected it from the snow. He lurched towards the white Florentine chair where he liked to read the *Wall Street Journal* and sip the finest champagne in the summer when the sunflowers were in bloom. A statue of Emperor Augustus stood on a pedestal behind the chair. He always imagined himself a Caesar, but now the truth had caught up with him. He was just a fat old man, and he was dying.

He slumped into his seat. Surely safe now. One of his staff would come and find him. Who was he kidding? He was alone. His robe flapped around him in the breeze. It was saturated with his blood. In Vietnam, he had enjoyed the sight of blood, but that was different. *Charlie* didn't count. Gooks were cheaper than rice. He, though, was one of America's most important men, the unofficial second-in-command of the Committee. He was within striking distance of being the most powerful man on earth. Had Clark uncovered his plan? Maybe these assassins were SMI agents. *Impossible.* No one else knew a thing. He'd done everything to cover his tracks.

His robe fell open over his groin. When he glanced down, he recoiled in shock. His dick was shrivelled and bloodstained. Looked dreadful, like some kind of amputated thing. *Holy, sweet Jesus.* He couldn't die, not here, not in the garden he loved. He was too important to die. Mother, what was happening to him? The Devil mask on his butt was hurting like hell, digging hard into his flesh.

He started to drift in and out of consciousness. *Am I dreaming of death or dying of dreams?* He heard his blood dripping onto the stone slabs. In the distance, the coloured landing lights of an airplane en route to LaGuardia were switching on and off in time with his fading breathing.

He thought about his life. What had he achieved? He'd created brainwashed assassins. Was that on the credit side? He remembered the experiments conducted on the Looking Glass subjects, week after week, month after month. The memory that lingered longest was of them floating in their individual glass isolation tanks, with all of their body hair shaved off – crash test dummies heading for a fatal collision. Their minds were no longer their own. Their memories, if they could be called that, were phantasms, created in a lab by SMI scientists and implanted in brains washed meticulously clean. The lives they thought they lived were fake. It was that ability to have their lives moulded to fit whatever plans SMI had in mind that made them so valuable, that made Alice the most powerful weapon of all.

His eyes began to close. The image of the young people in their isolation tanks had changed. Now the figures were fully dressed, their eyes wide open and staring, full of accusation. One of them was particularly special, the one he'd painstakingly hidden from Clark. He remembered all the shit he'd taken from the general in the last few years, the humiliation. No one could have tolerated the indignity, the ingratitude. It wasn't right, not after everything he'd done for Clark. Even after he saved the general's skin by taking care of Grissom, the thanks he received was grudging, the proper respect lacking. Payback was only days away, but now he'd never get the chance to see Clark's face when the Looking Glass world changed one last time. The twist would have made him the most powerful man on earth, but these killers were stealing his prize from him.

He heard steps. Not alone. They were *here*, in his little heaven. Hadn't shaken them off. They *knew*. Somehow, they'd discovered his secret. Got to face them, look them in the eye, show them they weren't dealing with a pussy. But... *Please don't do it. Begging you. Give you anything. Just... Stop.*

One of them was wearing one of those wrist gadgets – a digital music player. The bastard began to play something: *What a Wonderful World.* Sick fuck. It was the tune he played most often to Dexter and Sarah as a mockery of their doomed love affair. He'd been so jealous of that love. They were so into each other, so happy, so perfect for each other. It wasn't fair. Love like that deserved to be destroyed.

The four assassins pointed their pistols at him. He stared at their faces, but all he saw looking back at him was the Big Bad Wolf. One of them shot out the blue light above him. Broken glass cascaded onto the ground as darkness swept over him.

'Please, let me go,' he screamed into the blackness. It was futile. Dexter would never listen. 'It wasn't my fault. Clark gave the orders.' There was no answer; just the voice of Satchmo singing the song that Warren loved to listen to in summer when flowers of every colour transformed his garden into a living rainbow. Images of a perfect summer's day flooded into his mind, but that just made this moment harder to take. He watched as the killers took off their masks.

'*You!*' he gasped, gazing at the face of their leader, a face he knew so well. *Is this justice?* he wondered.

As the shots rang out, he knew it was.

18

Apollo Mission

A police roadblock brought Sarah to a halt. She rolled down her window and showed her FBI badge to the cop. 'I'm Sarah Harris, the CIRG's Incident Manager.' Her breath was visible in the cold air. 'I'm on my way to the Incident Command Centre.'

She was already agitated. Earlier, after she got out of the shower in her apartment, she'd switched on the morning news. The lead story was a car crash in Brooklyn. A woman and her boyfriend were dead. The newsreader said the incident was particularly tragic since the couple had just returned from France after living there for eight years. Sarah gazed in shock at the pictures that flashed onto the screen. The man seemed vaguely familiar. As for the woman…Christ, it was the crazy person from the restroom in Grand Central Station.

'Everything's in the castle's parking lot, ma'am,' the cop replied, shivering in the snow. 'There must be about twenty LDVs. Never seen anything like it.' He asked her to sign the entry log, then waved her through.

Twenty LDVs? These were the specially customised trucks that provided mobile offices for the different groups that needed to be present at a major incident. CIRG had its own LDV Incident Command Centre. Other LDVs came from the likes of the local Police Department, the IBM mobile communications team and the Coroner's office. There were rarely more than eight at an incident. Twenty was extraordinary. Had the Committee insisted on all this extra activity? It must have shocked the hell out of them to know they could be targeted.

Dromlech Castle loomed out of the mist. Already, Sarah knew today would be bad. David Warren, Director of the CIA, leading member of the Committee, was dead. This was off the chart. Dargo had told her he wanted all of his best people on the case. She should probably have refused, but she felt compelled to come. After all, she'd been here at Warren's party just thirty-six hours earlier. As usual, she was being shadowed by the secret service. They were in the car behind her, but she was increasingly irritated by their presence.

Luckily, most of CIRG's procedures were well rehearsed. Within minutes of a major incident, Sarah's team – all on standby 24/7 – would be alerted by the CIRG's emergency centre. Decisions would already have been made about whether negotiators were needed, or the Hostage Rescue Team or behavioural psychologists, or any of the other elements of CIRG.

Normally, Sarah would have little to do initially. Her job was to act as an escalation point, to use her extra authority whenever it was required, to think on her feet and overcome obstacles. With many incidents, she could step back and watch her team doing their jobs. She hoped it would be like that today, but there seemed little prospect.

She didn't like Warren and knew he'd made enemies, but she hadn't expected this. If Warren was vulnerable, anyone was. It made her worry about Robert. Assassination was an occupational hazard for high profile figures. Now the threat wasn't so theoretical.

As Sarah approached the parking lot, she noticed that the whole area was sealed off. A news helicopter hovered overhead. The *graveyard shift* – those morbid members of the public obsessed with others' deaths – were pressing hard against the blue and white crime scene tape, their faces lit by the flashing emergency lights of scores of police cars and ambulances. They were dying to know if they'd hit the jackpot – the thing the police called an Apollo case. It had that name for a simple reason – the ratings for the news coverage were always going to the moon. Every sonofabitch tuned in for an Apollo.

A police snowplough had cleared the parking lot of snow. Just as the cop said, an impressive collection of LDVs was lined up, providing an almost circus-like atmosphere. One of them was marked *Hazmat*: hazardous material. What the hell was going on?

Sarah was anxious to find the Incident Command Centre and get a rundown on what she was dealing with. When she got there, five control staff were making phone calls, poring over situation maps, gathering casualty information, preparing reports and entering data into computers, all the usual stuff. Sarah focused her attention on the bank of TV monitors broadcasting live pictures from Dromlech Castle.

A square building made from grey-yellow stone, Dromlech Castle was surrounded by a picturesque moat. It could be reached by two small drawbridges, one at the front and one the rear. It was stunning, a picture postcard image, especially in this wintry setting. Italian gardens, a maze, an aviary, sloping lawns, a lake – the Dromlech estate had everything. She wondered if the original in Scotland was as spectacular.

After being briefed by her team, she made her way towards the castle. All she could think of was how Warren died. The details were horrific. Shots were fired into each of his eyes, and one into his penis. Blood had splattered onto the slush, together with fragments of skull and chunks of raw brain. From footprints, it was known that there were four killers. One of the gang had sunk his teeth into Warren's lips and there was a suggestion that someone had licked blood off the corpse's naked belly. The final surreal touch was that a card resembling a kid's nursery rhyme card was found jammed into the mouth of the corpse. The words were weird:

Big fat pig, big fat pig, let me come in, said the big bad wolf. No, no, by the hair of my chinny, chin, chin, I will not let you in, said the fat pig. Then I'll huff and I'll puff and blow your fucking head off, replied the big bad wolf.

Sarah didn't want to see Warren's dead body. She'd decided to put it off as long as possible. Now, she was heading for the castle where other corpses awaited, but at least she didn't know any of these personally.

Approaching the entrance gate, she heard the sound of a police motor launch patrolling the partially iced-over lake at the foot of the long, snow-covered lawns. Ducking under the police tape that had been used to cordon off the front entrance, she made her way over the small wooden drawbridge. Two armed cops emerged from the shadows of the gatehouse, their eyes hidden by mirrored sunglasses.

'Stop right there.' One of them turned an Uzi machine pistol towards her. 'I need your security clearance.'

Sarah pointed at her purple armband and held up her FBI shield. 'Assistant Special Agent in Charge Sarah Harris, FBI. I'm the IM.'

'Go through,' the cop said when she'd signed in.

She stepped forward, then paused in front of the castle's heavy oak door, doubting she had the strength to open it. One of the cops heaved it open and she walked through into an inner courtyard, carpeted by untouched snow. On the far side was the black door leading to the main rooms of the castle. As she walked towards it, she felt the first thuds of a bad headache. She breathed in hard. Now she'd see for herself what happened here last night. They said Warren's death was nothing compared with what had occurred inside. This was an Apollo case heading for the dark side of the moon.

For a few moments, she stood in front of the locked door. *I'm terrified*, she realised. She knocked on the door and a young man in a silver boiler suit opened it. A gas mask dangled from his neck and he reeked of disinfectant. Behind him was a small anteroom, packed with equipment that looked like it came from a CDC lab for the investigation of contagious diseases.

'Put these on.' He handed Sarah a silver suit like his own, together with yellow boots and gloves, and a chem-bio protective hood fitted with a gasmask.

Prohibition A

She remembered the Hazmat sign on the LDV and began to panic. Chemical warfare; biological terrorism; dirty bombs. She wanted to turn round and walk back the way she'd come. 'What's the story?' she asked, trying to sound calm.

'Just put them on,' the man said. 'You can hang your coat on one of the hooks on the far wall.'

She recalled the old mantra: *Control the situation or it will control you.* 'I'm Sarah Harris, the IM.' She jabbed at her armband. 'Tell me what's going on.'

'Sorry, ma'am, I didn't realise. I was ordered to get any visitors suited up as soon as possible for safety reasons.' He gestured towards the plastic barrier. 'The victims were killed by hydrogen cyanide gas. We found the delivery mechanism in an upstairs room this morning. After that, the castle had to be checked for other devices. They're still sweeping, so we've had to take the appropriate precautions.'

Sarah nodded, but inside she was churning up. *Jesus, cyanide gas.* She thought of Nazi death camps, of smoke rising from charred flesh in crematoria. What was she doing in this nightmare? Her life was in real danger if she stepped inside.

Hesitantly, she took off her Puffa jacket and placed it on a hook next to a black anorak. Underneath, she had on a sky-blue fleece, a pair of blue jeans and short black boots – it was way too cold for regulation FBI gear. It took her several seconds to struggle into the one-piece suit she was given. She tried to blank her mind, to shut out the clamour of fear in her brain. The more she thought about it, the more convinced she was that the vagrant she saw in Red Square was in disguise. What was that weird thing he said? *Killed any boyfriends lately?* There was something about those words that petrified her. Somehow, that vagrant was linked with Warren's death. She didn't know how and she had no evidence, but she was certain all the same.

Her breathing changed when she put on the protective hood. She was conscious of the air going in and out of her lungs. Her sense of hearing altered too. Now, within the confinement of the hood, with the padded material pressing against her ears, everything sounded muffled. Finally, she put on the protective gloves and over-boots. When she was ready, she gave the man a thumbs-up and he waved her on.

A yellow plastic barrier had been placed over the entrance to a short corridor that connected the anteroom to the Great Hall: Dromlech Castle's centrepiece where she'd mingled with movie stars only the other night.

96

Apollo Mission

Gazing through the visor of her hood, she felt like an astronaut. She pushed through a gap in the plastic barrier and found herself confronted by a second identical barrier several yards on. Beyond, cameras in the Great Hall were flashing, throwing a green light into the corridor. For a moment, Sarah had a sensation of being trapped between two worlds, one of them safe and recognisable, the other terrifyingly unknown. *I have to go back*, she thought, and wanted to turn round and scramble backwards, but her legs drove her forward. A second later, she was in the Great Hall. She took one look and froze. *You must be fucking kidding.*

At least twenty naked bodies of young women and men were strewn over the floor, their faces hidden by outlandish masks of reptiles and birds. Black flags inscribed with scarlet swastikas formed a circle around the corpses. Vast steel shutters had slammed down from the ceiling to the floor, turning the place into a Panic Room from which there was no escape. Four investigators in camouflage protective gear and gasmasks were gathered round a black marble altar in the centre of the room, busily analysing evidence. Slumped between long black candles on either side of the altar was the body of a beautiful young woman, her flesh luridly pink.

Sarah had to lean against a wall to steady herself. The punky blonde hair was unmistakable, the nails still painted black. She shuddered as she remembered drinking and chatting with Carolyn Voronski so recently. Was this the 'adult' entertainment Carolyn had mentioned?

Dazed, she stepped closer. Carolyn, it seemed, had been wearing a mask of the Virgin Mary. It had fallen off and rolled to the foot of the altar. Pages torn from a Bible were scattered around it. Balanced between Carolyn's shoulder blades was a chalice containing what looked like semen.

Sarah turned away in disgust, only to find her eyes attracted to a slogan scrawled on the floor in blood-red capital letters. She stared at the words, transfixed. *SIN FOR SALVATION*. They seemed to flash at her, imprinting themselves almost violently on her brain. She thought she was going to hyperventilate.

A siren sounded. 'The all-clear has now been given,' a voice announced. 'You may remove your protective suits and gas-masks.'

She quickly shed her gear, took several deep breaths and ran her hand through her hair to untangle it. Blood pounded through her brain. Those words on the floor. Something about them…

'Hey, Sarah,' someone shouted.

Prohibition A

'*Mike* – what are you doing here?' Dressed in a black turtleneck sweater and white chinos Lacey looked like he was meeting some friends for a casual drink.

Don't give me any more bad news, she thought as she watched him hurrying over to her.

'You won't believe this,' he said eagerly. 'Apart from the woman on the altar, every dead person has ten red circles round their left wrist.' His eyes were jumping. 'And even the altar lady's got three circles. Does this qualify as a crisis now?'

Sarah peered at him. He was treating this like an intellectual game rather than the slaughterhouse it was. 'The woman on the altar is Carolyn Voronski,' she said sharply, 'Warren's girlfriend. I left you messages yesterday. She was the person I wanted to talk to you about. She knew exactly where she got the red circles done. When I last saw her, she only had one.'

'So, where *did* she get them?'

'She didn't say.'

'*Shit.*'

Sarah turned her attention to the flags. 'What's with those?'

'Neo-Nazi stuff?'

Sarah shook her head. 'None of this stacks up.'

'Behind you.' Lacey raised his eyebrows.

'What?' Sarah's headache was getting much worse.

'Someone's behind you.'

When Sarah turned, an agent from the Javits office, wearing a blue FBI jacket, was staring at her.

'I was told to give this to the IM.' The man held up a polythene evidence bag containing a damp piece of black paper. 'It was rolled up and stuck in the anus of the woman on the altar. It's covered with semen.'

Sarah was revolted. 'What is it?'

'There's a message on it.' The agent glanced at his notepad. 'It says: *Who is the Red Queen?*'

Sarah blinked rapidly. She wanted to say something, but her mouth went dry. Everything had turned red, as if a painter had transformed the world with a single, giant brushstroke. She fought back panic. Everywhere, nothing but red. Her hands were freezing cold. A noise like the buzzing of bees chain-sawed through her head. *What in God's name is happening to me?*

In her mind, she saw herself in Central Park once more. Police cars were all around her. A detective was talking to her. Lying at her feet was a body without a face. Bit by bit, features were appearing. She could hear voices, a cop speaking with the detective.

'*Any idea who the stiff is?*'

'*There's no ID card, no credit cards, nothing. He was carrying a hundred bucks in cash. As for the woman, you won't believe it. Name's Jane Ford: Secret Service.*'

'*Jesus.*'

'*Guess these spook broads don't want to be tied down, huh?*'

'*Hey,*' another cop said, taking a closer look at the gold ring. '*This is engraved. Says, "To Sarah with eternal love" on it.*' He guffawed. '*There you go, the sucker got shot for using the wrong frigging name! Probably had two girlfriends and got them mixed up.*'

'Hi, anyone at home?' Lacey said.

'I've not been feeling well,' Sarah said, realising she must have been gazing into space.

The Javits agent shrugged and walked off.

'What did it mean?' Sarah said. 'That message?'

'It could mean anything. These folks weren't using the same pack of cards as the rest of us.'

A pain tore through Sarah's guts. *I'm going down with something*, she thought. Food poisoning, maybe. She knew a bad dose could produce hallucinations. Was that what she'd experienced a few moments ago? That bizarre scene in Central Park. Why did it seem so real? Why did it keep coming back to her?

The buzzing in her head began again, like a pneumatic drill pressed against her ear. Weird pictures were filling her mind. Something was stepping out of the shadows, pushing forward into the light; a figure without a face. Then a single shot. Paramedics prepared a body bag for a corpse dressed in a yellow suit. *I'm wearing a red crop top*, she thought, *and I'm staring at an engagement ring. Men in grey suits are all around me.*

The Javits agent reappeared. 'A search team found hidden security cameras in the grounds of the castle,' he said. 'The cameras were fitted with night vision capability and motion detectors. One camera was located within feet of where Warren was murdered.'

Sarah struggled to compose herself, hardly registering what the agent had just said. She listened as he explained again. 'So, have you got the tapes?'

'They've all been removed.'

'By whom?'

The agent shrugged.

'Find out fast. I want those tapes.'

The agent nodded then handed her a single sheet of paper. 'The ICC asked me to give you this. It's the initial incident report.'

Sarah quickly read the report: 'A sex ritual was held in Dromlech Castle, the Long Island residence of CIA Director David Warren,' it said.' Just before midnight, a hallucinogenic drug in gaseous form was introduced into the room from a concealed pipe in the roof. While the guests were disorientated, hydrogen cyanide was released. Steel security shutters sealed off the room. Only the CIA Director escaped alive. All but one of the victims had ten red circles tattooed around their wrists. The exception was Warren's girlfriend Carolyn Voronski, who had three red circles. The meaning of the circles is unknown at this time. A note was found protruding from Voronski's anus. The note read as follows...'

Got to get some fresh air, Sarah thought.

'Are you all right?' Lacey asked. 'You don't look too good.'

'I'm done here.' Sarah tried to keep her voice firm. 'I'm going back to the ICC.' But she was thinking of only one thing. Did the vagrant kill these people?

Was the vagrant John Dexter?

19

The Hidden Danger

Is it over? General Clark gazed at the notes laid in front of him. Was this what the end of the world looked like? He felt sick, his body rebelling against the rigid control he had exerted over it for so long. In the last few hours, he had experienced extreme anxiety for the first time. He imagined it as a snake coiled around him, squeezing the air from his lungs. All his life, he'd played with the odds on his side. Now, he knew, he'd have to gamble. In the next few days, everything would be decided. Staring at the empty seat where David Warren always sat, he was shocked to discover that he was missing him, that in a strange way Warren had become his closest friend.

He looked around the table at the surviving members of the Committee. 'Before we discuss the matter that's on all of our minds, I'd like to hear what the progress is on the campaign.' He turned to Frank Doyle, the DIA Director. 'Frank, what's the latest?'

Doyle's eyes were sleepless. He spoke in a monotone. 'Our private polling puts the President on thirty-two per cent, Tom Lawson on thirty-one and Robert Montcrieff on thirty-seven. This is the first time Montcrieff has been clearly in front. He got a huge boost from his engagement to Sarah. The momentum is with him. Our latest model predicts he will reach forty per cent on Election Day, corresponding, we think, to fifty-four per cent of the Electoral College.' He placed his hands firmly on the table. 'Robert Montcrieff will be the next president.'

'Thanks, Frank.' Clark gazed down at a single sheet of paper he'd carefully separated from the rest of his documents. Speaking in a voice that he hoped communicated business-as-usual, he said, 'We know who killed David Warren.'

He saw astonishment flashing across his colleagues' eyes. 'We found out almost immediately.' He raised his hand to signal that he didn't want to be interrupted. 'Tapes from night-vision surveillance cameras at Dromlech Castle were taken to one of our monitoring stations. The memo I have in front of me is from Langley. It identifies the leader of the assassins. There's no doubt.' He couldn't bring himself to say the name. Instead, he pushed the memo to Frank Doyle. 'Pass it around,' he said, his mouth as dry as straw.

One by one, the other four men looked at the name. Clark wondered if any of them would speak, but, like him, they seemed too numb to react. They sat in increasingly upright positions. There was no sound in the room apart from the hum of laptop computers.

'It's almost laughable, isn't it?' It was Gary Lassiter, Director of the FBI, who broke the silence. 'Something as big as this, yet it changes nothing.'

'That's where you're wrong.' Clark took off his spectacles and placed them on the table. 'We're all in danger now.'

20

Lazarus

'That makes sense.' Dargo leaned back in his leather seat. 'We have to do something, but I don't think a search warrant is a good idea.'

Sarah was meeting her boss in his office in Pearl Street. She rarely ventured into Dargo's claustrophobic little room and already she was uncomfortable. A small, tidy room, it had a prominent bookcase packed with every edition of the FBI's Law Enforcement Bulletin. Dargo's favourite picture of J Edgar Hoover hung on the wall behind his chair. A silver plaque beneath the picture said: *Don't embarrass the Bureau.*

She'd briefed him about the latest news regarding the red circles and the fact that Warren mentioned Prohibition A. Searching the club seemed a logical move, but Dargo was hesitating.

'Getting heavy-handed with that club won't do us any favours. It has influential backers. We don't want to make unnecessary enemies. There's no firm evidence it has anything to do with this.'

'Well, how about going in discreetly? Lacey and I could go along and have a look around, see if we can dig up anything. My friend Nicki knows the place.'

'That sounds better.' Dargo picked up a photograph of a Death's-head Hawk moth that he kept beside his laptop computer. 'Also, get someone to contact the Cult Awareness Unit to see if they know anything about what "Sin for Salvation" might mean. There was something about "Red Queen" as well. Check that out too.'

Every time she heard the words 'Red Queen', Sarah felt nauseous. What was wrong with her? And it was stressing her out that no one could find the security tapes from Dromlech Castle, or any sign of who took them. They had simply vanished.

One thing that was no longer an issue was the incident with the man who resembled Dexter. Sarah was sure now it was a trick of the light. She hadn't really got a good look, and it had been over in a second. She was convinced those red circles had screwed with her mind. It was stupid of her not to have gone after the man and confronted him, but she hadn't been thinking clearly.

They were interrupted by a knock on the door. One of the security guards from reception came in, carrying a black envelope.

Prohibition A

'A guy came in a few moments ago and gave me this letter,' he said. 'He said you'd want to read it straight away. I asked him to wait, but he left.'

Dargo opened the envelope and took out a black card. It had names written on it in silver ink. He sprang to his feet and grabbed the security guard. 'Can you access the CCTV security footage for the reception area from my computer?' He was almost shouting.

'Sure. Give me a second.'

'I must see who gave you this envelope,' Dargo barked.

Sarah stared at Dargo who had started to sweat profusely.

'There you go.' The security man stood back as high-resolution pictures appeared on Dargo's computer screen. 'That's the man right there.' He froze the picture.

'It *can't* be, it just can't.'

'What is it?' Sarah was astonished by Dargo's behaviour.

'That's him, all right,' the security man confirmed.

'*Look.*' Dargo stabbed his finger at the screen.

Sarah joined Dargo behind his desk. Immediately, she felt the same numbing shock. '*Oh my God.*'

Dargo held up the black card.

'What's that?' Sarah's heart was drumming so hard she thought it would break through her ribs.

'It's headed TWEP.' Dargo was ashen faced. *Terminate with extreme prejudice.*

'An assassination list?'

'There are nine names on it. Six are the members of the Committee. Warren's name has been crossed off.'

'The others?'

'My name's on it.'

'This is impossible,' Sarah said.

'You haven't asked for the last two names.'

'Who?'

'Robert Montcrieff is one.'

Sarah turned away. She didn't need to ask the name of the last person.

****

They hadn't exchanged a word for fifteen minutes. Finding the office unbearable, Sarah had fled for fresh air to the private garden in the office's central courtyard. Dargo had followed her.

Her mind fought the avalanche of unwelcome facts that had buried her in the last few hours. She imagined herself with a thin rod, desperately poking upwards, trying to find air.

He's back. It was no look-alike she'd seen at Dromlech Castle. John Dexter had somehow returned from the dead.

Dargo rubbed his leg. Sarah noticed that he'd been doing that increasingly frequently. He had a limp that he tried in vain to disguise. Whenever he had to walk more than a few yards, it became more obvious. 'You're staring,' he said.

'Your leg.'

'Dexter,' Dargo replied enigmatically. 'I guess I should tell you the story.' He started massaging his leg again. 'It was a beautiful day. *What a Wonderful World* was playing on the radio. We were on an SMI mission, tailing the car of a terrorist suspect, following normal pursuit procedures. Dexter was driving. Suddenly, he snatched at the steering wheel. The car veered wildly. Moments later, we were chasing a different vehicle. I ordered him to stop, but he ignored me. When I looked at him, I could tell something had snapped.'

Dargo described how they smashed into a wall at 50 mph. Initially, Dargo thought he was paralysed but, after months of recuperation, he regained most of his mobility. He couldn't work for SMI anymore, but the Committee arranged for him to have his current job with the FBI.

As for Dexter, paranoid schizophrenia was the diagnosis. He ranted and raved about having been brainwashed. He denied known facts about his life and invented bizarre episodes that never happened. SMI were forced to discharge him from active duty. They didn't want to lose him and gave him a desk job, hoping he'd recover. But his delusions refused to go away. He behaved like a regular guy and would have seemed quite normal to most people, but he was always digging around, looking for evidence to support his theories. He tried to recruit others to help him.

'What drove Dexter crazy that day?' Sarah had always been intrigued by Dexter's story: the renowned agent, suddenly going off the reservation and plotting against the Committee.

'God knows. Maybe it had been building for years. Our line of work has a way of doing that to us.'

'Where did Dexter go?' Sarah pulled her scarf tighter. 'What happened to him?'

'*You did*,' Dargo said starkly.

Prohibition A

Sarah breathed in hard. Instantly, she pictured herself in that dark underground parking garage in Baltimore, waiting for Dexter to show up. 'When I think of my mission, my mind turns hazy,' she said. 'I have these vivid images in my head, but I don't remember what happened before or after. I don't know how I felt about it, or even if I felt anything at all.'

'You've blocked it out. A lot of agents do that.'

'But I *am* certain I killed him.'

Dargo nodded. 'He was confirmed DOA at the hospital.'

'So, what's going on?'

'I wish I knew.' Dargo bowed his head. 'The scary thing is I'm sure it really is Dexter and I've no idea how that can be.'

Sarah stared into space. 'Ghost or not, he murdered Warren.' She shivered and pressed her folded arms against her chest for warmth. She wanted to phone Robert, but he was on the campaign trail in Connecticut and uncontactable until after midnight.

'Question is – who's next? You should keep your secret service detail much closer in future.'

Sarah stood up. 'When did security men *ever* stop Dexter?'

'Where are you going?'

'I think it's time I visited Prohibition A.'

106

21

Prohibition A

Guide to New York nightclubs

<u>103:</u>   Prohibition A – 14 New Conway Street, Manhattan.

Kate Romero, *New York Listings Magazine*

We've saved the best until last. Give it up for Prohibition A, the club proving that nothing succeeds like sexcess. It hit the headlines in the summer when Cardinal Lenihan described it as 'an open sewer of depravity.' That was after supermodel Donna Cellini confessed to *Showbiz Gossip* what she'd got up to there. I'm sure you all memorised the sordid details (well, I did!), so I won't repeat them here. The club has been called a playground for the super-rich, a titanium-card paradise for highflying stockbrokers and their speedball-fuelled model girlfriends.

It would cost most of us a month's salary just to step through the doors of that funky black glass tower. It has a secret crypt where things go on that would have the Marquis de Sade reaching for his encyclopaedia. I reckon they've had to invent new sins because they've used up all the old ones. If you want an experience you'll never forget, this is it. Marry a millionaire, rob a bank, sell a kidney, I don't care. Just make sure you get your hands on enough dough to get your ass along there.

Specialities:

1) A cocktail called *Inferno*. If you want to enjoy the pleasures of the damned, this is your drink (but I guarantee you'll suffer the torments of hell the morning after).

2) Sexual shenanigans that reach ten on the *Prickter Scale*, if you catch my drift.

3) Hordes of rich and famous party people committing every sin in the cardinal's good book.

Rating: ***** (Unbeatable!). See you there after the lottery win.

****

Prohibition A

'Don't go in there.' The cab driver was practically begging as he pulled up in front of the black glass tower that provided the visible face of Prohibition A.

Most of the club, especially its controversial crypt, was underground.

Sarah watched as the driver reached over to the dashboard and touched a faded picture of the Virgin Mary. The man reeked of a vile perfume of bagels and cheap deodorant.

Mad, she thought. There was no danger inside the club. It was outside. *Him* – John Dexter. Her head was spinning, a carousel of images from the underground parking garage in Baltimore strangling her thoughts. Over and over, she replayed the moment when she pulled the trigger. Straight at the heart. A direct hit. She was a markswoman, top of her class at Quantico. It was impossible that she missed.

She couldn't decide whether to reply to the taxi driver. If this guy knew the club, he might be able to give her some useful info, but he was so weird, saying such freaky things, that she found it hard even to look at him.

'You seem familiar,' the guy said. 'Have you ridden in my cab before?'

'I don't think so.'

Never, she said to herself. *And never again, you creep.*

'Where are you from? Is it Boston? I can't tell.'

'I'm from Philadelphia originally. I've moved around.'

'Well, lady, you seem like a nice person.' The driver adjusted his rear-view mirror. 'I have to warn you – don't go inside.'

'It's just a nightclub.' Despite her reply, even Sarah didn't believe that. Some of the stuff that was said about this place was so incredible that many people regarded it as pure hype and ignored it. Yet, the word on the street insisted it was all true, that not one crazy rumour had been exaggerated. Whatever the truth, it had to be more believable than Dexter coming back from the dead. She killed him. He was DOA. A fucking ghost? Another thought dipped in and out of the chaos in her mind – an incomprehensible one – she was *glad* he wasn't dead.

'You don't understand,' the driver said. 'This place is built on the ruins of an old church.' His voice dropped. 'They deconsecrated it. The last priest...Jesus, the *crimes* that man committed.' He rubbed his forearms. 'It's so cold. May the Sacred Heart of Jesus Christ protect us.' The name Prohibition A – shining into his car from the club's neon lights – seemed to transfix him. 'They lynched him when they discovered the children's bodies in the crypt.'

'That was a long time ago,' Sarah said. 'The club hasn't broken any laws.' She was struggling to concentrate. Her mind had filled with new images of Dexter: strange, unfamiliar ones, different from those she remembered from the Baltimore op. He was happy, smiling, joking with someone.

'You don't know the truth.' The driver raised the crucifix he wore round his neck and kissed it. 'That crypt – I tell you, they've recreated *hell*.' His eyes were wild. 'I know people who went in there. They were good kids. Now...' He turned round to face her. He had crooked teeth and bad, flaking skin.

A religious nut, Sarah thought. He probably believed in ghosts. She shuddered: perhaps she did too now. She tried to avoid meeting the driver's gaze, but she was keen to ask him about Warren. Maybe he'd seen him here, might even have noticed the people he was with.

'Swastikas,' the man said. 'If you look down at the tiles in the reception area, that's what you'll see. Very faint, but they're there all the same.'

'The swastika is hundreds of years old.' Sarah dredged an answer from some magazine article she'd once read. 'It's a good luck symbol.'

'Yeah, but there are solar and lunar types of swastika, depending on whether the swastika points left or right. The solar swastika is a symbol of light and peace. It brings luck, just like you said. But the lunar swastika, well, that's something different. It's the symbol of evil, the one the Nazis chose.' He touched his crucifix. 'That's what this club uses. If you don't believe what I'm saying, read a book called *Gnostic Heresies* in the public library. It explains everything.'

'I'll do that.' Sarah had no intention, but she wanted to keep him sweet. There was something else she wanted – to go back to Baltimore, back to the underground parking garage where she shot Dexter, to the hospital where he was declared DOA. She wanted to talk to the paramedics and doctors who saw him.

'I've heard that David Warren sometimes came here,' she said. 'Did you ever see him?'

'Everyone comes here, lady. Everyone who isn't interested in saving their soul, that is.' He was almost hysterical now. 'I'm telling you, you're in danger. Those people in there, they *sell* sin.'

Sarah opened the door and stepped out onto the sidewalk. 'Here, keep the change.' She offered the driver two ten-dollar notes. *Loony tune*, she thought. *But is he any more nuts than I am?*

The man grabbed her hand. 'For God's sake, don't let them take your soul.'

Prohibition A

Sarah pulled herself away and walked towards the arched entrance of the club, pausing to glance back at the cab as it drove off. Soon it had disappeared from view, leaving behind nothing but silence. The cold weather had even driven away the Christian protestors who normally picketed the club. She shivered involuntarily. The city was frozen, every sidewalk covered with snow, the streets deserted. The darkness seemed almost physical. It could, she imagined, wrap itself around her and pull her down to somewhere she definitely didn't want to go – *her past*. God, why did it frighten her so much?

Looking up at the club's breathtaking tower with its gleaming black glass, she recalled that its designer said it was structured like an inverted cone. The tip of the cone was the futuristic tower while everything else was subterranean, a bit like an iceberg. The designer once declared, 'My aim is to bring to life the darkest fantasies of the unconscious.' The rumour was that he'd added something extra to the club's impressive range of features, a secret no one would believe. Would anyone believe hers? She glanced around. There was no sign of anyone, not even ghosts. She wondered if she should have brought her secret service men with her. They were sure to be furious when they discovered she'd sneaked out a side-door, but she didn't want anyone interfering with what she had to do. They wouldn't be able to protect her from Dexter in any case. He was the best in the business.

Climbing the remaining steps, she squinted at the club's weird name emblazoned over the entrance arch. It was a name that, despite the use of the word 'prohibition', suggested its opposite, hinting at absolute license, every form of degeneration and squalor, the celebration of all forbidden things.

Just below, written around the top of the arch in red gothic script, was an inscription. 'Sin is the Gateway. Salvation is the Reward.' Sarah felt her mouth going dry: *Sin for Salvation*.

22

Limbo

There was no question that this was the place: it was openly proclaiming it. She stepped into a marble reception area. Around the walls were huge skull-and-crossbones motifs in gleaming silver, like a bizarre parody of a corporate logo for some hi-tech Silicon Valley outfit. She stared down at the tiles to see if the crazy cab driver was right. Sure enough, a faint scarlet swastika was inscribed on the surface of each tile. Shit, there were swastikas at Dromlech Castle too: why hadn't she thought of it straight away?

If Dexter murdered Warren, and Warren was at Prohibition A...that meant Dexter must have been here too. He probably tailed Warren that night, following him to Dromlech Castle, or maybe he got himself invited back. She froze. *He could be in the club right now.*

She heard footsteps. Her pulse raced. *Him.* She stared into the dim light, paralysed. The Baltimore underground parking garage sprang into her mind. She remembered crouching in the shadows, waiting to shoot. She must have been nervous as hell, but if she thought hard about it – *real hard* – she couldn't remember feeling anything at all. It took place entirely visually. A complete emotional disconnection. Pictures without sound. *Why?*

She breathed out again. A young woman with long blonde hair in a ponytail was approaching – Trudy, according to her nametag. With large green eyes, a Miami tan and Miss America complexion, Trudy was blessed with supermodel looks, but it was what she was wearing over her visibly naked torso that grabbed Sarah's attention: a black, see-through, wasp-waisted jacket made from moulded lace. Tight black jodhpurs, knee-length shiny leather boots and a stylish gaucho hat completed her eye-popping outfit.

'Are you a member?' Trudy asked.

Sarah shook her head. Several heavies were standing near the door, ready to eject any unwelcome guests. She wondered how often that had happened. She'd never heard of any trouble here, apart from a few shoving matches with the regular religious protestors.

'In that case, smile please.' Trudy held up a digital camera.

'Why do you want to take my picture?'

'No need to be alarmed. The camera takes trick photographs, that's all.'

'*Trick?*'

111

Prohibition A

'You'll be able to see the results for yourself. We put the pictures on a wall near the exit. You can collect them on your way out. They're fun.' Smiling politely, Trudy snapped the picture. 'Now, who are you here to meet?'

'Nicki Murphy.'

Trudy walked over to a desk equipped with a matt black computer. She glanced at the screen. 'Sarah Harris, right? If I'm not mistaken, you're going to be Mrs Montcrieff soon. Congratulations, you're a very lucky woman.'

'Thanks,' Sarah replied, but she hated being so recognisable.

'Your friend's waiting for you in Limbo.'

'Sorry?'

'Go through the doors on your right. Limbo's the name of the lounge, that's all.' Trudy turned, as if about to leave, then stopped. 'Oh, I forgot to mention that Miss Murphy is with a companion.'

Sarah blinked in surprise. Nicki hadn't mentioned anyone else. When they spoke earlier to finalise arrangements, Nicki insisted it would be just the two of them.

She took Trudy's arm. 'Listen, I'm here for a good time with my best friend, that's all. A kind of hen night.'

Trudy nodded. 'I guessed it was something like that. Let me know if there's anything you need.'

Sarah walked towards the doors of the lounge. Over them was a sign that read: *The journey begins*. Pushing through, she found herself in a room resembling an airport departure lounge with gleaming black tiles and shining chrome. Groups of well-dressed men and women were laughing and chatting. They looked like rich people pretending to be 'street' but there was still an incredible vibe in the room. One man in a blue and white pinstriped suit with matching spats was talking loudly into a cell phone while his blonde companion, in a scarlet PVC cat suit, wrapped herself around him. The guy looked like a drug dealer but was probably a research analyst at one of the big investment houses.

It would be easy for Dexter to disguise himself as one of these people, Sarah thought. She figured he wouldn't prolong any assassination attempt. One shot. It would be done in such a way that no one would notice – not until he was long gone. All of his missions were like that. She had studied them when she was preparing for the Baltimore op. There was no 'fat' in any of his missions. Every one of them was lean, fast, untraceable. *Textbook*.

It didn't take her long to spot Nicki, sitting in a corner booth with her mysterious companion. Trouble was he wasn't mysterious. *What's Lacey doing here*? She had thought of asking him to come along, but decided against it.

She joined them at their candlelit table and sat down. The seats were upholstered in luxurious bottle green leather and must have cost a fortune, like everything else in the room. It was obvious that this place did everything as expensively as possible.

Nicki wore a black, off-the-shoulder cocktail dress made of see-through chiffon, with a slit on one side up to her hip, revealing hold-up stockings and several inches of well-toned bare thigh. Thick silver bracelets carved with intricate Celtic symbols covered her wrists. The overall effect was impressively glamorous.

Sarah glanced down at her own designer trouser suit in soft red leather, and her flat-heeled boots. She was sure she'd made the right choice – she might have to run.

Nicki raised her hand to give her a high five. 'Respect. After what Robert said about this place the other night, I never thought I'd see you here.'

Sarah smiled faintly. 'I didn't realise you two knew each other.' She tried to sound chatty.

'We don't.' Nicki smiled at Lacey. 'You've been keeping this young man a secret from me, haven't you? No one told me the Bureau hired such handsome agents.'

'God deals the cards,' Lacey said. 'I just play them.' He was dressed simply in a pair of smart black trousers and a crisp white shirt.

'I'm still waiting for an explanation of how you two managed to hook up.' Sarah glanced at Lacey. She had a weird feeling he was following her, *spying* on her.

'Dargo called me,' Lacey explained. 'He said you were coming here and thought you might need some help.'

'I heard him asking for you at reception,' Nicki interrupted. 'We've been here for twenty minutes, having a drink and a chat, waiting for you.' She winked. 'He's been telling me lots of stuff about you. I think you've got yourself an admirer.'

Lacey quickly looked away and Sarah did the same. Her eyes drifted down to a folded copy of the Manhattan Evening News lying on the table in front of Lacey.

'That thing has maxed it up, hasn't it?' Nicki said.

'What thing?'

'The Nursery Rhyme Killers case. What else would I be talking about?'

'The what?'

Prohibition A

Nicki held up the newspaper to show the headline: 'Nursery Rhyme killers slay CIA Director. Full story on pages 2, 3, 4, 5 and middle pages. Rumours of perverted sex denied by Justice Department. Mystery of *Sin for Salvation.*'

Sarah snatched it from Nicki and studied the garish pictures. For some reason, all she could think of was a line from an old nursery rhyme. *They couldn't put Humpty together again.*

'My paper has sent a team of ten journalists to cover the story,' Nicki said.

'Aren't you joining them?' Lacey asked.

'I'm doing another story.'

Sarah was about to ask what it was, but Nicki seemed eager to make sure she didn't. 'So, what are you drinking?' Nicki signalled to a waitress dressed like Trudy, except in red instead of black.

'Sparkling water.'

'Are you kidding?'

'I'm working, Nicki.' Sarah knew she needed a clear head. Anything might happen tonight.

'Working? What are you talking about? Tonight, you're supposed to be having fun. Jeez, what about you then, Mike?'

'I'm working too.'

Nicki shrugged her shoulders. 'So am I, but it's not stopping me.'

'What?' Sarah wasn't entirely sure she trusted Nicki. All journalists were always looking for the career-defining scoop, weren't they? They were the sort who would think nothing of ditching a friendship for the sake of a big story.

'I told you before, Sarah; I'm writing an article about this place.'

'Keep me out of it,' Sarah snapped.

'*Chill.* Of course I won't mention you.'

The waitress arrived. 'What can I get you?'

'I'm on Scotch on the rocks,' Nicki said. 'My dull friends would like fizzy water. Put the drinks on my account.'

'Coming up.' The waitress smiled and went off to the bar to collect the drinks.

'If you want something special to eat, I recommend scorpion dipped in chocolate,' Nicki said. 'I tried it last time I was here. *Fantastic.*'

Sarah felt sick most of the time these days. The last thing she needed was something that would definitely make her throw up. 'Incredible place,' she commented while they waited for their drinks.

Limbo

'I love it,' Nicki said. 'It's like a dreamscape.'

Lacey nodded. 'Coolest place I've ever been in.'

Nicki's cell phone beeped as a text message came in. 'Wow,' she said. 'I've a big day coming up. I must have mentioned that I'm up for the Journalist of the Year award at Craigavon Hall. That was my editor saying he's just heard I'm the favourite. The show's on cable. Nine o'clock tonight. I'm on at ten. Make sure you tune in.'

'Sorry, I'm going to see Robert at his TV debate.' It reassured Sarah to talk about future events, but increasingly Dexter contaminated all of her thoughts. How long would it take her mask to slip?

Nicki took Sarah's hand. 'Sorry, honey, I'm being so rude. I haven't asked how your wedding arrangements are coming along.'

Sarah shrugged. 'OK, I guess. We're having a rehearsal in a couple of days.' *A rehearsal for a funeral if Dexter had any say in it*, she thought grimly.

Just then, the candle on the table went out. Quick as a flash, Nicki clapped.

'What are you doing?' Lacey asked.

Nicki smiled. 'Haven't you read Peter Pan? When a candle goes out, a fairy dies. The only way to prevent it is to clap your hands.'

They were interrupted by the return of the waitress. 'Which circle is it tonight?' she asked as she placed the drinks on the table.

'Any recommendations?' Nicki said.

'I've tried three circles so far,' the waitress replied. 'Circle Two is my favourite right now.' She passed a receipt to Nicki. 'Just sign here.'

'What was that stuff about circles?' Lacey asked after the waitress left, giving Sarah a knowing look. He must be thinking the same thing she was – did these circles have any connection with the red circles?

Nicki took a sip of her Scotch. 'You can thank Dante for the circles.' She leaned forward, giving Lacey a close-up of her glossy, metallic-red lipstick. 'He wrote about the nine circles of hell, each more terrifying than the last, the final one reserved for the ultimate sinners, and Satan himself.'

Nine circles, Sarah thought. The victims at Dromlech Castle had ten. Why one more? There had to be a link, but what? She remembered the taxi driver's comment that the owners of this place had built hell itself.

'The lounge we're in now is called Limbo,' Nicki replied. 'It means *edge*. It's the edge of hell, to be more exact. From Limbo you can go up to Purgatory, and from there to Heaven, or you can go down to Hell.' She pointed at two adjacent black doors at the far end of the room. 'The door on the left takes you to Purgatory, the door on the right to…the *other* place.'

'What's the difference?' Lacey asked.

'Purgatory is a trendy nightclub, just like any other you'd find in Manhattan. It has a special elevated dance area called Heaven, with a glass floor. Men standing in Purgatory love the view, I'm told. So many short skirts, so little underwear.'

'Get me a ticket,' Lacey joked.

'Are you telling me that if we walk through the right-hand door we'll find hell?' Sarah asked. Maybe the cab driver was right all along.

'Finish your drinks and you can find out for yourselves,' Nicki downed her Scotch and stood up. 'Come on.'

Sarah and Lacey drank up then followed Nicki towards the right-hand door.

'Look at that sign,' Lacey whispered to Sarah. He pointed at a digital signboard above the door. The words on it were written in fiery letters.

I am the way to the city of woe,' the sign said.
I am the way to eternal pain,
I am the way to the damned.
Abandon all hope, ye who enter here.

'What happens now?' Sarah asked as the words flashed at her. They reminded her of the Sin for Salvation slogan written in blood at Dromlech Castle.

'Members can bring non-members as far as this door, but we're not allowed to take them any further,' Nicki explained. 'To go on you'll have to sign confidentiality forms and pay big money. Five hundred dollars, to be exact.'

'Ouch,' Lacey exclaimed.

'This one's on me,' Nicki said to Sarah. 'Call it a wedding gift.' She turned to Lacey. 'Sorry, that doesn't extend to single men.'

'I hope Dargo lets me claim this back on expenses,' Lacey grumbled as he brought out his credit card and stared at it ruefully.

'Plenty of room for the wicked and none for the poor, huh?' Sarah said.

'Not unless they're beautiful,' Nicki replied. 'The club always lets in the beautiful people, whether they can pay or not. It's good business – beauty attracts wealth, right?' She gestured to the waitress. 'Non-member forms, please. The gentleman will be paying by credit card. Put everything else on my account.'

The waitress brought over a couple of pink forms and said, 'Sign here,' pointing at the appropriate places on the forms. 'Virgins, huh?' She smiled as Sarah and Lacey signed. 'There's nothing quite like your first time, believe me.'

'I've never had to sign a form to go clubbing before,' Lacey complained.

'You've never been to a place like this...here, take these.' The waitress gave Nicki and Sarah masks made of fine lace. They were alluring creations, covering the whole face. 'I've picked them to match your outfits.'

Nicki got a black mask, Sarah red. As for Lacey, he was given a silver Zorro mask. Sarah couldn't help thinking of the masks the victims at Dromlech Castle wore: another echo of Prohibition A.

The waitress pressed a red button at the side and the door swung open, revealing a long, dark, rough-hewn stone corridor. 'Have yourselves a hell of a time,' she shouted as they tentatively stepped into the darkness.

23

The Nine Circles of Hell

The flickering torches lining the walls provided just enough light to show the way ahead. There were weird shadows and even weirder sounds as the corridor twisted and descended. Sarah thought she could smell aniseed. She started to rub her arms as it began to get cold. The large flagstone steps beneath their feet were marked, like the tiles in the reception area, with faint swastikas. After a minute, they emerged into a cavern, full of swirling white mist. It took several seconds for Sarah's eyes to adjust. Lacey squeezed past, a bemused look on his face.

They had reached a jetty, with water lapping against it. A black gondola was moored there, an antique lantern hanging from a pole on its prow casting a dim yellowish light. A ferryman in black robes and hood stood in the middle of the gondola, his face covered by a sinister ebony mask. Holding a bargepole in one hand, he held out his other hand to Sarah.

'You must give the ferryman a silver coin as payment,' Nicki whispered.

'I don't have any.'

'There's an old treasure chest over there.' Nicki pointed at a trunk several feet away, brimming with coins. 'I forgot to mention that you can't use cash in this club. The local currency is bronze, silver and gold coins. Bronze is five dollars, silver twenty dollars and gold one hundred dollars. You buy the coins from cashiers at booths around the club.'

'Why not use ordinary cash?' Lacey asked.

'There's some legal reason for it; a tax avoidance scheme, I think. Also, no one gets any change.'

'Nice scam, huh?'

'Well, the best things in life don't come cheap.' Nicki scooped up a coin from the trunk. 'You'll be glad to hear your first coin is free.'

Each of them collected a silver coin and paid the ferryman. The gondola rocked beneath their feet as they stepped in. Clouds of dry ice swirled around them. The ferryman stuck his pole into the water and pushed off from the jetty. The gondola glided into a long tunnel where flaming torches provided the only light.

'I wonder how deep underground we are,' Lacey said. 'It's creepy, huh?'

The Nine Circles of Hell

As they moved further into the tunnel, there was a sound like the murmuring of thousands of people far away. Then music began – Mozart's *Requiem*.

'What's going on?' Lacey whispered.

'The ferryman steers the gondola to different landing areas,' Nicki said, 'one for each of the nine circles of hell. The river is circular, so you eventually come back to the beginning.'

'Where do we get off?' Already, Sarah wanted to have the reassurance of solid ground under her feet. She was feeling queasy as the gondola rocked in the water. She found herself continually glancing at the ferryman. She'd never seen anyone quite so menacing.

'We'll go all the way round so that you can have a quick look,' Nicki said. 'Then we'll start at the beginning – *Circle One*.'

'Why that one?'

'You're not allowed to move to any new circle if you haven't visited the previous ones.'

'You can't just go straight to the final circle?' Lacey said.

'No. Each time you leave a circle, they give you a special coin with the circle's number on it. You show it to the ferryman whenever you want to move to the next circle. Oh, and the price of each new circle is five hundred bucks more than the one before.'

'You're saying it would cost four and a half thousand dollars to get into Circle Nine?' Lacey said. He did another quick calculation. Visiting all nine circles one after another would come to a grand total of twenty-two thousand five hundred dollars. 'Man, whoever's running this show is sitting on a goldmine.'

'This is an exclusive club, Mike,' Nicki said. 'Members pay top dollar for that.'

'Look,' Sarah said, 'we're coming to the first circle.' The gondola emerged from the tunnel into another large cavern. A crimson lamp lit Circle One's jetty. Above it was a sign saying *Acheron*. They could hear noises emanating from behind a black door set a few feet back from the jetty. 'What happens behind the door?' Sarah asked.

'That's for later.' Nicki winked. Turning to the ferryman, she said, 'We're not stopping.' He nodded and pushed the gondola forward.

Staring into the water, Sarah saw twinkling lights that seemed to be floating several feet beneath the surface. Looking closer, she thought she could make out hundreds of ghostly faces looking up at her.

Prohibition A

The ferryman pushed on. All along the route were stained glass windows, illustrating episodes in the life of Lucifer. One showed him as the Morning Star, the dazzling Angel of Light. A second revealed him as a grim warrior leading his doomed rebellion against God. A third window had him toppling through space, his face racked with horror, his rebellion crushed. The designs were as intricate as any in a Roman Catholic cathedral. Sarah wanted to see them close up, but the gondola increased speed and soon they arrived at the next circle: *Lust*.

'This is the one the waitress recommended,' Nicki commented. 'According to Dante, the sinners in the second circle of hell were guilty of the deadly sin of lust. Their punishment was to be blown about by a tempestuous wind, as wild as their passion was when they were alive. The wind stopped them from exchanging anything more than fleeting kisses.' She grinned. 'Romantic, huh?'

As they neared the jetty, they could hear a bizarre whooshing sound.

'Have they set up some kind of wind tunnel in there?' Lacey asked.

'*Exactly*.' Nicki's eyes were shining. 'It's awesome. Naked men and women are inside, getting blown around in a tunnel fitted with padded walls. You can spend only a few minutes with one partner before being blown onto the next.'

'Would you ever go?' Lacey asked.

'I've already been.' Nicki gave a provocative smile.

'I can't believe this stuff,' Sarah blurted. 'It can't be legal.'

'Who's telling?'

'No wonder everyone wears a mask,' Lacey commented.

They went past several other circles, variously called 'O', Sodom, Weird, Babylon, Sensation, Toledo and The Pit. The entrance to each circle gave a clue to what went on there. The entrance to 'O' was shaped like a woman's lips pumped up with collagen and painted with pink lipstick. As for Sodom, the entrance reminded Sarah of a scene from *Naked Lunch*.

Nicki explained that each circle offered kinkier sex than the one before, the final one being an indiscriminate orgy in pitch darkness in a pit where a guy in a spaceman suit came round every half hour with a high-pressure hose to wash everyone down.

Sarah tried to picture what was going on behind the plain black doors that protected each circle. She picked up a glossy brochure lying at the stern of the gondola and flicked through it. The description for 'O' said: *Imagine an elegant bar in Vienna in the middle of winter. A hot coal fire is crackling in the corner. Drinking schnapps, you're sitting at the bar, chatting to an attractive bartender. You have a warm glow in your belly. Suddenly you realise someone's moving about under the bar at waist level. One of the bar's wooden panels has been pushed to one side and someone has crept out from the other side and is pressing forward between your legs. You know you're about to have the most erotic oral experience of your life with a complete stranger whose face you will never see. In "O" you'll discover every oral technique used anywhere in the world. If oral is your thing, you've found your home.*

Babylon was described as: *This Circle conjures up the mysteries of the majestic east. Try our luxurious harem where the rarest, most exquisite and secret techniques of the east – formerly reserved for Sultans – are performed. Try the opium dens, the aphrodisiac fragrances and ointments, the deep and dark drinks of the East that will transport you to other worlds.*

Other phrases leapt out regarding other circles: *Make love in Moroccan mud baths or Siberian salt mines. Have sex in tundra, or permafrost, or with a fire raging around you. How about making love on a sandy, moonlit beach with waves gently lapping over you and your partner? Every sensation of texture, weather, temperature and touch is yours. Only your imagination sets the limits.*

Enter a dark world where you can touch the outermost limits of the erotic. Whatever you want, we have it. Personal requests are our speciality. Any scenario you can imagine, we can make it real. We are the ultimate dream-makers.

The crypt of a deconsecrated church. No light is allowed inside. Join scores of naked people in hell's lowest hole. Anything goes in the dark. No holds barred. No rules, no restrictions, no limits. Truly, Hell.

'Look, a fork in the river,' Lacey said as they rounded the final turn.

Sarah gazed ahead. A small tributary led into another tunnel and above it a sign proclaimed *Circle Ten*. Above the sign was a breathtaking stained-glass window depicting Lucifer being crucified, upside down, against a background of glittering stars. Sarah peered at it, but her mind was occupied with something else. Now she understood the significance of the ten circles. There was no doubt any more: this place was the key to the red-circle mystery.

It took her a second to realise the gondola had come to a halt. The ferryman was staring at her. Dexter in disguise? Anything was possible.

'We can't go any further,' Nicki said. 'I don't know what's at the other end of the tunnel. It's strictly off limits.'

Off limits? Sarah stared hard at Lacey.

'We must go back to Circle One now,' Nicki commented.

Sarah didn't say anything. She was busy thinking about how she could get to Circle Ten.

'Neither of you has asked the obvious question,' Nicki said.

'You've lost me.' Lacey shrugged.

Nicki leaned forward. 'If hell has nine circles then why is this called Circle Ten?'

'So tell us.'

'It's obvious really,' Nicki said. 'When you've committed every sin...' She faced the mouth of the tunnel. 'What comes next?'

24

You'll Fall in Love Again

Lacey stood alone at Circle One's upper balcony, scanning the dance-floor. He'd become separated from Sarah and Nicki half an hour earlier when he visited the main restroom.

The restroom had left quite an impression – all sleek black marble and elegant stainless steel fittings. The most surprising thing was that the attendant was dressed as a Spanish Inquisition judge. It didn't make it easy to take a leak, that was for sure. Afterwards, he couldn't find the two women. There was no signal on his cell phone, so he'd have to find them the hard way.

He heard someone sobbing and noticed a slim young woman to his left, leaning against a rail, dabbing her eyes. In hot pants, a boob tube and long boots, with the stars and stripes all over them, she was a dead ringer for *Wonder Woman*. Her black hair was tied back with a Stars-and-Stripes ribbon and she had a matching mask.

'*Bastard*,' she mumbled.

Lacey walked over and tapped her on the shoulder. 'Need any help?'

'Fuck off.'

Lacey started to walk away, but felt his arm being tugged.

'I'm sorry,' the woman said. 'I didn't mean to snap. Please stay.'

'I'm not hitting on you. I just wondered why you were crying; if there was anything I could do to help.'

'The usual frigging thing,' the woman said. 'Man trouble. I was getting on just great with this guy. Then a blonde appears. How was I supposed to know he was married?'

'You should avoid married men.'

'That's great advice, Einstein.'

'That mouth of yours will get you in trouble.' Lacey regretted the remark even as he said it.

'Oh, yeah? If I wanted your advice, I'd have written a cheque. Now get lost.'

'You have a bad attitude.' Lacey couldn't believe he was handling this so clumsily. He was a behavioural psychologist, for God's sake.

'What would you know about it, smart guy?'

Prohibition A

'You're upset because your lover boy has given you the kiss-off.' Christ, did he really say that? Just in time, he noticed the woman's left hand rising to slap him. He grabbed her by the wrist. 'Look, I was just trying to help you.' He couldn't help checking her wrist for any sign of red circles.

'Well, try helping someone else. Get out of my face.'

As Lacey turned to leave, he felt his sleeve being pulled once more.

'Don't listen to me,' the woman said. 'I need to be with someone.'

Lacey was confused, but curious too. 'OK, just for a few minutes.'

'I know I can be a bitch at times, but it's just a way of defending myself. I'm in Global Markets and Futures. It drives me nuts.' She lowered her head. 'My name's Fallen.' She smiled like a little girl. 'As in Fallen Angel.' She waved her hand...'I have weird parents.'

'Hi, Fallen,' Lacey replied. 'My name's Mike. I have *normal* parents.' He held out his hand. 'Pleased to meet you.'

They stood together, gazing down at the crowded dance-floor. A gang of clubbers dressed as vampires in black bat-wing masks were theatrically pretending to drink blood from each other's necks as they danced energetically to pounding Gothic music.

'Do you know what my favourite song is?' Fallen asked.

'Too many songs,' Lacey said, 'just too many songs.' It was a dumb question. What was wrong with this woman?

'OK, I'll come right out and tell you. It's real obscure. I can't even remember how I came to hear it. It's called "M" by *The Cure*. There's this line in it that I just can't get out of my head.'

Lacey thought it wise to indulge her. If her eyes got any more spaced-out, NASA would be employing her.

'Look, before I tell you, I don't want you to think I'm making a play or anything,' she said.

'I don't think that's likely, do you?'

Fallen smiled coyly. 'OK, the line is: *You'll fall in love with somebody else again tonight.*' She rubbed her arms. 'Doesn't it make you tingle? It gives me so much hope. I mean, don't you love the idea that your whole life can be transformed in a single night? You can go out, meet a special guy and fall in love there and then. The past is forgotten. It's a miracle, you know?'

'You think Mr Right comes to a place like *this*?'

'I thought he did tonight. Why are the best guys always taken?'

'Because they're the best guys?'

'Is this how you get your kicks – listening to sob stories?' Fallen snapped back to her old self. 'I hate do-gooders. Why don't you fuck off?'

124

'I'm gone.' Lacey was exasperated. He strode away, but for the third time she grabbed him to stop him leaving.

'I need help,' Fallen said. 'I'm cracking up.'

'I was just trying to be nice to you.'

'I know. Please, take me to the counsellors.'

'The *who*?'

Fallen pointed at a secluded upper level. 'Up there,' she said. 'There's a chill zone. They have trained counsellors.'

'On-site shrinks?'

Fallen nodded. 'I don't want to go on my own.' She led him by the hand up a glass spiral staircase to Circle One's top level.

Lacey was amazed to find a row of what looked like confessional boxes, six in total. Five of them had a red light above them with a sign saying *Occupied*. A welcoming green light illuminated the top of the last box. '*Vacant*,' the sign read, '*please come in*.'

They squeezed inside. Crimson velvet curtains hung round the interior of the little box. An orange light shone down from an overhead spotlight. They sat together on a leather seat. In front of them was a wrought-iron grating, with a black veil hanging down behind it. Lacey could make out a vague silhouette on the other side.

'We are all in pain,' a man said in a soothing voice. 'But that pain can end. Salvation is possible.' A metronome kept a hypnotic beat in the background.

'Help me,' Fallen said.

'You think you're a sinner,' the voice said. 'Sin is not an obstacle; it's the key that opens the door. The greatest truth of all is also the most surprising: salvation is only for sinners.'

Lacey's pulse raced. The guy had practically said *Sin for Salvation*. Theresa Martinez's words from the police video came back to him. '*The voice in the darkness*.' Then that other comment: '*The river can save us all. Back to the beginning*.' Was *this* the voice in the darkness? Was the river the one in Prohibition A – a circle that would take you back to the beginning?

'You're a special young woman,' the voice continued. 'There's a religion designed for extraordinary individuals like you. Sin for Salvation is one of the oldest religions in the world.'

There it was, as clear as day. Lacey's thoughts exploded in every direction. He put his hand on Fallen's shoulder. 'Sorry, I have to go.'

Fallen nodded and smiled. 'Thanks for everything,' she whispered.

Prohibition A

Outside, Lacey was desperate to find Sarah to let her know his news. As he moved towards the staircase, he noticed a room in the corner, past the confessional boxes, with a plain white door. He decided to check it out but when he tried to open it, it was firmly locked. He retreated a few steps and stared at it, not wanting to leave until he'd seen inside. Maybe it was just a storeroom, or a staff-room. Maybe something else. Why was it so close to the confessional boxes?

Seconds later, the door opened and a young woman came out, *maskless*. Wearing a fashionable grey trouser suit and pink blouse, she had classic Hispanic looks – large brown eyes, a cute upturned nose and sleek black hair in a ponytail. The amazing thing was that Lacey recognised her instantly – *Theresa Martinez*. She gazed past him with glassy eyes as the door closed behind her then made her way unsteadily to the staircase.

Despite getting only the briefest glimpse, Lacey had seen clearly inside the room. Several people were in there with helmet-shaped objects over their heads, like characters in an old sci-fi movie. People in black medics' uniforms were supervising the 'patients.'

There was a second part to the room…resembling a tattoo parlour.

25

Escort in a Devil Mask

Sarah didn't know where Nicki and Lacey had got to and felt more vulnerable than ever. Dexter might have agents all over the club. It was so dumb to have come to this place without backup. And what about Circle Ten? Was it off limits because that was where Dexter was hiding?

Calm down. She finished her glass of Martini – just one to steady her nerves, she'd told herself, but the idea of having more was so tempting. Chris Isaac's *Wicked Game* played in the background. She smiled sardonically.

Sitting at a table on an upper level of the club, she had a panoramic view. Circle One was quite simply the strangest place she'd ever been in. She figured it was directly below Prohibition A's black tower; the tower's floor providing Circle One's ceiling. The space was circular with three levels. Numerous small rooms fed into the main area. There were peep shows, live sex shows, porno movies, male and female lap dancing. The centrepiece was a gleaming black carousel in the middle of the dance-floor, with black horses spinning round to the sound of Saint-Saëns' *Danse macabre*. Naked couples got on and off as it went round. Many of them were openly making out on top of the horses.

Earlier, Sarah had noticed male and female escorts dressed as demons and devils circulating amongst the club's clientele. When she glanced up, she saw one of the males heading her way. She figured these guys were trained to approach single women and flirt with them. The escort stopped in front of her, but didn't speak.

I ought to leave, she thought, but decided it was safer to sit with one of these guys than be on her own. She went out of her way to catch the escort's eye. 'Can I get you a beer? she asked.

'Sure.' He sat down opposite her.

How ridiculous, she thought, *I'm in a sex club, talking to a guy dressed as the devil*. She signalled to a waitress and ordered a beer for the escort and a mineral water for herself.

The waitress returned a few moments later. 'That will be a silver, please.' She handed over the bottles and glasses.

Sarah paid the waitress from the stack of bronzes, silvers and golds Nicki had given her so she wouldn't run short.

Prohibition A

She turned to the escort, wondering if he knew Carolyn Voronski. He might have met her at the club, got chatting to her. 'So how much would it cost to go home with one of you guys?' she asked out of curiosity.

'Ten golds for the night.'

'You're not cheap, are you?'

'Pleasure has its price.'

'I guess.'

The light from the lamp in the centre of the table shone directly onto Sarah's engagement ring. The escort stared at it and seemed strangely transfixed. Sarah was certain he shuddered. 'It's just a ring.'

'Do you collect them?'

'*What did you say*?'

'Engagement rings – how many men have you taken for a ride?'

'Aren't you supposed to be nice to me?'

The escort didn't respond, but was now sitting rigidly upright.

'Why are you so quiet?' Sarah asked.

'Did you think the past would leave you alone?'

'The *past*? What has that got to do with...' Blood rushed from Sarah's skin and guts to her muscles. Adrenalin kicked in. She moved fast, slamming her fist down on the edge of the table, causing the other side to spring up. Bottles and glasses crashed onto the floor. Leaping out of her seat, she darted into the throng of onlookers, her mind filling with the colour red, a chaos of red flashes and dots. She barged through a group of men and women dressed in voodoo outfits. '*Get out of the way.*'

Sprinting along a gangway, she found a fire door leading to a stairwell. Rushing down several flights of stairs, she realised she had no idea where she was going. She burst through a door and found herself in a small movie theatre. The ushers directing people to their seats were stark naked, as were most of the masked audience. She glanced up at the screen and saw a hard-core porn movie reaching the money shot. She raced out again.

Pushing through another door, she entered some kind of freaky torture chamber. People holding candles and dressed in yellow tunics marked with little red devils were surrounded by guys who looked as though they were in the Ku Klux Klan, except they were wearing black robes instead of white.

Trying other doors, she was met by a succession of bizarre sights. It seemed she'd found the fire exits for each of the underground circles of hell. Barging through one door, she slammed into a wall. Through a Perspex porthole, she saw naked couples flying through the air – Circle Two's wind tunnel, unquestionably. Through another door, she blundered into a dark, echoing room. She heard sounds that made her think, weirdly, of pigs scampering around, sniffing from glue bags fitted to their snouts. Circle Nine, she realised – *The Pit.*

God, is there no way out of here? The only thing going right for her was that there was no trace of Dexter. Trying one more door, she found an elevator. She got in and pressed the button. Seconds later, she was back in the reception area. After throwing her mask into a basket, she made for the exit. Her mind now had time to process one piece of information she'd ignored earlier. Someone had called out 'Sarah' repeatedly while she ran, but she'd not stopped to find out who it was. As she neared the exit, she caught Trudy eyeing her curiously.

'Is everything OK?' Trudy asked. 'Have you seen your trick photos yet?'

Sarah ignored her. Her vision was going haywire, everything sliding into the red spectrum. Her heart thumped as she heard the fire door flying open behind her. She spun round.

'What's going on?' Lacey tore off his Zorro mask and tossed it into the basket.

'I don't have time to explain, Mike. Let's get out of here.'

Outside, Sarah futilely searched for a yellow cab. The streets were deserted. A frozen mortuary.

'My car's parked half a block away,' Lacey said.

Sarah gazed back at Prohibition A. Dexter might burst out of the doors at any moment. 'OK, let's go for it.'

Lacey's car was a black two-seater Smart car. They jumped in, Lacey started the car and they accelerated away.

'Little Italy – my apartment,' Sarah said. 'I'll give you directions.'

Once they had travelled a couple of blocks and Sarah was sure no one was following, she breathed out hard.

'Do I get an explanation now?' Lacey asked.

'I can't believe what happened back there.' Looking at herself in the rear-view mirror, Sarah recoiled. Her face had turned deathly white. 'I nearly got killed.'

'What are you talking about?'

She didn't respond. Her mind went back to Dexter. How had he pulled it off? – coming back from the dead like that.

Lacey slammed on the brakes and stopped the car.

'What the fuck are you doing, Mike?'

'We're not moving another yard until you've told me what the hell's going on.'

26

The Past

Sarah gripped a mug of black coffee. She'd talked Lacey into starting up his car again, but only on condition that she tell him the full story once they were safely back in her apartment. So, what now? – spin him a story or...

'I killed someone three years ago, Mike.'

'*What?*'

'I was in an FBI black ops unit. I was given an order to eliminate a mark and I did it. Simple as that.'

'Jesus, I had no idea.'

'The man I killed was a rogue agent called John Dexter. The man who tried to kill me in the club tonight was...' Sarah's voice tailed off.

'That's impossible.'

'Somehow, Dexter faked his death. It doesn't really matter. What counts is that he's back and he wants to kill me.'

'I can't get my head round this.' Lacey crossed his legs and leaned forward, clasping his hands. 'Prohibition A was the weirdest place I've ever been to. Now this stuff about Dexter.'

Sarah stared at her picture of the Peregrine falcon in Central Park. 'This is so fucked up.'

'I think I've figured out what's going on.' Lacey excitedly stood up. 'Sin for Salvation, Prohibition A, Warren, the red circles – they're all linked. I was wondering who the owner of Prohibition A was. If this John Dexter guy is alive, it has to be him.' He started pacing around the room. 'I think Prohibition A is the home of some sort of cult. It's a human laboratory, targeting fucked-up yuppies.' He raised his hand to stop Sarah interrupting. 'They're using brainwashing techniques. Victims are put in a strange, dark space and bombarded with music, flashing lights, incredible sex. They get so disorientated they seek help. I found out that the club uses psychological counsellors, but they're more like priests...And I know what their religion is.'

'*Sin for Salvation.*'

'Exactly.'

'Mike, I...'

'Hear me out. The victims are placed in the hands of one of these soothing, protective priests who promises to put everything right for them. Then they go to a room where they get full-scale brainwashing treatment. I'm certain that's where the dissociation's kicking in. I bet all the people I mentioned in my report went to Prohibition A. Everyone who died at Dromlech Castle probably went there too. Jesus, I even saw a tattoo parlour. That's where the red circles get done. You won't believe this, but I almost walked straight into that woman from the police video.'

'Who? Theresa Martinez?'

'Yeah. That club is a giant mind lab. I couldn't figure out what the point was, but now you've given me the final piece of the jigsaw. John Dexter is running it. He's picking out bright young men and women with emotional problems, then fucking with their minds.' He stroked the stubble on his chin. 'You said he'd gone rogue. I think he's turning them into agents for his organisation.'

'If Dexter recruited those people we found at Dromlech Castle, why were they murdered?'

Lacey hesitated.

Trouble was, the more Sarah thought about it, the more she suspected Lacey was on the right track. 'Prohibition A is connected with Sin for Salvation, that's for sure,' she said. 'I've seen the evidence myself. And we know Sin for Salvation is linked with David Warren's death.'

One thought she kept to herself: Lacey knew nothing about Dexter's TWEP list, but the fact that Warren's name was crossed off the list surely proved his case.

'You're saying I'm right?'

'We have to tell Dargo. He'll arrange for Prohibition A to be staked out, or raided.'

But there was another possibility, wasn't there? The Committee might contact her and order her to finish her job...She might have to kill Dexter all over again.

27

TV Debate

Stop pointing that camera at me. Sarah saw her face appearing on the overhead TV monitors. She and Lacey were in a Broadway TV studio where they'd come to watch Robert in his live presidential debate. Sitting in the second row of the studio audience, Sarah felt exposed. She turned and scanned for Dexter in the crowd. All day, she'd been on edge. Nine names were on his death list and one of them was already scored out. The final two names were Robert and hers. Did that mean he was leaving them till last? She was amazed that he imagined he could defeat the Committee. They'd already be taking countermeasures. Even though she didn't work for special ops any more, she suspected it was just a matter of time before the Delivery Manager contacted her to give her new mission orders. That was one of the things about special ops – you never truly left. But she'd long since lost her nerve. *I can't do it,* she thought. *Not before my wedding. It's impossible. I can't do anything like that ever again.*

'Are you alright?' Lacey asked.

Sarah stared ahead. The Delivery Manager was the last person in the world she wanted to hear from. Last time…

She closed her eyes. Why did she feel as if she'd met the Delivery Manager recently? She had a sick feeling in her gut. *Blood* – blood everywhere. Why was she associating blood with the Delivery Manager? Because he delivered the instructions that made people die? She opened her eyes again and gazed down at her cell phone nestling in her handbag. One of these days, it would ring and she knew she wouldn't want to speak to the person on the other end of the line. *Not ever.*

She'd phoned Dargo earlier to tell him what happened at Prohibition A. He said she and Lacey should get some rest. Rest? Impossible with Dexter on the loose. Every moment, she expected him to show up. When and where? Those were the only unknowns. Should she tell Robert? A zero-sum game.

Earlier in the day, Robert had flown to Chicago for another campaign speech. He got back a couple of hours ago – courtesy of a private jet – for the three-way TV debate with Democratic candidate Tom Lawson and President Rieper. She'd spoken to him briefly on his cell phone. He was upbeat, looking forward to the showdown.

'What's the story here?' Lacey asked.

TV Debate

Sarah explained that the format of the debate was for each candidate to talk for ten minutes. Then there would be half an hour in which a distinguished panel of political commentators would quiz the candidates. Each candidate could then make a concluding statement.

'Here they come,' Lacey whispered.

The candidates filed onto the stage and sat on raised stools. Sarah gazed at Robert. He had no idea of how much danger he was in. Sitting with the relaxed posture of a chat-show host, he was the only candidate who looked comfortable. Thirty-nine years old, he was some twenty years younger than his rivals and resembled a glamorous, successful son visiting his dad's elderly friends. The camera kept returning to him. It might as well be the Robert Montcrieff show.

The chairman of the panel gave a brief introduction, announcing that Robert, as the independent candidate, would be the first to speak.

'There they are.' Robert extended his hand in the direction of President Rieper and the Democratic candidate. 'Our very own Wizards of Oz. Pull back the curtain and see for yourselves the pathetic reality. Washington DC is the Emerald City, all smoke and mirrors, pretending to be the centre of vast power when in fact it's run by buffoons. They'll say I have no experience, but when it comes to experience, you have to ask yourself a simple question: have you had a thousand different experiences or the same experience a thousand times? Look where *their* experience has led us – to a nation in reverse gear with vast debts...humbled and humiliated by failed military operations abroad, and lack of security at home.'

Sarah was impressed, and it was obvious the rest of the audience agreed. A political outsider, Robert could say the things no one else dared, and the voters, in rapidly growing numbers, were taking him seriously as someone who could restore America's standing in the world.

'Look!' Lacey nudged Sarah and pointed at one of the overhead monitors. An external feed showed a huge explosion at Craigavon Hall where the Newspaper of the Year ceremony was being held.

'Jesus,' Lacey mumbled, 'wasn't Nicki due on stage about now?'

28

Picking up the Pieces

S uicide bomber, that's what the survivors were saying. A beautiful young woman, apparently. It was the following morning and Sarah was standing in the centre of the bomb wreckage, trying to absorb its scale. A few days earlier, Robert had proposed to her right here. It seemed a lifetime ago.

Craigavon Hall's roof had caved in, taking the walls with it. A burned-out shell was all that was left. Bizarrely, snow was falling inside. A canopy had been erected to protect the site from the weather. Structural engineers had announced there was no danger of additional collapse. The cloakroom was still standing and Sarah set up the Incident Command Centre there. Her team was stretched, with many still on site at Dromlech Castle, but they were doing OK, getting help from the Javits office.

She studied the damage, trying not to inhale the smell of burned flesh. Dozens of FBI forensic operatives were sifting through the ruins. The NYPD's specialist bomb squad had arrived. *Good luck to them*, she thought. Earlier in her career, she'd turned down the chance of working for the bomb squad. It was hard to think of anything more depressing than that job, trying to...

'One at a time, one at a time,' Dargo bellowed, marching past her. Agents, all trying to get his attention, surrounded him.

'OK, the story so far,' he said. 'A Hispanic woman at a table of twelve gets to her feet at ten o'clock, just as the Newspaper of the Year award is being announced. She detonates a bomb. Only five of the survivors see or hear anything. One is an usher at the rear of the hall. This eyewitness swears that the bomber shouted a slogan just before the explosion. He didn't hear clearly but he thought he could make out two words: "Cindy" and "station." We're assuming the bomber actually said "Sin for Salvation."' He turned to Sarah. 'Have you found out what that means yet?'

'The Cult Awareness Unit is sending me a report by lunchtime.'

'Make sure they do.'

Minutes later, he took Sarah to one side. 'What do you make of this?' He held up a partially melted silver locket inside a plastic evidence bag. 'We found it in the bomb wreckage. We think the bomber was wearing it. It's a locket with a skull and crossbones design.'

'Skull and crossbones?'

'Does that mean something to you?'

'They've got that design all over Prohibition A.'

'That figures.' Dargo frowned. 'The locket has some words inscribed in it. *How long will death reign? As long as women bear children.* Mean anything to you?'

'Not a thing.'

'Well, it's something else to think about.'

'What about Prohibition A?' Sarah asked. 'We have to get agents over there to check it out properly. I think we should close the place down.'

'No,' Dargo said sharply. He glanced at his watch. 'Sorry, I have a press conference. We can talk about this another time.' He left the room and walked over to a table crowded with microphones. After taking his seat, he poured himself a glass of water.

Sarah tried to understand why he was stalling over Prohibition A. It made no sense. She watched him as he addressed the large media contingent that had been herded into a small corner of the room. There was a strange atmosphere – uniquely, no newspapers had been printed that day as a mark of respect for the dead.

'I'm Special Agent in Charge James Dargo of the FBI's New York Critical Incident Response Group,' Dargo declared. 'I have a statement to make regarding last night's bombing. At ten pm, just as the Newspaper of the Year award was being announced, an unidentified young woman stood up and shouted, we believe, "Sin for Salvation," before detonating a plastic explosive bomb concealed in her handbag.

'One hundred and twenty-three people were killed immediately. Ten died en route to hospital or on the operating table. Thirty individuals are in intensive care. A further fifty people have been detained in hospital for the treatment of less serious wounds, shock etc. Seventy-six people were allowed to go home. Of those, only five were able to give us any information about what happened. That completes the statement. I'll take questions now.'

Sarah, gazing at a monitor in the ICC, saw Nicki step to the front. She'd tried to phone her friend for hours, but got no answer from her cell phone. She'd checked the police's casualty list earlier, though, and was relieved to see Nicki's name in the uninjured column.

'Nicki Murphy, *The Washington Post*,' Murphy said, as everyone else respectfully retreated. 'I was fortunate enough to leave the hall just before the explosion. If I'd waited another five minutes...' Her face filled with anger. 'I want to know who did this. What *is* Sin for Salvation? That was the slogan painted on the floor at Dromlech Castle and now we hear that the suicide bomber said the same thing. That means these two incidents are connected. Is Sin for Salvation a terrorist organisation? Are they waging a campaign in the run-up to Election Day?'

That remark caused a commotion amongst the reporters.

'Have the lives of any of the presidential candidates been threatened?' one journalist shouted.

'Do you have any clues about who's behind this?' another voice said.

'Quiet please.' Dargo gestured for calm. 'OK, everyone has lots of questions. I can't answer everything right now but I can tell you we do have a prime suspect. I won't be providing any more details about his identity just this minute. We are presently unaware of the precise meaning of Sin for Salvation. The Cult Awareness Unit will be providing a full report shortly.'

Sarah wasn't listening any more. *This can't be*, she thought. She'd just been handed a piece of paper identifying the bomber. Again, she stared at the name and felt a shudder passing through her. There was no mistake: *Theresa Martinez*.

Martinez's left arm had been blown a hundred feet across the room and was horribly charred, but a DNA analysis succeeded in finding a positive match in the NYPD database. Forensics detected traces of plastic explosives on Martinez's hand. They were also able to make out one final feature.

She had ten red circles round her left wrist.

29

Alters

'**I** can't believe it. I saw Martinez just the other night.' Lacey shook his head. 'I knew this thing was huge. We have to round up everyone with red circles on their wrists.'

Sarah stared at the TV in the corner. She'd arranged to meet Lacey for breakfast in the *Baluga Bar* in Pearl Street, but her appetite had gone. Lacey's too. All they could manage was a glass of orange juice each. The smell of burned flesh still clung to Sarah's clothes. So many people had died in the explosion. Why would a beautiful, wealthy young career woman throw away her life like that? On the TV, Martinez's friends were being interviewed and each was expressing bafflement, though they conceded Martinez hadn't been herself for some months.

Sarah felt sick. If she'd taken Lacey's worries more seriously, Martinez might have been stopped and none of those people would be dead. Now Lacey was suggesting that the red circle people should be detained. 'I suppose so,' she said wearily.

'You don't sound convinced.'

'I'm wondering how much good it would do. It would be easy to conceal those red circles with bracelets or whatever. Besides, there's no clear evidence we're dealing with a conspiracy. Maybe Martinez was a lone nut. I mean, we know for a fact she was suffering from dissociation.'

'She was brainwashed in Prohibition A,' Lacey said. 'There are at least a hundred others like her. We could be facing a wave of bombings. We must act fast.'

Sarah frowned. 'OK, everyone listed in your report will be brought in.'

'Don't forget, there could be new recruits by now.'

'We'll put out an alert.' Sarah's head ached again. This wasn't going to be easy. She took a sip of her orange juice. It was so acidic she almost spat it out. 'Tell me more about your brainwashing theory. Did Martinez have two personalities: her normal one, and another one created by the brainwashing? Is that why she was so different in the video? Is it like multiple personality syndrome?'

'Yes, and no. Multiple Personality Disorder was renamed Dissociative Identity Disorder because psychiatrists thought *multiple personalities* was misleading. The technical definition of someone suffering from DID is that they have within them two or more entities, or personality states. The word I prefer is "alters" as in "alter ego." The alters can think, act, feel and remember in their own individual way. Sometimes they're aware of each other and in direct conflict; or aware of each other and cooperating; or completely unaware of each other. In the last case, the patient may suffer severe memory loss.'

He struggled to explain himself better. 'What I mean is that if one alter is in charge for, say, one week, and then another alter takes over the following week but knows nothing about the first alter, then the second alter is faced with trying to figure out what was going on the previous week when the other alter was running the show. Sometimes one alter has completely different friends from another alter and a patient can literally find himself talking to someone he thinks he's never met before if the switch from one alter to another takes places at an inconvenient time.'

'Jesus, that's rough.'

'DID is difficult to pin down,' Lacey said. 'You need to study a patient for a long time to find out what's really going on. Sure, Martinez seems to have suffered from extreme alters which had no knowledge of each other. That would account for her amnesia on the police video. When she blew up Craigavon Hall, her normal self knew nothing about it. It was done by the brainwashed alter.'

'So, with brainwashing, is it possible for a person to do things and have absolutely no memory of them?'

Lacey nodded. 'At the best of times, memory is tricky. False Memory Syndrome is about people remembering things that never happened. Real Memory Suppression allows them to bury things that did. A thing called cognitive dissonance can change a person's memories to whatever causes them least distress. Throw in drug-induced distortions of reality, dreams, hallucinations, fantasies etc and you have to wonder what it is we're remembering when we talk about our memories. As for brainwashing, it can artificially create alters, and replace true memories with false ones. To be blunt, it can do pretty much anything with a person's memory.'

'I'm confused, Mike.'

'Maybe this will help. A psychologist called Douglas Henderson reasoned that it was bad memories that made people mentally ill and claimed he could cure them by substituting good memories for the bad. When the CIA heard about his work, they were intrigued. The health angle was unimportant. They wanted to know if it were possible to put manufactured memories in place of real ones. If you can change people's memories, you can change *them*.' He locked his hands together. 'You can make them into anything you like – a tinker, a tailor, a candlestick maker. Even a president '

'So, was Henderson right?'

'Probably. Not that it did him any good. His work was ridiculed professionally. When critics heard of the CIA links, they were horrified and said his research was unethical, with no practical applications.'

'But what did he really prove?'

'That nothing is as it seems. How can any of us be sure our past is genuine? Maybe we've just had a false set of memories implanted. How would we know the difference? Maybe every day when we wake up we're actually someone new. Thanks to artificial memories, we might think we have history; that today we're the same person we were yesterday. But how could we prove it? If you can't be sure of your past, you can't be sure of anything. If what you've done in your life isn't what you think you've done then who are you? Who's taking the decisions? Is it you or a *you* created in a laboratory by a scientist five minutes ago?'

'You're scaring me, Mike.'

'I'm scaring myself. Fact is, Henderson abolished history. No one can make predictions based on the past. They can't be sure it even existed. The past isn't a foreign country, Sarah, it's science fiction.'

'What happened to Henderson?'

'With a Senate Committee breathing down their neck, the CIA withdrew their backing for Henderson's work. He couldn't get funding from anyone else. He became depressed. Retired early. Died about twenty years ago.'

'But there's no proof that brainwashing actually works,' Sarah said. 'Not that I've heard of, anyway.'

'Who knows? No one claims to be doing any brainwashing these days. That doesn't mean they're not. That stuff in Prohibition A has convinced me – someone has cracked it.'

'Dexter?'

'Maybe that's the reason you were ordered to eliminate him. Maybe people knew what he was up to.'

Sarah said nothing. She felt the same uneasiness sweeping over her as she had when she first heard of the red circles.

'Haven't you seen *The Manchurian Candidate*?' Lacey asked. 'You know, the old black and white movie with Frank Sinatra and Lawrence Harvey?'

When Sarah admitted she'd never watched it, Lacey explained it was based on a novel about the attempted assassination of a president by a brainwashed patsy. The movie was released in 1962 and withdrawn in 1963 after Jack Kennedy's assassination. It didn't resurface for twenty-five years. Incredibly, it was said to be JFK's favourite movie. It told the story of how the Chinese, working with the Soviets, captured several American soldiers in the Korean War and took them to Manchuria where they brainwashed them. One of the American prisoners was selected as an assassin, to be used in a plot to assassinate the President and put a Communist mole in the White House as the new President.

'The CIA uses the term "zombie state" to describe the condition a brainwashed person goes into when they carry out pre-programmed commands,' Lacey said. 'I'm sure you've heard stories about people claiming to be zombies when they carried out high-profile assassinations. There was that Palestinian guy Sirhan Sirhan who shot Robert Kennedy. Then there was Mark Chapman who killed John Lennon, and John Hinkley who stalked Jodie Foster and tried to shoot Ronald Reagan. Some people have said Lee Harvey Oswald and James Earl Ray were both brainwashed.'

Sarah looked away. She hated this stuff. Any chance that people might not be in control of their actions terrified her. She put down five dollars to pay for her drink.

'Going somewhere?' Lacey asked.

'I'll organise the detention of everyone with red circles. Then I have something else to take care of.'

'Such as?'

'I'm going to follow up a tip a crazy cab driver gave me.'

30

Reading it in Books

'Over here,' Sarah said.

Dargo glanced to the right and saw her sitting at a table with books piled in front of her. He wondered why she wanted to meet him in the New York Public Library of all places. With the media going berserk, he badly needed information about Sin for Salvation.

'What's the deal?' he asked.

'Sin for Salvation – it's all here.' Sarah held up a folder with FBI markings. 'I got the report back from the Cult Awareness Unit.'

'So why aren't we looking at this in Pearl Street?'

Sarah showed him a thick book with a black cover: *Gnostic Heresies*. 'You won't believe it, but a taxi driver told me to read this and I decided to check it out. It's got all the same stuff that's in the report, plus a lot more.'

'You're telling me a New York cabbie had the answers all along?' Dargo scowled. 'OK, tell me the score.'

'Sin for Salvation is about jailed souls.'

'Come again?' Dargo rubbed his forehead with the heel of his hand. 'Tell me it from the top. Just the main points.'

'Do you remember the story about Satan rebelling against God?'

'Sure. He lost, got his ass kicked out of heaven, then created hell.'

'Right, but according to Sin for Salvation, hell isn't what you think it is. It's not an inferno far away in some spooky dimension. It's a lot closer to home. In fact, *this* is the world Satan created – the earth.'

Dargo was amazed as Sarah explained about this outlandish religion. Apparently, the universe consisted of two components – spirit and matter. The spiritual universe was a perfect paradise, heaven itself, populated by beautiful souls, while the material universe was full of drones – bodies without souls – and was a hell of desire, deceit and violence.

But some souls became curious about matter, something so enticingly different from the spiritual world they inhabited. Sex, in particular, fascinated them. To some souls, sex and the human world were impossibly tempting and they became obsessed with the idea of getting inside a physical body. So, they left heaven and came to earth where they took over human bodies, the drones. What they didn't realise was that they were then imprisoned. There was no way out of the physical world, no way back to heaven. At least, no easy way. Sin for Salvation was the gospel showing jailed souls the only escape route. Salvation was possible only if a soul learned to despise everything connected with the material world. The pleasures of the flesh were the main dragon that had to be slain.

Sarah said that the cultists believed that the only thing that could overcome sexual desire was satiety. The greatest sins produced the greatest overindulgence, and therefore the trapped souls' best chance of freedom. According to Sin for Salvation, it wasn't sin that kept people out of heaven, it was the lack of it.

'Jailed souls, huh?' Dargo said. 'And by the time you've committed every sexual perversion, every crime, every sin, then you've overcome your desire and freed yourself of the world of matter. You've bought your ticket out of jail, right?'

Sarah nodded. 'Each sin brings you closer to heaven. The bigger the sin the nearer you get. They say salvation can be achieved not by being good but by liberating yourself from your body. Heaven is for souls, not for good people. Sin gets you to heaven, not goodness. Once you've sinned enough, you can return to the spiritual world, purged of all material desire. If you don't sin enough, you'll remain curious about flesh and you'll stay ensnared in the physical world, reincarnating in new drones as old ones die.'

Dargo stared at the floor, bemused.

'Devils, demons and the fires of hell don't exist as far as Sin for Salvationists are concerned,' Sarah went on. 'In their religion, the good guys and the bad guys from the Bible are swapped around. Cain, Judas, Pontius Pilate, even the serpent in the Garden of Eden, are all proclaimed as heroes because they opposed the creator of this world.'

'Think how dangerous this is,' Dargo said. 'If it caught on, no one would know right from wrong.'

'There's another thing. Because Sin for Salvationists believe Satan made the earth, they think that anyone else who claims to have made earth must be Satan too. So God, Jehovah, Allah are just different names for Satan.'

'Everyone else's God is their Devil?'

'They have other names for him. One is Rex Mundi, the King of the World. The name they use most of all is the Demiurge.'

Dargo frowned. 'These people hate God, hate the world, hate their own flesh. They don't give a damn about human life. Guilt means nothing to them. They're capable of *anything*.'

'I'm certain Warren was mixed up with Sin for Salvation,' Sarah said. 'That thing at Dromlech Castle must have been one of their ceremonies.

That's why everything was so freaky. I think they committed mass suicide as their big sin to get them back to heaven.'

'But why was Warren killed?'

'Dexter's behind the whole thing. He's controlling all of these Sin for Salvation people. They'll do whatever he wants. The reason he was at Dromlech Castle was revenge. Warren was first on his list. The mass suicide might have been some kind of perverse victory ceremony once Warren was dead.'

'It's far-fetched,' Dargo said.

'You remember that transcription you found in the locket at Craigavon Hall, the thing about *How long will death reign? As long as women bear children*. This book explains it. It says the quotation is by Jesus and appears in a suppressed gospel. It means that souls will be safe only when there are no more bodies left on earth to trap them.'

Dargo shook his head. 'These guys want to annihilate the human race.'

'The book also mentions Prohibition A – what the name means for Sin for Salvationists.'

'Let's hear it.'

'It says, "The First Prohibition of *their* God is: Thou shalt not kill. Our *Anti*-Prohibition, our Prohibition A, is: Thou *shalt* kill. What is prohibited? *Nothing*. The crime that cannot be named, the perfect sin, is the ultimate Prohibition A.'

Dargo gasped. For a second he thought he glimpsed a world of universal crime, a planet of slaughter.

'As for the Prohibition A nightclub,' Sarah went on, 'the sign at the entrance says, "Sin is the key. Salvation is the Reward."'

'So, everything ties up.'

'The club is based on a fantasy sex journey through hell. Every sexual taste is catered for. I think the idea is that by the end of your journey you've had so much sex that you're sick of it and your soul is ready to go back to heaven. You reach a final destination beyond hell – called Circle Ten – where all your physical desires have been expunged.'

'The launch pad to heaven, huh? That explains why they have ten circles on their wrists. That's the sign that they're ready to leave this world.'

'Then throw in the fact that John Dexter was at the club.'

Dargo took a seat beside Sarah. 'It all makes sense. Dexter is using Prohibition A to recruit people into a cult and converting them into suicidal killers.' He shook his head. 'But why? What's the point?'

'What do you mean?'

Prohibition A

'If he's here for revenge against the people on his list, why is he blowing up newspaper people?'

'Maybe he actually believes in this stuff.'

'It doesn't matter. He has to be stopped.'

'When are we going to make our move against him?'

'Soon.' Dargo rubbed his sore leg. 'There's no way he'll make any basic mistakes, but if we can guess where he's going to strike next we can be waiting for him.'

'Any ideas?'

'There's only one place I can think of.'

'Where?'

Dargo couldn't meet her gaze.

'Where?' Sarah insisted.

'*Your wedding.*'

31

Pictures on the Wall

As she listened to her deputy, Lee Baynes, Sarah realised she wasn't taking in half of what he was saying. She and Baynes were meeting in the Pearl Street office to discuss the CIRG operations at Dromlech Castle and Craigavon Hall. Baynes was bringing her up to speed with the additional data the team had gathered, but she knew they were way behind the game. Lacey's theory was the key.

She studied Baynes's face. There were no wrinkles, no bags under his eyes, no signs of restless nights. His face seemed a miracle of stress-free life, something that seemed inconceivable to her. The whole time, Dargo's prediction went round in her head. There was no doubt about it – Dexter was coming to her wedding.

Her cell phone rang. *For God's sake, she thought, leave me alone.* Baynes paused and waited for her to answer. She walked a few steps to a discreet area, cell phone to ear. 'Hello.'

'Sarah, I must see you right away.'

'What is it, Robert?'

'I'm with Tommy Henshaw. We need to show you something. We're on our way to the Holography Museum in Mercer Street. Can you hook up with us? Please, it's urgent.'

'What is it?' Sarah repeated.

'I can't talk on the phone.'

Sarah drew in a long breath. 'OK, I'm on my way.'

****

A crowd had gathered. Robert's supporters were waving placards, with women, as usual, outnumbering men. Sarah parked her car in a reserved space. As she got out, she was recognised and everyone started clapping. She scanned around for Robert, trying to hide her embarrassment at all the attention. Robert was standing on a podium, surrounded by campaign workers and advisers. Judging by his body language, he'd just finished a speech and was winding down. Tommy Henshaw was standing behind him directing a large security team. Robert beckoned her over and several security men cleared a path through the crowd for her. Sarah had her own

145

secret service men back in tow, but their presence was increasingly annoying her. For their part, they said they couldn't do their job properly if she refused to cooperate fully.

'What's going on?' she asked Robert.

'Let's go inside.'

The Museum of Holography in Mercer Street was a sleek, hi-tech building with a gleaming metallic facade. Sarah had never visited it, but it was something she'd always planned to do some quiet Sunday. The museum had a mock-up of FATS, the FBI's *Firearms Automated Training Centre* that featured prominently at the Quantico training academy. It was a kind of souped-up kids' video arcade, the idea being that criminals and civilians would pop up on screen and trainee agents had to kill the bad guys and save the innocent.

Sarah heard an announcer in the background addressing the crowd: 'The next president and his fiancée are about to try their luck at taking out the bad guys. We'll bring you their score as soon as we get it.'

Inside, the Holography Museum's staff were lined up, with their manager in pole position. Sarah realised she was expected to follow Robert along the line, shaking everyone's hand. It was surreal. Robert wanted to tell her something critical and yet they had to deal with all of this palaver first. She forced a smile onto her face and dutifully made her way along the line.

When it was over, she and Robert went alone into FATS. Robert muttered something about everything having been checked out. They entered via electronic sliding doors, then found themselves in a dark, circular room, with blue airplane guide lights on the floor. The main lights had been dimmed, but there was still enough light for them to see each other.

'We have a couple of minutes before the game starts,' Robert said.

'What's this all about?' Sarah asked as she started fitting a holster containing a laser pistol.

In the faint light, Robert reached inside his jacket and pulled out a small, ornamental dagger with a white ivory handle.

'What the hell is that?'

'I found it lying on my pillow this morning.' He pressed the tip of the blade against the palm of his hand. 'It's a signal.'

'What do you mean?'

A tiny dot of blood appeared in the middle of Robert's hand. 'Tommy explained it to me. It's what the original assassins did centuries ago to scare their victims. They placed a dagger on the pillow of their target to show them how easy it was to get to them.'

Pictures on the Wall

'You mean, if they could put a knife on the target's pillow they could just as easily have killed him?'

Robert nodded. 'It's the final warning. Next time it's for real.'

'Who's behind it?'

'I don't know. Death threats are an occupational hazard for a guy like me, but this is no ordinary threat. A pro did this.' He put the knife back in his pocket. 'I need the FBI's help.'

A voice crackled over the tannoy. 'Roll up, folks, and see a facsimile of the FBI's training centre where those fine men and women of the Bureau fight it out with virtual criminals. What sort of score can you get in the Feds' most famous shooting house? Are you good enough to join the FBI?'

'Game on,' the voice said as the lights were switched off.

Ten video screens flickered into activity. Sarah gasped. Every screen showed an identical image – John Dexter holding a pistol fitted with a silencer, like James Bond. All ten Dexters opened fire.

'I wasn't ready,' Robert complained.

Sarah stared at him, numb.

'What is it?'

'Low score! Low score!' flashed up on each screen. 'Sorry, you haven't made the grade. Why not try running for president instead?'

'What's up, Sarah?' Robert repeated.

'We have to get out of here.' Sarah darted towards the doors. They were meant to slide open automatically, but nothing happened. She slammed her hand against an emergency red button at the side. Again, nothing.

'What's going on?' Robert insisted.

Sarah sprinted to the other side of the room. There was no response from the doors there either. 'Shit, we're trapped.'

'Sarah, tell me what's happening.'

'I know who left that dagger on your pillow.' Sarah stared at the screen directly in front of her.

'Who?'

'The man right in front of you.'

'What are you talking about?'

'That guy on the screen is John Dexter, an ex-special-ops agent. He wants to kill both of us. He's after you because you're marrying me.'

As Robert fixed his gaze on Dexter's image, Sarah closed her eyes and rubbed her temples, desperately trying to soothe away the panic exploding inside her.

'What the hell's happening now?' Robert exclaimed.

Prohibition A

Sarah opened her eyes. A new set of pictures had appeared on the screens: a simulation of Robert and her on their wedding day. An out-of-tune version of the Wedding March began to play. Two words formed underneath each picture: *Poor Judgement*. Then the images turned red, as if blood were streaming down the screens. A new tune began: the Funeral March.

Noises erupted outside. Sarah heard Henshaw screaming something. She didn't catch it first time round because of the music, but the second time she got the message. A man was explaining about some technical malfunction. They had someone working on it and if there was no progress, they'd break down the doors. They were to hold on for five minutes.

Robert stood still. 'It's no technical malfunction, is it?'

'Dexter must have hacked into the computer and set up all of this.'

'What's going to happen now? Gas? A hand grenade?'

There were more noises outside. 'This is the Hostage Rescue Team,' a voice said over a tannoy. 'The building is surrounded. If you don't come out in thirty seconds with your hands above your head, we'll force our way in.'

'Do they mean us?' Robert asked in confusion.

Moments later the only window in the room – a small, darkened pane ten feet above the ground – shattered. A smoke canister landed in the middle of the floor and white smoke billowed out.

'They're coming in,' Sarah shouted. 'Whatever you do, don't move.' Seconds later, the doors were smashed out of the way. Through the smoke, Sarah could see vague shapes entering the room, moving stealthily, taking up position.

When the smoke cleared, HRT team members in black body armour, wearing gas masks and pointing assault rifles at them, surrounded Robert and her. The laser sights of their assault rifles generated red beams that cut across the room.

'Are you OK?' the leader of the rescue team asked.

Sarah didn't answer. Robert was staring past her. She turned to see what he was looking at. Goosebumps erupted all over her. The electronic screens had flashed up a new message.

'*RIP*,' they all read.

32

Confession

What's he thinking? Sarah watched as Robert paced backwards and forwards. The HRT had hustled both of them out of FATS and into the manager's office. Outside, cops, the HRT and Robert's security team were sweeping the building, looking for any trace of Dexter.

She knew they'd find nothing. This was just for show, to demonstrate how Dexter could get to Robert and her at any time he chose, but he'd make his real attack at the wedding. What else could those images in FATS mean?

'I didn't want to tell you,' she said quietly.

'Who the hell is that guy?' Robert stabbed his finger in the direction of FATS.

Sarah said nothing. Her face was pale, her lips pressed tightly together, sealing in a feeling that had been troubling her more and more. Something in her relationship with Robert had changed. It was tiny, imperceptible, yet it was there. She knew the precise moment when it happened – when she saw Dexter at Dromlech Castle. A shiver rippled through her. His face hadn't changed one bit. The appalling thing was...Christ, how could she think that? There was no denying it, though. She found him exceptionally attractive. It was as if she were walking along a dark corridor and someone had switched on a light in a hidden room and now she could see the light streaming out from beneath the door. It was Bluebeard's room, wasn't it? She didn't want to think about it. She had no desire to open the door to the forbidden.

As she explained Dexter's story to Robert, she watched the astonishment growing on his face. 'It's true,' she repeated. 'I shot him in an underground parking garage in Baltimore. He was DOA at the hospital.'

Robert thumped his fist against his thigh. 'So, he's an elite agent, so good he can apparently come back from the dead.' He stared out of the window. 'When will the real attack come?'

'Our wedding.' As the words left her mouth, Sarah could see they'd stunned Robert. It was as if she'd named the date of his death.

'But that would be crazy. 'How could he pull it off? It would be suicide.'

'You've just seen what he can do.'

'You knew about this before today, didn't you?'

'A couple of days.'

'And you didn't say anything?'

'I didn't want to worry you.'

Robert tugged the lobe of his ear. 'If this Dexter guy was so good, why were you ordered to kill him?'

'I told you. He'd gone rogue. He was a threat.'

'And now they're letting him run around on the loose? Isn't the FBI going to do anything?'

'The position is being evaluated.'

'Evaluated? That makes me feel real safe.'

Sarah had never seen Robert like this. She bowed her head, her hair falling over her face. She remembered studying Dexter's file before the Baltimore op. He wrote the SMI handbook on dry-cleaning: every way to detect surveillance and take countermeasures. Was that why the Committee were so uncertain about what to do? The irony was that John Dexter was the person they'd once have turned to for cleaning up a mess as big as this.

Robert looked out of the window again. 'I'll get Tommy to flood St Patrick's with security people. It will be impossible for any assassin to get through.' He took Sarah's hands and helped her to her feet. They hugged each other. 'Ready for a fight?' he whispered.

Sarah felt an icy tingling spreading down her back. *The fight of our lives.*

****

Don't hassle me. Sarah pushed the microphone away from her face. She and Robert were about to give a press conference in his campaign headquarters and were surrounded by impatient journalists and newsmen.

'Was the incident at the Museum of Holography a *Sin for Salvation* attack?' someone shouted.

'Your wedding's a potential target,' said a young brunette. 'Are you calling it off?'

'Is it true you already know who did it?' a slim black woman bellowed.

Robert was silent, still in obvious shock. Sarah knew she probably looked just as bad. 'I wish to read a statement,' she said. 'Special Agent in Charge James Dargo of the FBI's Critical Incident Response Group stated at an earlier press conference that we have a prime suspect for the *Sin for Salvation* attacks. I am now authorised to put a name to that individual. He is John Dexter. He is armed and extremely dangerous.

'The public are warned not to approach this individual under any circumstances. Anyone who knows his whereabouts or recognises him should notify the FBI immediately. Photographs of John Dexter are being issued to all relevant media.' She gazed at the camera. 'I repeat, this man is armed and dangerous. Do not approach him. Call the FBI.' She glanced at another piece of paper that she'd received minutes earlier. 'I have an additional announcement to make. In the last few minutes, the Director of Homeland Security has put the country on Code Red alert in anticipation of new Sin for Salvation attacks. All National Guard troops must report for duty immediately. Units will be deployed throughout areas deemed at particular risk. Citizens may be stopped and searched at random. The Director has ordered emergency roadblocks to be set up in key areas. Every vehicle will be searched. All citizens should be vigilant.' She lowered her head. 'That concludes this statement.'

'James Taylor of NBC,' a man shouted. 'Yes or no – was Dexter a highly decorated secret agent?'

'I have no further comment to make.' Sarah put her hand in front of her face to shield her eyes from the bright camera lights. She looked at Robert, wondering if he wanted to say anything. He shook his head.

The NBC man wasn't finished. 'Sarah, is it true you know Dexter personally?'

33

The Delivery Manager

Another headache. In the last few days, Sarah's head seemed to be splitting apart. She took a couple of aspirins every few hours. They weren't doing much good. Her poor performance at the press conference had depressed her, but what could she do? Even Robert was subdued and he was the consummate showman. It wasn't surprising. When an elite agent returned from the 'dead', anyone would get nervous. Even the Committee were running scared.

She and Robert were sitting in the back of his Mercedes limo as they made slow progress through Manhattan's crowded streets. Her sore head wasn't being helped by drivers sounding their horns, newsvendors screaming the latest headlines, schoolchildren squealing as they fooled around in the snow. She'd left her own car at the Holography Museum, not feeling well enough to drive.

'Why have we stopped outside Bloomingdale's?' she asked. 'You're supposed to be taking me back to Pearl Street.' Henshaw's security car was behind them, but she'd finally parted company with her own secret service men. Robert wasn't happy about it, but he didn't make it an issue. Maybe he'd realised Dexter rendered standard security measures redundant.

'I have a surprise for you,' Robert said. 'Something to cheer you up.'

'You didn't like that press conference either, did you?'

'I wasn't feeling right. It didn't look too good, did it?'

'No one's going to hold it against you.'

'Can I ask you for a huge favour?' Robert put his hand on her knee. 'I got a call from Pino Monzelli. Your wedding dress is ready. It was flown over from Rome last night.'

'Fantastic!' But Sarah's joy evaporated almost instantly. 'What's the favour?'

'I know I'm pushing it, but I'd like you to be filmed in your wedding dress. I want to show people that it's business as usual, that the wedding's on track.' He took her hand in his. 'To show that Dexter hasn't intimidated us.'

But he has, Sarah thought. Robert was right, though. She had a duty to let people see that life would continue as normal, at least on the surface.

She nodded unenthusiastically. A bride-to-be ought to feel elated about her dress, but everything had gone flat. Dexter had wrapped her emotions in thick, insulating gloom.

'The camera crew is inside,' Robert said. 'My mother's there too.' He leaned over and kissed her. 'I know this is difficult for you, but you'll be happy when you see your dress.'

They got out and made their way towards the store, protected on all sides by Henshaw's security team.

'Over here,' a voice cried.

Robert's mother was standing at the entrance of the store, beckoning to them. Sarah had met Mrs Montcrieff just once before, at a cocktail party months earlier. Mrs Montcrieff had a Welsh accent, diluted by years of living in the States. Her claim to fame was that she'd been an accomplished violinist in the London Philharmonic Orchestra.

All three of them were greeted by the manager of the bridal suite who escorted them to the lavish rooms that comprised the luxury suite. As they made their way through the store, some people applauded and others wished them good luck. Sarah, with a fake smile stuck to her face, now understood why Robert always felt so phony on the campaign trail.

Soon, they were in the safety of the bridal suite. A camera crew was there, with a beautiful blonde interviewer. All the other customers were asked to leave.

The suite's centrepiece was the *Room of Mirrors*, featuring a 360-degree mirror. As she went inside and changed into her Monzelli dress, Sarah felt more optimistic. This was what she'd always wanted, to see herself in a gorgeous white wedding dress. Standing there on her own, gazing at her reflection, she thought of Miss O'Mallen's childhood curse. It could go into the garbage can now. For the first time that day, for a long time really, she felt happy.

'Can we look?' Robert shouted from outside.

'You know the rules. The groom isn't allowed to see the bride in her dress before the wedding.'

'Well, can the camera team see? I have a lady here who's dying for a peek.'

'Send them in, I guess.'

The door opened and a cameraman, the interviewer and Mrs Montcrieff squeezed in.

'Wow, you look fantastic, Sarah,' the interviewer said. 'That dress is amazing.'

Sarah smiled. It was true – Monzelli had performed his usual miracle.

'Are you finding it difficult to concentrate on the wedding?' the interviewer asked. 'I mean, with everything that's been going on.'

'Things aren't perfect,' Sarah responded, 'but I think it's important to get on with things even when times are tough. We can't let terrorism wreck our lives.'

Mrs Montcrieff nodded approvingly.

'Is John Dexter stalking you, Sarah?'

'I don't want to comment on that.'

'People are saying that Dexter is planning a spectacular, with your wedding as the target.'

'I told you, I'm not getting into any of that.' Sarah felt as if every word was being scrutinised. Was this what life as First Lady would be like? She picked up her wedding veil and began to fit it.

Then her cell phone rang.

She looked down and saw it sticking out of her handbag. Instantly, she knew who it was. *Please, don't do this to me.* It continued to ring, throwing out the sound of the helicopter blades from *Apocalypse Now*. It kept ringing. She felt like Martin Sheen at the start of the movie, having a breakdown.

'Aren't you going to get that, Sarah?' Mrs Montcrieff asked.

'I suppose so.'

The blonde interviewer was staring curiously at Sarah and directing the camera team to point the camera at her handbag.

The cell phone kept ringing, the sound breaking like storm waves against Sarah's ears. It drilled into her head. Still it rang. It was the call that had to come, that could never be avoided.

Mrs Montcrieff moved towards her.

Sarah felt dizzy. The ringing continued. It was never going to stop, *never*. Those helicopter blades had become a soundtrack for a nightmare. Then she had another thought. Maybe it wasn't the call she'd been dreading. Maybe Dexter had got hold of her number. Against every particle of reason, she longed to hear his voice.

Fighting to keep her hand from shaking, she picked up the cell phone. 'Hello,' she whispered, hoping it was a wrong number, that the person at the other end would never speak.

'Red Queen,' a voice announced.

'What did you say?'

A high-pitched tone sounded.

The Delivery Manager

Sarah froze. An image seized her mind – of a man in a grey suit coming into the mirrored room and throwing a silver coin at the ceiling. Every mirror shattered, showering her with glass. In a moment, she was bloodstained from head to toe, her white dress transformed to blood red.

'This is the Delivery Manager.'

Every gland in Sarah's body went into hyper-production. *I'm stepping into Bluebeard's room.*

'Please confirm the delivery number.' The voice was cold and metallic, as if it had been fed through a synthesizer. No trace of humanity.

'Sorry, I…' It had been so long since Sarah last heard that voice.

'Please confirm the delivery number,' the voice insisted.

'It's 505, uh, 921.' She dredged up a number from she didn't know where.

'Here are the delivery details.'

'Can't this wait? It's not a good time.' She glanced at the interviewer and saw her smiling back with awkward politeness.

'This is a priority delivery. Customer is a VIP.'

'I…OK…'

'The customer is…'

'Sorry, can you hang on a moment?'

'Customer is *Robert Montcrieff*,' the voice said.

The words crashed through Sarah.

'I…I…don't understand.'

'Repeat: customer is Robert Montcrieff.'

'There must be a mistake.' Blood pulsed through Sarah's head, dissolving words, sights, sounds, making it impossible for her to think straight.

'Customer identity is confirmed. Customer is Robert Montcrieff.'

'I don't understand.' Still that throbbing of blood. Sarah's hands shook. She could see them reflected in the lens of the camera.

'Delivery is to be made on Monday, 5th November,' the voice continued. 'Delivery address is St Patrick's Cathedral. Delivery must be made on schedule. Customer services are monitoring.'

'I…*What*?'

The line went dead.

'Bad news?' Mrs Montcrieff asked.

Sarah couldn't look at Robert's mother. 'No, it's nothing.' *This couldn't be happening.* But the Committee never made mistakes, did they? And they never changed their minds.

155

Prohibition A

'You've gone very pale, Sarah.'

She struggled to breathe. She wanted to vanish, to be transported instantly to somewhere else, *anywhere*. 'No, it was just, em, a Delivery Manager confirming some details for the wedding.'

'What's he delivering?' the interviewer asked. 'Our viewers are interested in all the details.'

Sarah couldn't answer.

'Didn't you hear the lady, Sarah?' Mrs Montcrieff asked.

'Sorry,' Sarah mumbled, 'I'm miles away.' She struggled to prevent her body from trembling. If it began, it would never stop.

'We were only enquiring what the man was delivering,' Mrs Montcrieff persisted. 'Anything I can help with? You know I want the wedding to go without a hitch.'

'It's nothing. Some, er, silk gloves for my Maid of Honour.'

'Are you poorly?' Mrs Montcrieff asked.

'I feel dizzy.'

'You've had a rough day.'

'Is there a problem?' the interviewer asked.

'Sarah's not feeling so good,' Mrs Montcrieff said.

'Listen, I'll have to cut this short.' Sarah clutched her stomach. 'I think I'm going down with that bug that's going around.'

'I'm sorry to hear that,' the interviewer responded. 'Anyway, I think we have enough material. I hope you're fine for your wedding. Best of luck.'

Sarah waited until the interviewer and her cameraman left and then changed back into her normal clothes. Lacking the energy to say anything to Mrs Montcrieff, she made a feeble gesture to indicate she was leaving.

'I'll send Robert in,' Mrs Montcrieff said. 'Then I should go home and get a good rest.'

A moment later, Sarah was alone with her fiancé. What the hell was that strange acoustic tone she'd heard? It had gone straight through her, setting every part of her on edge. She stared at Robert and no words would come. Surely the Committee meant to say the target was John Dexter, not Robert.

'Are you all right?' Robert said. 'You're as white as a sheet. I saw the others leaving, then my mother said you weren't feeling well.'

Sarah waved her hands futilely. 'I have to...'

'Shall I drive you home? Do you want to see a doctor?'

'The restroom,' she said. *Christ...Can't...Have to...What's happening to me?* 'Back in a minute,' she managed to say. She fled for the nearest restroom, her legs barely carrying her. Blinding tears filled her eyes. Finding an empty cubicle, she threw her head over the toilet bowl. The vomit came instantly – thick, yellow, blood-streaked, reeking of rancid chemicals. *I can't do this any more.* The hard floor was agony against her knees. Nightmares of God-knows-what flashed through her mind as she watched the hands of her watch going round.

The thudding of her heart was so strong it frightened her. An image gripped her mind. She was naked, in an isolation tank, without any hair. *They're staring at me. Men in white lab coats, writing insults about me on clipboards.* They all turned their clipboards towards her. Each one bore exactly the same word – *Robert*.

It was a couple of minutes before she got to her feet and left the cubicle. She splashed cold water over her face from one of the washbasins. When she looked in the mirror, a ghost stared back at her. Picking up her handbag, she made her way back to Robert. There was so much to do. It was Thursday and their wedding was on Monday. She had four days to save his life.

34

The Committee

Sarah headed along the corridor towards her office. Earlier, Robert had taken her back to her apartment and told her to get some rest. As soon as he left, she called a cab to take her to Pearl Street.

She kept telling herself that the Committee had made a mistake. Something crazy was going on and it was up to her to sort it out. She opened a linking door and slammed straight into someone coming from the opposite direction.

'Sarah, what's the hurry?' Mike Lacey said.

'I…well…' Sarah's mind felt like jelly struggling to set.

'You look like you need a timeout. Listen, I'm going to meet my friend Terry Redpath in the computer department. He's doing some computer-aided enhancements of my Dromlech Castle photographs. Do you want to come?'

Sarah didn't answer.

Lacey gripped her arm. 'I think you need to sit down. Let's go to the canteen. We'll grab a couple of coffees and you can tell me what's on your mind.'

Mechanically, Sarah went along with him. The canteen was on the ninth floor and they had to walk down a flight of steps to get there. It was empty when they went inside. They collected their coffee in white plastic cups from the dispenser, then sat in the booth in the far corner where they could see anyone coming in.

'I hear we've already detained some of the red circle folks,' Lacey said. 'When's the announcement going out on TV to advise the public to be on the lookout for the rest of them?'

Sarah stared out of the window. The red circles seemed almost trivial now.

'You're not listening,' Lacey said.

Sarah watched Lacey's lips moving and heard sounds coming out of his mouth, but all she could think of was the Delivery Manager's orders.

Lacey grabbed her hand. The sudden physical contact made her sit upright. 'What is it?' she blurted.

'Do you realise what you're doing.'

'What?'

The Committee

'You're acting just like the red circle people. I half expected to see circles on your wrist.'

'I have things on my mind, Mike, that's all.' She pulled her hand away. 'I didn't come here to be psychoanalysed.'

'I just want to help. Is it your wedding? Nerves?'

Sarah placed her thumb on her wrist. Her pulse was out of control.

'Cold feet?' Lacey prompted.

'Mike, what is this?'

'It's my job. I'm interested in the way people behave.' He coughed then reached awkwardly for his coffee. 'Particularly people I like.'

I'm not answering any more questions, Sarah thought. She had to steer Lacey onto another subject. Outside, a red advertising balloon drifted over the dark city, tracked by a spotlight. As soon as she saw it, Sarah's heartbeat accelerated. Pins and needles spread through her hands and arms. Her mind was swamped with red. Red Queen – *Kill*. Red Queen – *Kill who*? Red Queen – *Kill Robert Montcrieff*.

'God help me,' she said aloud. She grabbed Lacey's hand. 'Red Queen,' she mumbled.

'I don't understand, Sarah. What is it?'

'Red Queen. What does it mean?' She closed her eyes. 'Mike, please help me. I can't concentrate any more. My head's screwed up. Maybe you're right. Maybe I do have some kind of dissociation. I...'

'Sarah, something's got its hooks in you and it's not letting go.' He leaned towards her. 'Come on, you know you can trust me.'

Sarah's head throbbed. Pressure was building up. If she didn't find some way of releasing it, she was in big trouble. She couldn't tell anyone about the Committee's orders. What *could* she do? She had to confide in someone, talk it through. In Bluebeard's castle, who do you turn to? The handbook said that in an emergency you should use your instincts. Those pointed to just one person...the man sitting in front of her right now. She'd already confided in him about Dexter and he knew as much as she did about what had been going on in the last few days.

He didn't look like one of Bluebeard's henchmen and maybe, at some crazy level, that meant he wasn't. It was mad to turn to him, but there was no one else. Nicki was out of the question because she would take the story straight to her editor. She couldn't tell Robert – the Committee would act instantly to protect themselves. She couldn't get any other friends involved in something as heavy as this. Her own team was out of the question. She

159

certainly couldn't ask Dargo. Doors in Bluebeard's castle were slamming shut all around her. She had to choose one before they all closed.

'Mike, I'll to have to trust you whether I like it or not.'

'You know you can, Sarah.' Lacey lowered his voice. 'You know how much I care about you.'

'Please don't talk that way.'

'I mean friendship, that's all.'

Sarah nodded, but struggled to look at him. 'Have you ever heard of the Committee?' She stared at the door to check for people coming in. When Lacey looked at her blankly, she clasped her hands. 'Mike, what I have to tell you is really big.'

'You know how to get someone interested, don't you?' Lacey edged forward on his seat. 'OK, tell me what this Committee thing is.'

'It's a group of six men,' Sarah said, 'the Directors of the CIA, FBI, the National Security Agency, the Defence Intelligence Agency, the National Reconnaissance Office and Special Military Intelligence.'

'That's serious firepower,' Lacey said. He looked puzzled for a moment. 'So, when Warren gets replaced, are you saying the new guy will have been vetted by this Committee and he'll join them?'

'Yes.' Sarah peered at Lacey. 'I didn't realise you knew about Special Military Intelligence. Most people have never heard of it.'

Lacey smiled sheepishly. 'Actually, I was just about to ask you about that.'

'It provides intelligence relating to future threats to America,' Sarah explained. 'It's the most secretive of the intelligence services, a hi-tech wonderland. You know – boys with toys, men with smart bombs, scientists with dumb theories.' She took another sip of her coffee, but it tasted foul. 'They do all the weird research that you see in bizarre documentaries. Remote viewing, psychic spying, narco-hypnosis, psycho-electronics – all the mad shit. I have no idea if any of it works.'

Lacey nodded. 'I get the picture.' He lifted his finger. 'One thing before you go on – why is the Committee called that?'

'The French Revolution.'

'*What*?'

'In those days, France was run by a group of men known as the Committee of Public Safety. They were the guys who sent you to the guillotine if you didn't cooperate.' Sarah moved her coffee cup over the coffee table, as if making a chess move. 'The Committee sees itself as doing the same kind of thing for America.'

The Committee

'These Committee guys are left wing revolutionaries?'

'They like the name, that's all.' Sarah almost conjured a smile. 'Take it from me, none of them has any left-wing sympathies.'

'So, tell me more.'

'Some of us in the intelligence services have sworn an oath of allegiance to the Committee. Their orders come above anyone else's.'

'Including the President?'

'The Committee is above the President and the Supreme Court. It's above the Constitution itself. That's what you sign up to when you take their oath.'

'And you did?'

'A lot of what they say makes sense.' She frowned. 'At least, it used to. Listen, Mike, no one gets in the way of the Committee. Sooner or later, every opponent is taken care of.' She chose her words. 'One way or another.'

'Let me get this straight. There are six big shots called the Committee. They decide from time to time that the White House or Capitol Hill isn't working and they take steps to put things right.'

'Whatever "right" means,' Sarah replied. 'Sometimes, they use plain old assassination, or they set people up. They might arrange for them to be involved in a scandal, or leak damaging information about them. They use illegal surveillance operations, claiming it's part of America's counter-intelligence efforts, but it's really about digging dirt on VIPs.'

'Scary.' Lacey edged closer. 'Did the Committee kill Warren?'

'Whatever went on in Dromlech Castle was way too strange for them.'

'That leaves only one thing.'

'What do you mean?'

'Come off it. You haven't told me about the Committee to pass the time of day. They've been in touch, haven't they?'

Sarah was regretting getting into this with Lacey, but she'd gone too far to backtrack now. Could she tell him everything? Was it suicidal?

'Fuck,' Lacey cursed.

'What is it?'

'I missed it, didn't I?'

'Missed what?' She could almost see Lacey's mind working. Would he figure it out? No, impossible.

'Something you said before has got me thinking. You told me you were ordered to kill Dexter. The Committee gave the order, didn't they?'

She nodded again, scared of what Lacey might say next.

'Now you've said the Committee have been in touch with you again.'

'What are you saying, Mike?'

'They've ordered you to do another job, haven't they?' His eyes gleamed. 'It's Dexter again, isn't it? And they want you to do it before your wedding. That's why you're so upset.'

A mixture of relief and horror washed over Sarah. Lacey had half guessed the answer. Close, but not the whole thing. What would happen now? *I can't tell him*, she thought, I *can't*.

'What are you going to do?' Lacey asked quietly.

What am I going to do? Sarah bowed her head, trying to remember how to pray.

'Listen,' Lacey said, 'let's go down to the computer room like I suggested before. You'll feel better. I have my best ideas down there. We can think of something.'

'Even a miracle?'

35

Computers and Dead Ends

Lacey led Sarah to the back of the IT room where Terry Redpath had his workstation. Peering out from behind thick round glasses, Redpath was a black guy with crooked teeth and a geeky outfit consisting of a lime green shirt, orange flares and, despite the weather, open-toed Jesus sandals. A fashion car wreck.

Lacey linked his digital camera to Redpath's PC and started downloading images onto the hard disc. 'We'll be a while, Sarah. 'Why don't you look around?'

Sarah wandered off, trying to think. She had no plans, no ideas, zilch. If the Committee hadn't made a mistake then it meant they were terrified of Robert becoming President. Why? Did they want him dead because they knew he wanted to make the Intelligence bosses more accountable? He'd said so in several speeches. But assassinating him for that?

She glanced at what the IT staff were doing. A young woman with long greasy hair was looking at a computer file showing details of candidates for the now-vacant post of CIA Director. 'What are you doing?' Sarah asked.

The woman peered at Sarah's ID card before answering. 'A routine security check. Just making sure there's nothing in this individual's record that the President ought to know about.'

'Are you telling me that everyone connected with the Government has a file stored in that database you're looking at?'

'Ma'am, nearly everyone in America is on this database.'

'Can you show me Robert Montcrieff's file?'

'If you mean presidential candidate Robert Montcrieff then I'm afraid I don't have access to that one. He's on the A-list.'

'The *what* list?'

'About a thousand people are on it. They're all big shots – politicians, CEOs, military, media, education, the Intelligence community, that kind of thing.'

'Who has authority to view that file?'

'Try Terry Redpath. He's a senior op.'

Sarah hurried back to Lacey and Redpath. 'Guys, I have to interrupt you.'

163

'What's up?' Redpath asked. 'It's not often we get one of the sky people down here.'

'Sky people?' *Geek speak*, Sarah thought. That was all she needed.

Redpath gave an enigmatic smile.

'Tell her, Terry,' Lacey said.

'The people who work at the top of the building are the sky people. Below them are the earthlings. Us at the bottom, we're the Capones.'

'Capones?' More mumbo jumbo. She didn't have time for this.

'Al Capone was a gangster, gangsters are the Underworld, and this place down here is fifty feet below street level.'

'Do me a favour, Terry,' Sarah said. 'Access Robert Montcrieff's file for me.'

'What's this about?' Lacey asked.

'I can't access that file without authorisation,' Redpath said.

'I'm involved in a Priority One investigation that requires this information. I'll take full responsibility.' Sarah was stretching the truth, but if anyone challenged her, she could say Robert was a known associate of Warren. She was convinced the file would reveal some clue. A start, a way into the labyrinth.

'OK,' Redpath said, tapping a few keys.

Searching for database file – please wait declared an on-screen message. Moments later a new message appeared. *File found. This file is classified Top Secret. Confirm your user identity and password, your authorisation to carry out this activity and the category three password. You are advised that all access to this file is logged. Unauthorised access is a criminal offence.*

Redpath looked up. 'This is heavy. Are you sure you want to go ahead?'

'Do it,' Sarah snapped.

Redpath keyed in the information. A computer file appeared, featuring a recent picture of Robert and a short biography. In the bottom left-hand corner was a small green box entitled *Special Details: Restricted Access*. The box contained a single line of text: Reference – *Alice Through the Looking Glass*.

'What's that?' Sarah asked.

'It's the first time I've ever seen anything in that box.' Redpath scratched his head.

'Alice Through the Looking Glass must be another file,' Lacey said.

Redpath searched for it within the database, but got nothing. 'I'll look for it on all the drives,' he said. 'It will take a few seconds.' The result soon came back: *no files found.*

Just my luck, Sarah thought.

Computers and Dead Ends

'It could be hidden,' Redpath muttered. 'Some secure files are deliberately concealed. I have authority to unhide them.'

'Go ahead,' Sarah urged. The moment she saw those words, there was something about them. Call it intuition. Call it whatever. She knew that file was vital.

'Well, what do you know?' Redpath pointed at the screen. 'Alice has come out to play.'

'Show me what's in there.'

Redpath clicked on the file. Instantly, an alarm sounded. Everyone spun round. Redpath's computer screen turned red. Flashing yellow words declared: 'Your name is Terry Redpath, employee number NA123 62F; security level three beta. You have committed a level-one security breach. Remain where you are.' Then the screen went blank.

Redpath stared at Sarah. 'You're assuming responsibility, right?'

Sarah stared back, then felt a tap on her shoulder. When she turned round, Lacey pointed at the doorway with a strange expression on his face.

Looking in the same direction, she immediately understood why. The doorway was filled with a squad of heavily armed soldiers in black uniforms and balaclavas, carrying submachine guns – pointing straight at her.

36

No Way Out

Red dots from the laser sights of assault rifles tracked over Sarah's torso. Most of the IT staff had dived for cover beneath their workstations. A few were frozen in their seats. The room was silent, apart from the unanswered ringing of one telephone. Dargo, standing in the middle of the commandos, showed no emotion. They fanned out, taking up positions all round the room.

'Area secured, sir,' their leader shouted to Dargo.

Sarah's eyes switched to one of the computer monitors. Its screen saver had come on and showed Jesus Christ rising from the dead then ascending into heaven in the centre of a dazzling light.

Dargo stepped forward. 'Do you think this is a game, Harris? Alice Through the Looking Glass is off limits to you, to me, to everyone. Full stop.'

'We need to talk.' Sarah shielded Lacey and Redpath. 'National security is at stake.' She was desperate to buy time to find out more about Alice.

'Move out of the way so that I can talk with your two friends,' Dargo said.

'They have nothing to do with this. I take full responsibility.'

'I told you to move.'

Sarah swapped glances with Redpath and Lacey. Shaking her head, she stepped to one side.

'You've let me down, and you've let yourself down.' Dargo said to Lacey. 'You and your friend are suspended with immediate effect. You'll be escorted off the premises and your personal belongings will be forwarded once they've been searched. Don't attempt to contact any outside group or individual regarding this matter.' He gave them an icy stare. 'We'll be in touch.' Commandos escorted the two men away.

'Come with me,' Dargo said to Sarah.

Without speaking, they made their way to Dargo's office. He took his seat and picked up his prized picture of a Death's-head Hawk moth.

'Well?' Sarah asked.

Dargo ignored her. A second later, his phone rang.

'Aren't you going to get that?' Sarah said after it rang for the third time.

'It's for you,' Dargo replied flatly.

'What do you mean?'

'It's for you,' Dargo repeated.

Sarah shook her head, failing to comprehend.

'You don't get it, do you?' The phone continued to ring. 'The Committee – *I work for them*.'

The words slammed into Sarah. She stared at Dargo as he thrust the receiver towards her. Now she understood. He'd said in the courtyard garden that he knew she shot Dexter. How could he possibly have that information? The Committee must have told him.

Trembling, she took the phone. 'Sarah Harris,' she said quietly. She heard someone breathing on the other end of the line. The person was hesitating, as if fighting some overpowering emotion. *Why?*

'You do it,' a man's voice said. Sarah realised the first person was getting someone else to deliver the message.

'This is the Committee,' the new voice stated.

'How do I know?'

'You know.'

'What do you want?'

'The delivery. Yes or no?'

'You're insane if you think I'd ever do that.'

There was no response, just an odd mechanical sound.

'What is Alice Through the Looking Glass?' she asked.

The line went dead.

Her hand trembled as she put down the phone. 'How much do you know?' she demanded, staring at Dargo.

'The Committee told me to watch you. That's all.'

'Don't play games. You must know what I've been ordered to do.'

Dargo got to his feet and walked towards the window. 'I told you. I don't know a thing.'

'I'm not in the mood for this.' Sarah had to concentrate on controlling her breathing. She thought she might have a panic attack.

'This is an FBI office, not a fortune teller's parlour,' Dargo said. 'I don't do telepathy. Say what's on your mind or get out.'

'You'll tell the Committee everything, won't you?'

'Naturally.'

Sarah thought about that. Dargo was a direct route into the Committee. If she told him exactly what was happening, maybe he'd realise the orders were a mistake. Maybe he could talk to them, put them straight. 'The Delivery Manager rang this afternoon,' she said hesitantly.

Dargo sat down again. 'I assume the customer is John Dexter.'

Sarah couldn't hold his gaze.

'No? Then who?'

Her answer seemed to travel an immeasurable distance to reach her mouth.

'*Robert.*'

Dargo poured a drink from a bottle of mineral water, his face strangely blank.

'There's something else,' Sarah said, trying to interpret Dargo's lack of reaction. 'Our wedding day is the delivery date.' The muscles in her face twitched. 'How could anyone order someone to kill their fiancé on their wedding day? It's sick.'

Something flickered over Dargo's face. He admired the theatre of it, didn't he? *Bastard.* She felt a flash of murderous hatred towards him. 'If I don't kill Robert they'll kill me, won't they?'

Dargo again looked at his Hawk moth photo. He didn't reply.

'What they're asking me to do is deranged. You must see that.' Sarah's mind went back to the hesitation at the beginning of her conversation with the Committee. The first person was unable to speak to her. Maybe their decision to order Robert's death wasn't unanimous. Maybe some could be persuaded to change their vote.

'If you're thinking of taking on the Committee, forget it,' Dargo said. He turned the picture of the Hawk moth towards her so that she could see it clearly. 'The scientific name of this is *Acherontia atropos*.' He ran his fingers over the Hawk moth's outline. 'Acheron is the river of pain in hell. Atropos is the name of one of the Fates.' He placed the photograph back on the table. 'The one who cuts the thread of life.' His meaning was all too clear.

'My life's over, whatever happens.'

'Get a grip, Harris.' There wasn't a trace of sympathy in Dargo's voice.

Sara fixed Dargo with her stare. 'You have to talk to the Committee. You must stop this.'

'I don't have to do anything.'

'Why do they hate Robert?'

'I don't have any information suggesting he's a security threat, and nor do I have any influence over the Committee. You know as well as I do that they tell all of us the absolute minimum. What I can say is that the Committee wouldn't be able to arrange a delivery date so quickly. This must have been in the pipeline for months.'

No Way Out

'I don't believe you. You must be involved.'

'I've told you, I'm completely out of the loop.' He glanced over to the window. The city was dark and quiet. Snow was falling. 'Will you carry out the Committee's order?'

'How can you ask that?' Sarah shook with emotion. 'I love Robert.'

'In that case, you'll pay the price. That's the game we're in.'

'Then maybe it's time someone changed the game.' Sarah didn't care any more. There was no way she would help the Committee. 'You know, I used to laugh when I heard left-wingers reciting their paranoid fantasies about the secret services. Now, I realise we're the ones who spread conspiracy theories: to discredit the conspiracy theories of our enemies so that no one realises we *are* conspiring.'

She felt as if the threads that linked her to existence were being severed one by one, leaving her as a broken puppet in a show that had been over for years. When she gazed out of the window at the long shadows falling over the city, she imagined they were reaching towards her.

'You shouldn't talk that way,' Dargo said. 'It won't do any good.'

'What good is your way to me?'

Dargo sat down again and picked up the phone.

Sarah stormed out of the office. She had absolutely no idea what to do now.

37

Modern Art

'It's all my fault,' Sarah said. She had arranged to meet Lacey at the Guggenheim Museum, adjacent to Central Park, and now they were standing on one of the spiral ramps leading to the higher galleries, watching a stream of art lovers drifting by.

'Don't worry about it,' Lacey said. 'Dargo called half an hour ago. The damage is one week's suspension without pay. No big deal, but he did tell me to steer clear of you.' He shrugged his shoulders. 'I followed his advice, obviously.'

'What about your friend?'

'Terry's cool. Got the same deal I did.'

'Aren't you worried about your career?' In an odd way, Sarah felt she'd done Lacey a favour. Otherwise, in a few years' time, he might be lured into the Committee's web and have to endure all the shit she was experiencing.

Lacey shrugged. 'My problems are a joke compared with yours.'

Sarah didn't react, gazing instead at an exhibit of an African tribal chief's mask. A death mask.

'Hey, did you know I used to be a photographer?' Lacey said. 'I still do some stuff whenever I get any free time. I wouldn't mind doing a session with you. It will cheer you up. You're a ringer for Louise Brooks with that hairstyle, you know. I could do some stylish, noir photos.'

'I don't think so, Mike.'

'Well, if you change your mind, my private cell phone number's on this.' Lacey handed her an old business card. It said: 'Mike Lacey. Professional Photographer – New Future Studios.' It gave an address in Brooklyn and a cell phone number.

'Nice,' Sarah said unconvincingly. It was extraordinary that Lacey was being so casual after everything that had happened. Wasn't he freaked out that soldiers were pointing guns at him a few hours earlier? That his career was probably over?

'You know, I only found out today that *beach time* means a suspension,' Lacey remarked. 'I heard someone talking about it last week and I thought he meant his vacation. I'll pick up all the jargon one day, I swear it.'

Sarah managed to smile. At least Lacey's chatter had taken her mind off the delivery for a few moments. The *delivery*. Even now, hours after she got

170

Modern Art

the call from the Delivery Manager, she couldn't take it in. What the Committee had asked of her was deranged. No one would carry out those orders. Regardless of anything else, it was impossible. No agent could kill someone in St Patrick's Cathedral in front of a priest and the two thousand members of the congregation, not to mention the millions who'd be watching on TV, and get away with it.

Her head thudded with a dull, thick ache. She knew she was being dragged back to the past, the long ago, her childhood. There she was, aged twelve, standing in front of Miss O'Mallen, the convent schoolmistress with her black gown and frightening eyes.

'Why did you do it?' O'Mallen shrieked, her gown flapping like a bat's wings, her stubby finger pointing at the defaced wedding photographs. 'Every child but you brought in a picture of their parents on their wedding day. You must have had parents. Weren't they married? Yesterday, we put the photos on the wall and this morning they've all been cut up. I know you did it, I know it. You're a wicked child, full of sin.' Then the witch's curse. 'What you've done is a sin against the sacrament of marriage. You'll never wed, Sarah Harris, never. You'll never be happy. Trouble will follow you wherever you go.'

'There's only one piece of jargon I can relate to right now, Mike,' Sarah said. 'The *too-hard* box.'

'The what?'

'It's an imaginary box between the in-box and the out,' she explained. 'It's for things that are too difficult to handle. I've fallen in and I don't think I'll ever get out.' She massaged her neck, trying to find some relaxation in the pressure of her fingers against her skin. 'I shouldn't have got you involved with any of this. It was unprofessional.'

'Anyone would have done the same in your position.'

As they walked down the spiral ramp, a neon sign hanging overhead flashed up a message: *Professionalism is roboticism*. Sarah glanced up at it. An artist had programmed many slogans into the thing and a new message popped up every few seconds.

All work and no play makes Jack a dull boy, the board said. It repeated the message over and over, getting faster and faster until the words almost blurred.

'That was the line Jack Nicholson typed out a hundred thousand times in *The Shining*,' Lacey said. 'That was when you knew he'd gone mad.'

Prohibition A

'I remember.' Sarah gazed at the words until the screen went blank. There was nothing for a few seconds, then a new slogan appeared. *What did Alice see through the looking glass?* the board signalled in scarlet letters.

'Look at *that*,' Sarah blurted.

'Relax,' Lacey said. 'This is an art gallery, not the Twilight Zone.' Even as he spoke, a new message took shape: *She saw both of you.*

Sarah stared incredulously. The Committee must have got access to the signboard's computer program. They probably had cameras trained on them right now. 'I'm getting out of here.' She strode fast down the ramp.

'Whatever you say.' Lacey hurried after her.

They left the museum and emerged into Manhattan's perpetual snow and darkness. Sarah glanced back at the Guggenheim and felt sick.

'Shit, another traffic snarl-up,' Lacey said. Dozens of cars were honking their horns. A stressed-out female cop, looking half-frozen, blew a whistle and struggled to restore some order.

'Keep moving,' Sarah said.

'Why are you so freaked?' Lacey asked. 'It was just a random message back there. Pure coincidence.'

'There's no such thing in our business, Mike. They're following us.'

'Who is? Dargo?'

'Think, Mike.'

'Dexter?'

'I'm sure he doesn't know about Alice Through the Looking Glass.'

'So, you mean the Committee? Look, let's go into the park. We'll grab ourselves a coffee and an apple Danish at the late-night café. Then you can explain precisely what's going on.'

They were yards from one of the gates leading into Central Park's east side.

Once inside, they headed for *Segovia*, a fashionable café on the edge of Conservatory Water, the boat pond. After a minute, Sarah came to a dead stop. Her eyes locked onto one of Central Park's most famous sights – a bronze statue of Alice in Wonderland, lit by a yellow spotlight. Gazing at it, something inside her gave way. She'd tried so hard to remain composed and tough, but now, all at once, her defences caved in. Sobs poured from her. She thought her legs would give up on her and she'd topple pathetically into the snow. Strong arms gripped her – Lacey was propping her up.

'Thanks, Mike,' she whispered.

Lacey didn't say anything. He just stood there, not releasing her.

172

Modern Art

Sarah looked over his shoulder at Alice. *I can't escape you, can I?* Alice was sitting on a giant mushroom surrounded by the March Hare, the Mad Hatter and the Dormouse, with the Cheshire Cat right behind her. The Mad Hatter's Tea Party? *That's about right*, she thought. She'd gone to a crazy world without a return ticket. She half expected the statue to open its eyes and wink at her, but it was more likely to be the Cheshire Cat that did that, wasn't it? The cat's mysterious grin was like the Committee. Even when it wasn't there, it was.

She felt Lacey's hand brushing her forehead, tidying strands of hair. His body, she realised, was trembling.

'I have feelings for you, Sarah. Strong feelings.'

'Don't say that to me.' She recoiled.

'I can't help it.' The words were coming out of Lacey like treacle, sticking to his mouth, making his lips move painfully slowly.

'We can't talk about this, Mike. We have to forget it happened.'

Lacey nodded, a film of tears forming over his eyes.

Sarah turned and walked rapidly towards the *Segovia*. She couldn't believe what had happened. She liked Mike a lot, but she hadn't given him any encouragement. There was that dumb Christmas kiss, nothing more. Jesus, she was about to get married.

When they reached the café, it was almost empty. A woman wearing a baseball cap scribbled in a notebook while a couple of waiters chatted to each other and glanced at their watches. A couple of men in black jackets argued in the corner.

Sarah and Lacey sat down on one of the wooden benches. Sarah nervously tapped her right foot against the floor while Lacey spoke to one of the waiters. The guy returned a minute later with two filter coffees and apple Danish pastries.

Lacey took a sip of coffee, then bit into his apple Danish. He brushed away some crumbs. 'Not eating?'

Sarah was glad Lacey was trying to normalise things. 'Maybe later,' she replied.

'Let me in, Sarah. Please, I can help.'

Sarah looked out of a window and found herself focusing on a teenage boy in a red ski-jacket pushing a miniature boat into the floodlit pond. Her brain felt as if it were turning to mush. Every thought that tried to form dissolved instantly.

'It's obvious that something's eating you.' Lacey's face wrinkled. 'Did you tell the Committee you were refusing to do the op?'

173

Prohibition A

Sarah switched her attention to some workmen putting up scaffolding for a rock concert scheduled for the following night. One of them kept glancing at her. 'I don't believe it. Look at that guy.'

'He's got the hots for you, that's all.'

'Get real. He's a member of a surveillance team.'

'You think they're watching you because of Alice Through the Looking Glass? I don't get it, Sarah. You're marrying a guy you love. You should be ecstatic, but look at you.' He peered at her. 'Is something up with Robert? Is that what's worrying you?'

'It's not what you think. I haven't got cold feet, if that's what you're driving at.'

'Health? Is that it? Robert's got a heart condition?'

'It's nothing like that either,' Sarah replied sharply. 'Neither of us is sick.' She knew that answer would only encourage Lacey to probe more.

'God,' he said quietly. 'I know what it is.'

No way. He couldn't have worked it out.

'There's been a threat against Robert, hasn't there? A death threat?'

She looked away, but that was the worst thing she could have done.

Lacey stared at her. 'Christ, I'm right.'

I can't do this, Sarah thought. 'It's the Warren investigation,' she managed at last. 'There's something wrong.' She needed to get away from Lacey. He was coming too close.

'This is bullshit,' Lacey said. 'Why are you lying?'

Sarah closed her eyes.

'I know what's happening,' he whispered, 'I *know*.' His fingers stretched towards Sarah's hand. 'You've heard from Dexter. He's vowed to kill you and Robert at your wedding. You have to get him before he gets you.'

Sarah gazed down at her plate. This was all fucked up. Hell, she realised, has infinite entrances, but no exits. Not a single one. She couldn't go on with these lies. 'It's more complicated than that.' Tears were welling in her eyes.

Lacey stood up. 'Jesus H.' He'd guessed the truth – the look in his eyes was proof enough. 'That's the sickest thing I've ever heard.' He quickly sat back down again, his voice fading to a whisper. Then he made her dilemma concrete. 'It's not Dexter, is it? It's *Robert* they want you to kill.'

Sarah breathed in so hard she thought her ribs would snap. '*Yes.*'

No way back. Now she had no choice but to follow through. 'How can I kill the man I love, Mike?' They were such incredible words, words that no one should ever have to say. And they wanted her to do it on her wedding day. It took truly perverted minds to devise that.

'They'll kill you if you don't do it, won't they?'

Sarah stared numbly at the skin forming on the surface of her coffee.

'It doesn't get any worse, does it?' Lacey shook his head. 'Your fiancé's life or your own. It's the choice from hell.'

Sarah's eyes scanned Lacey's face, searching for something…she didn't know what. Lacey was in the loop now, for good or ill. 'Should I tell Robert?'

'Wouldn't the Committee simply kill both of you?'

It was true. It would do no good, just guarantee a quick end for both of them.

Lacey glanced at her furtively. 'I feel awkward saying this, but what if Alice Through the Looking Glass proves Robert is guilty of something?'

'I told you, the Committee often fabricates evidence.'

'So, you're not interested in Alice any more?'

'It's the only clue I have.'

'I'm glad you said that. Terry's on the case even as we speak.'

'What are you talking about? He's suspended.'

'He has everything he needs at home.'

'You're saying he's hacking into the FBI's central computer system?'

'Listen, he loves a technical challenge. He's determined to find out what's in Alice. This time he won't leave any traces. No one will know where he's been.' He checked his watch. 'I'll give him a call and see how he's getting on.'

Lacey took out his cell phone and made the call. 'Hi there, Terry, it's Mike. How's tricks?' There was a pause. 'A headache, huh? Why's that? Yeah…'

Sarah gazed out of the window. *Where's my exit*? she wondered. There had to be a way out.

Lacey put his cell phone away. 'Terry says Alice is a mean son-of-a-bitch. He's never seen security like it. He'll crack it, though. He reckons he'll have the answers by tomorrow, if he doesn't fall asleep. He's drinking lots of black coffee.'

'God, I hope he doesn't get caught.'

'Sarah, how about this? You write down everything you know about the Committee in a notebook and you put it in a safe place. You tell the Committee that if anything happens to Robert or you, the notebook goes to *The Washington Post*.'

Sarah leaned back in her seat. 'They might be scared of publicity.' She nodded slowly. 'What about your theory regarding Prohibition A and

Dexter? Where does Robert fit in? Why the hell does the Committee want him dead?'

Lacey's pager went off, an irritating sequence of high-pitched beeping sounds. From where she sat, Sarah could see the small screen clearly. The message comprised just two words: *The Committee*. She blinked rapidly, trying to comprehend. She could never beat these people. They were too smart, too powerful. They were everywhere, even on Mike's pager.

Lacey read the message too. 'What the hell's going on?'

Something flashed across his eyes, a look Sarah couldn't decipher. She needed to get out. If hell had no exit, she'd have to make one herself.

38

The Underground View

John Dexter had never forgotten the rusty swings. Tomorrow, a bulldozer would demolish them to make way for a new kids' play area. He was sitting on a park bench only feet from where Harris shot him two years ago. *Two years*, he thought, since he last saw her in the flesh. Then he walked straight into her that night in Dromlech Castle.

Of course, she'd changed her appearance. They always did, thinking a makeover would alter their past, erase their sins. A dark bob had replaced the long, free-flowing blonde hair. Her eyes, once copper, were now blue thanks to coloured contacts. Fake, like everything else about her. She had so many masks she'd probably forgotten which was her real face. Despite her attempts at disguise, he'd recognised her instantly. She was still beautiful, maybe better looking than ever, but that just made him angrier.

'How could a woman do that?' He had spent the last ten minutes telling the story to the man sitting beside him. Even now, it seemed impossible. Yet it happened, on that beautiful summer's day.

Mike Lacey nodded. 'It takes some believing.'

'Has she ever spoken about it?'

'Just once. She said you were a rogue agent. She got the order to eliminate you and she carried it out. Simple as that.'

'Simple as that,' Dexter repeated. 'When I think of her now, I picture a machine...nothing human.' He stooped, picked up some snow from the ground then watched it melt in his hand. 'She shot me after I proposed to her. I was actually reaching out to give her the engagement ring.' He shook his head, reliving it yet again, as if he were trapped in an endless loop. 'You know what she whispered in my ear. I'll never forget it.' Even now, the words could slice him in two. '*I love you to death.*'

When he first met her, it amazed him just how quickly she beguiled him. She didn't do anything in particular, she just *was*. Something about her electrified him, switched him on and kept him lit up every second they were together. She was everything he desired: beautiful, intelligent, intriguing, an odd mixture of insecurity and decisiveness. Every day, he was curious about which version he'd get.

'What are you going to do?' Lacey asked.

177

Prohibition A

'Something big. That's all you need to know.' Dexter sat back. 'What do you think of them, Harris and Montcrieff, the happy couple?'

'They remind me of a story I once read, about a young man who never grew old because he owned a magic painting of himself that grew old instead. They seem too good to be true, if you know what I mean.'

Dexter nodded. *'The Picture of Dorian Gray.'* He managed a grim smile. *Lacey's right*, he thought. Harris and Montcrieff were a couple living on the surface, like insects standing on water. They looked good and sounded good and that was all it took to make people think they *were* good. No one saw the layers hidden beneath, the underground view, the faces of two Dorian Grays that told the real story. Justice, if it were anything, was drawing back the curtain that concealed what these people wanted to hide at all costs – the truth.

He gazed at the horizon, searching for something he knew he'd never find: the blind spot. They always come at you from there, the place where you can't see, where you have *no* defences. He'd done it to others many times in the days when he worked for the Committee, but he'd become sloppy. When Harris pulled the pistol from her handbag that day, he realised how stupid he'd been. Of course, it would be her. Harris had played him for a clown. How she must have laughed at him afterwards.

Much as the thought sickened him now, he'd been besotted with her, carrying a photograph of her wherever he went, in a silver locket on a chain round his neck.

So, the first law of assassination stated that she – the *impossible* assassin – would be the assassin. In Central Park that day, his senses became magnified. He'd seen the flash in the chamber of the pistol, had heard the explosive blast and watched the bullet rocketing along the barrel. Just as his mouth filled with the disgusting taste of a cocktail of emergency fight-or-flight chemicals, the bullet crashed into his chest at almost point-blank range. The only thing that saved him was his bulletproof vest with its special pressurised layer, filled with blood so that anyone who shot him would believe he'd been fatally hit and wouldn't attempt a headshot.

The force of the blow against his chest stunned him. An impact like that, he learned afterwards, could have stopped his heart. He collapsed and smashed his head against the ground, knocking him out cold. The paramedics told him later that when they saw him lying there in all that blood with what seemed like a clear entry wound over his heart, they assumed he was dead. Of course, they soon discovered the bulletproof vest, but even that shouldn't have helped him given how close Harris was when she pulled the trigger. It was a miracle he survived, they said.

A miracle? Fucking stupidity more like. Why didn't his intuition warn him? When he kissed Harris, he should have tasted poison. Touching her, his fingers should have blackened. When he looked at her, his eyes ought to have burned. They said the lowest circle of hell was reserved for the greatest traitors. Could there be a worse traitor than her; that *whore*? *My one mission in life,* he thought, *is to send her to the most stinking ring of hell, where the light never appears, where one moment she's frozen to death and the next burned alive.*

He rubbed his forehead. 'I knew they'd come for me,' he said aloud. 'I thought I was ready, but the one thing that didn't occur to me was who they'd send against me. I never saw *that*. The only thing I managed to do right was wear my bulletproof vest.'

'But they must have found out you didn't die.'

'Before I left the hospital, I hacked into its administration computer and made sure I was registered as DOA,' Dexter explained. 'The computer showed that there was an unidentified body in the morgue. I "identified" it as me. The Committee would have checked the computer records and found exactly what they were expecting: John Dexter listed as DOA and his body present and correct in the morgue.' His face moulded itself into a hard sneer. 'Virtual death is so much more convincing than the real thing.'

'They'll correct their mistake when they find out you're back.'

'They already know. We've been infiltrated.' He didn't elaborate. 'Did you find out anything about who killed Warren?' he asked.

'Not a thing.'

'Then improve your hearing. It could answer a lot of things.' He pressed his fingers against the stubble on his jaw, wondering who had a stronger motive than he did for getting rid of Piggy. At least it had saved him the effort, allowing him to scratch Warren's name from his TWEP list.

'I told Sarah that *you* killed Warren,' Lacey said.

'Why?'

'See if I could smoke out any information. Nothing doing, sorry.'

Dexter shrugged. 'What other news from the magic kingdom?'

'The Committee have ordered an emergency delivery.'

Dexter thought Lacey sounded over-eager, as if he were taking pleasure in the information he had, as if it were particularly special. It was always a mistake to be too impressed by secrets. They betrayed you, like love. 'Me, I assume. I guess Dargo didn't appreciate it when I showed up on his doorstep.'

'Not you.'

'No?' Dexter wondered who else it could be. What sad jerk was next in the firing line?

'I think you'll like it,' Lacey said.

'Tell me.'

Lacey blurted out the name. '*Robert Montcrieff.*'

'What?' Dexter felt a shiver of morbid excitement, as if a part of paradise had fallen from the sky, touching him as it passed.

'It gets better.'

How could anything get better than that? Dexter wondered. 'Are they dragging Dargo out of semi-retirement to do the job?'

'Have another guess.'

Dexter had an intuition, but it was so far-fetched. 'Who?'

'*Sarah Harris.*'

The name passed through Dexter like a ghost. He remembered lying on his back in Central Park, staring at the blue sky, with pain radiating from his heart to every nerve cell. One image was imprinted in his mind – Sarah Harris looking down at him without a flicker of emotion, as if she thought he were an insect in a formaldehyde jar.

'Aren't you pleased? Isn't it some kind of poetic justice?'

Dexter pulled up his collar. 'Has Harris agreed to deliver?'

'She says she won't do it. She loves him.'

'Love? What would *she* know?'

'She's convincing,' Lacey said.

Dexter heard the answer and noticed something in Lacey's tone. Lacey liked Harris, didn't he? Maybe more that. In the past, the thought would have infuriated him, but now he just felt sorry for Lacey. The fool was well on his way, sailing into the Sirens' rocks just as he had.

'That type always is,' Dexter replied. He looked up at the sky. More snow was falling. It was the right weather for a season in hell, wasn't it? The ninth, the lowest circle of hell, wasn't full of fire. It was ice, a nightmare frozen for eternity. 'Does she know she'll be sanctioned if she doesn't do it?'

'She knows.'

'So, what secret does the Committee know about Montcrieff that I don't?'

'There's one lead,' Lacey said. 'A secret project. I think it contains classified information on Montcrieff.'

'There's a *but* in there somewhere.'

'It's a top secret computer file with state-of-the-art protection.'

'Look, this city is full of geeks who can hack into the Pentagon's computers. Get one of them on the case if you have to.' Dexter turned face-on to Lacey so that their heads were only inches apart. 'I want that information.'

Lacey nodded. 'There's something else,' he said hesitantly. 'I've been suspended because of this thing. It's, um, awkward.'

'Isn't life a bitch?' Dexter shook snow off his shoe. 'Any other business?'

'I suppose not. I'll meet Sarah and find out what she intends to do.'

'You do that.' Dexter watched as Lacey got up from the bench. 'One last thing.' He stared into the darkness, avoiding eye contact with Lacey. 'I told you we'd been infiltrated. There were two of them.' He switched his attention back to the kids' swings. 'There's only one now.'

Lacey's cell phone rang. He looked at it, then gave Dexter a strange look. 'What's up?'

Lacey didn't answer.

'Who's calling?'

'Sarah,' Lacey responded after a long pause.

The answer produced a completely unexpected effect. Dexter bowed his head, hoping Lacey wouldn't see the tears pricking the corners of his eyes. He remembered the first time he discovered Sarah wasn't everything she seemed. Even then, he forgave her. All it proved was that Phineas T Barnum was right all along.

There's sucker born every minute.

Eight Years Earlier

East Campus Residence Hall, Columbia University, Manhattan

For eleven months, Dexter had watched his girlfriend jumping out of bed at 7.30 every morning to perform a ritual that didn't make any sense. Then, on 25 June, she didn't budge.

Dexter rolled over and gazed at Sarah. She was lying on her side with her back to him. As he strained to see any movement, he noticed that her shoulder was vibrating, like a fly's wing fluttering in slow motion. The movement was accompanied by a sound so quiet it was almost inaudible. It

181

took a moment for him to realise what it was telling him – Sarah was sobbing.

The more he gazed at Sarah's skin the more he thought she was becoming translucent. She once told him that she liked to imagine that love made couples transparent and they could walk around holding hands like miraculous glass angels. They ought to shatter at any second but never did. Now, Dexter was terrified the glass was about to break.

This was the first time he'd been with her on her birthday. Every previous year she'd gone away. He didn't know where and he never asked. That was the way they both liked it. Now, he wasn't sure what to do.

Give her some space, he decided. Quietly, he lifted the duvet from his side of the bed and got out, slid his feet into flip-flops and put on his blue bathrobe. He glanced back at Sarah as she lay awkwardly at the edge of the bed with her blonde hair hanging over her shoulder.

With the morning light filtering through the curtains, he left the room and padded downstairs to the pigeonholes, determined to carry out Sarah's ritual for her.

East Campus was the first stop on the mailman's delivery run and he invariably arrived punctually at 6.30 am. Dexter wondered why, if Sarah was so keen to check the mail each morning, she always waited that extra hour. Whatever she was expecting, it obviously never arrived. Maybe she had finally realised it was never coming.

There was only one item of mail for Dexter – a postcard. He put his hand in Sarah's pigeonhole expecting to find a clutch of colourful birthday cards from her friends, but there was nothing except a white envelope. It had no stamp on it and no indication of the sender.

Surprised, he switched his attention back to his postcard. Peering at it in the dim light, he thought he was looking at some kind of modern art. The image was baffling and yet in the back of his mind he was sure he recognised it. The pixels, initially a scramble of reddish meaninglessness, slowly resolved themselves. When he realised what he was looking at, he almost dropped the card in revulsion.

He held up the card and the envelope side by side. The typefaces used for his name and Sarah's were identical. Did the envelope contain the same sick garbage that had been sent to him? Then something clicked. Sarah *knew* this was coming, didn't she?

He returned to the bedroom where she was lying in exactly the same position as before. He got back into bed, wondering what to do. Everything about the card had freaked him out. How was it connected to Sarah?

The Underground View

This wasn't the only strange thing that had happened lately. In the last few days, wherever he and Sarah went, he'd seen men of middle height and undistinguished features, wearing unremarkable grey suits. They were so anonymous you wouldn't be able to pick them out in a crowd. Yet he'd done exactly that. Whenever he pointed them out to Sarah, she said he was imagining it.

'Why would anyone be following you?' she asked. Yet there was something about the way she said it that made him think she knew exactly who they were.

'Sarah,' he whispered, 'there's mail for you.' He felt as if someone had pulled the pin from a grenade and now he was waiting for the detonation.

He had been anticipating a fantastic time today, especially with what he had in mind for later. Instead, something loathsome had entered their lives. He stared at the postcard, trying to understand. The more he looked at it, the more nauseated he felt. The message that was typed under the image in an almost unreadable font couldn't have been more disturbing: *Coming your way*: *Vagina Dentata*.

That was what he was looking at – the magnified opening of a vagina lined with blood-covered, razor-sharp teeth.

'I didn't want you to be here today,' Sarah whispered. 'I didn't know how to tell you.'

Dexter absorbed the words, trying to unpick their meaning, trying to map them to the message on the card.

'I love you so much,' Sarah said. 'It was wrong. You're the last person I should have got mixed up with this.'

Dexter felt as if every word were like an iceberg, the substance hidden deep beneath the surface. 'I got mail too,' he said. He wondered if he were crazy to reveal what he'd received.

Sarah's sobbing stopped. She rolled over and for the first time that morning he saw her face. Her eyes were red and wet. 'Give it to me,' she demanded.

He was astonished by the forcefulness in her voice. As he handed it to her, her face blanched and she closed her eyes.

'I can't bear this any more,' she said in little more than a mumble. When she slipped out of bed, she was wearing nothing but white knickers and Dexter was startled by how slender she was. He realised he hadn't seen her eating for days. Maybe he'd ignored it because he thought she was dieting so that she could fit into some slinky new dress for her birthday. Now he understood – her birthday wasn't her best day of the year; it was her *worst*.

183

Prohibition A

She couldn't eat, couldn't sleep, couldn't do anything except try to pretend that everything was OK. Now the day was here and she couldn't pretend any longer. She ripped the card apart and scattered the pieces over the floor.

'Tell me what's going on,' Dexter pleaded.

'Please give me the other one,' Sarah said.

He handed over the letter, expecting Sarah to open it, or at least look at it, but she tore it up without a glance. She went to the wardrobe, pulled out a shoebox from the bottom drawer and knelt down, staring at it as though she were about to throw up.

Dexter had looked inside the box months before. It contained old Christmas cards from Sarah's friends, nothing more.

Sarah rocked herself back and forth, her eyes glued to the box.

Dexter had never asked her about her past, just as she never asked about his. It was a no-go area for both of them, an invisible world of fluttering shapes. They never went there and that was the way they both liked it. He'd yet to meet any orphan who was comfortable with the past. It was one of the reasons they got on so well. Others didn't get it. Their eyes were never sharp enough to see the scars from the little cuts on their arms, wrists and legs where he and Sarah had tried to let out the pain over the years. When they first met, both recognised the signs instantly. They knew that when they closed their eyes they travelled to the same dark destination. They didn't want to discuss it. All they needed to know was that they were with someone who understood.

But this was different.

'Tell me what's in the box.' Dexter got up from the bed, walked over to Sarah and crouched down beside her.

'There's a false bottom,' she said.

Dexter gently took the box from her, opened it up and saw all the cards he remembered from before. He reached in, yanked aside the false bottom and pulled out a collection of envelopes that looked identical to the one Sarah had just destroyed.

As soon as she saw them, Sarah turned away and began to cry. 'Please, John, don't look at them. I'm begging you, please don't look at them.'

Dexter couldn't believe it. He'd never trusted anyone as much as Sarah. Now he felt numb. She was holding back secrets from him, things from before they met.

'You don't have to explain anything to me.' He moved back to the bed, sat on the edge of the mattress, rubbing his head in frustration.

Sarah slid down the wall, shaping herself into a protective ball with her knees drawn up to her chin, her hands grasping her knees. *'I'm not an orphan.'*

Dexter heard the words but couldn't take them in. He thought of the life-changing gift he had for Sarah in its expensive black velvet box and wondered if he were going mad.

'My parents didn't die when I was five,' she whispered.

As Sarah spoke, Dexter imagined she was disintegrating in front of his eyes. Sometimes he thought there was nothing she could do that he wouldn't forgive. Now he scarcely recognised her.

'The truth is that my mother left my father. She couldn't afford lawyers to fight him and was too scared to take me with her. The last thing she said to me was that she'd write when she could. She said it might take a long time, but I was to be patient and always check my 7.30 post, wherever I was.'

A tremor ran through Dexter. Now it all made sense. Each morning Sarah was a child again, praying that today was the day when her mother wrote, telling her she was coming to get her.

'Do you hate me?' Sarah's blonde hair straggled lifelessly over her face.

'Sarah, your father…'

She turned her head away.

Dexter thought of the marriage proposal he was planning to make to Sarah that very evening. He went over to her and took her hand. They sat in silence for several minutes.

'You don't want to know about my father. He…' Sarah began shaking. 'I can't tell you.'

Dexter tried to understand what it meant that the mail was unstamped. Her father had come round personally to deliver it, hadn't he? It was a deliberate, calculated gesture. *I know where you are. I can come for you at any time.*

'Are you leaving me?' Sarah's head was resting on her knees. Her voice was muffled. 'I won't blame you.'

Dexter looked at the envelopes he was holding. There were ten, three untouched. He opened them and collected the cards together. They were all images of women tempting men, betraying men, luring men to their deaths: Eve, Jezebel, Delilah, Clytemnestra, Medea, the Empress Messalina, the witches from Macbeth, Cleopatra, the Sirens, the Harpies, Medusa; a catalogue of the deadliest women imaginable, real and mythical. Each had a message on it. 'The sins of the mothers shall be visited upon their daughters,' one said. 'Like mother like daughter,' was another. 'Mothers are the crime, daughters the punishment'; 'The original sin – when God created woman'; 'Adam's first wife – Lilith, the hell-demon.'

Dexter was appalled by how much hate they contained. As he ripped them up and scattered them angrily over the floor, Sarah spoke again.

'John, if you stay with me, he'll kill you.'

****

Dexter watched as Mike Lacey walked away, disappearing into the falling snow. Sarah was the consummate liar, wasn't she? She had lied about being an orphan, and, above all, she had lied about who would attempt to kill him.

39

Triple Agent

No more fucking mind-games. Lacey wanted to punch something to release his anger. The Committee had screwed up big-time, almost ruining everything with that insane message they'd sent to his pager. Why did they do it? Was it a test? If they'd sent the message while he was with Dexter, it would have blown everything. He was sure Sarah was unconvinced by his reaction. She suspected something. Maybe not consciously, but it was in her head now, the first suspicions. Jesus, she'd go crazy if she ever found out he worked for the Committee.

It was becoming a real struggle to keep his cover. It was so difficult to pretend to Sarah that he'd never heard of the Committee, or of Dexter. He had to fight a powerful desire to confess everything to her.

One of the objectives the Committee gave him was to get as close to her as possible, to become her confidant. Incredible, wasn't it? The mountain had come to Mohammed, or some shit like that. He had a special connection with her, he was sure of it, and he guessed she felt it too. Was that why the Committee assigned this mission to him? But it was high risk. He was already in way too deep.

He couldn't get Sarah out of his bloodstream. What if she somehow went ahead and got rid of Montcrieff? Then he could make a move on her. Christ, he must be losing it. He was suffering from what he often accused others of – magic thinking, anticipating some bizarre chain of events that would suit him down to the ground. Nothing was ever going to happen between Sarah and him.

In spite of everything, Dexter still had the Sarah sickness, didn't he? For a moment when they last met, he could swear Dexter started crying. He once asked Dexter about a locket on a silver chain that he kept round his neck. 'It looks like there's a picture of someone in there,' he said. Dexter had glanced at the locket, then put his hand over it and clenched it in his fist. The crazy thing was, Lacey was convinced he knew whose picture it contained – Sarah's. Why the hell would Dexter permanently wear her picture round his neck? To remind him? But he hardly needed reminding. Those memories were destroying him.

Lacey shuddered. Sarah was now destroying him too. The sensible thing was to distance himself from her. Everything connected with her was dangerous. Had Dexter told the truth? Did he really propose to her then get shot by her? What kind of woman would do that?

But why should he believe Dexter? It was in Dexter's records that he went psycho, and suffered a complete breakdown after a car accident. He'd started fantasising, and for some reason his greatest fantasy centred on Sarah.

He looked up at the dark windows of the Hudson Tower. No one could see in, but the hundreds of agents inside could certainly see out. They were watching all the time, watching everyone. Apart from being the Committee's secret meeting place, the tower was the home of the National Security Agency, responsible for intercepting the communications of foreign countries. The National Reconnaissance Office was also based there. They operated the most powerful spy satellites on earth. Their boast was that they could read the newspaper lying on your kitchen table before you could.

The lobby was full of soldiers dressed in black uniforms with no insignia – members of a Special Forces unit assigned the task of protecting the country's most sensitive installations. Each man carried a Steyr AUG assault rifle.

Lacey hated the way they scrutinised him as he approached the elevator, but before he even got that far he had to negotiate the retinal scanner. He couldn't deny it was an impressive piece of kit. It was so sensitive that if it was your left eye that was scanned originally and you happened to put your right eye in front of it, an alarm was triggered. A couple of awkward incidents had taught him never to repeat that mistake.

Two guards accompanied him to the elevator. The Committee occupied the penthouse floor, incorporating an impressive aluminium-clad boardroom where they held their meetings. It was a brightly lit room, but for Lacey it seemed touched by darkness. Everything connected to the Committee was dark. Now there was a new darkness – Sarah Harris. He thought about her all the time. Sometimes, when she had that pained, doomed look in her eyes, all he wanted to do was take her in his arms and comfort her. She seemed so sad, so vulnerable. He'd actually done it back there in Central Park and, for just a moment when he pressed himself against her, he thought he was a kid again, pulling back a curtain and seeing every Christmas present he'd ever desired. *Madness.* The last person in the world he should be thinking of romantically was Sarah Harris.

Soldiers escorted him to the boardroom. As he walked along the black-tiled corridor, CCTV cameras tracked his steps. The guards ushered him into the boardroom then shut the door.

Triple Agent

I hate this place, Lacey thought. It had the atmosphere of an autopsy room. Everything he said was analysed in minute detail, dissected and deconstructed. He always had an urge to visit the restroom, even if he'd taken a leak just minutes earlier.

As for the Committee, he was never allowed to see them in the flesh. They used an opaque partition to divide the boardroom. He was on one side, they on the other. Although he saw shapes, it was impossible to make out any features. Whenever a member of the Committee spoke, the person's voice was fed into Lacey's half of the room by a voice synthesiser, making it impossible for him to recognise the speaker's real voice. Often, he wondered why they bothered going to all of this trouble. After all, apart from the Director of Special Military Intelligence, the members of the Committee were all public figures. Was all of this just to protect one man's identity?

'Good evening, Mr Lacey,' a voice said. It was the one Lacey heard most often and belonged, presumably, to the leader of the Committee. He wondered which of them it was.

'Please sit down.'

He flopped into a leather swivel chair.

'Is Sarah planning the delivery?' the voice asked.

'She won't do it.' Lacey still couldn't understand why they thought there was any chance she'd carry out such a mad order.

'Did you tell Dexter?' a second voice asked.

'Yes.'

'His reaction?'

'It got his attention.'

'Did he say if he was planning to do anything?'

Lacey hesitated. 'No, but he wants to know what Alice Through the Looking Glass is.'

'How's your friend getting on with that?'

'He'll have it cracked by tomorrow.'

'That's too soon. It's ahead of schedule.'

'Schedule? What are you talking about? Anyway, why can't you just give me the damned thing? Why does Terry have to crack into it?'

There was no answer.

'I'm sure you guys know best.' Lacey wondered if he could rattle them. 'I think Eva Kranic is dead,' he said. 'Dexter knows we've infiltrated his organisation. He said he'd dealt with one agent. Now he's looking for the other.'

'Has your own position been compromised?'

189

'I don't think so.' Lacey leaned forward. 'But before I go back, I want to know a heck of a lot more about Dexter. I've met him five times so far and each time I get uneasier. Now he's saying this weird stuff about Sarah.' He stared hard at the partition. 'Why are you so scared of him?'

'Dexter was our top plumber.'

'Plumber?'

'A plumber fixes leaks, Mr Lacey.'

Now Lacey understood. Dexter tracked down double agents. He had taken care of Eva Kranic and now it was only a matter of time before it was his turn. A shiver rippled through him. 'If I deliver Alice to Dexter, I think he'll trust me.' He was trying to convince himself.

'That's the plan, Mr Lacey.'

'Shall I go now?' The Committee had done it again, pulling the levers that left him feeling utterly powerless.

'One last thing,' the voice said. 'We know what's going on between you and Harris.'

40

The Shrine

Sarah found it impossible to raise her head. What if Robert asked the right questions? Would she lie to him? They had just run through a full-scale rehearsal of the wedding ceremony. She'd tried so hard to behave normally, but how could she? The Committee's fatal order infected every breath she took.

It was Friday and her wedding was on Monday. She and Robert were in the Shrine of Saint Elizabeth Ann Seton, one of the few places in St Patrick's Cathedral where they could get privacy. She felt like an open nerve being picked at by a scalpel.

'It's Dexter, isn't it?' Robert said. 'You don't think we'll stop him.'

She could sense Robert analysing her body language, calculating why it didn't seem authentic. His stare had become intense, his pupils widening, sucking in more light, more data. *He knows there's something else*, she thought.

'Have you any other surprises for me?' Robert kept probing her, seeking a weak point, the way in.

She shook her head, but she couldn't look him in the eye.

'You have something else to tell me, don't you?' His voice was insistent, inquisitorial, as though he were in a courtroom, cross-examining a witness. He just stood there. Waiting. There was no way out.

'I hardly know how to say this.' She gazed at the floor, hoping an escape-door would appear. 'They say in these situations you should just come out and say it.' She tried to go on, but her mouth was dry like paper, the words imprisoned inside her. She imagined choking on them if they ever escaped.

Robert was studying her, still waiting.

'OK,' she said at last. 'The people who ordered me to kill Dexter have ordered me to assassinate someone else. To kill...' She stared straight at him, then quickly dropped her head. The last words were never said, but the damage had already been done. Robert's eyes burned into her, scrutinising her face for signs of God knows what. His pattern of breathing altered, long breaths changing into short gasps. Would he think it was some appalling joke? But it was too serious, wasn't it? It was the truth because it couldn't be

191

anything else. Robert came here to rehearse his wedding and now he was not only facing assassination by an elite former agent, but by his own bride too.

'They want me to carry out the order at our wedding.'

Robert stood there frozen, the oddest expression in his eyes. 'What the hell are you telling me here? Who, exactly, has ordered you to kill me?'

She explained to him about the Committee. Somehow, she managed to dredge up the most pathetic of smiles, hoping it would reassure him. 'I'm never going to kill you, you know that. I'd rather die.' It was incredible that she should be saying such a thing to her fiancé. She raised her engagement ring to her mouth and kissed it.

'But if you don't, they're not going to stop, are they? They'll use someone else and kill both of us.' Robert gritted his teeth. 'That's if Dexter hasn't got us first.'

'What are we going to do, Robert?'

'I can only deal with this after I've won the election. If we do or say anything now, the Committee will deny everything. We don't have any evidence and they wouldn't be dumb enough to provide us with any.' He made a fist with one hand and slammed it into the palm of his other. 'When the time comes, I'll have all of them arrested.' He shook his head. 'Jesus, why on earth at the wedding?'

His next comment stunned Sarah. 'Have the Committee joined forces with Dexter?'

41

Grand Central Station

Was it possible? Had Dexter made a temporary alliance with the Committee? Sarah paced up and down the snow-covered sidewalk outside St Patrick's, while four cops kept an eye on her. She would kill Robert and then Dexter would kill her – was that the Committee's sick plan?

Robert was still inside the cathedral, discussing the situation with his security chief, Tommy Henshaw. Sarah had been desperate for some fresh air, so she left them to it and got out. Now her mind was in more turmoil than ever. When a hand pressed on her shoulder, she spun round wildly, her heart thumping. 'Mike! Christ, you scared the life out of me.'

'The office told me I'd find you here.' Lacey said. 'I needed to see you straight away. Terry called. He says he's discovered something we have to see straight away. He wants us to go over to his apartment right now.'

Sarah nodded and spoke to one of the cops, asking him to pass on a message to Robert that she'd been called away on urgent business. She hailed a cab and asked for Grand Central Station. Lacey gave her a quizzical look.

'I have something to do first.' She reached into her jacket and brought out an envelope. 'It's a letter to the Committee about the stuff we spoke about back at the Segovia café. You know, making it clear I'm prepared to go to the newspapers if they continue with their plan.'

Lacey nodded.

Twenty minutes later, they were inside the rail terminal. It was one of Manhattan's top landmarks, but Sarah was always uneasy here because of its connection with the Committee.

'Where are we going?' Lacey glanced around the crowded concourse. 'A luggage locker?' he said moments later as he stared at locker 66.

'It's a dead drop,' Sarah explained. 'Senior agents leave their documents here. Later, the Delivery Manager collects them.' She could see that Lacey hadn't understood. 'The Delivery Manager's the go-between, the only person who gets to talk to the Committee, except in emergencies. He's their voice, their link to the outside world. If there's a reply he leaves it in locker 99.'

'Isn't this a bit low-tech?'

'It's always been done this way, Mike. The box is under 24/7 surveillance in case anyone gets curious. Anyway, tomorrow we'll get the answer.' She slammed shut the locker. 'Now let's go and see Terry. I hope to God he's got good news.'

They went outside and hailed another cab. Downtown traffic was at a standstill because of a snarl-up, but there were no problems in the opposite direction. As they neared Terry's apartment in Upper East Side, NYPD patrol cars and an ambulance raced past. When the cab reached Terry's apartment block, the police cars and ambulance were lined up outside.

'What's going on?' Lacey asked.

As Sarah paid the driver, Lacey hurried over to the entrance of the block. Kids listening to iPods were hanging around, and a baby in a buggy wouldn't stop wailing. Lacey stopped, waiting for Sarah to catch up.

When they went inside, they found several cops. Two stood in front of the elevators and two protected the stairs. Lacey walked past them. At first they ignored him, but then one said, 'Hey, buddy, you can't go up there.' Lacey paid no attention and began climbing the stairs to Terry's apartment.

'Official business,' Sarah said, flashing her FBI shield at the cops. They didn't react and Sarah followed Lacey up the stairs. Two more cops were standing outside a first-floor apartment, getting crime scene tape ready.

'Where do you think you're going?' one of them said to Lacey. 'No one gets through this door until the boys from Homicide say so. They'll be here any time.'

'Homicide?' The word seemed to make no sense to Lacey. 'What are you talking about?'

'I'm talking about the stiff inside.'

'Terry's dead?'

'If the guy who lived in there was Terry then, yeah, Terry's dead.'

'What? We spoke on the phone an hour ago.'

'In that case you'd better wait for Homicide.'

'Let us through.' Sarah joined Lacey outside the door.

'This is our turf,' the cop answered. 'No one goes through this door without Homicide's OK.'

'Get out of the way,' Sarah snapped. 'Terry Redpath worked for the FBI. That makes it our business.' The cop gave up and Sarah and Lacey went into the bedroom.

A peculiar smell was the first thing Sarah noticed, then the red streaks on the far wall. Terry's body was slumped over his computer, half his skull missing. It looked like someone had used a shotgun at close range against the back of his head.

Lacey was open-mouthed, as if a scream had frozen as it tried to emerge.

'I'm so sorry,' Sarah whispered.

Lacey backed himself up against the wall. His legs gave way and he slid down to the floor. What he said next sliced through Sarah.

'*I hate you.* If it wasn't for you, Terry would still be alive.'

42

Mad World

'I'm not going back. He *knows*.' Lacey was still shaking. 'Terry was my best friend. We'd known each other since we were kids. You can't send me back, you can't.' He bent forward in his leather seat in the Committee's boardroom, holding his head in his hands.

'Dexter had nothing to do with your friend's death.' The synthesised voice of the Committee's spokesman was more mechanical than Lacey had ever heard it.

'What do you mean? Of course he did. Who else could it have been?'

'Mr Lacey, *we* ordered your friend's death.'

Lacey's breath left him. Staring at the bright lights that were trained on him, he thought he was going crazy. '*What?*' It seemed so inadequate.

'It was the only way to convince Dexter that Alice was authentic.'

'Are you out of your fucking minds?'

'Don't you think Dexter suspected you were the other double agent? He'll calculate that because we killed your friend you're in the clear.'

'You killed...you *executed*...my best friend.'

'It was necessary.'

'Necessary? You crazy sons of bitches.'

'You're emotional, we understand.'

'Emotional? You've blown away a guy I've known all my life.'

'It couldn't be helped. There's too much at stake.'

'Blow it out of your ass.' Lacey stood up, but two soldiers blocked his path, their assault rifles jabbing into his chest.

'You don't leave without permission,' the leader of the Committee said. There was a long pause. 'There's another reason for what we did. Your friend cracked Alice earlier than we anticipated. He discovered something...'

'Like what? That you killed Kennedy? That aliens landed at Roswell? Maybe he found out that this whole thing was one giant fraud.'

Lacey realised how silent the room had become. His mind leapt to a bizarre conclusion. 'Jesus, that's the answer, isn't it? There's no such thing as Alice Through the Looking Glass. Terry died because he found out you guys were pulling off a huge scam.'

'We'll be in touch,' the voice said and the two guards stepped aside.

43

Surveillance

General Clark didn't knock. He barged into the monitoring room in the bowels of the Hudson Tower and found Gary Lassiter, the FBI Director, staring at a bank of TV monitors, all tuned in to Montcrieff's Campaign HQ in Fifth Avenue.

'What's so damned important?

Lassiter swivelled round on his seat. 'We've set up the surveillance equipment in Montcrieff's HQ, as per your orders. Something's going on over there, something big. They're planning...Jesus, I must have got it wrong.'

'Planning what?'

'It's to do with the wedding...I can't be sure, but...' He shook his head. 'Just fragments, you understand. They haven't come out and said it outright.'

'Lassiter, what are you talking about?'

'I...maybe I'm being dumb. I'm trained to detect nuances...'

'So, you have a hunch...'

Lassiter turned towards the monitors. 'I know this sounds mad, but I think there's major trouble. I mean, like, it's unbelievable.'

Clark took a seat, realising Lassiter wouldn't be making this fuss over something trivial. 'Spit it out.'

'The wedding – Montcrieff is planning to...' Lassiter's face twitched. '...Christ, *to assassinate Sarah.*'

'Are you out of your fucking mind?'

'It's crazy, I know, but I've joined the dots and that's the picture they're showing me.'

'Believe me, you've joined the wrong dots. You're getting mixed up with *our* plan. We're using Sarah to assassinate Montcrieff at the wedding, remember?'

'*Are we?*'

Clark peered at him. Was Lassiter getting cold feet? Did he think it couldn't be done?

'Sarah has gone the same way as Dexter,' Lassiter said. 'We both know it. She's not responding to the programming. You heard it yourself: she's refusing to carry out our order. She'll never go ahead with it. *It's over.*'

Prohibition A

Clark wasn't surprised by Lassiter's comments, only by how long it had taken him to get round to saying them. 'Don't be so sure,' he replied. 'You're right that Sarah is no longer with the programme, but she'll still do what we want.'

'How?'

'Leave that to me.'

Lassiter shifted uneasily. 'What about my Montcrieff theory?'

'I'm sure you're worrying about nothing, but keep monitoring it. Let me know if anything breaks.'

'And Dexter? He's using sophisticated counter-surveillance techniques. He has two teams shadowing him at all times, looking for any signs of our guys. I've had to order our agents to stand down for fear of blowing Lacey's cover.'

'What about the trace we planned to put on Lacey?'

'Forget it. We can't take the risk. From what we can make out, Dexter has all kinds of bespoke detection equipment. He'd find any bug easily.'

'That guy's a nightmare.'

'There's something else. We think we've spotted Eva Kranic.'

'But Lacey told us she was dead.'

'I think Dexter turned her,' Lassiter said.

Clark scratched his head. Shit, if Dexter had turned Kranic, what about Lacey? No, that was one thing that *definitely* could not happen.

'Regarding what we were talking about earlier…' Lassiter said.

'What about it?'

'We can get rid of Montcrieff at any time. Why does it have to be at the wedding? Why Sarah? It's too complex, too ambitious. We should amend the plan.'

Clark bristled. 'We're not amending anything. The plan is perfect. It always has been.' It annoyed him that none of his colleagues possessed his vision. They were technocrats, blind to the value of propaganda. If, in 1963, JFK was shot in a forest, out of sight of cameras and cheering crowds, his death would have been shocking, but not the defining moment it became thanks to Zapruder's film.

Killing wasn't the point. It was how it was performed, how it was *presented* that was critical. Robert Montcrieff would stand in front of the high altar of St Patrick's Cathedral. Within seconds of the end of his wedding ceremony, he would collapse and die. The watching nation would think it was a shocking natural tragedy. A doctor would examine the body. Everyone would be expecting him to pronounce death by natural causes, but that wouldn't happen. The doctor would point in horror at the sobbing bride and accuse her of poisoning her husband. Screaming, Sarah would be led away in handcuffs by FBI agents as pandemonium erupted around her. Like Lee Harvey Oswald, she'd be killed afterwards to ensure she didn't give anything away about what really happened.

No one who witnessed the fatal wedding would forget it. It would be the perfect symbol of society's breakdown, and it would trigger the final apocalyptic events of the eve of the presidential election.

Quite simply, Alice Through the Looking Glass was about ensuring that Election Day never took place. Everyone in the presidential succession and everyone likely to resist the Committee would be eliminated. The attacks would be presented as Sin for Salvation outrages, with Sarah's iconic assassination of Montcrieff the most diabolical of all. The Committee would claim that the nation was in mortal danger from the terrorists and seize power. No one would resist. Everyone who counted was already in their pocket, or dead, or about to be dead. Of course, as soon as the Committee assumed control, the terrorism would end and a grateful nation would give eternal thanks.

He wondered why Sarah couldn't figure it out. She and Lacey believed that Dexter was in charge of Sin for Salvation. How dumb could they get? Only one group on earth was capable of pulling off something like this. He put a reassuring hand on Lassiter's shoulder. 'Don't worry, we'll deal with all of your concerns. You're doing a great job. Nothing will stop us.'

A new dawn was coming, a thousand years in which American righteousness would illuminate the globe. To achieve it wasn't difficult provided the will was there. He thought of what was needed, *demanded*. It was time to use Manchurian Candidates to assassinate leaders of all hostile powers; to wipe out every enemy both domestic and foreign; time to capture terrorists, brainwash them and send them back to wipe out the others in their terrorist cells. In short, it was time to stop fucking around. Negotiation, politicking, compromising – all were symptoms of decadence, of inveterate weakness. They were long past their sell-by date. The future was clean and pure: *America leading, and everyone else following*.

44

The Funeral

Snipers scanned the crowd from rooftops while hundreds of National Guard troopers patrolled the streets around the Capitol. Washington DC had never seen a security operation like it Secret service and FBI agents were dotted throughout the crowd, and squad cars were parked at every vantage point. Checkpoints had been set up so that everyone arriving at the Capitol could be searched. All the time, police helicopters hovered overhead.

'Here it comes,' someone said as the horse-drawn hearse made its way along the road towards the Capitol. The Stars and Stripes flew at half-mast on every flagpole on either side of the route. The ninth floor of the Pearl Street FBI office, where Sarah was working for the afternoon, came to a halt as everyone crowded round the TV to watch. Sarah's eyes tracked the hearse and, like everyone else, she wondered if Sin for Salvation cultists would attack the funeral. Yesterday, they'd sent a one-line statement to *The New York Times*. 'David Warren will never be buried,' the statement said starkly.

Looking at the flags fluttering in the rainy breeze, Sarah thought of the Committee. They claimed to be the true guardians of America. Once, she'd agreed with them but now she knew they were insane. She'd checked luggage locker 99 in Grand Central Station an hour earlier and there was still no reply. Were they making alternative plans? Getting pally with Dexter?

The hearse halted at the foot of the Capitol where two files of US Marines in ceremonial uniform lined the steps to the Rotunda. They stood to attention and saluted while a drummer kept a single beat. The drizzle turned to rain. Black umbrellas popped up amongst the mourners like dark flowers.

Eight Marines advanced to the rear of the hearse in time with the drumbeat. They stopped and their leader saluted with a stiff, white-gloved hand. After hoisting the coffin, draped in the Stars and Stripes, onto their shoulders they turned to climb up the thirty-five steps of the Capitol, with the rain driving into their faces.

Sarah held her breath. The soldiers' faces showed the strain as the rain mixed with their sweat. At the top of the steps, a presidential guard of honour representing the army, navy and air force came to attention, before carrying out an intricate drill manoeuvre with their rifles.

Without warning, the TV filled with a blinding light, followed by a thunderous rumble. Sarah watched in confusion. The cameras filming the

200

The Funeral

funeral shook like children's rattles as a blast wave swept through the Capitol. Windows in offices were blown out. Thick black clouds obscured everything as fragments of wood, metal and plastic flew into the air before crashing down again, accompanied by body parts and scorched, still-burning, fragments of uniforms...like a billion shooting stars.

Then the screaming began.

Everything on the TV seemed to slow down, moving frame by frame. Sarah barely noticed that an agent had thrown open the doors at the far end of the office and was running towards her, his face pale, gleaming with sweat. The pounding of his feet grew louder. In a room in which everyone else was motionless, it was extraordinary that this man contained so much energy. Everyone turned from the TV to look at the running man.

In the background, a commentator spoke solemnly: '...Unbelievable pictures. One moment a sense of dignified grief...ambulances and fire trucks arriving...speculation that bomb was concealed in the coffin...going back to the studio... many feared dead...suspected Sin for Salvation outrage...'

The agent stopped in front of Sarah. He stared at the TV screen, then dropped his arm by his side. 'I...' He couldn't complete his sentence. 'Dargo,' he gasped eventually. His lips moved slowly. It took Sarah several seconds to absorb his words.

'Dargo has been murdered.'

****

Sarah sat alone in Dargo's office. It was half an hour since the news broke. Work had come to a halt. People were gathered in every corner to discuss what had happened. She was certain that she was the subject of many of the conversations. It wasn't simply that her boss was dead, it was the other factor. *The other factor*, she mumbled to herself...Nicki Murphy was Dargo's killer! Afterwards, Nicki turned her gun on herself. An examination of her body brought the final revelation: ten red circles round her left wrist, just like Theresa Martinez. Her thick silver bracelets had concealed them.

Sarah stared at Dargo's picture of a Death's-head Hawk moth. Death had surrounded her in the last few days. She imagined she'd become part of some ancient curse. Her mind filled with images of Dargo and Nicki, a weird collage of the serious, weighty cases she and Dargo had dealt with, and all the happy nights out, full of laughter and lightness, with Nicki.

She couldn't bear this any longer. *She had to confront the Committee.*

45

The Gothic Chapel

Hearing footsteps, Sarah stood up, anxious to see who was coming. 'Mike, what's this all about?' They were meeting at The Cloisters – an outpost of the Metropolitan Museum of Art – located in the sixty-six acres of upper Manhattan's Fort Tryon Park. Sarah had never been there before and she wished that was still the case. The feeling of nausea that permanently clung to her made it impossible for her to admire the beauty all around her. She'd been sitting on a low stone wall in the Pontaut Chapter House, surrounded by medieval artefacts from Europe, as lifeless and pointless as she felt inside. The clock was counting down and nothing had been resolved. She hadn't heard from the Committee. Had they already given the orders for Robert and her to be killed? *I'm on Death Row*, she thought. The only consolation was that Lacey had calmed down and was no longer blaming her for Terry's death. She wasn't convinced she deserved his forgiveness.

When he called two hours earlier, she wondered why he wanted to meet her here. It was such an odd choice. He said he had important news that he needed to discuss in person. So here she was, hoping it was good. When they parted after his outburst at Terry's apartment, he'd tried to look brave, but she could tell he was cut-up. The more she went over their phone conversation in her mind the more she realised he'd sounded scared.

Lacey half-heartedly returned her smile. He was badly dressed in thick winter-wear clothes that didn't suit him. *What the hell's wrong with him*? she wondered, shocked by his appearance. He was normally one of those guys who didn't seem capable of choosing the wrong things to wear, but today was the exception. 'So, what's new?' She tried to sound upbeat as they sat together on the wall.

'The Committee,' Lacey commented, partially concealing his face with his hand. Everything about him was hesitant. He seemed tired, older. 'They've been in touch with me. They asked me to pass on a message.'

Sarah was astonished. 'The Committee has spoken to *you*? But I thought they only communicated via the Delivery Manager.'

'Don't you want to hear what they said?'

'I can guess.' Sarah stared glumly at the stone slabs. '*No deal*.'

'No one would publicise your story, Sarah. They wouldn't dare. Everyone who counts is in the Committee's pocket, bought and sold.'

The Gothic Chapel

'They still expect me to murder Robert?'

'Can we go for a walk?'

Without speaking, they trudged around the floodlit gardens of the Cuxa Cloister. Talking had become too difficult. A group of tourists emerged from one of the side rooms, led by a guide in a blue raincoat.

Sarah didn't want any company. 'Isn't there somewhere quieter?'

'Let's go to the Gothic Chapel. It's just round the corner.'

They made their way to the small chapel that contained four thirteenth-century sarcophagi of the Catalan Counts of Urgel, transported from their original resting place in Spain. The stained glass windows laid beautiful patterns of coloured light over the stone coffins.

'I have a plan,' Lacey said. 'You don't want to kill Robert and you want to stay alive. That's the puzzle you have to solve.'

Sarah looked at one of the stone sarcophagi. *Puzzle*? That was one way to describe it. 'Go on,' she said.

'There's no choice, you know that.'

'I want you to say it.'

'Very well – *you have to kill the Committee, Sarah.*'

She gazed at the cold statues in the chapel. 'They can't be killed,' she whispered. 'They're too powerful.'

'They want to meet you. There's a helicopter waiting for you outside.'

'A helicopter? What are you talking about?'

'It's in the park a hundred yards away.'

'You're serious, aren't you?' Sarah stared into the shadows. 'The Committee think I'm going to jump when they call? Like a dog?'

'I'm not sure you have any choice.'

Sarah grabbed his arm. 'If I don't get into that helicopter, I'm not leaving this place alive, is that it?'

Lacey didn't respond.

Sarah watched the tourists drifting by outside. Not tourists, she realised with a sickening jolt – Committee agents.

'You'll need this.' Lacey handed her a small Uzi machine pistol. 'It's a special edition from the experimental lab, made of wood and plastic. It won't trigger a metal detector. The ammo is made of stone, wood and plastic. It's effective at short distance. You need to get close.'

Sarah looked at the weapon and shook her head. 'I'll talk to them, make them understand.'

'Take it.' Lacey pushed the gun into her handbag. 'You know the time for talking is over.'

46

Trap

'Ever been in a military helicopter before, ma'am?' The pilot had a strong Tennessee drawl. They'd taken off from a heli-pad in Fort Tryon Park, flying into a grim, murky night. With snow and wind engulfing the aircraft, conditions were horrendous.

Sarah didn't reply. She thought of Lacey's Uzi in her handbag. Had it really come to this? If this didn't go right, she'd be dead within hours.

'No?' the pilot remarked. 'Then it's going to be fun.' Wearing night-vision goggles, he didn't seem worried by the poor weather.

'What do you mean?' Sarah got no response other than a weird laugh. She tried again. 'Where are we going?'

'Oh, it's not too far. The Committee chose it specially. It's not their usual meeting place, but this isn't an ordinary occasion, is it?' The pilot grinned. 'You won't have any problem recognising this place, ma'am. Everyone knows West Point.'

Why there? Sarah couldn't figure it. She wondered what would happen when she was brought in front of them. It was impossible to believe they would change their orders. When she refused to carry them out, what then? Would they shoot her on the spot, or send another agent to the wedding to kill Robert and her? Or leave it to Dexter to do their dirty work? Was that why they weren't using all their resources to take him out of the equation? He was their Plan B.

What a mess. Maybe by meeting them face to face she'd get some straight answers. Maybe, somehow, they'd listen. She looked out of the window. It was pitch black, a darkness so deep it was seeping into her flesh. As the pilot made a course adjustment, she saw the twinkling lights of Manhattan in the distance, shimmering like fireflies amongst the falling snow.

The pilot nudged her. 'Some kind of problem,' he shouted over the noise of the engine and the rotor blades. A red light flashed on his control panel. 'I've got an indicator showing low fuel. It doesn't make any sense. I had enough to make this trip three times over.'

Flying scared Sarah at the best of times, but this was petrifying. 'A leak somewhere?' Her voice was dwindling to nothing.

'I'll have to take her down. We're flying over farmland right now and I saw a cottage. There's a Land Rover outside. We can requisition it. The base isn't too far away.' The pilot's smug expression had disappeared. 'When we land, go to the farmhouse and explain the situation to the owners. Ask them if they can drive us to West Point, or let us take their vehicle.'

Sarah nodded. A minute later, the helicopter settled in a field close to the farmhouse. Sarah leapt out and hurried over the frozen, snow-covered farmland towards the cottage and the small outhouses surrounding it. Lights were on in the cottage and the door was open by a few inches. She knocked on it and shouted, but there was no answer. Pushing it open, she looked inside.

Jesus.

She couldn't stop the scream that erupted from her. The cottage was deserted, apart from one thing – black rats feeding on a rotten sheep's carcass in the hallway.

Sarah covered her nose and mouth with her hand to block out the revolting smell and fled. As she made her way back to the helicopter, its engine burst into action, the blades started to spin and, within seconds, it was airborne.

A set up!

A movement behind her made her spin round. A man in a black trenchcoat stepped out from behind a half-demolished wall of one of the derelict outhouses, pointing a pistol straight at her. Now she knew – there would be no meeting, no talking. The freezing wind blew straight into her face.

A shot rang out. She jerked back, gasping. The man crashed forward into the snow. She tried to move, but her legs refused. A second man stood in front of her. *No stranger.* Two emotions flared in her: fear, and something she couldn't identify, filling her with confusion.

She closed her eyes. She wanted to drift into unconsciousness, to fade away. Nothing happened. Why hadn't Dexter fired? She was aware of his breathing. As she stood there, she had the weirdest feeling. She wanted to say something to him. She didn't know what. *Something.* Was her mind cracking? *It's him or me*, she thought. Her hand edged towards the Uzi in her handbag.

Another shot. Her handbag dropped into the snow, its strap shot through. Unsaid words fluttered in her mind like butterflies.

'St Patrick's,' Dexter said. He fired a second shot over her head.

Prohibition A

She threw herself to the ground, her mouth filling with snow as she landed in a heap. A motorbike engine revved up. When she looked up, Dexter was riding away. Her heart pumped wildly.

The darkness pressed in on her. She tried to get up, but her limbs rebelled, refusing to cooperate. She lay there, shattered. *I'm so alone*, she thought. Not just physically alone, but separated from everything. Shutters had slammed down all around her, sealing her off from everyone else. Not even Robert offered any hope of escape. She was in a jail without doors, windows or any possible escape route.

She bowed her head. 'God save me,' she said aloud. She imagined herself as a single, minuscule atom floating through space, through eternity, surrounded by the infinite dark. Maybe the best thing was for her to stay here and die. Would anyone miss her? Robert was obsessed with his campaign. In a crazy way, only Dexter cared.

Staring at the snow in the faint light, she noticed something lying a few feet away, close to where Dexter had stood. She shuffled over on her knees and picked it up. It was a red rose petal, completely dry and flat as if pressed in paper. An image flashed into her mind of a tall man putting a rose into the buttonhole of his lapel. She couldn't see the man's face and the image vanished. The strangest feeling seized her. As she stared in the direction in which Dexter had gone, something inside her wanted to go the same way. She gently kissed the rose petal and put it in her pocket.

After wiping away tears, she got to her feet and walked towards the Land Rover, collecting her handbag on the way. The door was open and the keys in the ignition. The Committee agent had obviously expected to make a sharp exit. *Bastard.*

She climbed in and took a moment to look at herself in the rear-view mirror. Her hair was filthy, hanging in clumps. Mud covered her face. She couldn't recognise herself. Had she *ever* been able to recognise herself? Opening her mouth, she stared at the gap between her teeth. In a way, that space was the only constant in her life, the one place where the truth still existed. Sometimes a feeling of fakeness overwhelmed her. She rarely met anyone who seemed genuine, but there was nothing phony about Dexter's hate for her, was there? She almost admired its purity. It wasn't something she could complain about. She'd tried to kill him. He had every right to reciprocate.

What should she do now? Go after Dexter? But that would be suicide. What about the Committee? They'd tried to kill her. Maybe she should do what Lacey suggested and return the gesture. But they probably weren't in

West Point. Even if they were, they'd be heavily guarded. *Just get moving,* she thought. *Back to Manhattan.*

****

She'd been driving for about twenty minutes over miles of relentlessly flat land, devoid of trees and buildings, when soldiers appeared from nowhere, as if they'd grown out of the land. In white camouflage uniforms with their faces covered in white face-paint, they resembled ghosts. They flagged her down with flashlights. One of them stepped in front of her car, pointing an assault rifle at her. He motioned to her to wind down her window. 'Step out of the vehicle,' he said. 'Don't make any sudden movements.'

Sarah got out slowly. 'Hey, what are you doing?' she shouted when the soldier shoved her against the side of the car and kicked her feet apart. He frisked her all over and wasn't shy about where he put his hands.

'She's clean, captain.'

'Search the car,' the captain ordered.

'What's going on?'

'Shut up, bitch.'

'Captain, Uzi in her bag. Special edition.'

The captain slapped Sarah with the back of his hand, sending her sprawling into the snow. For a moment, she thought he was going to kick her, but he backed off. She looked up and saw a jeep speeding towards her.

'Captain, what's happening here?' a man barked from the jeep as it came to a stop. Like the others, he was in winter camouflage. He had a colonel's insignia.

'Armed female, sir,' the captain said. 'Suspected terrorist.'

Sarah got back to her feet as the colonel climbed out of the jeep. Her body was shaking so violently she had to struggle to steady herself.

'Who are you?' the colonel demanded.

'Check my ID. It's in my bag.'

One of the soldiers found her ID card and read it out. 'This thing says she's in the FBI.'

'We got intel. that a Sin for Salvation terrorist was in this area,' the colonel said. 'A woman carrying fake FBI ID.'

Sarah stared at the colonel in disbelief. 'I can't believe I'm hearing this. You must know who I am. I'm marrying Robert Montcrieff on Monday.'

Prohibition A

'Of course you are.' The colonel grinned. 'Presidential brides always go for a walk in the wilderness, armed with a customised submachine gun, the weekend before their wedding day, don't they? It's a tradition.'

The soldiers laughed. The sound cut through Sarah, like the mocking of the schoolchildren who ridiculed her all those years ago when she tried to spell Mississippi. 'Phone Robert,' she demanded. 'He'll tell you himself.'

'I don't think we'll be doing that. I doubt Mr Montcrieff would appreciate a call from a terrorist. We're taking you in for interrogation.'

'I've found another card,' the first soldier shouted.

Sarah glanced at what the soldier was holding – the business card Lacey gave her in the Guggenheim.

'Sir, it says, "Mike Lacey, Professional Photographer, New Future Studios." It gives some address in Brooklyn and a cell phone number.'

'Who's this?' the colonel asked. 'Your boyfriend?'

'Phone him,' Sarah urged. 'He'll vouch for me. He works for the FBI too.'

'Indulge her,' the colonel said.

She wondered if Lacey would be able to persuade them. He had been acting so strangely.

The soldier walked to the back of the Land Rover to make the call, using Sarah's cell phone.

She tried to hear what he was saying, but the wind made it impossible. The soldiers stood around her in a semi circle, staring. For a second, she imagined them all in white lab coats, like scientists. *Psychiatrists*? She shuddered.

The soldier calling Lacey soon reported back. 'Colonel, I've spoken to a Mr Lacey on that number. He claims he's a photographer from Brooklyn, just like it says on his card. He's never heard of anyone called Sarah Harris and he's never had any dealings with the FBI.'

Sarah blinked rapidly, hardly able to comprehend what was happening.

'You must take us for idiots if you think we'd believe you were FBI,' the colonel said. 'And, for Christ's sake, marrying a presidential candidate – do me a favour. I thought you people were supposed to have good cover stories.' He signalled to the soldiers. 'Take her away, and have this Lacey guy picked up. He's probably not as innocent as he's making out.'

Two soldiers grabbed Sarah. They tied her hands behind her back and put a gag over her mouth. She swallowed a mouthful of blood: the blow to her face must have bust her lip open. A billowing sensation of nausea made her jam her hands against her stomach, trying to hold herself together. The soldiers bundled her into the back of the jeep.

They drove off. Closing her eyes, she tried to shut out the pain. How could Lacey have betrayed her like that? They told you to trust no one. It was always a mistake to break the rules. She'd regarded him as a friend, but now she remembered the odd sensation she'd had in Prohibition A when she thought he was spying on her. Then something else – how could she have missed it? – they'd sent a blatant message direct to his pager. He was working for the Committee all along.

She tried to figure a way of escaping, but it was hopeless. It had always been hopeless. Everything. *Her entire life.*

After half an hour, they reached West Point where she was hauled out of the jeep. The first thing she saw was the black military helicopter she'd travelled in earlier. The creepy pilot was standing next to it, grinning.

'Told you it would be fun.' He walked over to the colonel and handed him a piece of paper.

'I've been asked to release you into the custody of this pilot,' the colonel said with obvious irritation, removing Sarah's gag. 'I don't understand. You've to go back to Manhattan in that helicopter, with two of my soldiers.'

'Where am I being taken?'

'I'm not sure,' the colonel replied. 'There's a diagram with scribbles on it...*ten circles.*'

47

The Final Circle

Sarah stood at the jetty of Prohibition A's underground river. In the dim light, the dark water threw rippling reflections round the cavern. There were odd sounds, like whispers of the dead. Questions were piling up. What were the Committee doing here the middle of Sin for Salvation's HQ? Did that prove they were conspiring with Dexter?

She looked at the soldiers and pathetically hoped for some answers that they could never conceivably provide, but they turned away. *I can't do this any more.* She mouthed the words as if giving them shape would somehow make them false, but with each repetition they simply became truer. The water in front of her was full of twisted shadows and weird underwater lights. For a moment, she thought of jumping in, becoming part of this subterranean world forever.

The soldiers pushed her onto the gondola and stepped in behind her. The ferryman set out, just as he did the last time she was here. They travelled round the river until they reached the familiar fork: one branch leading back to the main jetty, the other to Circle Ten, through a tunnel so dark, so brooding, it looked like the entrance to Hell itself.

All the while, Sarah tried to make sense of the puzzle. Dexter wanted the Committee dead. He would never cooperate with them. So why did he seem to have hooked up with them? But, in that case, why did he save her life at the farmhouse? She just wasn't getting clear pictures. Too much static. She was missing something, some clue, something obvious. As for the Committee, one minute they wanted her dead; the next, they were prepared to talk. Why were they here in Circle Ten, the unlikeliest place in the world?

She turned to face the ferryman, wondering why he'd stopped. He was anchoring the gondola with the bargepole, a flickering red light falling on him and shimmering over his dark robes. Dexter in another disguise? Or a Committee agent about to drown her? *Do whatever you're going to*, she thought.

A green light flashed and the ferryman propelled the gondola forward again, steering it up the narrow channel. He brought the craft to a halt at a small jetty, painted in lurid red.

'Get out,' one of the soldiers barked.

The Final Circle

Shakily, Sarah stepped out of the gondola, searching for something to hold onto. Above the jetty, a sign said: *If nothing is true, everything is permitted.* This place was full of cryptic signs, symbols and statements, but that was the most enigmatic of all. The *Assassins* used this slogan hundreds of years ago, if she remembered right. It seemed equally well suited to the Committee. Ahead was a long corridor lit by red neon, with a plain black door at the far end.

'Put this on.' One of the soldiers handed her a blindfold.

The blindfold had been in the man's pocket and smelled of urine and semen. Sarah wanted to gag.

'Walk,' the soldier ordered.

Sarah edged her way along the corridor, holding her hands out in front of her, bracing for a collision. As she shuffled along, she heard the breathing of the two soldiers behind her. 'What about the door?' she asked.

'We'll tell you when to stop.'

Moments later, she collided with the door.

'Open it,' one soldier barked.

Sarah fumbled for the doorknob. The door creaked as she nervously opened it. When she stepped forward, the door slammed behind her. Before she could react, the floor rose beneath her feet – *an elevator.* It stopped after a few seconds. She removed her blindfold and tossed it away, then emerged into a circular room. A bizarre film was being projected onto the walls and even the ceiling. It was hard to make any sense of the images. The movie showed a red moon stamped on a black sky, throwing an eerie light over a wasteland stretching in all directions. There were pools of black water, heaps of black slag, forests of charcoal trees. Fast-moving black clouds, lit by indigo lightning, raced across the sky. Skeletally thin people in grey rags wandered in long lines over dunes of black sand, wailing pitifully, going round and round in circles.

The picture changed. Thousands of hands appeared and started pounding against a transparent wall, like prisoners trying to escape from an unbreakable glass jail. *This,* Sarah realised, was hell itself.

Words in vivid scarlet flashed up on the screen directly ahead of her: *Jailed angels. Dungeons of flesh. The body is the tomb of the soul.*

So, this was where the Sin for Salvationist cultists came to hear the truth of their religion. But how was any of this connected to the Committee?

Someone switched on a dim light. In the middle of the room stood a fabulous tree made of gleaming black glass like some conceptual art exhibit. It had fruit shaped like the human brain, made of the same smooth black

211

glass. There was one other item – a table, covered by a white tablecloth, looking like something from Leonardo da Vinci's *Last Supper*. But there were no Apostles sitting at the table, just five men dressed in grey suits...

The Committee.

There they were, the men who'd ruined Sarah's life. They seemed almost pathetic sitting there like that, nothing like the larger-than-life apparitions she'd cast them as in her imagination. She was familiar with all of them, except one. He must be the mysterious Director of Special Military Intelligence. He stared at her with undisguised malevolence then nodded at Gary Lassiter, the FBI Director.

Lassiter stood up. He was an imposingly tall man whom Sarah had met several times. Each time, she had regarded him in the same way – a desiccated, empty human being with the strangest eyes, like a corpse's.

'Why did you try to kill me?' she asked.

'Lacey phoned us to say you were on your way to assassinate us.'

'It was Mike who gave me the gun. I just wanted to talk, to see if we could work something out.'

Lassiter turned to his leader. 'I was afraid of that. We need a new Delivery Manager.'

Mike was the Delivery Manager? Sarah wanted to scream, to release everything that she'd been holding inside her in one primal outburst of sound. But no cry came...*nothing.*

'You're not going to kill me, are you?' She tried to shut out all thought of Lacey's deceit. 'What made you change your minds?'

Lassiter walked over to the black tree. 'You want to *know*? This place, Circle Ten, is where you find out. He tapped the bark of the tree. 'Recognise it?'

'Should I?'

'If you were a believer in Sin for Salvation this is where you would come for the answers to your life. This is Eden's fabled Tree of Knowledge.'

Sarah realised how dumb she'd been. '*You're* Sin for Salvation, aren't you?'

'You already know most of the story. Sin for Salvation was a religious doctrine preached by Carpocrates, a notorious heretic from the second century CE. One of our top analysts said Carpocrates' ideas were perfect for risk-takers, giving them the chance to behave as badly as they liked. Believers in Sin for Salvation would make ideal killers. They hated the material world and longed to commit sins to earn their return ticket to their heaven. The bigger the sin, the better they liked it. They'd feel no guilt no matter what they did. *Perfect* criminals.

'We agreed. But we wanted to guarantee our control over them, to make sure they did exactly what we wanted. This club was the result – our factory for manufacturing brainwashed assassins. Here, we short-circuit people's senses, seize their minds and turn them by hook or by crook into Manchurian Candidates. David Warren, the world's top expert in mind control, was in charge of the operation.'

Sarah trembled. These old men were insane killers, responsible for the deaths of hundreds of people in the last few days. Nicki was one of their puppets, and Lacey too. She remembered the Jonestown massacre in Guyana in the late 1970s when over 900 members of *The People's Temple* perished. Some people said Jonestown was the product of a CIA mind control experiment; that Jim Jones, the cult's leader, worked for the CIA all along and that brainwashed assassins murdered any cultists reluctant to swallow the poison each had been given. Now, she didn't doubt it was true. Sin for Salvation was *The People's Temple* on a new, terrifying scale.

'Where does Robert fit in?' Sarah asked. All the time, she was aware of the SMI Director staring at her so malignantly it was as if he were willing her to die. For some reason, she suspected she'd seen him recently. An image crashed into her mind – of her blowing off the head of her cat. A man in a grey suit lay dead at her feet. *God Almighty.*

Lassiter signalled to one of his colleagues. 'Show the video.'

Hell vanished, replaced by images of a fat, naked old man being murdered in snow and darkness. There was no doubt about the victim's identity. The silhouette of Dromlech Castle stood in the background, while the foreground revealed four men in suits, wearing Big Bad Wolf masks. They stalked CIA Director David Warren, trapped him in his garden and executed him.

When the leader of the killers removed his mask and inspected the body, Sarah felt a cold force hurtling through her veins and arteries, sending her core temperature into free-fall. A voice screamed in her mind, trying to deny the truth, to deny everything. The world could not be this way. One word thudded inside her head, pounding out a devastating beat.

Robert.

'You remember the footage from the surveillance cameras at Dromlech Castle that went missing?' Lassiter said. 'You've just watched it.'

Prohibition A

'I don't believe you. You've faked it. You substituted Robert's face for someone else's.' Sarah's legs threatened to give way beneath her. She found a seat and slumped into it.

Lassiter touched the trunk of the glass tree. 'Knowledge of good and evil,' he said enigmatically. 'We recorded this conversation in the last hour.' He signalled to one of his colleagues and moments later a new film appeared on screen, showing Robert sitting in a private room of his Fifth Avenue HQ with his three cronies: Spiegel, Longbottom and Henshaw. 'Turn up the volume,' he instructed after explaining that the Committee had installed surveillance equipment in Robert's HQ.

Sarah grew colder still. The men were going over the details of a plan to assassinate a bride at a wedding – *her* wedding. Tears rolled down her cheeks. The Assassins' motto above Circle Ten's jetty came back to her: *If nothing is true, everything is permitted.* She was in the middle of the Looking Glass world. There was no truth. There never had been.

Some part of her still insisted that Robert was innocent, that the Committee had used sophisticated technology to stage the whole thing: body doubles and computer-generated images. The chill spreading through her body told a different story. Through it all, the SMI Director stared at her. There was something horrifically familiar about him. *I've known him all my life*, she thought, and she had no idea how that could be. Not her Guardian Angel – *the opposite.*

'Come with me.' Lassiter led her to a small alcove at the back of the room. He pressed a button on the wall, causing part of it to slide upwards. Behind it was a two-way mirror. 'See for yourself. They're here right now.'

Sarah realised she was staring into the Limbo Lounge. Circle Ten must back on to it. In front of her were Robert, Spiegel and Longbottom. There was no sign of Henshaw.

'I don't understand. What are they doing here?'

'They arrived half an hour ago, via the rear entrance,' Lassiter said. 'It's not the first time. Montcrieff uses the club for meeting business clients.'

'Can we hear them talking?' Sarah remembered that Robert had claimed he'd never been here before. Another lie.

'I promise you, we didn't know Montcrieff was planning this.' Lassiter pressed a second button and the room filled with voices.

'Remember, Jacob,' Robert said to Spiegel, 'bottom line is I need a dead bride.' He broke into a grin 'You know, I couldn't believe it when Sarah told me she'd been ordered to kill me. She said she'd rather die than go through with it. When she kissed her engagement ring, I nearly laughed. It was *so* pathetic. The thing that really freaked me out was how similar the Committee's plan was to my own. I never thought they'd try to assassinate me at my wedding. You have to hand it to them.'

'Switch it off.' Sarah was sure no one other than Robert knew about that incident with the engagement ring. It had taken place so unexpectedly in the shrine at St Patrick's Cathedral. The Committee couldn't have faked it. Part of her wanted to break down. Another part...

'Why?' she asked. It seemed so feeble.

Lassiter shook his head. 'We don't know what he's trying to achieve. It's a lunatic's plan.'

'You think he's gone mad?'

'First Warren and now this. Don't you? It's almost as if he believes in Sin for Salvation.'

'What about Alice Through the Looking Glass?'

'You don't need to know anything about that,' the SMI Director snarled.

Instantly, Sarah realised this was the same person who'd hesitated on the other end of the line when the Committee phoned her in Dargo's office.

'All you need to know is that your fiancé cannot become President under any circumstances. He can be killed in such a way at his wedding that no one will suspect anything. You're the only person who can do it.'

'What about Dexter?'

'Forget him. In a few hours, he won't be a problem.'

'So?' Lassiter said. 'The time for bullshit is over.'

Sarah's world was collapsing. Her flesh seemed to be retracting, her whole body shrinking, as if she were trying to become a tiny, invisible creature that no one could hurt.

'Tell me what to do,' she whispered.

48

Phoenix

When the black limousine headed straight for him, Lacey froze. He'd been walking aimlessly down Eleventh Avenue towards the financial district, feeling as if his emotions had been stripped from him and placed on the sidewalk so that everyone could trample on them. Terry was *dead*. That word still refused to make any sense.

The limo stopped a few feet in front of him, spraying slush over his shoes. The doors opened and two men in black uniforms got out.

'Mr Lacey, please step into the car,' one of them said in an odd voice.

'Do I have a choice?'

'Step into the car,' the soldier repeated.

Some kids ran past screaming at each other. For a moment, Lacey wondered if he could make a break for it, but he knew he wouldn't get far. When he climbed into the limo, the soldiers sat on either side of him and the car moved off again. Its engine could scarcely be heard within the cocoon that Lacey found himself, but he was concentrating on something else – the silver-haired man sitting opposite in a black uniform, with four silver stars on his cap and epaulettes.

'I'm General Frederick Clark, Director of Special Military Intelligence,' the man said then sat back in his seat. 'What did you hope to achieve, Mr Lacey?'

Lacey closed his eyes.

'I've seen many things,' Clark said, 'but you're something special. Sarah thought you were her friend.'

Lacey felt sick. Even now, he could hardly believe what he'd done.

'Look at me.' Clark kicked Lacey's shoe.

Lacey reluctantly opened his eyes again.

'Revenge for Terry's death?' Clark shook his head. 'No, I don't think so. This is something else.'

'I don't know what you're talking about.' But Terry's death *was* Sarah's fault, Lacey thought. If she'd never mentioned Alice, everything would be cool. Clark was right, though – it was something else.

'Of course you don't.' Clark smirked. 'Listen to me: every top agent has faced a situation like this. I suppose you might think of it as your initiation.' He leaned forward. 'But no one ever reacted like you.'

Phoenix

'What do you want?'

'We need you to do something for us.'

'If you think I'm going to cooperate with you, you're crazy.'

'Did I say you had a choice?'

'An offer I can't refuse, huh?' Lacey smiled bitterly. He looked at the partition separating them from the limo's driver. It was bullet proof and bombproof, he knew. These guys didn't take risks, especially after what happened to Warren.

'It's the illusion of control that causes people to suffer,' Clark said. 'Your friend couldn't be saved. There was nothing you could do, except get yourself killed.' He brushed a speck of fluff off his lapel. 'I'm going to tell you a story you probably won't believe.'

Lacey looked out of the window and saw a white van overtaking them. It had an advertisement on the side saying, 'Time to get out of Dodge?' He had no idea what the ad was for, but the message was all too appropriate.

'It's time to introduce you to the adult world,' Clark said. 'I'll come straight to the point. Do you recall the Phoenix programme?'

Lacey said nothing, but his mind locked on and retrieved the necessary information. *Operation Phoenix*: a classified CIA black ops initiative during the Vietnam War. Object: to assassinate the enemy's leadership. Success: limited. The CIA couldn't infiltrate the higher levels of the Viet Cong and the NVA. The enemy's top brass escaped.

'Phoenix was abandoned,' Lacey said.

'You've been misinformed, Mr Lacey. We never truly abandon anything. After Vietnam, the project was handed over to Special Military Intelligence. It was combined with another project, the one investigative journalists have been writing about for decades.'

'*MK-Ultra*,' Lacey said. The limousine speeded up.

'That's right…the infamous MK-Ultra. The combined project was given a new name.'

'To something original like Phoenix II?' Lacey couldn't resist the jibe.

'To Alice Through the Looking Glass, actually.'

'Alice Through the…but I thought…so, it's real after all.'

'It's real all right,' Clark said. 'Information, Mr Lacey, is what we deal in. It's our currency, our most precious commodity. I'm about to give you the equivalent of 24-carat gold. This information bears our highest security markings, and only four other people have knowledge of it. I'm telling you for one simple reason – you need it to complete your mission.'

Lacey glanced at the soldiers. They were hearing this too.

Clark smiled, evidently realising what Lacey was thinking. 'Don't worry. These guys have 20/20 vision, but they're stone deaf and can't lip-read.'

Now Lacey understood why the soldier had talked so oddly. He sat back, more disoriented than ever. 'Go on,' he said quietly.

'You saw a reference to Alice Through the Looking Glass on Robert Montcrieff's computer file, in a special green box. If you'd done more digging, you would have found that the President's file mentioned it too. In fact, everyone in the presidential succession has such a box.' He paused. 'More investigation would have revealed something else – that the files of scores of rich young people in Manhattan also have a reference to Alice Through the Looking Glass. This time, in a red box.'

'The red circle people,' Lacey mumbled.

Clark smiled. 'Finally, two people – you know them well – have a reference to Alice Through the Looking Glass in a blue box.'

'What are you talking about?' Lacey felt his stomach lurching as the limousine made a sharp turn.

Clark took off his silver-rimmed spectacles and wiped them with a cloth. 'I'm talking about John Dexter and Sarah Harris.' He replaced his spectacles. 'They were students at Columbia University, looking for extra cash, so they signed up for a psychology research programme; just a few routine sensory deprivation sessions, the sort that students all over America were familiar with at the time. The money on offer was fantastic. One thousand dollars a week. No one objected.'

'But you neglected to tell them the real point of the experiments?'

'We neglected to mention that the programme was being run and funded by Special Military Intelligence, if that's what you mean.'

'A minor oversight.'

'If you'd let me go on,' the general said. 'Of all the students who signed up, only Dexter and Harris were deemed suitable for the second phase of the programme. Their unique gifts were exactly what we were looking for.'

'What about their families? Didn't they have any say?'

'Dexter had no family. He was an orphan.'

'What about Sarah?'

'She's an orphan too.' Clark coughed. 'She and Dexter were to be our star agents, the ones assigned the toughest jobs.'

'The Mission Impossible team, huh?'

'Call them what you like.'

'They're Manchurian Candidates, aren't they?' Somehow, all along, Lacey had guessed the truth about Sarah. He just didn't want to admit it to

218

himself. That's why the Committee fully expected her to carry out their mad orders.

'Exactly, Mr Lacey. The future is here. We can brainwash people, programme minds, invent lives for people that they never lived.'

Lacey looked out of the window at the scores of people on the snow-covered sidewalk. He thought he could see through them, as though they were ghosts. 'So what went wrong?' He struggled to contain the anger rising within him.

'Dexter's programming broke down. His mind became a mess, a mixture of recovered memories that we'd suppressed and false memories we'd implanted. He knew something was badly wrong and began to ask questions. We couldn't risk letting him find out anything.'

'So you decided to get rid of him.'

'No choice.'

'And you had no choice about whom you selected to do it?'

'Dexter was the SMI's top agent. Sarah was the logical person to do it – another Manchurian Candidate, and his lover.'

A shiver ran through Lacey. Jesus, Dexter was telling the truth all along.

'Their relationship made it easy,' Clark said. 'Easy to get them together; complete trust between them; no suspicions. I think you know the rest of the story.'

Lacey nodded. 'Dexter told me about it, but Sarah has never mentioned any romance between them.'

'She remembers nothing about it. We reprogrammed her to think that something different happened, that she assassinated an agent who'd gone rogue. She believes the man she loved for so long was another man.'

Lacey shook his head in dismay.

'Remember, this is the Looking Glass world.' Clark peered at Lacey. 'In this world, it's Montcrieff and Sarah who are lovers. In the real world, Sarah cared for only one man – *Dexter*.' Again, he hesitated. 'I made it my business to know that.' Another nervous cough followed. 'I've never seen a couple so besotted with each other. They say that ordinary people make eye contact sixty percent of the time, while lovers gaze at each other seventy-five percent of the time. I think those two stared at each other ninety-nine percent of the time. They would have married...' He clasped his hands together, almost in prayer. '...if Alice hadn't intervened.

'But bring to bear a multi-billion dollar research programme featuring the most advanced mind reprogramming techniques ever devised and, hey presto, Sarah believes Montcrieff is the true love of her life. After we introduced them to each other, they were all over each other instantly.' He grinned. 'I assure you, a laboratory-manufactured love affair is at least as intense as anything nature has to offer, without the inconvenience of both parties having to be in any way attracted to each other.'

'What do you mean?' Lacey's exasperation was increasing. He found all of this hard, impossible, to take in. 'OK, maybe you can control Sarah, but that doesn't explain Montcrieff.'

Clark nodded. 'You're right. We got lucky there. We'd been monitoring Montcrieff for years – that's something we do for every influential person in the country. We produced a psychological profile on him. We knew what type of women he went for. Sarah was a perfect match.'

Lacey's unease flooded back. He stared out of the window at the Hudson River. It reminded him of the Committee – a huge power flowing past the lives of millions of unaware citizens.

'And what happens to...'

'To Sarah?' Clark leaned forward. 'You like her, don't you? But it's more than that, isn't it?'

Lacey couldn't speak. What possessed him to make that phone call to the Committee last night? If anything had happened to Sarah...

Clark's face was stony. 'What is it you like? A pretty face, an intriguing personality? Harris is a creation of an SMI research project, that's all. There's nothing there, *nothing at all.*' He waved his hand dismissively. 'Sarah Harris is a phantom.'

There was venom in the general's voice. Something didn't stack up.

'Hundreds of people must know the truth,' Lacey said. 'Everyone who knew them.'

'They've all been dealt with in one way or another.'

'How?'

'Don't underestimate our resources. It would be more practical to believe in us than in God. Believe me, we're as close as you'll ever get. Do you need me to remind you of the kind of the power we have?' Clark traced his finger across his forehead, as though he were about to open his skull and let endless secrets pour out. 'Sarah shot Dexter in broad daylight in Central Park in front of scores of people and was arrested within seconds. She wasn't charged. No police report was ever filed. The story didn't appear on TV or in any newspaper. You won't find a mention of that incident *anywhere.*' He leaned forward. '*That's* how powerful we are. We control everything worth controlling. Forget ZOG, Bohemian Grove, the Bilderberg Group. When you hear conspiracy theorists saying that the people who control the world can sit around one table and have lunch together, they mean *us*.'

'What gives you the right?'

'*What gives us the right*?' The general repeated the question and seemed almost amused. 'If not us then who? Someone has to be in charge.'

'I detest you.' Lacey tried to sound braver than he felt. 'I'll never cooperate.'

'You'll come to your senses. Only the Committee stands between this nation and chaos.' Clark gazed out of the window. 'Son,' he said, 'you'll have to learn the hard way. You're young, immature, but we have faith in you. You'll be an important man some day.'

'This is going nowhere.'

'Whatever your opinions, I'm going to cut to the chase.'

'What chase?' Lacey felt the limousine slowing down at the same time as his heartbeat speeded up.

Clark leaned over until their faces were practically touching. 'We want you to kill John Dexter in the next three hours.'

49

Russian Dolls

'Let me out,' Lacey said. 'I need air.' The limo stopped adjacent to North Cove Yacht Harbor, not far from *Memoriam*, the hi-tech, titanium-plated art gallery that stood on part of the old World Trade Center site.

Clark gestured to one of the soldiers to open the door for Lacey.

As he clambered out, Lacey loosened his collar and took a deep breath. He trudged through the snow to the edge of the water, conscious that Clark was right behind him. He felt sick and yet oddly exhilarated. Whether he liked it or not, Clark's revelations had mesmerised him. They'd killed his best friend, so he could never help them. Yet he felt drawn, irresistibly, towards them, the moth to the flickering flame. But what Clark had asked for – that was impossible.

'You don't mean it, do you?' he said when Clark stood beside him. 'I haven't killed anyone in my life. I'm a psychologist. I'm hopeless on the firing range. I got the lowest score in my class at Quantico. Even if a chance came my way, I couldn't take it.' He shivered in the cold. 'I'm telling you, I don't have what it takes. You're expecting me to take out a trained killer.'

'There's no alternative,' Clark answered. 'Dexter has a TWEP list and every member of the Committee is on it. If he succeeds, the country will be plunged into chaos, exposed to every kind of terrorist attack and foreign interference.' He checked his watch. 'Now, Mr Lacey, time has caught up with us. Are you in or out?'

Despite his protests, despite the anger he felt over his best friend's death, despite everything, Lacey heard himself saying, 'What do I have to do?' It seemed there was never any real possibility he could say no, as if it was all decided long ago. Anyway, how could he hope to fight people who were capable of the things Clark had described?

It was only a trace of a smile that crossed Clark's face. He took something from inside his jacket: a DVD disc. 'This is Alice Through the Looking Glass.'

'*That's* what my friend died for?'

'We want you to give it to Dexter.'

'You're not going to let Dexter know what you did to him, are you?' Lacey was astonished.

'We tell people only what we want them to know. Dexter can't be allowed to find out about the real Alice, but that doesn't stop us giving him an alternative Alice.'

'It's junk on that disc?'

'Junk wouldn't be convincing. Our material must look like the truth or it wouldn't be believed. We pride ourselves on the quality of our misinformation.'

'So, what's the truth according to the fake Alice?'

'This says that Robert Montcrieff and his three best friends murdered Warren.'

'That's nuts. Dexter would never swallow it.'

Clark smirked. 'Montcrieff *did* kill Warren. We have the whole thing on a security video that we removed from Dromlech Castle.'

'All on film?' Lacey spluttered. 'What possible motive could he have?'

Clark didn't answer.

'That's why you ordered Sarah to assassinate him, isn't it? But she's not going to do it, is she?'

'I wouldn't be so sure.'

'You give her some kind of codeword, don't you? That's how you programme her. That's what turns her from a lover into a killer.' Lacey didn't wait for a reply. 'I know what the codeword is.' He remembered his weird conversation with Sarah in the canteen in Pearl Street. 'It's *Red Queen*, isn't it?'

'How do you know that? That's classified information.'

Lacey managed a faint smile.

'Very good, Mr Lacey. Actually, the words *Red Queen* have to be accompanied by an acoustic tone of a specific frequency. Otherwise, Sarah could be accidentally programmed if someone just happened to say those words.' He stepped closer. 'What else do you know?'

'The codeword doesn't work properly any more.'

Clark nodded. 'We don't know why. Perhaps the programming loses effect after a few years. Our scientists haven't gathered enough data.'

'What are you going to do?'

'We've already taken care of it. Sarah *will* do the job.'

'What have you done to her?'

'That's not your concern. Dexter is your priority now.' Clark turned to look at *Memoriam*. 'We can't allow him to jeopardise our plans any longer.'

'Will Dexter be told why Montcrieff killed Warren?'

Prohibition A

'Alice says Montcrieff is trying to create a crisis using a terrorist organisation. He'll then pose as the solution to the crisis.'

'What else does it say?'

'It says the Committee has discovered Montcrieff's plans and must stop him. To prevent a political scandal, the assassination must be presented as a personal love tragedy. Enter Sarah Harris.'

'Will Dexter buy it?'

'Why not? It fits all the available facts. It's believable from the viewpoint of anyone who works in our world.'

'Is there a real Alice?' Lacey asked. 'I mean a real, solid thing I can touch that spells out all the true details about Alice Through the Looking Glass?

Clark considered for a moment. 'Yes,' he said eventually. 'It's on the hard drive of a computer in my office. There's one copy in a safe location. That's it.'

'There's no other record?'

'None.'

'That's some project.'

'Alice is the most secret project in the world, Mr Lacey.'

'So, I hand over the fake Alice. What then?'

'Once you give the disc to Dexter, his guard will be down. He'll be preoccupied, digesting the information. The last thing he'll expect is an assassination attempt. You'll be alone with him. It's the perfect time.'

'How do I do it?'

The general reached into his pocket and pulled out a small white tube. 'This contains two L pills.'

'L for lethal?'

Clark smiled wryly. 'Drop them into anything he's drinking. They dissolve in a second.'

Lacey was surprised. Christ, he might actually get away with this.

'Do you think you can do it?' Clark asked.

'I think so.'

'Then let's do it.'

'One last thing,' Lacey commented as the general turned away. 'Once or twice, I've seen Dexter drinking something I've never seen before.'

'A rust-coloured soft drink?'

'Yes, exactly.'

'It's *Irn-Bru*, from Scotland.'

'Iron what?'

Russian Dolls

'That's spelt I R N hyphen B R U. One of the pioneers of the CIA's embryonic mind control programme originally came from Glasgow in Scotland.'

'Douglas Henderson, I presume.'

'That's right. He was brought up on this *Irn-Bru* stuff. Apparently, everyone drinks it over there. He never shook off the habit and he used to have crates of it shipped over from Glasgow. He amused himself by conditioning some of his experimental subjects to acquire the habit. The tradition was carried on even after Henderson left the programme and SMI took over.'

'You guys have a sense of humour, huh?'

'It's time to go,' Clark said.

'I suppose so.' Lacey shrugged his shoulders and followed the general back to the limousine, wondering why Clark was so confident about Sarah. If her programming had broken down and she was no longer obeying mind commands, the Committee must have tried a different tactic. The answer came to him in a flash. They'd shown her the footage of Montcrieff and his cronies butchering Warren, hadn't they? That was the only possible answer. He started to dream of what might happen between Sarah and him when Montcrieff was out of the picture. Who was he kidding? Sarah would never forgive him.

Then another thought. If Sarah changed her mind and refused to do it, they'd have to kill her. He knew exactly who'd be given the task. *Him.*

50

Alice in Wonderland

Lacey always met Dexter in disused offices, abandoned warehouses, public parks, fly-by-night locations: never in the same place twice. Today they were in small offices undergoing refurbishment in Manhattan's Tribeca district. Paint cans, brushes, rollers, buckets and white sheets lay strewn everywhere.

What's keeping him? Lacey wondered. Twenty minutes earlier, Dexter had disappeared into another office to study the DVD. Now Lacey was sitting uncomfortably on a rickety wooden stool, waiting for his chance to use the pills.

Dexter returned, tapping the DVD against the palm of his hand. Wearing a black suit, shirt and tie, he looked as though he was on his way to a funeral.

'The computer was playing up,' he said.

'I hope it was worth it.' Lacey tried to sound confident.

'I haven't offered you a drink, Mike. What can I get you?' There was something about Dexter's tone.

'Nothing for me, thanks.'

Dexter vanished into the other office again and returned with two glasses and a bottle of an odd-coloured drink.

Lacey instantly realised what it was. 'Terry was my best friend,' he said as Dexter poured the Irn-Bru. 'We'd known each other since junior school.' He tried to think of a diversion to allow him to slip the L pills into Dexter's drink.

Dexter ignored him. 'Alice Through the Looking Glass – did you take a good look?' He ran his fingers over the silver pin on his black tie. 'What did you think of the Montcrieff story?'

'He's mad. It's obvious, isn't it?'

Dexter shook his head. 'Montcrieff had nothing to do with Warren's death.'

'I'm not following. Alice Through the Looking Glass. It's categorical.'

'Categorical *shit*, Mike. Why would Montcrieff jeopardise everything days before the election?'

'I...I...'

'You don't know what I'm talking about, huh?' Dexter frowned. 'Sometimes I think secret agents must have the lowest IQs on earth. We

226

Alice in Wonderland

spend all of our time saying we don't know this and we don't know that, we don't know *any* fucking thing.' He held up his glass and watched the bubbles rushing to the surface. 'I have crates of this shipped over from Scotland. It does an incredible thing – it improves my sense of smell. Makes it acute. Like, right now, I can actually smell your fear.' He poured a second glass and offered it to Lacey. '*Drink.*' It wasn't an invitation this time.

Lacey's hand shook as he tried to take the glass.

Dexter grabbed his wrist and forced him to grip the glass. 'Drink up, Mike.'

He's going to kill me. A pathetic realisation hit Lacey. The last taste in his mouth would be this Irn-Bru.

'Do you remember *Blade Runner,*' Dexter remarked, 'when the last-surviving Nexus 6 android was about to die? The android said, "I saw attack ships on fire off the shoulder of Orion. I watched C-beams glitter in the dark near the Tannhauser gate."'

Dexter gazed out of the window. 'Such astonishing things. I also saw an astonishing thing recently. I was standing outside a black glass tower…'

Lacey felt a deadening cold creeping through his body.

'Guess who I saw going into the building?'

Lacey shook his head. *I'm about to die*, he thought. *I have to get out of here.* He was furious with himself. Why had he been so dumb? It was so fucking obvious now – Dexter was spying on him all along.

'I thought maybe I should go and ask your best friend what was going on,' Dexter continued. 'When I arrived at Terry's apartment, I saw men in grey suits leaving fast. The front door was open and your friend was inside. No need to check his pulse. But, surprise, surprise, on-screen were those magic words: Alice Through the Looking Glass. This is what I saw: *File – Alice Through the Looking Glass. File size 0 bytes. Warning: file is empty.*' He paused, allowing his words to have their full impact.

File is empty, Lacey mouthed to himself. He wanted to run for the door, but he knew he wouldn't stand a chance. His stomach felt as though it had fist-sized chunks of ice in it.

'Alice Through the Looking Glass is a sham,' Dexter said, 'a shell with nothing inside. Just bait, nothing else.' He stared through Lacey as if he were glass.

'Yet here you are hand-delivering Alice. Now things have changed. Now it's full of information. Question is – how can an empty file have stuff in it hours after the man who downloaded it has bought his ticket to the mortuary? Obviously, someone added data to the file after your friend's death. That same person copied it to a disc and gave it to you to bring to me.' The expression on Dexter's face was glacial. 'Am I going too fast, Mike? Maybe you'd like another drink. Maybe you'd like to slip something into mine.'

'I...what...'

'You're carrying a couple of L pills, aren't you, Mike? Probably strychnine. Do you know what it does?' Dexter set down his drink. 'It attacks the central nervous system, causing every muscle in the body to contract simultaneously then release, making the victim jack-knife backwards and forwards. Some victims break their necks during their convulsions. The victim's neck and face stiffen. His arms and legs go into spasm. Shortly after, he chokes to death. Rigor mortis sets in instantly, locking the body in its last position. The eyes are always wide open, the face frozen in a death scream.' He ran his finger round the lip of his glass. 'Were you going to drop a couple of L pills into my drink, Mike?'

'I...no...I...'

'You wouldn't dream of it, right? In that case, take the white tube out of your pocket and empty the pills into your own drink.'

'How...I...'

'How do I know what you've got in your pocket? Because I used to carry them myself when I worked for the Committee. Now take them out of your pocket.'

'That, uh, drink you like,' Lacey stammered, 'when did you start drinking it?'

Dexter studied him. The question must have sounded odd, but it stopped him.

'Why?'

'They don't sell it in this country.'

'I told you – I import it from Scotland.'

'Have you ever been to Scotland?'

'No.'

'So who introduced you to the drink?'

Dexter suddenly seemed confused. 'What are you telling me?'

'If I tell you...'

'Will I agree not to kill you? I'll tell you what, if you give me a heads up, I'll consider it.'

'How can I trust you?'

'If you don't, I'll kill you. If you do, well, I might do something different.'

'That's not a deal.'

228

Alice in Wonderland

'It's the only one you've got.'

'OK,' Lacey mumbled. 'That drink has a weird name: *Irn-Bru*.' He could read the curiosity in Dexter's eyes. 'The CIA had a top scientist called Douglas Henderson, born in Scotland. His team conducted experiments on people's minds.'

'Experiments?'

'Mind control, psychological manipulation, brainwashing. When the CIA lost interest, SMI took over. They chose you as their main guinea pig. False memories were implanted in your mind.'

Dexter gazed ahead, unblinking.

'Henderson thought it would be amusing to give his subjects a taste for his favourite childhood drink. SMI continued the tradition.'

Dexter's face seemed to freeze in place.

'You'd never heard of Irn-Bru until you became part of Henderson's programme.'

'This is the real Alice Through the Looking Glass, isn't it?'

'*Yes*.' Lacey was thinking fast. He didn't want to tell Dexter everything that he'd learned from Clark. Feed him half-truths, that was the lesson Clark had taught him. Then get back to the Committee and let them sort out this mess.

'It explains the fucked-up memories, the flashbacks.' Dexter was ignoring Lacey now, almost talking to himself. 'Which are my real memories and which were implanted?' He took a slow sip of his drink. 'Any ideas?'

'Only the Committee can tell you.'

'Why the pretence that Alice was connected with Montcrieff?'

A weird thought flashed into Lacey's mind. Without thinking, he used it. 'Montcrieff is part of the programme too.'

'*Jesus*.' Dexter slammed his drink down. 'That explains so much. Maybe he did kill Warren, after all. He probably hates the Committee as much as I do.'

He's not going to kill me, Lacey thought. Relief washed over him. But then another thought: Dexter couldn't afford to let him go.

'They've done some job,' Dexter said. 'Not just on Montcrieff and me.'

'I don't understand.' Lacey breathed in hard.

'If they can fuck with my mind...'

'What are you saying?'

'You have no idea, do you?'

'What are you talking about?' Lacey's eyes closed involuntarily. His mind raced through everything General Clark had told him. Why had the general given away so much? It was far more information than he needed to complete his mission. Was it because Clark knew it didn't matter a damn?

'Alice Through the Looking Glass isn't the only top secret project the Committee have been working on,' Dexter said. 'Yesterday, thanks to a mole I've got working in the Hudson Tower, I hit the mother lode. Alice has a sister project.'

Lacey wasn't listening. His body temperature had gone into free-fall. Goosebumps covered every part of him.

'To be more accurate, it's the sequel to Alice Through the Looking Glass.' Dexter waved a piece of paper in front of Lacey.

Lacey's head was spinning, his vision blurring, but he was still able to make out what Dexter was holding – a printout of a computer file headed *Mike Lacey*. There was a blue box at the foot of the printout. It said, *Special Details: Restricted Access*. The box contained a single line of text: Reference – *Alice in Wonderland*.

'If I'm the star of the original, guess who's playing my part in the follow-up?'

'What are you saying?'

'Do you know who the Delivery Manager is?'

'No idea.'

'According to Alice in Wonderland, the Committee's current Delivery Manager is…' Dexter didn't need to finish the sentence.

A wave of horror swept over Lacey. Holes were opening all around him. Holes in his thoughts, his memories, his whole life. All that stuff about alters, zombie states, DID and cognitive dissonance – it all applied to *him*. He stared at his left wrist, expecting to see red circles. It was clean, but it made no difference. The circles might as well be tattooed all over his body. *I'm just a patsy, a big-time dupe.*

Dexter was still peering at him. 'Join the marionettes, Mike.'

'But I'm not programmed now, am I? Why didn't the Committee programme me when they sent me here?'

'I was the top Plumber in the game. If you'd come here as a programmed assassin, I would have spotted you straight off. The Committee did the right thing – sending you here just as you are was their only move. If I hadn't done my job, I'd be lying on the floor with two L pills in my gut.'

Lacey said nothing. He was thinking of Sarah. Did he love her because, deep down, he'd always known the truth – that they were the same?

'You never had a chance, Mike.'

'What do you mean?'

Alice in Wonderland

'You can come through now.' The door opened and a woman came in. 'Hello, Mike,' Eva Kranic said.

'You see,' Dexter commented, 'I knew about you right from the start.'

'What are you going to do with me?'

'Programming you is easy.'

'What are you saying?'

'You know what a zombie state is, don't you?'

'Please, don't,' Lacey pleaded. 'I beg you.'

'Alice in Wonderland says that if you hear a certain phrase accompanied by an acoustic tone…I think you know the rest.'

'I don't believe you.'

Dexter signalled to Eva Kranic and she raised a silver coin-sized gadget.

'What's that?' Lacey stared at the object and felt his heart racing. An indefinable fear seized him. Somehow, he knew he'd seen this gizmo many times before; that whenever it was shown to him, he was engulfed by a void, timeless and infinite. He would be trapped in some weird dimension, with the certainty he could never escape under his own volition.

'It's a tone generator,' Dexter remarked.

No, it's so much more, Lacey thought. *It's oblivion, extinction, the end of all things.* 'What does it do?' he whispered, but he didn't need an answer.

Kranic took two steps forward until she was almost touching Lacey. 'Mad Hatter,' she said, pressing the gizmo. A single high-pitched tone pierced the room.

Lacey felt his body shuddering with an incredible inner violence. His lungs desperately tried to expand, to suck in a single breath of precious air. Burning pains radiated out to every part of his body. His arms and legs went numb. All he could see now was a long, black tunnel. His mouth hung open, futilely gasping for air. Every light in his head was switching off.

51

Wanted

Dexter edged open the curtains and peered at the screen of spruce trees surrounding his log cabin. The last 24 hours had brought proof he wasn't mad, but his mind had been screwed around with so much he might as well be. How can you live when true and false memories sit side by side, melded together, incapable of being separated? You can't be certain of a single thing you did in your life.

The only consolation was that at last he'd got to the heart of the Committee's inner world. *I know your secrets*, he thought. *I can hear your heartbeat. I'm going to destroy you.* He felt like an Old Testament prophet summoning the Almighty to smite Pharaoh and his armies. Only one other person had made him feel the hatred he was experiencing now.

Thick snow lay round his cabin. There were no other properties within half a mile, no prying eyes. Few people would be out searching for him in these conditions. He'd chosen this hideout in Great Kills Park on Staten Island months earlier. Any moment now, he would have his first guest. After reprogramming Lacey, he'd made him call the Committee to tell them he'd failed to deliver. He wrote Lacey's script for him: *He was too suspicious. I didn't get the chance to use the poison pills. He didn't buy the story about Montcrieff.*

He was hoping that if the Committee had any real evidence about Montcrieff, they'd use Lacey to deliver it to him. Other questions were worrying him. Why did the Committee want Montcrieff killed at his wedding? It didn't make sense. Why use Harris to do it? There had to be more to this.

Lacey was on time and Dexter ushered him inside, following him along a small corridor and into the lounge.

'The whole country's looking for you,' Lacey said stiffly.

Dexter walked over to the window, hung with thick blackout curtains, and checked one of his CCTV monitors. He had hi-tech motion-detection equipment installed all round the house. No one would take him by surprise. He stared at the package Lacey was carrying. 'What have you got there, Mike?'

'A DVD. It was left in locker 99 at Grand Central Station.'

Wanted

Dexter studied Lacey's face. He seemed confused, as if struggling to recall the exact connection between the locker and him.

'Am I the Delivery Manager?' Lacey said slowly.

The poor sap has really lost it, Dexter thought. He knew the feeling, remembering the days when crazy things had crowded into his head. It still happened from time to time. 'Sure, *you're* the Delivery Manager,' he replied, 'and soon you'll be delivering my regards to the Committee.' His attention switched back to Lacey's disc. 'You were telling me about the DVD. Something to do with Alice Through the Looking Glass?'

'The note that came with it said I was to tell you it was mailed to me by Terry before he died. It's video, proof that what Alice says about Montcrieff is true. I've to try again with the L pills. I mustn't fail.'

'Video footage?' Dexter took the disc from Lacey and went over to his DVD player. Reaching down to insert the disc, he glanced back at Lacey. 'I'll be settling down to watch this, but you have a call to make. I'll tell you what to say.'

'Who am I calling?'

'Friends of yours: the Committee.'

'The Committee?'

This guy's a zombie, Dexter thought. 'You know all about the Committee, don't you, Mike? We've just been talking about them.' He sat down and picked up the remote control. 'Have you noticed that Sarah Harris never smiles properly for the cameras? She always keeps her lips shut tight.' He glanced at Lacey, standing there as motionless as a shop dummy. 'It's because she's embarrassed by the gap between her front teeth.' He pressed the *play* button. 'One day soon it's going to get a whole lot fucking bigger.'

233

52

Messages

S arah was alone in her apartment, staring at her picture of a Peregrine falcon in Central Park. She took it on a beautiful sunny day. Now it was impossible to imagine sunshine in her world. It was Saturday night. In just over thirty-six hours, all of this would be over – one way or another. She might as well be lying in a coffin, waiting for the end. When the lid closed, who would care?

According to the Committee's latest intel, Robert's plan to kill her at the altar was designed to guarantee him the presidency. He would be propelled into the White House on a tide of public grief, he thought. He'd carry her, in her blood-spattered white wedding dress, out of the bronze doors of St Patrick's Cathedral, an image that would become as iconic as the Zapruder film, haunting the American imagination.

She could picture all of it, especially Robert carrying her body. There was something perversely comforting about it. The bride, on the day when she's never looked more beautiful, is slain, like something from a tragic ballad. Peace at last.

Get a grip, she urged herself. She couldn't let that bastard, that *monster*, win. The Committee had asked her to go back to Prohibition A tomorrow night to collect the weapon they wanted her to use to stop him, together with their plan of action. It had to be good, unbelievably good.

The whole situation was as bad a nightmare as she could conceive. She was helping crazy mass murderers kill a madman who might become president. Who was worse – she or they? If it wasn't for Robert plotting her assassination, she'd be doing everything she could to bring down the Committee. When the wedding was over, what then? If she survived, what would happen? They'd try to kill her, wouldn't they? She knew far too much.

She looked in a mirror and an exhausted face gazed back. Her hair had lost its sheen and hung lifelessly around her face. The harder she stared, the more the mirror seemed to turn into something else – a gleaming surface of blood. She thought of Clever Kitty being run over, of Carolyn Voronski naked on the altar at Dromlech Castle. She thought of Terry Redpath with half his head missing, of Dargo murdered by Nicki. The world had gone insane. Warren was dead. So many people she knew had joined him. She was

Messages

a death star. Everyone who came within her orbit was sucked in and destroyed.

She needed something to take her mind off it. For the past week, whenever she got a moment, she had read books about weddings. Lots of trivia was burned into her mind now, like the meaning of the word wedding. It came from the old English word *wed*, meaning promise. There would be many promises on her wedding day, all of them counterfeit. But there was also an older, deeper meaning – *to gamble*. That was right, wasn't it? It would be the biggest gamble of her life, with her life as the wager.

She stared at Robert's beautiful engagement ring. A circle with no beginning and no end – a symbol of eternity. Her marriage wouldn't last seconds. The third finger of the left hand was chosen as the ring finger because it was once believed that it had a special vein, 'the vein of love', running directly to the heart. *Love*? She hoped Robert would choke on the word.

And Dexter? Whenever she thought of him, everything went loco. Some part of her was terrified, but there was another feeling she couldn't pinpoint. She tried to kill him, and now he was determined to kill her. It seemed straightforward, but there was something else between them, she was certain. Even now, she found it oddly comforting that he might be watching her apartment. A Guardian Angel? He'd make sure no harm came to her before the wedding. But what then?

She had well and truly entered the Looking Glass world. The more she thought about it, the more Dexter seemed like the good guy. Everyone on his TWEP list, including her, deserved to die. They were all guilty. Only his motives were pure.

The phone rang. She stared at it, terrified. It sat next to her model of a Mississippi steamer. Phones had become nightmarish. They always brought bad news, like fluttering crows delivering messages from the heart of hell. She let the answerphone kick in. Her recorded message played and she waited for the person to speak. Madly, she hoped it was Dexter.

'Hi, Gorgeous.' Robert's voice was sickening, like treacle smeared over maggots. He was more than two-faced: he had a face for every occasion.

'Dreaming of Monte Carlo?' he said. 'Not long now. Everything will be fine. Speak to you soon.'

Monte Carlo? A dead dream, a destination that would never be reached. She leapt up, grabbed her Mississippi steamer from its glass cabinet, and hurled it against a framed picture of Robert hanging on the wall. '*Fuck you*,' she screamed then slammed her foot into a stack of wedding books on her coffee table, scattering them over the floor. In her mind was that idyllic image: she and Robert holding hands under a cherry blossom tree. How could he have fooled her so easily? Unlucky in her career, unlucky in love, unlucky in every fucking thing.

She remembered a story about why the marriage ceremony involved a best man, groomsmen, a maid of honour, and bridesmaids. It dated back to the days when a man would literally have to fight to get a wife. He and his companions, the groomsmen, would raid a village and drag away the victim. The woman's friends, the bridesmaids, would struggle to save her from being captured. The idea of marriage as an extension of war now made perfect sense to Sarah.

She switched off the light then sat in the dark on the floor, rocking back and forth. She imagined she was a baby again, being soothed to sleep by her mom. But she couldn't remember her mom. Nor her dad. Not even a photograph. Just a *No one at home* sign.

There was nothing for her to look forward to. She heard the siren of a police car in the street outside. Another emergency. Always an emergency. Some people went through life as if they'd never woken up. Others had a siren permanently ringing in their ears. She put her hand to her neck. In a clear locket hanging from a silver chain was the red rose petal she'd found. That pathetic, dried-up petal, with its sad, fading colour somehow gave her a glimmer of hope. Against all the odds, she'd found it in the wilderness. Would someone find her too? She clutched the locket as if it were a heartbeat. Tears rolled down her cheeks. All she did now was cry. Struggling over to the window, she opened the blinds and stared out into the night. The snow was falling. It was always falling.

In desperation, she tried to imagine a different wedding ceremony, one with the proper, happy ending. The organ would be playing the Wedding March as she left the cathedral with her handsome new husband, to the accompaniment of the cathedral's majestic bells, with rainbow-coloured confetti showering down. Then they would go on the most fantastic honeymoon. Thoughts like that were so *enticing*. But what was it that prayer said? – *Lead us not into temptation*. It was time to forget the dream and face the nightmare.

Thinking of a happy wedding had made her think of the ideal groom. The person whose face flashed up in her thoughts was the least likely imaginable.

It was John Dexter.

53

Betrayed

Sarah clutched the small black box the Committee had given her. It was Sunday night, the eve of her wedding, and she was back in Circle Ten. The box contained the weapon she was to use against Robert. As the Committee explained, it was the kiss of death. In every sense.

The Committee said their next appointment was with Mike Lacey. He would be going on an enforced vacation, starting that night. A new Delivery Manager would be assigned, and a new role found for Lacey.

Two soldiers escorted Sarah back to the jetty, but the gondola wasn't there. It appeared moments later with a single passenger – *Lacey*.

'Bastard!' Sarah screamed. 'I trusted you.'

Lacey looked uncertainly in her direction. He gave no sign that he even recognised her. He was much bulkier than normal, as if he'd put on a stone in weight. She tried to grab him as he stepped off the gondola. *Look me in the eye*, she wanted to shout. *Tell me why*. But before she could speak, one of the soldiers dragged her away while the other grabbed Lacey.

'Come with me, sir,' the soldier said to Lacey.

Sarah watched in amazement. Lacey was moving like a sleepwalker. They'd become so close over the last few days but now it was as if he didn't know her. Her rage leaked away, defused by Lacey's odd indifference.

The remaining soldier ordered Sarah into the gondola. She did as she was told, bewildered by Lacey's behaviour. The next few minutes passed in a blur. Before she knew it, she was at the front entrance.

'I've called a cab for you,' the soldier said, ushering her outside.

She stepped onto the snow-covered sidewalk and glanced around, shivering. The darkness seemed blacker than ever. As she looked for the cab, a desperate new idea formed. Maybe she could make a run for it; try to get out of the country. Why not leave the rats in their sack to fight to the death amongst themselves? The idea disintegrated. The Committee had eyes all over the world. Wherever she went, they'd track her down. Truth was, she couldn't get out of this. Going forward was all she could do because there was no way back.

Without warning, her pulse raced. She spun round and stared at the club. How could she have been so stupid? Now she understood why Lacey looked so overweight. She started to sprint back to the entrance. *Too late*. A blinding flash lit up the street, followed by a gut-wrenching noise. A blast wave hurled her to the ground. Windows and doors blew out all along the street, while clouds of smoke, dust and debris swirled around her. Hard snow, displaced by the explosion, fell back to earth with an eerie tinkling sound.

Sarah frenziedly patted herself, searching for signs of blood. *Nothing.* In the light of the fires blazing all around her, she saw a soldier's severed leg. When she shook her hair, glass sprayed everywhere. Scorching air was in her throat and chest, making her cough uncontrollably. The black box had dropped from her hands and now lay a couple of feet away, still intact.

Jesus fucking Christ – Lacey has blown up the Committee! Then another occurred to Sarah.

Was Robert in the club?

54

Cursed

It was Monday morning. What little sleep Sarah had managed in the last few days was always leaden and dreamless. Whenever her eyes closed she imagined going into a black tunnel and never coming out. Yet here she was, sitting in a hairdresser's, making the futile pretence that such a thing as normality still existed. Amanda, her usual stylist, was doing the honours. She could be relied on for her discretion.

Sarah's next appointment was with a beautician. She had arranged for her to come round to her apartment, but what was the point? She'd be the most beautiful corpse in the morgue, that's all. Now she understood why Lacey looked so weird. All that stuff about dissociation and Manchurian Candidates – it was all about him. He'd been turned into an uncomprehending Delivery Manager. Then Dexter – or Robert – had got to him and reprogrammed him, making him into a suicide bomber.

Again, she thought of running away. The Committee weren't there to stop her. But Dexter and Robert would never let her disappear, would they? They'd come after her one way or another. There would never be any rest. If she wanted to sleep easy ever again, she had to end this thing once and for all.

She remembered her freaky conversation with Robert on her cell phone minutes after the explosion. He had called to say that CNN was reporting a huge downtown explosion. Was she OK? She wasn't to worry about him. *Worry*? That was a laugh. It didn't matter any more. Robert was alive and that was that. He was supposed to love her but in reality he wanted her dead. Not that he'd do it himself. The Committee had heard much of his plan, but not the fine detail. A shooter, probably a sniper, would fire at the climax of the ceremony, but his identity and position were unknown. As for Dexter, whenever she pictured him, she imagined a ghost walking through walls. Somehow, some way, he'd get through. He had promised to kill her at her wedding and he wasn't one to break his promises.

She didn't speak while her hair was being cut. Staring into the mirror, all she could think of was how much of a failure she was – a freak, friendless and alone. There wasn't even someone to give her away at the cathedral, though Robert had said he would take care of that. From what she could make out, he'd done everything to make the wedding appear as normal as possible, practically inventing friends and companions for her. She would have bridesmaids, a Maid of Honour, the works – and she didn't know even one of them. All so that the pretence could be maintained to the end.

When she left the salon, Sarah passed a row of self-serve newspaper stands. Most of the headlines were screaming about the Prohibition A bombing, but it was the odd one out that caught her eye. She slammed some coins in and snatched out the paper. 'The Curse of the Wedding Dress,' the headline proclaimed. Underneath, it said, 'The awful secret Pino Monzelli didn't tell the bride.'

She read in astonishment that the design she'd chosen for her wedding dress wasn't one of Monzelli's new creations after all. Instead, it had a unique and dark history. Twenty years earlier, a beautiful Italian heiress commissioned the dress from Monzelli. The night before her wedding, she hanged herself in her bedroom, with the dress laid out in front of her. No one wanted anything to do with it after that. Monzelli said he'd longed for someone to wear it and was overjoyed when Sarah chose that design. Her measurements were identical to those of the tragic heiress.

Sarah threw the newspaper in a garbage can. Could things get any worse? She would walk down the aisle in the dress of a dead woman.

55

Till Death do us Part

As soon as Sarah stepped out of the limousine, the media surged forward. Two paparazzi, wildly clicking their cameras, dodged past the line of policemen. Sarah quickly lowered her veil. St Patrick's Cathedral loomed over her, dark and Gothic amidst the bright snow.

Her Maid of Honour greeted her with an extravagant air kiss while ten bridesmaids in pink satin dresses stood in a choreographed line on the cathedral steps. Robert had told her they were sisters, cousins and nieces of Tommy Henshaw and Jacob Spiegel.

Sarah stared up at St Patrick's twin spires, trying to avoid thinking of what lay ahead. *Those who are about to die, salute you.* She wanted to focus on her appearance, the only thing that day that gave her any pleasure. Her hair – perfectly cut, glossy, with sharp, stylish edges – looked as good as it ever had, while her face was superbly made up. Diamond earrings and matching bracelets, gifts from Robert's mother, made her feel that she was literally sparkling, on the outside if nowhere else.

Making her way towards the cathedral's entrance, she felt she'd joined Bluebeard's band of doomed brides. The bouquet of red roses she was clutching looked like a wound against the white of her wedding dress. Miss O'Mallen got it right all those years ago. Marriage was never going to work out for her. Maybe she'd always known it: that was why she cut up those dumb wedding photos.

More snow was falling. The flakes twinkled like stars before melting on her dress. St Patrick's always looked better in the snow, she thought. Gazing at the cathedral's bronze doors, she wondered if anyone had ever been murdered inside.

The wind was getting up and she struggled to keep her dress under control. As she walked up the steps, a man in a black hoodie and dark shades pushed past the police cordon and ran towards her. *Hell, this nut's going to attack me.*

'Don't marry the Trickster,' he yelled. Several security men hustled him away.

Trickster? Already, Sarah's nerves were fraying. *I'm Dead Woman walking.*

Prohibition A

A dozen birds flew into the air just ahead of her. An usher had opened a cage of white doves and there was an incredible cacophony as the birds soared into the frozen sky, wings fluttering. One dove was left behind. With one of its wings caught in the door, it twisted wildly, making a pathetic chirping noise. Sarah remembered the Peregrine falcon from her childhood, and how its owner was forced to kill it. She stared at the dove. *I'm so sorry.*

She again turned towards the cathedral's entrance. The doors were wide open. The ushers stood aside and she and her entourage went inside. After taking a few steps into the vestibule, she found a font of holy water. She dipped her right hand in then made the sign of the cross, just as she had as a kid when she was marched along to Mass every Sunday.

A young guy in jeans and red fleece, wearing a harness to support a mobile TV camera, filmed everything she did. Her death, or Robert's, was about to be immortalised on film. The media would get the coup of a lifetime, the Apollo to beat them all. What could be better: the death of the next president or his FBI bride – or both – in the perfect setting of St Patrick's Cathedral? Plus a surprise bonus: a ghost from the past in the shape of John Dexter, America's best agent whose own bosses had arranged his assassination.

An usher opened the doors leading to the nave and Sarah and her Maid of Honour stepped through, followed by the colourful procession of smiling bridesmaids, prompting the hundred-strong choir in the organ gallery to start singing. Handel's *Messiah* was their choice, or rather Robert's.

Everyone in the cathedral turned round to look at Sarah. A dozen TV cameras trained their lenses on her. She felt embarrassed and was glad she had her veil. Ahead, Cardinal Lenihan, the leader of New York's Catholics, waited in front of the altar, accompanied by an entourage of priests, deacons and altar boys. In front of them stood Robert and his best man Ian Longbottom. They too turned round to look at her.

Even from a distance, Robert, impeccably dressed in his morning suit, looked devastatingly handsome. Why had he chosen Longbottom as his best man? She realised she knew almost nothing about the *real* Robert.

Walking slowly down the aisle, she concentrated intently on each step. The cathedral's organ was playing, filling the building with a huge, majestic sound. She knew everyone would be whispering about her, commenting on how peculiar it was that she had no one to give her away. Her single act of defiance was to refuse to let Robert arrange for one of his friends to assume that role.

Till Death do us Part

Everywhere she looked, she saw blood-red roses. *Funeral wreaths.* She imagined casting them from the back of a black barge into a fast-flowing river, like bloody tears.

Some men were staring at her with that special glint in their eye, wondering, no doubt, what she had on under her dress. The answer, ridiculous in the circumstances, was the most expensive lingerie – new silk French knickers, white stockings, a garter belt and the traditional blue ribbon round her thigh. *Something old, something new, something borrowed, something blue.* She had even managed to squeeze herself into a white whalebone basque. If there had been enough time, she would have had it specially treated to make it bulletproof. *A Kevlar basque*, she thought. *How absurd has my life become?*

Two silver Heckler & Koch P9S pistols were strapped to her thighs. What kind of nuptial tradition was that? She'd been forced to get a seamstress to make a last-minute adjustment to her dress, to place two slits in the sides. The seamstress had been baffled by the request, but, then, it wasn't her life at stake. Now Sarah had easy access to her pistols. They were 'break glass in emergency' weapons, the last resort.

She wondered if anyone had ever been stabbed in the cathedral's aisles, if shots had rung out in the nave, if blood once ran down the steps of the high altar. There were only two spots where a sniper could get a good position. One was the organ gallery, but it would be too difficult for the shooter to conceal himself there, under the noses of the choir. There was one other place – the high-level camera gantries. Six of those camera positions, about twenty feet above the ground, were dotted around the cathedral. One of those six cameramen must be a fake, maybe two. Dexter could be up there too, but he might prefer to step out of the crowd with a silencer, or emerge from one of the dark alcoves, then vanish in the confusion.

Whichever way Sarah sliced it, she was certain she'd die here in St Patrick's, wearing the ring of the very man who had plotted her death.

Despite everything, there was incredible beauty in this place. Ravishing patterns of coloured light fell on her from stained glass windows. Glancing upwards, she took in the grand vaulted ceiling. Above all, she focused on the baldachin – the ornate bronze canopy that overarched the high altar. She'd read somewhere that the sculptures on the baldachin represented the theme of redemption. No such thing, she reflected. *Just damnation.*

This ceremony was a farce, complete madness. At any second, a shot could ring out. How long could she hold herself together? She was running on nerves and they were already stretched to the limit.

Prohibition A

She overheard women commenting on her dress, saying how enchanting it was. *The dress of a ghost.* She reached the end of the aisle and there she stopped. Mr and Mrs Montcrieff were sitting in the front pew. Mrs Montcrieff smiled at her and gave a little wave. As for Mr Montcrieff, he stared straight ahead. A small man with a weasel's face, he was so unlike Robert you'd never believe they were related. Grace Rebello sat on the other side of Mr Montcrieff. Sarah wondered if Rebello had any inkling of who her running mate really was.

She walked forward again, up several broad marble steps, aware of the shuffling feet of her bridesmaids. All the while, she was conscious of the TV cameras pointing at her, charting the course of her likely death. Over two thousand people were crammed inside the cathedral, while the TV cameras were broadcasting pictures to tens of millions. But none of them could *see* a thing.

As she glided over a marbled section of flooring decorated with black and white diamond tiles, two lines of young altar boys in white vestments stood on either side and waved censers back and forth. The sickly smell of incense was almost too much.

The part of the cathedral Sarah had entered was known as the Sanctuary, but it offered her no safety. At the far end stood Robert himself, with his back turned to her, shoulder to shoulder with Ian Longbottom.

Robert looked tall, strong, healthy – perfect husband material. Apart from the fact that he was a murderous psychopath. He twisted round and glanced at her. Then he smiled, such a curious smile. She forced herself to smile back then took her position beside him, on his left. Her Maid of Honour and bridesmaids stood several feet behind. The game had to be played to the end. *Thy kingdom come, thy will be done.*

Robert was wearing a blood red rose in his lapel, matching the roses in Sarah's bouquet. The sight of the red petals again made her think of the wound that would stain her dress when the sniper opened fire. She'd slump to the ground, scattering the roses around her.

Standing at the top of the red and white patterned marble steps in front of the high altar, Cardinal Lenihan looked magisterial in his pristine white vestments bordered with red silk. His head was directly in line with the tall golden crucifix rising above the altar.

'The Lord be with you,' he said into his microphone.

Several sound booms were positioned around the altar, to make sure the viewers at home heard every word clearly. This place had incredible acoustics. When the shooting began, it was bound to be unforgettable.

Till Death do us Part

'And also with you,' the congregation responded.

'Dearly beloved,' the cardinal said, 'we are gathered together here in the sight of God, and in the face of this congregation, to join together this man and this woman in Holy Matrimony. My brothers and sisters, to prepare ourselves to celebrate the sacred mysteries, let us call to mind our sins.'

The congregation gave the required response: 'I confess to Almighty God, and to you, my brothers and sisters, that I have sinned through my own fault, in my thoughts and in my words, in what I have done, and what I have failed to do...' Sarah found the words disturbing. Until the rehearsal, she'd last heard these words when she was a kid. They spooked her then...and they still did.

She let her tongue rest against the back of her lips. An hour earlier, she'd put on her lipstick – from the black box the Committee had given her. Bizarrely, it was pure style, a fantastic shade of metallic pink. But it came with a fatal ingredient – *potassium cyanide*. When Robert kissed her, it would be deadly. She never thought that lips could be a weapon, but, when Judas kissed Jesus, wasn't that murder? What had made the Committee think of this as an assassination method? It was so subtle, so *feminine*.

When she applied the lipstick, it made her so nervous she scarcely breathed. Was she about to kill herself? The Committee had supplied her with a newly developed antidote that they claimed would last for three hours. She'd taken the antidote, resembling a mini aspirin pill, just before putting on the lipstick. Now she had just over two hours left. If the lipstick wasn't removed by then, she'd die from cyanide poisoning. *Two hours*? How could anyone know for sure? Maybe she only had minutes. If anyone tried to give her the kiss of life, it would be the opposite.

Glancing at Robert, Sarah was amazed by how unruffled he was.

'May Almighty God have mercy on us and bring us to everlasting life,' the cardinal said. 'If any of you know cause why these two persons should not be joined together in Holy Matrimony, let him now speak, or forever hold his peace.' He glared at the congregation, as if inviting someone to come forward. Part of Sarah felt like doing it herself. Causes didn't come much bigger than knowing your groom wanted you dead in the next few minutes.

Out of the corner of her eye, she noticed someone stepping out from the front pew. Her heart thudded. Then she recognised the face – Jacob Spiegel. He went into the marble pulpit on the right of the Sanctuary. Standing in front of a lectern, he opened his Bible, coughed to clear his throat and waited for a signal from the cardinal.

Prohibition A

'A reading from the First book of Corinthians,' he began. 'Love is patient, love is kind...' As Sarah listened, part of her mind switched off, just as it had when she was a young girl enduring her weekly trip to Mass.

She kept looking around. When would Dexter make his move? At least she could keep an eye on Robert. The only one of his close friends she hadn't seen yet was Tommy Henshaw. That meant *he* was the shooter. He was Robert's head of security, had military training, and enjoyed access to all parts of the cathedral. It figured he'd do it. She looked up at the camera operators but couldn't see any of their faces.

Spiegel closed the Bible. 'This is the word of the Lord.'

'Thanks be to God,' the congregation replied.

'Robert and Sarah,' the cardinal declared. 'You have come together in this church so that the Lord may seal and strengthen your love in the presence of the Church's minister and this community.'

The further they went into the ceremony the more surreal it became. Sarah wasn't sure if she was in Wonderland or inside the Looking Glass.

'Christ abundantly blesses this love,' the cardinal continued. 'He has already consecrated you in baptism and now he enriches and strengthens you by a special sacrament so that you may assume the duties of marriage in mutual and lasting fidelity. And so, in the presence of the Church...'

The cold metal of Sarah's pistols pressed against her thighs. Her eyes darted around then focussed on one of the bronze carvings on the baldachin. It showed a man holding a dagger against the throat of a small boy: a depiction of Abraham and his son Isaac. Death in the cathedral. A bullet, a dagger...

A poison kiss?

Just behind the altar, a set of steps led down to the crypt. Was that where they'd take her body? She pictured herself on a cold slab, her skin waxy and pale, blood red flowers resting on her chest.

'I shall now ask you,' Cardinal Lenihan said, 'if you freely undertake the obligation of marriage, and to state that there is no legal impediment to your marriage. Are you ready freely and without reservation to give yourselves to each other in marriage?'

Robert searched for the nearest camera. 'I am.'

The cardinal coughed. Sarah realised it was a not-so-subtle prompt. 'I am,' she said too. A stranger's voice.

'Will you love her, comfort her, honour her, and, forsaking all others, keep only to her, so long as you both shall live?'

'I will,' Robert said.

246

Till Death do us Part

Then it was Sarah's turn. 'I will.' She wondered if the words would crack like glass and slash her mouth. *I'm ashamed of myself.* This was supposed to be a solemn ceremony, with eternal, once-in-a-lifetime vows, but everything she and Robert said was a lie. The ceremony was a charade and these words meant nothing. There was one truth only – that at least one person would die today.

'Robert Francis Montcrieff, will you take Sarah Veronica Harris for your lawful wife, according to the rite of our holy Mother the Church?' the cardinal asked.

'I will.' Robert smiled. It made Sarah want to retch.

'Sarah Veronica Harris, will you take Robert Francis Montcrieff for your lawful husband according to the rite of our holy Mother the Church.'

'I will.' The words sounded ridiculous. The only thought in Sarah's mind was of a clock ticking. How many seconds of life did she have left?

The cardinal instructed them to join their right hands, the symbol of their union. As their flesh touched, a shiver ran through Sarah. She didn't attempt to look at Robert. She wondered if she'd be able to kiss him. The closer the moment came, the more outlandish it seemed.

Not long now until Robert placed the ring on her finger. Jacob Spiegel kept glancing up at the choir gallery. That must mean that Henshaw was up there after all instead of one of the camera gantries. Spiegel was probably signalling to him to get ready.

The cardinal began to recite the climactic words of the ceremony. Robert carefully repeated his words. 'I call upon these persons here present to witness that I, Robert Francis Montcrieff do take thee, Sarah Veronica Harris, to be my lawful wedded wife, to have and to hold from this day forward, for better for worse, for richer for poorer, in sickness and in health, to love and to cherish.'

Sarah waited for Robert to say the final words. Would he choke on them? 'Till death do us part,' he declared without hesitation. Sarah's stomach lurched. When she glanced at a clock on the wall, the hands were moving impossibly slowly.

Then it was her turn to say the binding words. More than ever she felt they were shrapnel and that as each emerged it would gash her mouth. Mad images stampeded through her mind. She saw herself as a queen in a red dress standing in a field of red poppies, a queen walking through a forest of red trees, stepping into a red boat about to cross a lake of blood. She was in a graveyard, full of red graves, red coffins, red headstones as far as the eye could see. Christ, she was terrifying herself. Her eyes had become enormous.

Prohibition A

She gazed at the world through a film of tears. Who would protect her from Dexter? No sign of him yet. When would the ghost appear?

The cardinal blessed them, and sprinkled holy water over their joined hands. The time had come for the ring to be placed on Sarah's finger. As soon as it was, she was as good as dead.

'The ring?' the cardinal prompted. Ian Longbottom took a simple gold ring from his pocket and placed it on the prayer book offered by one of the cardinal's assistants. The cardinal sprinkled more holy water on the ring and made the Sign of the Cross over it. 'May the Lord bless this ring,' he said, 'which you give as the sign of your love and fidelity. Amen.' He then handed the ring to Robert.

Sarah trembled as Robert turned to her. When she stretched out her left hand, Robert gripped her wrist. With his right hand, he placed the ring against her thumb. He said, 'With this ring I thee wed.' Then he moved the ring to her next finger. 'With my body I thee worship.' Then the next finger. 'And with all my worldly goods I thee endow.' He slipped the ring over her wedding finger.

'In the name of the Father, of the Son, and of the Holy Spirit. Amen,' Lenihan said. It was time for the end of the ceremony. Closure, *one way or another*.

'You have declared your consent before the Church,' Lenihan announced. 'May the Lord in his goodness strengthen your consent and fill you both with his blessing. What God has joined together, let no man put asunder. Amen.' He gave a signal and a deacon stepped forward with a censer and waved it backwards and forwards, producing a cloud of choking incense.

'I now pronounce you man and wife,' the cardinal said finally.

Sarah felt nauseous.

'The groom may now kiss his bride,' the cardinal said.

The crisis Sarah knew had to come was only seconds away. *In the midst of life, we are in death.* That's what it said in the Bible, wasn't it? *A time to live and a time to die.*

Robert took a step forward and gently lifted Sarah's veil. He lingered, preparing for the spectacular kiss that he no doubt believed would clinch him the presidency.

Glancing at the cardinal, Sarah was astonished to see his eyes darting everywhere. Then she saw it – a tiny red dot from a rifle's laser aiming system tracking across his white vestments. Instantly, she understood – *Henshaw was lining up his shot.* The cardinal probably didn't understand

248

what was going on. At any moment, the red dot would switch to the back of her head and Henshaw would fire.

The deacon holding the censer dropped it and pushed the cardinal to the ground.

'Where the fuck is he?' he shouted.

The congregation gasped. Sarah couldn't believe what had just happened. Her gaze switched to Robert. He was equally astonished. The deacon put his hand up to his face and began to peel away the flesh. Sarah screamed. Everyone screamed.

A *mask*, the deacon was wearing a mask – *Dexter*!

Sarah once heard a survivor of a car wreck saying that, just before impact, time lost its meaning. Now, staring at that face, she understood. A new set of chemicals flooded her body and they obeyed different rules, existed in an alternative universe where a second might as well be the age of the earth. Before the Big Bang, there was no such thing as time. How could that be? She heard a loud crack. Something slammed against her with tremendous violence. She crashed to the ground, her shoulder blazing with pain. As she lay on the cold marble steps in front of the high altar, a sensation of sickness overwhelmed her. She was going into shock.

It had actually happened. A boiling hot bullet was inside her body. Somehow, she was still here, still breathing, still alive. All the commotion must have distracted the sniper and he didn't get off a clean shot. Wave after wave of agony pulsed through her. All around her, people were screaming, most of them stampeding towards the exits. With her ear against the floor, she could hear their scuffling feet, feel the vibrations of their panic.

Then she heard Spiegel's voice. 'Take out the fucking deacon, Tommy. For God's sake, take him out.' Another shot rang out, but the bullet crashed into the altar, sending up a shower of marble fragments. Sarah raised her head as best as she could, trying to shut out the pain, struggling to see what was happening.

Blood pumped out of her shoulder. It wasn't a mortal wound, not yet at least, but if she didn't get some medical treatment soon, she'd bleed to death. Then there was her cyanide lipstick. If she didn't re-administer the antidote in time, she'd die from that instead. She tried to wipe away the lipstick, but her arm flopped uselessly.

Help me, she mouthed.

Life became a mosaic. Her visual field split into compartments. Dexter was in one, raising his robes and pulling out two pistols from holsters strapped to his sides. In another, Robert was punching him, sending him sprawling backwards. In a third, Dexter was springing back to his feet, wheeling and firing. There was rapid gunfire. Every kind of noise broke out. The slaughterhouse had come to life.

Robert threw himself behind one of the pews at the side of the Sanctuary. Sarah could see him looking over at her, no doubt praying she was dead. *Bastard.* She wished she'd given him the fatal kiss she'd planned. *I hope Dexter shoots him*, she thought. But even that thought struggled to survive in the black void that was locking her, increasingly tightly, inside her own skull.

Another shot went off. Sarah couldn't see where it came from but she saw Dexter falling. Blood spurted from his left arm. He rolled over and fired off several more shots. Someone groaned in one of the pews behind Sarah. More shots. She couldn't work out who was doing the shooting. Robert's security team probably. She wanted to crawl to a safer position, but was practically paralysed. *I can't reach for my pistols*, she thought, *I can't do anything*.

Dexter had taken cover behind the altar. As for Robert, his best man Ian Longbottom was crawling towards him, pistol readied.

'Dexter got Tommy and Jacob,' Longbottom said. 'You'd better get out of here, Robert. I'll cover you.'

Sarah couldn't keep her eyes open any longer. She lay still. Her breathing had become shallow, but she could still hear.

'What about Sarah?' Robert said. 'Is she dead?'

'I don't know. She's definitely been hit.'

The words were tailing off, disappearing into a growing haze in Sarah's mind. She was so sleepy. *I'll lose consciousness soon*, she thought.

Now she realised how her life would end – as a fake bride in front of an altar of a God she didn't believe in, with cyanide on her lips. There was nothing she could do about it, nothing she could do about anything. The lights in her head were going out one by one. Soon, shadows and whispers were all that remained. A faint, monochrome world, with a fading heartbeat.

****

A blast of freezing air revived Sarah. She was outside. As her eyes focused on the doors of the cathedral, she tried to figure out what was happening. Robert, she realised, was carrying her, but he'd come to a halt and was staring at a silent crowd packed into Fifth Avenue.

Till Death do us Part

People scarcely seemed to be breathing. There was something about them, as if they were too shocked to move. Even the paparazzi were frozen in place.

She managed to tilt her head towards a bank of TV monitors in the back of one of the multitude of TV vans parked outside the cathedral.

Then she understood.

Three sets of unbelievable images were stamped on the screens, as astonishing as those on the day the Twin Towers came down.

One showed hysterical people being led away by police from a shattered, blazing building surrounded by fire trucks and ambulances. Twisted pieces of metal and broken glass lay strewn around. Fire fighters and paramedics, looking stunned, rushed past camera crews while priests administered the last rites to horribly mangled and charred bodies. Smoke, dust and debris were everywhere. The wrecked building was very familiar – the *White House*.

The second set of pictures showed a woman in handcuffs, surrounded by FBI agents. A caption ran along the bottom of the screen saying, 'Breaking News – the presidential candidate was taken to Montgomery Naval Hospital. An emergency operation is underway. Mr Lawson is not expected to...

But it was the third set of pictures that held Sarah's attention. Robert's face dominated every image. He was defiling the corpse of Director David Warren, licking blood off the bloated belly.

Now Sarah understood the thoughts going through the minds of the crowd. In the last minutes of the wedding ceremony, horror had come to America. The President had been blown up and someone had shot the second presidential candidate, Tom Lawson. As for the third candidate, the favourite to win tomorrow's election...

They thought he was insane, didn't they?

Sarah coughed. She was desperately ill. When two paramedics started edging towards her, Robert let her go and she slumped to the ground. Lying there, she had a weird view of Robert. He took out a pistol and pointed it at the crowd.

'Back off or I'll blow the whole fucking lot of you away,' he snarled like a B-movie gangster. A path through the crowd cleared for him. The police didn't attempt to intervene, probably fearing a shoot-out. He advanced down the steps, pointing his pistol at anyone who moved. Then he sprinted towards a yellow cab that had stopped at a red light.

Where can he go? Sarah wondered. She saw a paramedic preparing an injection for her. From one of the TVs, she heard an announcer's voice: *The Pentagon has declared Martial Law. Curfew will commence at six o'clock.*

251

Prohibition A

All National Guard soldiers must report for duty immediately. The Joint Chiefs of Staff issued the following statement...

She couldn't keep her eyes open any longer. Everything was growing dark.

56

Love Hurts

Dexter's clothes were heavily bloodstained, but no one was looking at him now that he'd got rid of his deacon's robes. He'd managed to escape from the rear exit of the cathedral where he was caught up in the flood of hysterical people squeezing through the doors and scattering in all directions. A rumour was going round that the President had died in an explosion at the White House. An irrelevance, Dexter thought. He cared only about his mission. Got to get patched up quickly.

It took him ten minutes to reach his back-up unit, waiting nearby in a Land Rover. Eva Kranic was in the back, getting an emergency medical kit ready. She jumped out and helped him inside. He lay down in the back and let Kranic examine his wound. His head swam as she probed the area with her fingertips. He wanted to vomit.

'Good news and bad,' Kranic whispered as the Land Rover got going, making its way past a convoy of police cars racing towards the cathedral. 'The bullet went clean through, but there's a lot of damage and you're bleeding heavily.'

Dexter was hardly listening. His mind flashed back to what happened in front of the altar. He'd seen Harris lying face down a few yards away, her white dress red with blood. Probably dead. A sniper beat him to it. Who was the shooter? He hadn't expected that, not at all. He couldn't work out why right now, but he knew Montcrieff was behind it. That sonofabitch. Wasn't Harris supposed to kill him?

He'd seen Montcrieff crawling out from behind a pew towards Harris's body and couldn't figure out what he was up to. He tried to line up a shot at Montcrieff, but as soon as he moved, he came under fire from at least four shooters. They had to be Montcrieff's men or secret service. Either way, they pinned him down. Then he looked at the blood pumping out of the gaping hole in his upper left arm. Not good, not good at all.

Momentarily, he'd thought of the real deacon lying drugged in the crypt. He'd ambushed him shortly before the ceremony began, giving him a knockout drug then hiding him. He told the man's colleagues that the deacon was taken ill with appendicitis and he was the last-minute replacement. It would be hours before the deacon was discovered, not that it mattered.

Prohibition A

He wondered why he'd let the ceremony go on for so long. Every minute that passed had increased his chances of being discovered. He should have fired as soon as Harris arrived at the altar and stood beside Montcrieff. There they were – together – right in front of him. But he'd let it drag on. He knew why. He wanted to make this assassination a work of art. He'd planned it meticulously night and day since news of the engagement broke, wanting people to marvel at it, to talk about it for years. It would be a memorial, a warning to every other Harris and Montcrieff who thought they could get away with it.

But he waited too long. Now he was in no shape to go after them. Got to cut his losses and get out. Anyway, he had Plan B, didn't he? Whatever happened, Montcrieff was finished. He'd made sure Lacey's DVD showing Montcrieff murdering Warren had just received its world premiere.

It was only as he got close to the exit that he became conscious of tears in his eyes. The sight of Sarah's body – it had been unendurable. He found himself praying it wasn't true. How could *that* be? It was impossible. He'd lived for this moment.

Kranic waved her hand in front of his eyes. 'Are you listening, John? We need to get you fixed up properly. We have a safe-house organised, and a doctor.'

He ignored her, concentrating instead on the radio traffic of the emergency services at the cathedral. Frantic shouting was punctuated by hysterical messages about the President and other members of the Cabinet. Army units were on their way to New York, Washington and Chicago. Then he heard the news he was waiting for – a message that Harris was being taken to hospital in an ambulance.

'Intercept that ambulance,' he barked.

'You're not up to it, John. That wound is bad. There will be other days.'

'No, it's today or never.'

There was a long pause, then Kranic said abruptly, 'Do you still have feelings for her?'

Anger surged through Dexter. He had to fight to control it. 'I failed, didn't I?' He threw out his hand. 'Roll down the window.' He took a deep breath of the cold, fresh air that rushed in. The sun broke through some clouds.

'Know what a sucker's gap is?' he asked, gazing at the unexpected sunlight. He didn't wait for a reply. 'It's when there's a brief break in the weather. The shit stuff goes away and the sun shines. Everyone thinks the worst is over, but soon the shit is back, twice as bad.'

Love Hurts

'I don't understand, John.'

Dexter noticed Kranic staring at the locket round his neck. 'Just concentrate on getting me to Harris's ambulance.' When he closed his eyes, all he could think of was what Sarah said to him in Central Park just before she shot him. As the Land Rover accelerated along Fifth Avenue, he mouthed her words: *I love you to death.*

57

Soul River

General Clark stared at the pictures from the cameras monitoring the street outside Prohibition A. Montcrieff would come here. There was nowhere else, was there? Scaffolding had been erected to stabilise the exterior of the building, but there were no workers here today. There were no security guards.

Clark winced as another pain ripped through him. He ought to have stayed in hospital but they'd assured him his wounds were superficial. Even so, they hurt like hell. Last night, they gave him morphine for the pain. Now, he only had aspirin. It was essential that his head remained clear. But he was the lucky one. No one else had survived. When the bomb went off, he was questioning one of the soldiers about what happened between Lacey and Sarah. The soldier took the full force of the blast. It was a Dexter op, wasn't it? Somehow, he'd managed to reprogramme Lacey. The bastard was as good as ever. He'd have to be dealt with fast. But first things first.

Clark shivered. A fever was coming on, but today he couldn't afford to be ill. He was at the centre of the web. Everything depended on him. He had unleashed the greatest forces and if he wasn't there to control them, disaster was certain. The operation at the White House went perfectly, the entire Cabinet being wiped out. It hadn't stopped there. Tom Lawson was dead. The Speaker of the House had joined him. The Supreme Court went the same way as the White House. Every symbol of the old regime was wiped out; everyone in the presidential succession had been eliminated. The Constitution was silent on what should happen next. So, he would take over. The military would offer unconditional support. He'd spent years cultivating the friendship of senior generals, admirals and airforce commanders. He shuddered, recalling a line by Yeats. *Things fall apart; the centre cannot hold*. It was his job to make sure it held. He was prepared to do anything.

First, every loose end had to be addressed. He hadn't hesitated to get rid of Dargo when he started finding out more than was good for him. It was always dangerous to let people know too much. Most organisations carried out their cleaning operations when things got messy. His philosophy was to start cleaning before anything was spilled.

He dangled his hand in the water. Was it dumb to have chosen to sit in this gondola to await Montcrieff's arrival? He glanced up at the boatman and wondered if the soldier took any pleasure in dressing up in those odd black robes and that mask. His peculiar assignment would soon be ending.

Clark glanced around. It was amazing how little damage had been done down here in the cavern. The blast from Lacey's bomb was directed upwards thanks to the solid granite that lined Circle Ten.

There was a sudden movement on the monitor in front of Clark. A smile crept over his face. A cab was heading at speed down the street towards the entrance. The cab screeched to a halt and a figure leapt out into the snow.

Microphones picked up every sound. 'Get lost,' Montcrieff growled at the driver, then watched as the cab sped away. He turned and gazed at the scaffolding. There was something about his body language. He knew he was expected. Everyone is searching for the golden thread that leads them out of the labyrinth, aren't they? Montcrieff knew exactly where to come.

Montcrieff stepped inside, cameras tracking his every step. He stopped briefly to listen to the sirens of the police cars closing in from all directions. A huge posse was in pursuit. Detectives, cops, FBI agents, journalists, ordinary Joes – they were all chasing him down. The hunt was on, the hounds in full cry, baring their teeth.

They all want a piece of Montcrieff, Clark thought, a souvenir to hang on their walls as a trophy. *What do I want from him*? He found it odd that he was asking himself that question. After all, there was never any doubt. They had spotted years earlier that this man was smart and charismatic enough to go all the way. Warren, in particular, took a special interest in Montcrieff's career. Would he have made a good president? There was no doubting his ruthlessness and ambition, but it was all academic now.

Warren and the Committee had gone. Clark alone was left to ensure they lived up to their billing and did great things. There was nowhere to hide, no excuses. At least he had Alice in Wonderland in the pipeline – the key to everything.

Alice Through the Looking Glass was all about manufacturing brainwashed assassins. Alice in Wonderland was quite different – its purpose to make mind control an everyday occurrence, to allow the manipulation of others' thoughts and memories during a casual conversation. Ultimately, to allow entire populations to have their behaviour fully controlled. Every nation would bow to America. The American Dream would be elevated to the World Dream. Lacey was the prototype of the new project. How did Dexter find out about it? The irony almost amused Clark – the star of the original wiping out his replacement in the sequel.

257

Prohibition A

There was still a long way to go with Wonderland, but Clark had no doubt it would come good. Then everything was possible. He shuddered. Did he believe it? Did he *really* believe it? In a lifetime of plotting, double-dealing, betrayal, assassination, he thought he'd seen everything. Human nature had been laid bare for him, and it was repulsive. He believed he could no longer be astonished by anything. But one thing today changed all of that, bringing him more pain than all of his wounds. Even now, it was hard to accept. He closed his eyes. The moment when Sarah was shot flashed into his mind. For a moment, he caught the sickening scent of his own fear. His panic had one cause – his terror that his daughter was dead.

He'd always imagined he would be indifferent when the moment came. Or even happy. But it was the opposite. Some part of him – a deep, hidden, terrified component within the relentless, single-minded machinery of his life – felt nothing but infinite love for Sarah. *God help me*, he thought, recalling how beautiful Sarah had looked in her white wedding dress. He'd felt the aching pride of a father in his talented, smart, radiant daughter.

He breathed in hard. The cold air was sharp, like a blade cutting through the stale air in his lungs. Shutters in his mind were being thrown open for the first time, allowing all kinds of screams, nightmares, every kind of dread, to rush out. Was he losing his nerve? Was he – he thought of the right word – *afraid*? One moment everything made sense, the next it was falling apart. Was this how Montcrieff felt too?

Anxiety rose in him like flames. He was breathless, his lungs struggling to restore a vanishing equilibrium. Doubts plagued him. Would his plan work? If it did, he himself would be President by the end of the day. Was he ready? He had to be.

He watched as Montcrieff made his way through the foyer, through the Limbo Lounge, through the doors and then down the long, descending corridor to the underground river. In the end, they all come to hell.

Finally, Montcrieff was standing at the jetty, looking unsurprised.

Clark gestured at him to get onboard.

Montcrieff, giving only a glance in the direction of the ferryman, didn't argue. He slumped into the seat opposite Clark. Lazily, he lifted his pistol. 'Who are you?' he asked.

Cop cars were outside the club. There was a clamour of shouting voices upstairs. Not much time left.

'Does it matter?' Clark replied.

'You *know*, don't you?'

'What do you mean?'

Soul River

Montcrieff stared into the water. 'I loved her. You know that, don't you?' A sentimental smile flickered over his face. 'I remember the exact moment when I knew I was in love with her. We were beneath a cherry blossom tree. I reached out and took her hand.'

Clark's spine tingled. He started to shiver. *Oh my God.* He'd once heard Sarah giving exactly the same answer when she was asked how she fell in love with Montcrieff. Warren had told him that a cherry blossom tree played a prominent part in her brainwashing. *Why didn't I realise?* It was so obvious, staring him in the face all along. His shivering grew stronger. Sarah and Montcrieff couldn't have fallen in love at exactly the same moment in exactly the same place in exactly the same way so soon after being introduced to each other. That meant one thing – it was an *invented* episode, an implanted memory, a fabrication created by brainwashing. Warren's work.

Instantly, Clark understood everything. Warren had taken such a close interest in Montcrieff's career because he was secretly brainwashing him. He had added him to Sarah and Dexter as the primary subjects of Alice Through the Looking Glass. All along, Warren was plotting against the Committee. He must have had his own plans. Maybe he wanted to eliminate the rest of the Committee, to put Montcrieff in the White House as his puppet. He remembered one of Warren's most provocative comments: *I want to be the perfect conman, capable of conning everyone all of the time.* The bastard had come terrifyingly close.

Now he understood another thing that had baffled him. Montcrieff's plan to kill Sarah at the wedding was no aberration, but something horrifically deliberate – a calculated, methodical, logical outcome of a particular philosophy, a very familiar philosophy – Sin for Salvation. This was nothing less than Montcrieff's Prohibition A, his ultimate sin providing him with his instant passport to paradise. Warren must have used Montcrieff as the first guinea pig for Sin for Salvation. Christ, Montcrieff was probably the leader of the cult. Was Warren insane? Nothing could have been more dangerous than having the President as the high priest of the most lethal cult ever devised.

'Why did you kill Warren?' he asked.

'There's something wrong with me, isn't there?' Montcrieff's voice was trembling. 'Warren did things to me. I have these flashbacks. Nightmares. I'm suspended in a tank of yellow fluid. I don't have a single hair anywhere on my body.'

'Revenge?'

Montcrieff nodded. 'You're one of Warren's colleagues, aren't you?' He half-heartedly pointed his pistol again. 'I ought to kill you too.'

'You won't,' Clark said.

'Why?' Montcrieff asked.

'You know the answer.'

They both heard *What a Wonderful World* playing on a ghetto blaster in the street outside, the sounds being picked up by Clark's hidden microphones. The moment had come.

Clark signalled to the boatman. The gondola moved off into the middle of the first tunnel, then stopped. The water lapped gently against its sides. The only light came from a couple of flickering torches.

Clark studied Montcrieff's face and was sure he detected the faintest of smiles. Montcrieff *knew*. He was going home. A second later, it was over. The ferryman broke Montcrieff's neck with one expert twist.

Cause and effect.

They quickly dumped the body into the water. It floated for a moment, surrounded by bubbles, before sliding under. Already, Clark's thoughts were moving on. Now they focused on one thing only.

Sarah.

58

End Game

Sarah's eyes flicked open. *I'm still alive.* For a moment, she felt a surge of almost drunken exhilaration. She'd gazed into the abyss and it had gazed right back. Yet, somehow, she was still here.

The joy disappeared. Her vision was blurred and she wasn't sure where she was. A vehicle of some kind. She could tell that much from the noise and vibrations. Gradually, her eyes focused. The vehicle had a white roof and white sides. There was a metal apparatus and various tubes. So, an ambulance. They were taking her to hospital. But why no siren? She shook her head. The Committee had reached out from the grave and killed the President and Tom Lawson. So, who would take over now? Did it matter? New songs, same old tunes. She was too depressed to care.

No one was in the back of the ambulance with her. She had tight strapping on her shoulder. They'd given her a strong pain-killing injection. She felt better than she had in the cathedral. Still groggy, but at least the sick feeling had gone. Gazing down, she saw that she was still in her wedding dress. Was she a married woman? Maybe a widow, maybe something else. It seemed so long ago, a lifetime.

What had happened to Robert? To Dexter? Maybe the nightmare was over. She guessed they were either both dead or in custody. The next moment she sat bolt upright. *I haven't taken the antidote.* In panic, she raised her right hand. Her own ring was safely in place on her middle finger. Using her left hand, she flipped open the Celtic cross in the middle of the ring. Underneath was a secret compartment, containing four tiny white antidote pills, but as she tried to pour the pills into her hand, the ambulance rocked. The pills spilled out and scattered over the floor. Horrified, she tried to get out of the stretcher to retrieve them, but a searing pain ripped through her shoulder, and she slumped back.

The ambulance came to a halt. She prayed they'd reached the hospital. The rear doors opened and cold air rushed in. All she could see was snow. A man in a luminous yellow paramedic's uniform, wearing a baseball cap and shades, climbed in.

'Which hospital are we going to?' she groaned. 'I've dropped my pills on the floor. Please, you have to get them.'

261

Prohibition A

The man sat down beside her, with his back turned to her, and slowly removed his hat and sunglasses. Puzzled, she looked up at him. As he turned towards her, the world moved into slow motion.

John Dexter was pointing a pistol at her head.

'Till death do us part, isn't that how it goes?' he said in a brittle voice.

He peered at her bloodstained dress and seemed to take satisfaction. 'The lowest circle of hell is reserved for traitors. Cassius, Brutus, Judas – *you*.' He leaned forward. 'What sort of dreams does someone like you have? Do you wake up in the middle of the night, screaming? Does the dark haunt you? Do you dread being alone with your guilt? But people like you don't feel anything, do you?'

Sarah closed her eyes and turned her head away. Her heart was thudding. Darkness gripped her mind. Then, slowly, almost imperceptibly, tiny points of light pierced the dark as if dozens of people were shining torches into a hole. Eventually there was so much light she could see perfectly. What she was looking at was her own private movie in perfect Technicolor.

She was in Central Park on a beautiful day, wearing a red crop top and rainbow-coloured hot pants. A little kid in a Spiderman costume ran past a tall figure in a yellow suit. She strained to see who the man was. Indistinct at first, his face gradually became clearer. Soon, she could see it in sharp focus. It was the face she'd always known it would be.

Dexter's.

A deadening realisation seized Sarah. Dexter was no rogue agent that she shot in an underground parking garage in Baltimore. He was the love of her life whom she gunned down in broad daylight in Central Park moments after he asked her to marry him. Her heart, stricken, contracted so hard she thought she'd die.

'The day I proposed to you was the happiest of my life,' Dexter whispered. 'If I hadn't been wearing my bulletproof vest...'

Memories bubbled up in Sarah's mind like pages of books she'd read long ago. She remembered a man in a grey suit standing in front of her. *Red Queen* – that's what he said. Then he pressed a button on a gadget that emitted a piercing tone. She remembered it all, the silver pistol, the red balloon, the little kids playing on the rusting swings. She recalled the single shot. Most of all she remembered how much she loved John. Tears rolled down her cheeks.

In an instant, she understood everything. The Committee had played with her mind, changed her memories, just as John always claimed had been done to him. Every part of his story was true. The Committee had twisted their minds, brainwashed them, turned them into unwitting Manchurian Candidates. Maybe it was done to Montcrieff too. All of them were marionettes. The puppet-masters had controlled every part of their lives, but now all the strings were cut. They were cast adrift in a senseless universe.

If she ever escaped, she'd have to reconstruct herself, retrace her life, separate false memories from the truth, discover who she really was. Was it even possible? Somehow, she'd have to track down Alice Through the Looking Glass and learn everything that was done to John, to her, and Montcrieff too. Did her parents really die when she was young? Maybe she had brothers and sisters. Her life, once so solid and real, was dissolving in front of her eyes.

She and Dexter were the same: two victims smashed to pieces on rocks they could never have avoided, with no chance of things ever going back to the way they were. She knew what had to happen. Putting her right hand through the specially cut hole in her wedding dress, she placed her hand round the pistol grip and manoeuvred the gun into position.

'You were my life,' Dexter said. 'How could you do it?' He gripped her jaw with his left hand, forcing her to open her eyes and look at him. 'Don't you remember? For God's sake, tell me you remember.'

For a moment, all Sarah could think of was that delicious physical contact but, as more memories rushed in, a deep horror settled on her, offering only one way out. Her mind filled with an image of the falcon she saw in her childhood. It was born to fly higher, to go further than ordinary creatures, travel places others couldn't go. Wounded, it would never do those things again, never fly as high, never be so strong. In time, it would hate itself. Its wish, she knew, would be to be put out of its misery. *The strong can't be weak.* Hot tears welled in her eyes.

She wondered how badly wounded Dexter was, mentally as much as physically. Could he ever again be the way he was, do the things he'd done, the things he was born for? *The strong can't be weak*, she said to herself, thinking of what she must do. She'd fire a single shot through her wedding dress, through the blanket partially covering her. A headshot this time, to make sure. It would be over, forever. Peace, for both of them. She owed it to him.

Dexter grabbed her arms. 'Even now,' he said, 'even now.' He was making it impossible for her to move her arms. He knew about the pistols. 'Tell me you remember,' he said again. '*Tell me*,' he repeated, but his voice was less firm than before. Maybe it was emotion, or maybe he was weakening from his wounds.

Prohibition A

His eyes tracked down to the locket around her neck where she'd placed the red rose petal she found near West Point. A shuddering jolt convulsed through her as she recalled John putting a red rose in the buttonhole of the lapel of his yellow suit just before he proposed to her. She knew this rose petal was from that same rose and that John had saved it all this time, losing it that night, where she picked it up. A link through eternity, despite all the odds, all the obstacles – their hearts connected, entwined forever.

'Tell me,' Dexter insisted.

He can't forget, Sarah thought; *he can't let go. He has to know it was true, that it really happened, that I once truly loved him. I did*, she said to herself. *I do. More than I can bear.*

Closing her eyes again, she relived every moment they had spent together. Especially, she remembered his kisses – sometimes tender, sometimes passionate, always blazing with love. She loved him then and loved him still. She would always love him. It was the only true thing in her life. Even though the Committee had done everything to destroy her love, it had survived in her heart. That's why she was so confused in the last few days, why John was always on her mind. It was why she'd found him so attractive even when she thought he was going to kill her. It was why she wanted to hear his voice on her answerphone the other night, why she wanted to speak to him in the wilderness near West Point when he saved her life, why she thought of him almost as a Guardian Angel, protecting her against all threats, at least until her wedding. Her love for John was the one thing she could be sure of, the only certainty amidst all the lies that had been force-fed to her for God knows how many years. It was always calling to her, making her feel unsettled with Robert, telling her something was terribly wrong.

Could they put the past behind them, forget what they had done and what had been done to them? It was futile. The past would never give them peace. This was a man she'd shot at point blank range. Things like that can't be set aside. They're too extreme. Everything is coloured by them.

Dexter placed his fingers lightly against her lips. 'Speak to me,' he said. 'You remember, don't you?'

When he did that, Sarah knew what she had to do. 'Kiss me, John.' She kept her eyes closed, imagining the look of astonishment in his eyes. Part of him would be repulsed, appalled, trying to figure out what was going on. Another part would be overwhelmed with remembrance of how things used to be, with memories of those priceless whispers of love. There would be so much desire to bring those memories back to life, to sculpt them again, fuller, more beautiful than ever. Against his better judgment, he would lean forward and press his lips against hers.

She knew he would do that because that's exactly what she wanted to do too. She waited. In the next second, John would either shoot her or kiss her. But choice is an illusion, isn't it? A second later, she felt his lips on hers. A tremendous rush ran through her body, as if every cell were electrified at once. She could taste his saliva and, as their tongues touched, she knew they loved each other as much as they ever had, a wonderful love, beyond space and time, impossible and unbearable. She wanted to cry, to die. This, she imagined, was how it must have been with Judas, the apostle who, of all of the disciples, loved Jesus most.

'I've found you again, Sarah.' John's voice broke with emotion. 'I never stopped loving you, not ever. I swear to you, you were inside me like the beat of my own heart. I would have done anything to be with you now like this. We can't be parted again.' He stroked her hair. 'Promise me we'll always be together.' His next words imprinted themselves on Sarah's heart with the pain of a branding iron. '*I love you more than life itself.*'

She was being sucked into a black hole with no return path, no possible escape, no way out. She felt John running his tongue over her lips and she kissed him back as passionately as she could. Her eyes hurt with the tears filling them. She knew what this kiss was – the *cyanide kiss*, the kiss that ends kisses. In her mind, she could hear a tune: *What a Wonderful World*. But the world wasn't wonderful, it was the opposite.

As Dexter bent over her, Sarah's eyes flashed wide open. A silver locket fell forward from around his neck and swung open. It contained a tiny picture. She gasped, recognising her own face. A memory exploded in her mind of John taking that picture moments after their first meeting. Love at first sight, he said. Now she could no longer stem the burning tears that flooded down her cheeks. She was crying so much she could hardly breathe.

Through her tears, a dreadful realisation gripped her. She realised why she'd never been able to remember taking the picture of the Peregrine falcon in Central Park. Quite simply, she never took it. The memory was implanted. All that stuff about killing the things you love if they were damaged...*lies*. How could she ever have believed any of it? She just wanted John back again, in any condition. But it was too late, always too late, a million too lates.

He hardly made a sound, just a brief gurgling noise as some blood trickled from his mouth. His limbs twitched and he slumped forward. She clutched his lifeless head to her chest and stroked his dark hair, just as she used to do years before. She would give anything to be with him again on a bright summer's day in Central Park. As she looked at the tiny white antidote pills lying on the floor, she knew she was broken forever.

'I remember,' she mumbled, answering John's last question, 'I *remember.*' She said it aloud over and over again, until she wished she could forget.

Her body froze, locking itself in a dreadful posture of suffering. *I can't bear this.* Every part of her felt the emptiness of life without John. She imagined she'd been skinned, and that ice-cold air was blowing over her flayed flesh. Staring at the white walls, she felt she was floating in some universe of her own, alone, damaged beyond repair, irredeemably cut off from love, from hope, from life itself.

How long was it before she became aware of a commotion? Time seemed to have been suspended. The ambulance had stopped, she realised. She heard raised voices, a gunshot. Normally, those sounds would have spurred her into action, but now she remained in the same position, uncaring. She was alive but death was in her blood, stretching out to every part of her. Her life was over. With her own lips, she'd killed love. *There's no criminal worse than me*, she thought, *no one more despicable.*

The back doors of the ambulance were thrown open and icy air again blew into the ambulance. Sarah's eyes locked onto a man in a general's uniform, climbing into the ambulance. *Him* – the leader of the Committee. So, they hadn't all been killed in the explosion. He was pale and bruised, his jaw and left cheek scarred by deep, stitched wounds.

She stared at him with glassy eyes, scarcely reacting to his presence. What did it matter that he'd survived? What did anything matter? She noticed his eyes darting over the scene inside the ambulance, fitting the jigsaw together. A moment later he was down on his knees, scooping up the antidote pills. He got back to his feet and turned to face her. Before she could grasp what was happening, he gripped her jaw. With frantic speed, he wiped off her lipstick with a tissue then prised open her mouth and forced the pills in.

'Take them, for God's sake.'

Almost reflexively, she swallowed the pills. As she did, she felt an overwhelming surge of rage. This man had saved her life and condemned her to live with her sin, her crime, her *hell.* No hope of redemption, no pardon possible – a life sentence. Despairingly, her eyes drifted back to John's lifeless body.

'Did he harm you?' the general said.

End Game

The words slammed into her. *Harm me*? Her mind was stunned by the absurdity of the remark. She had nothing to fear from John. It was precisely the opposite. She was the killer, the assassin, the thief of life. John's love for her had been limitless, beyond the laws of nature. She'd repaid him like the lowest, slimiest snake, full of deception and fatal venom.

'Harm me?' Even as the words left her mouth, she comprehended that the man in front of her bore every bit as much a responsibility for John's death as she did. The Committee were the puppet masters. What they willed, she did. It was their design, their plan, not hers. She reached for one of the pistols under her dress. With mechanical efficiency, she slipped off the safety and positioned the pistol.

The general gazed at her, his expression an extraordinary mixture. She tried to think of the correct words. Revulsion was in the mix, and horror, perhaps also pity. But there was something else. The word seemed preposterous and yet she could swear it was the right one. *Love*. How was it possible? This man was a monster. Now her whole body flooded with hate, and every nerve in her body sparked with an unquenchable desire for revenge, for some pathetic justice for John. She fired and the shot crashed into the general's guts. A vivid gunpowder mark appeared round the hole in her dress made by the bullet as it raced to its target.

There was a look of astonishment in the general's eyes, then he collapsed. He lay groaning on the floor, death rattling in his throat. Almost pathetically, he threw up his right hand. 'Your hand,' he wheezed pleadingly, his own hand flailing in Sarah's direction. 'Please, your hand,' he begged.

Incredulous, Sarah understood that he wanted her to hold his hand. Was he insane? This vile old man was about to die and yet the only thought in his head was to hold her hand, to feel some kind of physical contact with her, some human bond. It made no sense.

Then he said his last word on this planet, a word that filled Sarah with infinite horror. It pierced the few remaining protective layers of her mind, penetrated to her heart until she felt she must howl with final, terminal madness.

She mouthed that last dying word to herself and knew she'd never escape from it as long as she lived. It was the word that made her understand everything, that condemned her, finally and irrevocably, to the lowest, deadliest circle of hell.

Daughter.

Also available:

THE ARMAGEDDON CONSPIRACY

by Mike Hockney

When an SS officer commits suicide at the end of WWII, he leaves behind a document called *The Cainite Destiny* that hints at an incredible link between the Nazis and the Bible's greatest pariah…Cain. Only one person – Cambridge professor Reinhardt Weiss – appreciates the document's significance. His research is ridiculed when he claims he has begun to uncover an unimaginably dangerous conspiracy going all the way back to Adam and Eve. All of history's best-known conspiracies, he insists, are different aspects of a single *superconspiracy* that directly connects the Nazis to the Knights Templar, the Cathars, the Alchemists, the original Freemasons and the early Gnostic sects. His work unfinished, Weiss dies in obscurity.

In 2012, the fate of the world hinges on whether *The Cainite Destiny's* ultimate objective, which always eluded Professor Weiss, can be discovered. Adolf Hitler supposedly attempted to perform the final cataclysmic act, but failed for reasons unknown. Now the members of America's most elite Special Forces unit have deserted en masse and they appear to be the latest inheritors of history's oldest and deadliest secret mission.

When their backgrounds are checked, an extraordinary fact emerges. All of them are grandsons of American intelligence officers who, at the end of the Second World War, interrogated senior officials responsible for the treasure hoard that the Nazis had looted from all over Europe.

The deserters carry out a coordinated set of daring robberies, targeting holy sites associated with the three greatest religious icons of the Western World: the Ark of the Covenant, the Holy Grail, and the Spear of Destiny…the Roman lance used to pierce Christ's side at the Crucifixion, and which was coveted by Hitler.

It seems the American soldiers are the instruments of Cain's ancient revenge. Are they planning the greatest crime of all?

To kill God.

ISBN: 978-1-84799-474-5

Also available:

THE MILLIONAIRES' DEATH CLUB

by Mike Hockney

When 23-year-old Sophie York, a forgotten Reality TV contestant, receives a card from a mysterious stranger saying, 'How far will you go for ultimate pleasure?' she doesn't realize she's about to embark on a journey that will change her life forever. Hollywood movie mogul Harry Mencken and his two most glittering A-list stars, Sam Lincoln and Jez Easton, think she's the perfect person to help them discover the truth of an urban legend.

Mencken is obsessed with a story he heard from an upper-class English student at a party in Beverley Hills. The student claimed that an elite Oxford University dining and drinking club had discovered the secret of ultimate pleasure.

Now Mencken and his stars are determined to track down the rich students and find out if the incredible rumour is true. No sooner have they and Sophie begun their search than they have a series of odd encounters with glamorous young men and women dressed in a succession of bizarre costumes. It soon becomes clear that these are the Oxford students and these episodes are no accidents – the students have targeted them.

The president of the students is a breathtakingly beautiful 21-year-old blueblood called Lady Zara Hamilton. In the following days, Sophie and her famous clients are drawn further and further into Zara's shadowy world, involving stunts performed in public and strange rituals surrounded with the utmost secrecy.

It all seems like harmless student fun until two of the students show up dead, and one of the Hollywood stars receives a black card, embossed with a terrifying holographic skull, saying, 'Congratulations, you have been selected by the Millionaires' Death Club.' It doesn't take long for Sophie and her glamorous clients to discover the first rule of the Millionaires' Death Club...

If you're in, you're dead.

ISBN: 978-1-84753-679-2

ABOUT THE AUTHOR

www.meritocracy.org.uk